Praise for *Updraft*

Winner of the Andre Norton Award
Winner of the Compton Crook Award
Nebula Award Nominee for Best Novel
Publishers Weekly Fall 2015 SF Fantasy &
Horror Top 10 Book
Library Journal Debut of the Month

"I long to know more about the world and where Wilde's imagination will soar next. In the meantime it's all I can do to slow-clap this powerfully engaging debut: Wilde's world and characters—as is entirely appropriate—blew me away."
—NPR

"Extraordinary world-building and cascading levels of intrigue make Wilde's debut fantasy novel soar. . . . This well-written and fascinating exploration of a strange land is an extremely promising start for an exciting new writer."
—*Publishers Weekly* (starred review)

"Captivating . . . Kirit's journey to find her place is satisfying, but the real draw is a world that readers will be anxious to revisit in future volumes of this exciting new series."
—*Library Journal* (starred review)

"An absolute delight to read, a coming-of-age story set in a truly original world, blending romance, conspiracy, awesome training montages, and some good old-fashioned adventure to create a book that's impossible to put down. [Wilde has] planted herself firmly in the 'authors to watch' category."
—Andrew Liptak

"Fran Wilde has written a compelling debut, and I for one look forward to seeing what she does next." —*Locus*

"This book has political intrigue, action, airborne wind tunnel combat, and voracious flying monsters with tentacles. Seriously. You want to read this." —Ann Leckie, award-winning author of the Ancillary series

"*Updraft* promises many good things to come from Wilde." —Scott Lynch, *New York Times* bestselling author of *The Republic of Thieves*

"A wonderful fantasy world unlike any other!" —Elizabeth Bear, author of the Eternal Sky trilogy

"A vivid, beautifully written tale of loyalty and hidden secrets." —Max Gladstone, author of *Full Fathom Five*

"Rife with so many of my favorite tropes—wings, layers of secrets, a heroine who deals with the consequences of being talented—all at a roller-coaster pace." —Sherwood Smith, author of *Treason's Shore*

TOR BOOKS BY FRAN WILDE

Updraft
Cloudbound

UPDRAFT

FRAN WILDE

TOR

A TOM DOHERTY ASSOCIATES BOOK
NEW YORK

UPDRAFT

Copyright © 2015 by Fran Wilde

A Tor Book
Published by Tom Doherty Associates, LLC
175 Fifth Avenue
New York, NY 10010

www.tor-forge.com

Tor® is a registered trademark of Tom Doherty Associates, LLC.

The Library of Congress has cataloged the hardcover edition as follows:

Wilde, Fran.
    Updraft / Fran Wilde.—First edition.
        p. cm.
    ISBN 978-0-7653-7783-8 (hardcover)
    ISBN 978-1-4668-5820-6 (e-book)
    1. Single women—Fiction.   I. Title.
    PS3623.I5355 U74 2015
    813'.6—dc23

                            2015019191

    ISBN 978-0-7653-7784-5 (trade paperback)

Our books may be purchased in bulk for promotional, educational,
or business use. Please contact your local bookseller or the Macmillan
Corporate and Premium Sales Department at 1-800-221-7945, extension
5442, or by e-mail at MacmillanSpecialMarkets@macmillan.com.

First Edition: September 2015
First Trade Paperback Edition: September 2016

Printed in the United States of America

0 9 8 7 6 5 4 3 2 1

To Iris & Tom

PART ONE

ALLMOONS

1

DENSIRA

My mother selected her wings as early morning light reached through our balcony shutters. She moved between the shadows, calm and deliberate, while downtower neighbors slept behind their barricades. She pushed her arms into the woven harness. Turned her back to me so that I could cinch the straps tight against her shoulders.

When two bone horns sounded low and loud from Mondarath, the tower nearest ours, she stiffened. I paused as well, trying to see through the shutters' holes. She urged me on while she trained her eyes on the sky.

"No time to hesitate, Kirit," she said. She meant *no time to be afraid.*

On a morning like this, fear was a blue sky emptied of birds. It was the smell of cooking trapped in closed towers, of smoke looking for ways out. It was an ache in the back of the eyes from searching the distance, and a weight in the stomach as old as our city.

Today Ezarit Densira would fly into that empty sky—first to the east, then southwest.

I grabbed the buckle on her left shoulder, then put the full weight of my body into securing the strap. She grunted softly in approval.

"Turn a little, so I can see the buckles better," I said. She took two steps sideways. I could see through the shutters while I worked.

Across a gap of sky, Mondarath's guards braved the morning. Their wings edged with glass and locked for fighting, they leapt from the tower. One shouted and pointed.

A predator moved there, nearly invisible—a shimmer among exploding gardens. Nets momentarily wrapped two thick, sky-colored tentacles. The skymouth shook free and disappeared. Wails built in its wake. Mondarath was under attack.

The guards dove to meet it, the sun dazzling their wings. The air roiled and sheared. Pieces of brown rope netting and red banners fell to the clouds far below. The guards drew their bows and gave chase, trying to kill what they could not see.

"Oh, Mondarath," Ezarit whispered. "They never mind the signs."

The besieged tower rose almost as tall as ours, sun-bleached white against the blue morning. Since Lith fell, Mondarath marked the city's northern edge. Beyond its tiers, sky stretched uninterrupted to the horizon.

A squall broke hard against the tower, threatening a loose shutter. Then the balcony's planters toppled and the circling guards scattered. One guard, the slowest, jerked to a halt in the air and flew, impossibly, backwards. His leg yanked high, flipping his body as it went, until he hung upside down in the air. He flailed for his quiver, spilling arrows, as the sky opened below him, red and wet and filled with glass teeth. The air blurred as slick, invisible limbs tore away his brown silk wings, then lowered what the monster wanted into its mouth.

By the time his scream reached us, the guard had disappeared from the sky.

My own mouth went dry as dust.

How to help them? My first duty was to my tower, Densira.

To the Laws. But what if we were under attack? My mother in peril? What if no one would help then? My heart hammered questions. What would it be like to open our shutters, leap into the sky, and join this fight? To go against Laws?

"Kirit! Turn away." Ezarit yanked my hand from the shutters. She stood beside me and sang the Law, Fortify:

Tower by tower, secure yourselves,

Except in city's dire need.

She had added the second half of the Law to remind me why she flew today. Dire need.

She'd fought for the right to help the city beyond her own tower, her own quadrant. Someday, I would do the same.

Until then, there was need here too. I could not turn away.

The guards circled Mondarath, less one man. The air cleared. The horns stopped for now, but the three nearest towers— Wirra, Densira, and Viit—kept their occupied tiers sealed.

Ezarit's hand gripped the latch for our own shutters. "Come on," she whispered. I hurried to tighten the straps at her right shoulder, though I knew she didn't mean me. Her escort was delayed.

She would still fly today.

Six towers in the southeast stricken with a coughing illness needed medicines from the north and west. Ezarit had to trade for the last ingredients and make the delivery before Allmoons, or many more would die.

The buckling done, she reached for her panniers and handed them to me.

Elna, my mother's friend from downtower, bustled in the kitchen, making tea. After the first migration warnings, Ezarit had asked her to come uptower, for safety's sake—both Elna's and mine, though I no longer needed minding.

Elna's son, Nat, had surprised us by helping her climb the

fiber ladders that stretched from the top of the tower to the last occupied tier. Elna was pale and huffing as she finally cleared the balcony. When she came inside, I saw why Nat had come. Elna's left eye had a cloud in it—a skyblindness.

"We have better shutters," Ezarit had said. "And are farther from the clouds. Staying higher will be safer for them."

A mouth *could* appear anywhere, but she was right. Higher was safer, and on Densira, we were now highest of all.

At the far side of our quarters, Nat kept an eye on the open sky. He'd pulled his sleeping mat from behind a screen and knelt, peering between shutters, using my scope. When I finished helping my mother, I would take over that duty.

I began to strap Ezarit's panniers around her hips. The baskets on their gimbaled supports would roll with her, no matter how the wind shifted.

"You don't have to go," I said as I knelt at her side. I knew what her reply would be. I said my part anyway. We had a ritual. Skymouths and klaxons or not.

"I will be well escorted." Her voice was steady. "The west doesn't care for the north's troubles, or the south's. They want their tea and their silks for Allmoons and will trade their honey to the highest bidder. I can't stand by while the south suffers, not when I've worked so hard to negotiate the cure."

It was more than that, I knew.

She tested the weight of a pannier. The silk rustled, and the smell of dried tea filled the room. She'd stripped the bags of their decorative beads. Her cloak and her dark braids hung unadorned. She lacked the sparkle that trader Ezarit Densira was known for.

Another horn sounded, past Wirra, to the west.

"See?" She turned to me. Took my hand, which was nearly the same size as hers. "The skymouths take the east. I fly west. I will return before Allmoons, in time for your wingtest."

Elna, her face pale as a moon, crossed the room. She carried a bowl of steaming tea to my mother. "For your strength today, Risen," she said, bowing carefully in the traditional greeting of lowtower to high.

My mother accepted the tea and the greeting with a smile. She'd raised her family to the top of Densira through her daring trades. She had earned the greeting. It wasn't always so, when she and Elna were young downtower mothers. But now Ezarit was famous for her skills, both bartering and flying. She'd even petitioned the Spire successfully once. In return, we had the luxury of quarters to ourselves, but that only lasted as long as she kept the trade flowing.

As long as she could avoid the skymouths today.

Once I passed my wingtest, I could become her apprentice. I would fly by her side, and we'd fight the dangers of the city together. I would learn to negotiate as she did. I'd fly in times of dire need while others hid behind their shutters.

"The escort is coming," Nat announced. He stood; he was much taller than me now. His black hair curled wildly around his head, and his brown eyes squinted through the scope once more.

Ezarit walked across the room, her silk-wrapped feet swishing over the solid bone floor. She put her hand on Nat's shoulder and looked out. Over her shoulders, between the point of her furled wings and through the shutters, I saw a flight of guards circle Mondarath, searching out more predators. They yelled and blew handheld horns, trying to scare skymouths away with noise and their arrows. That rarely worked, but they had to try.

Closer to us, a green-winged guard soared between the towers, an arrow nocked, eyes searching the sky. The guards atop Densira called out a greeting to him as he landed on our balcony.

I retightened one of Ezarit's straps, jostling her tea. She looked at me, eyebrows raised.

"Elna doesn't need to watch me," I finally said. "I'm fine by myself. I'll check in with the aunts. Keep the balcony shuttered."

She reached into her pannier and handed me a stone fruit. Her gold eyes softened with worry. "Soon." The fruit felt cold in my hand. "I need to know you are all safe. I can't fly without knowing. You'll be free to choose your path soon enough."

After the wingtest. Until then, I was a dependent, bound by her rules, not just tower strictures and city Laws.

"Let me come out to watch you go, then. I'll use the scope. I won't fly."

She frowned, but we were bartering now. Her favorite type of conversation.

"Not outside. You can use the scope inside. When I return, we'll fly some of my route around the city, as practice." She saw my frustration. "Promise me you'll keep inside? No visiting? No sending whipperlings? We cannot lose another bird."

"For how long?" A mistake. My question broke at the end with the kind of whine that hadn't slipped out in years. My advantage dissipated like smoke.

Nat, on Ezarit's other side, pretended he wasn't listening. He knew me too well. That made it worse.

"They will go when they go." She winced as sounds of Mondarath's mourning wafted through the shutters. Peering out again, she searched for the rest of her escort. "Listen for the horns. If Mondarath sounds again, or if Viit goes, stay away from the balconies."

She looked over her shoulder at me until I nodded, and Nat too.

She smiled at him, then turned and wrapped her arms around me. "That's my girl."

I would have closed my eyes and rested my head against the warmth of her chest if I'd thought there was time. Ezarit was like a small bird, always rushing. I took a breath, and she pulled away, back to the sky. Another guard joined the first on the balcony, wearing faded yellow wings.

I checked Ezarit's wings once more. The fine seams. The sturdy battens. They'd worn in well: no fraying, despite the hours she'd flown in them. She'd traded five bolts of raw silk from Naza tower to the Viit wingmaker for these, and another three for mine. Expensive but worth it. The wingmaker was the best in the north. Even Singers said so.

Furled, her wings were a tea-colored brown, but a stylized kestrel hid within the folds. The wingmaker had used tea and vegetable dyes—whatever he could get—to make the rippling sepia pattern.

My own new wings leaned against the central wall by our sleeping area, still wrapped. Waiting for the skies to clear. My fingers itched to pull the straps over my shoulders and unfurl the whorls of yellow and green.

Ezarit cloaked herself in tea-colored quilted silks to protect against the chill winds. They tied over her shoulders, around her trim waist and at her thighs and ankles. She spat on her lenses, her dearest treasure, and rubbed them clean. Then she let them hang around her neck. Her tawny cheeks were flushed, her eyes bright, and she looked, now that she was determined to go, younger and lighter than yesterday. She was beautiful when she was ready to fly.

"It won't be long," she said. "Last migration through the northwest quadrant lasted one day."

Our quadrant had been spared for my seventeen years. Many in the city would say our luck had held far too long while others suffered. Still, my father had left to make a trade during a migration and did not return. Ezarit took his trade routes as soon as I was old enough to leave with Elna.

"How can you be sure?" I asked.

Elna patted my shoulder, and I jumped. "All will be well, Kirit. Your mother helps the city."

"And," Ezarit said, "if I am successful, we will have more good fortune to celebrate."

I saw the gleam in her eye. She thought of the towers in the west, the wealthier quadrants. Densira had scorned us as unlucky after my father disappeared, family and neighbors both. The aunts scorned her no longer, as they enjoyed the benefits of her success. Even last night, neighbors had badgered Ezarit to carry trade parcels for them to the west. She'd agreed, showing respect for family and tower. Now she smiled. "Perhaps we won't be Ezarit and Kirit Densira for long."

A third guard clattered to a landing on the balcony, and Ezarit signaled she was ready. The tower marks on the guards' wings were from Naza. Out of the migration path; known for good hunters with sharp eyes. No wonder Nat stared at them as if he would trade places in a heartbeat.

As Ezarit's words sank in, he frowned. "What's wrong with Densira?"

"Nothing's wrong with Densira," Elna said, reaching around Ezarit to ruffle Nat's hair. She turned her eyes to the balcony, squinting. "Especially since Ezarit has made this blessed tower two tiers higher."

Nat sniffed, loudly. "This tier's pretty nice, even if it reeks of brand-new."

My face grew warm. The tier did smell of newly grown bone. The central core was still damp to the touch.

Still, I held my chin high and moved to my mother's side.

Not that long ago, Nat and I had been inseparable. Practically wing-siblings. Elna was my second mother. My mother, Nat's hero. We'd taken first flights together. Practiced rolls and glides. Sung together, memorizing the towers, all the Laws. Since our move, I'd seen him practicing with other flightmates. Dojha with her superb dives. Sidra, who had the perfect voice for Laws and already wore glorious, brand-new wings. Whose father, the tower councilman, had called my mother a liar more than once after we moved uptower, above their tier.

I swallowed hard. Nat, Elna, and I would be together in my still-new home until Ezarit returned. Like old times, almost.

In the air beyond the balcony, a fourth figure appeared. He glided a waiting circle. Wings shimmered dove gray. Bands of blue at the tips. A Singer.

A moment of the old childhood fear struck me, and I saw Nat pale as well. Singers sometimes took young tower children to the Spire. It was a great honor. But the children who went didn't return until they were grown. And when they came back, it was as gray-robed strangers, scarred and tattooed and sworn to protect the city.

The guards seemed to relax. The green-winged guard nudged his nearest companion, "Heard tell no Singer's ever been attacked by a skymouth." The other guards murmured agreement. One cracked his knuckles. Our Magister for flight and Laws had said the same thing. No one ever said whether those who flew with Singers had the same luck, but the guards seemed to think so.

I hoped it was true.

Ezarit signaled to the guards, who assembled in the air near the Singer. She smiled at Elna and hugged her. "Glad you are here."

"Be careful, Ezarit," Elna whispered back. "Speed to your wings."

Ezarit winked at Nat, then looked out at the sky. She nodded to the Singer. Ready. She gave me a fierce hug and a kiss. "Stay safe, Kirit."

Then she pushed the shutters wide, unfurled her wings, and leapt from the balcony into the circle of guards waiting for her with bows drawn.

The Singer broke from their formation first, dipping low behind Wirra. I watched from the threshold between our quarters and the balcony until the rest were motes against the otherwise empty sky. Their flight turned west and disappeared around Densira's broad curve.

For the moment, even Mondarath was still.

❦ ❦ ❦

Nat moved to pull the shutters closed, but I blocked the way. I wanted to keep watching the sky.

"Kirit, it's Laws," he said, yanking my sleeve. I jerked my arm from his fingers and stepped farther onto the balcony.

"You go inside," I said to the sky. I heard the shutter slam behind me. I'd broken my promise and was going against Laws, but I felt certain that if I took my eyes off the sky, something would happen to Ezarit and her guards.

We'd seen signs of the skymouth migration two days ago. House birds had molted. Silk spiders hid their young. Densira prepared. Watchmen sent black-feathered kaviks to all the tiers. They cackled and shat on the balconies while families read the bone chips they carried.

Attempting to postpone her flight, Ezarit had sent a whipperling to her trading partners in the south and west. They'd replied quickly, "We are not in the migration path." "We can sell our honey elsewhere." There would be none left to mix with Mondarath's herbs for the southeast's medicines.

She made ready. Would not listen to arguments. Sent for Elna early, then helped me strip the balcony.

Mondarath, unlike its neighbors, paid little mind to preparations. The skymouth migration hadn't passed our way for years, they'd said. They didn't take their fruit in. They left their clotheslines and the red banners for Allmoons flapping.

Around me now, our garden was reduced to branches and leaves. Over the low bone outcrop that marked Aunt Bisset's balcony, I saw a glimmer. A bored cousin with a scope, probably. The wind took my hair and tugged the loose tendrils. I leaned out to catch one more glimpse of Ezarit as she passed beyond the tower's curve.

The noise from Mondarath had eased, and the balconies were empty on the towers all around us. I felt both entirely alone and as if the eyes of the city were on me.

I lifted my chin and smiled, letting everyone behind their shutters know I wasn't afraid, when they were. I panned with our scope, searching the sky. A watchman. A guardian.

And I saw it. It tore at my aunt's gnarled trees, then shook loose the ladder down to Nat's. It came straight at me fast and sure: a red rip in the sky, sharp beak edges toothed with ridge upon ridge of glass teeth. Limbs flowed forward like thick tongues.

I dropped the scope.

The mouth opened wider, full of stench and blood.

I felt the rush of air and heard the beat of surging wings, and I screamed. It was a child's scream, not a woman's. I knew I would die in that moment, with tears staining my tunic and that scream soiling my mouth. I heard the bone horns of our tower's watch sound the alarm: We were unlucky once more.

My scream expanded, tore at my throat, my teeth.

The skymouth stopped in its tracks. It hovered there, red and gaping. I saw the glittering teeth and, for a moment, its eyes, large and side-set to let its mouth open even wider. Its breath huffed thick and foul across my face, but it didn't cross the last distance between us. My heart had stopped with fear, but the scream kept on. It spilled from me, softening. As the scream died, the skymouth seemed to move again.

So I hauled in a deep breath through my nose, like we were taught to sing for Allmoons, and I kept screaming.

The skymouth backed up. It closed its jaws. It disappeared into the sky, and soon I saw a distant ripple, headed away from the city.

I tried to laugh, but the sound stuck in my chest and strangled me. Then my eyes betrayed me. Darkness overtook the edges of my vision, and white, wavy lines cut across everything I saw. The hard slats of the shutters counted the bones of my spine as I slid down and came to rest on the balcony floor.

My breathing was too loud in my ears. It roared.

Clouds. I'd shouted down a skymouth and would still die blue-lipped outside my own home? I did not want to die.

Behind me, Nat battered at the shutters. He couldn't open them, I realized groggily, because my body blocked the door.

Cold crept up on me. My fingers prickled, then numbed. I fought my eyelids, but they won, falling closed against the blur that my vision had become.

I thought for a moment I was flying with my mother, far beyond the city. Everything was so blue.

Hands slid under my back and legs. Someone lifted me. The shutters squealed open.

Dishes swept from our table hit the floor and rolled. Lips pressed warm against mine, catching my frozen breath. The rhythm of in and out came back. I heard my name.

When I opened my eyes, I saw the Singer's gray robes first, then the silver lines of his tattoos. His green eyes. The dark hairs in his hawk nose. Behind him, Elna wept and whispered, "On your wings, Singer. Mercy on your wings."

He straightened and turned from me. I heard his voice for the first time, stern and deep, telling Elna, "This is a Singer concern. You will not interfere."

2

SENT DOWN

The Singer came and went from my side. He checked my breathing. His fingers tapped my wrist.

Elna and Nat swirled around the table like clouds. I heard Elna whisper angrily.

When I found I could hold my eyes open without growing dizzy, Nat had disappeared. The Singer sat at my mother's work-table. His draped robes puddled on the floor and obscured her stool. As the sun passed below the clouds, he sat there finger-ing a skein tied with blank message chips.

In the dark, his knife scraped against one bone chip, then another.

The room felt tight-strung, an instrument waiting to be played.

With the sunrise, Densira neighbors began clattering onto our balcony. They brought a basket of fruit, a string of beads.

"The tower is talking," Elna said. "About the miracle. That it's a skyblessing."

The Singer waved away our visitors. He positioned a tower guard on the balcony.

Occasionally, the guard peered through the shutters and shook his head, like kaviks did when they were molting. "Laws-breaker," he muttered. He told any who would listen how stu-pid I'd been.

I caught pieces of his words on the wind.

"It came right for her. The fledge stood out on the balcony with the lens of that scope glinting in the sun. Should have gobbled her up. Would have shot her myself, attracting a mouth to the tower like that." He waved our neighbors away. "Don't waste your goods on her. She's not skyblessed. She's bad luck. Should tie enough Laws on her that she'll rattle when she moves."

The people of Densira did not listen. Elna scrambled to find places for everything they brought.

She took the guard a cup of tea. "Luck was with her, Risen. The tower has luck now, because of Kirit. The skymouth fled."

The Singer cleared his throat loudly. Elna jostled the cup. Nearly spilled the tea. The Singer looked as if he wanted to have Elna swept from the tower and silenced.

I tried to say something helpful, but my voice rasped in my throat.

"Don't try to speak, Kirit." Elna returned to my side. The Singer glared again, then rose, muttering about needing a new sack of rainwater. He must have decided to keep me alive a little longer.

She propped me up. Around me, the bone lanterns' glow cast halos and small stars against the pale walls. The rugs and cushions of the place I'd shared with my mother since the tower rose were swathed in shadow.

Elna wrapped me in a quilt, tucking the down-filled silk beneath me. Instead of warming, I shook harder. The Singer returned and held my wrist between his thumb and forefinger. He reached into his robe. Took out a small bag that smelled rich and dark. Metal glittered in the light.

A moment later, he handed me a tiny cup filled with sharp-smelling liquid. It burned my throat as it went down, then warmed my chest and belly. It took me a moment to realize I wasn't drinking rainwater from my usual bone cup. He'd given me a brass cup so old the etching was nearly worn away. It warmed in my hands as the glow crept up my arms. Calm followed warmth until I was able to focus on the room, the smell of chicory brewing, the sound of voices.

Elna disappeared when the Singer glared at her a third time. He gave me a stern look. Waited for me to speak. I wished Ezarit sat beside me.

"They think you are skyblessed," he said when I did not speak on his cue.

I blinked at the words and closed my eyes again. Skyblessed. Like the people in the songs, who escaped the clouds, or those who survived Lith.

The Singer's tone made it clear that he thought me nothing of the sort.

"Your example will tempt people to risk themselves. We have Laws for a reason, Kirit. To keep the city safe."

I found that hard to argue. I sat up straighter. My head pounded. I looked around the empty tier, at the lashed shutters, anywhere but at the Singer standing before me, his hands folded into his robe.

"You are old enough to understand duty to your tower. You know our history. Why we can never go back to disorder."

I nodded. This was why we sang. To remember.

"Yet you are still part of a household. Your mother is still responsible for you. Even while she's on a trading run."

He was right. She wouldn't learn what I'd done until she flew close enough to the north quadrant for the gossip to catch up with her. I imagined her sipping tea at a stopover tower. Varu, perhaps. And hearing. What her face would look like as she tallied the damage to her reputation. To mine. Bile rose in my throat, despite the calming effect of whatever was in that cup.

The Singer leaned close. "You know what you did."

I'd broken Laws. I knew that. I'd attracted a skymouth with my actions. A punishable offense. Worse, I drew a Singer's attention, which could affect Densira. Councilman Vant, Sidra's father, would sanction me, and my mother too, for my deeds.

But that fell below the Singers' jurisdiction. They only dealt with the big Laws. I sipped at the cup to conceal my confusion. Cut my losses. "I broke tower Laws."

He lowered his voice. "Not only that, you lived to tell about it. How did you do that, Kirit Densira?" His eyes bored into mine, his breath rich with spices. He looked like a hawk, looming over me.

Elna was nowhere to be seen. I looked at my fingers, the soft pattern on the sleeve of my robe that Ezarit brought back from her last trip. Stall, my brain said. Someone would come.

I met the Singer's gaze. Hard as stone, those eyes.

"I am waiting." He spoke each word slowly, as if I wouldn't understand otherwise.

"I don't know."

"Don't know what?"

"Why I am still alive."

"You've never been in skymouth migration before?"

I shook my head. Never. Wasn't that hard to believe. Everyone knew the northwest quadrant had been lucky.

"What about the Spire? Never to a market there, nor for Allsuns?"

Shaking my head repeatedly made the room spin. A low throb gripped the base of my skull. My voice rasped. "She said we'd go when we were both traders."

He frowned. Perhaps he thought I lied. "Don't all citizens love to visit the Spire's hanging markets at Allsuns, pick over the fine bone carvings, and watch the quadrant wingfights?

I shook my head. Not once. Ezarit never wanted to go, nor Elna. They avoided the Singers more than most. How could I convince him I told the truth?

"Do you know what you've done?"

I shook my head a third time, while pressure pounded my temples. I did not know, and I felt nauseated. I could see no way for me to get away from this Singer. Even seated, he loomed over me, tall and thin and sour-faced. Despite this, his hands were smooth, no deep lines marked his face beneath the tattoos; he might not have been much older than me.

"I don't know what you want me to say. I went on the balcony. A skymouth came. I screamed, and it—"

I stopped speaking. I'd screamed. The skymouth had halted. Why? People who were close enough to a skymouth to scream died.

The Singer's gaze bored into mine. His frown deepened. He turned away from me and looked at the balcony. Then back to me.

"There are those who can hear the city all the time. Not only when it roars. They learn to speak its language. You know that, right?"

I bowed my head. "They become Singers. They make sure we continue to rise, instead of falling like Lith." Our Magister, Florian, had taught us this long ago. If tower children became Singers, their families were rewarded with higher tiers; their towers with bridges. But the Singers themselves were family no longer. Tower no longer. They severed themselves from city life; enforced Laws even on those they once loved. Nat's father, for instance. Though I'd been too young to see it, I'd heard stories. I imagined now a Laws-weighted figure thrown to the clouds. Arms and legs churning in place of missing wings. Failing. Falling. Tears pricked my eyes.

This Singer took my arm and squeezed hard. I locked my teeth together to avoid crying out. His fingers pressed into my skin, dimpling pale rings around the pressure points. "Kirit Densira, daughter of Ezarit Densira, I place you under Spire fiat. If you reveal anything that I say now to anyone, you will be thrown down. If you fail to tell the truth, you will be thrown down. Do you understand?"

My head throbbed worse than ever, and I leaned hard against his grip. "Yes." Anything to get free of this man.

"Some among the Singers can speak to monsters."

"What do you mean?"

"There are five people in the city who can stop a skymouth with a shout. All Singers. Except one."

He stared at me. He meant me. I was the fifth.

"Kirit." He paused. "You are not skyblessed."

I bowed my head. I hadn't thought so.

He released a breath. Scent of garlic. "But you could be something more. Someone who helps to keep the city safe in its direst need."

As my mother did. I raised my eyebrows. "How?"

"You must come into the Spire with me."

The way he said it, I knew he didn't mean for a visit. I jerked backwards. Neck and shoulder muscles tensed into a rejection of him. And yet he held me. Tried to shake me out of it. *No.*

I would not leave the towers. I would not go into the Spire. Not for anything.

Traders flew the quadrants freely, making elegant deals. They connected the city, helped weave it together. Better still, traders were not always tied to a single tower and its fate; they saw the whole city, especially if they were very good, like Ezarit. That was what I wanted. What I would choose when I was able.

I stalled. "I have already put my name in for the next wingtest."

His turn to shake his head. "That hardly matters. Come with me. Your mother will be well honored for your sacrifice. Your tower too."

Sacrifice? No. Not me. I would ply the winds and negotiate deals that let the towers help one another. I would be brave and smart and weave beads in my hair. I would not get locked in an obelisk of bone and secrets. I wouldn't make small children cry, nor etch my face with silver tattoos.

I yanked my arm away. Scrambled off the table, my knees wobbly, toes tingling. Two steps, and I hit the floor. I tried to crawl to the balcony, to get to Aunt Bisset's, to get back to Elna.

The Singer grabbed me up by the neck of my robe. His words were soft, his grip fierce. "You have broken the Laws of your tower. Endangered everyone here. Some think you're skyblessed, but that will wear off. Others think you are a danger, unlucky."

"I am no danger!"

"I will encourage these thoughts. What then? Soon the tower will grow past you. Your bad luck will sour your trades and your family's status. You will be left behind. Or worse. You will be Densira's pariah for every bad thing."

I saw my future as he drew it. The tower turned against me, against my mother. Ezarit, living within a cage of shame.

"As a Singer, you will be respected and feared. Your mother and Elna and Nat will be forgiven your Lawsbreaks."

The household. He would punish Elna and Nat too. And Ezarit. For my decisions. I needed to bargain with this man. How did I do that? How would Ezarit have done it? I groped for memories of her trading stories, for how she would have turned him away. She would have tried to trade, to haggle. If she'd nothing to trade, she'd bluff.

"I am too old to take." I'd never heard of someone nearly at wingtest being taken by the Singers.

"You are still a dependent in the eyes of your tower."

"In that case," I said, resisting the urge to argue his point, "my mother would never permit this." I was certain of that.

"Your mother is not here. Won't be back until nearly All-moons."

"You can't take me without her permission," I said. "It says so in Laws." *And once I have my wingmark, Singer, I will be an apprentice. Able to decide my own path. Singers do not take apprentices from the city, except for egregious Lawsbreaks.* I coughed to conceal my shudder at that possibility. Then I straightened. "Ezarit would bring down a storm on the Spire so great, you'd be begging the clouds to pull you back up." I yanked my arm from his grip.

The Singer smiled, all but his eyes. My skin crawled. "Singers are more powerful than traders, Kirit. Even Ezarit. No matter what your mother thinks."

I drew a deep breath. "I will not go with you."

The Singer straightened. "Very well. You would be unteachable at this age if you did not desire to become a Singer anyway."

I'd changed his mind. I couldn't believe it. It felt too easy.

"You will stay in Densira until the wingtest. Then we will talk again." He rose and reached back to release his wings. He was leaving. Then he paused. Frowned. The tattoos on his cheeks and chin creased and buckled.

"Of course," he said, "you did break tower Law." He drew a cord from his sleeve, tied with four bone chips. "The tower councilman has sent you, Elna, Nat, and your mother a message. Vant is of the opinion, which I have reinforced, that you are in no way skyblessed, no way lucky. That the guard must have driven away the skymouth with noise and arrows. That you must be censured severely to avoid future danger to the tower."

I took the chips. Freshly carved. Approved by Councilman Vant. Two were thin, light: Nat's and mine. We were assigned hard labor, cleaning four tiers downtower.

I gasped. That could take well past the wingtest to finish.

Heavier still were Elna's and Ezarit's chips. They felt thick. Not the thickest, I knew, but still true Laws chips. Permanent, unless Ezarit could bargain with Vant so that he let her untie them.

As promised, they were punished for my deeds. For both the Lawsbreak and for refusing the Singer. Nat and I could miss the wingtest. We would certainly miss the last flight classes, when the Magister did his most intensive review. I could lose my chance at becoming an apprentice this year. Perhaps forever.

My head ached, and I tried hard to swallow. I knew I could have been thrown down for endangering the tower. But censure was bad too. Everything was wrong now.

And not just for me. I held Elna's, Nat's, and my mother's fates in my hand.

The Singer raised his eyebrows. Would I change my mind? Would I give in and go with him?

I stared back at him. Swallowed. Shook my head. Densira seemed to fall silent as we stared each other down.

"My name is Wik. Remember it," he said. "I will find you at Allmoons, Kirit Densira. By then, you will want to come with me."

Trapped behind walls. Gray wings and robes, silver tattoos. Lawsbreakers thrown down, arms flailing. No family. No tower but the Spire.

I would find a way to avoid that. I had to.

🖋 🖋 🖋

The sound of Elna and Nat returning startled the Singer. He swept from our quarters, unfurling his wings as he crossed to the balcony. Nat dodged left to avoid being struck.

I walked unsteadily to greet them, waving my hand to dissuade Elna from bowing in custom.

Shading my eyes against the sunset, I watched the Singer's silhouette shrink as the breeze carried him away. He soared towards the city's center, towards the Spire.

My shoulders dropped. I sank down to rest on my mother's

stool. Nat came to stand by me. "I'm sorry," he murmured. "For locking you out."

I looked up at him. Wished I had words. But anything I said could reveal me, break the Singer's fiat, and endanger Nat and Elna even more. They had enough trouble coming because of me.

I held out the markers, with their sentences on them.

Elna read hers and sucked in her breath. Then she read Nat's and mine, saw they were blessedly temporary. Her eyes watered. "Serves you right," she said. But she heaved the words at us with such relief, I knew she'd been afraid.

I did not want to think of Naton, Nat's father, now. But I was sure Elna thought of the bone markers she'd held the day Naton was thrown down. A skein of Treason Laws, making him first chosen for Conclave, the ritual to appease the city.

Those chips were the heaviest the Singers dispensed.

Ours were much lighter. Tower Laws. Warnings. We would not have to wear them forever.

After he read his chip, Nat's face was a puzzle. "Why do I get punished for what Kirit did?"

Because I would not sacrifice myself for you, Nat. Because I would not go with the Singer, you are punished. I opened my mouth to tell him. To say I was sorry.

But Elna turned on him. "Oh, you're not innocent. You stood by and watched." Her look stopped him cold. He glanced at me from under his lids instead. She huffed and began piling foods from the offerings into a basket. "Might as well get packed up, then. The council will be up."

"Packed?" I couldn't fathom why.

"They'll want you two as low as they can send you," Elna said. "Closer to your duties, but also much more shameful, isn't it? So they'll move you down, to my tier."

I walked towards the back of our quarters to retrieve my

sleeping mat and to get away from Nat's glare. My new wings leaned against the inner wall, dark beside the slick bone column. Vant had nicked "no flight" on our punishment chips. Fine.

I would find a way to finish the cleaning in time. I would fly the wingtest. I promised myself this as I fed the silk spiders and the whipperling. Watered the kavik. They'd survive on their own until Ezarit returned. I hoped she would be quick.

My hands went through the motions while my mind whirred. I saw the skymouth's teeth flash once again. Felt the heat of its breath.

Nat shook me by the shoulders. "Stop it!"

"What?"

"You were keening. It sounded horrible. Hurt my ears. Worse than your singing."

I touched my face. My cheeks were wet. How had that happened? I hadn't cried in front of someone since my first flight group, when I was very young.

Back then, the meanest among them, Sidra, had pretended Nat didn't exist at all. "He's nothing. His father broke Laws. Singers said so." But she'd rounded on me. Teased me for my tuneless renderings of the first Laws we learned. "Your father must have fed himself to a skymouth to keep from being there to hear you cry." The flight group, young as chicks, collapsed into laughter until the Magisters came with their nets to take us into the sky for our first flight. Then everyone's voice froze tight in fear.

We'd only flown for a few minutes that day, tumbling into the tightly woven nets as we learned the winds around Densira. I'd rushed home and, in answer to Ezarit's "how was it?" my nose and eyes had run like rainspouts.

"Sidra's father talks too much, up at the top of Densira," she'd said bitterly. "Your father didn't return from a trade run. He could have been taken by a skymouth, but no one knows for certain. It wasn't your doing." And that was all she ever said.

She'd walked away from me, shoulders hunched, while I buried my face in my sleeping mat. She'd left early the next morning for the Spire, stopping to kiss my head. "Don't let them tell you who you are, Kirit. Don't let them see you cry." I'd pretended to be asleep. But I heard her.

She'd petitioned the Singers that day, though she would not say for what. But her trade routes got better, and, when the tower grew, we were allowed to move to the new tier. Above Vant and his family. A great honor.

Now she was on a trade, and I'd wept again. For whom? For what? Nat still shook me, gently. "I'm all right," I sniffled. He let go.

"What did the Singer say?" he asked.

My mouth went dry. I shook my head.

"Fine, Kirit."

"It's not that, Nat. I can't say what he said."

He opened his mouth to press me for more, but a clatter at the balcony signaled Councilman Vant's arrival, along with the tower guard from this morning. They held a net basket between them.

"I'm not getting in that thing," Nat said.

"No." The councilman shook his head. His jowls jiggled. "You're not. Kirit is."

My jaw dropped. To be sent downtower was one thing. To be sent by basket like an invalid or a cloudbound offering was entirely another. I began to protest, but the councilman held up a finger. "Singer's orders." He smiled with pleasure.

The councilman's enjoyment of my mistake made my stomach clench. Perhaps he hoped this was the first of many small falls.

My mother was not here to ease the way with kind words or gifts. I must do what he said, without making things worse.

I looked around once more before climbing in the basket. Our wide quarters were so recently grown atop the tower that the inner walls hadn't yet begun to thicken. The space was comfortable, for all its newness. We had cushions from Amrath tower, and woven storage baskets in elegant patterns from Bissel. Chimes made from reclaimed metal so old they'd worn smooth of their past hung from the ceiling in the center of the room.

I realized too late that I didn't want to leave this height for downtower's stink and worry. Councilman Vant's family had likely felt the same, as the tower grew past them. They'd been accustomed to being at the top. But towers rose according to need. Densira hadn't risen for years, until Singers arrived with their rough scourweed and chants. Until they'd coaxed the bone tower into growing a new level. But Densira kept groaning. Once, while I'd lived downtower, Nat and I had skipped flight to cruise over the expanse of new-grown bone, and I had spotted the beginnings of a second tier, a natural one, emerging atop the one the Singers had called in the traditional way. After two seasons where the walls creaked and the wind cut ghost patterns around the emerging core, the tier thickened and steadied enough to be occupied.

My find was a tiding, my mother said to anyone who'd listen. She conferred with the Singers and they named our family the occupants, though we waited another season to move. No one had wanted to interfere with the tower's rise. Then we'd climbed, all of us, past Vant's tier, while quite a few other families filled in our former quarters below. Nat had been right to tease yesterday that we were only newly risen, our tier as well. It still stung.

Even now, as I prepared to leave, the central wall creaked and settled. It whispered tower dreams to us and to its cousins all across the city. I wished that the city would speak at this moment. Then the Singers would focus on its message, and not on me.

Elna and Nat descended the rope ladder and left me in my home. Two days ago, I would have given anything to leave it. Now I wished I could stay.

The guard cleared his throat. I heaved my things into the basket, and the councilman helped me in.

"Kirit Lawsbreaker, you're a poor example to your tower. Let your penance make you humble. Let it be of service to Densira," he said. I waited for him to say more. Instead, he and the councilman swung me over the edge of the balcony, making the basket spin. I twisted in the air, wingless, like an infant, as I sank below the floor where my family lived.

Above, the guard played the rope across the cleats cut into our balcony. As the basket jerked down and down again, people emerged on Mondarath's and Densira's gardens to watch. My skin prickled with the attention, but there was nothing I could do. The fiber net held me tight against the wind, which pushed it dizzyingly against the edge of the balcony. The ropes groaned as they bore my weight.

My eyes raked the sky for another mouth or more teeth, found none.

The basket stopped and then started moving again precipitately. Perhaps the guard and councilman had argued about whether to let the rope go, whether to drop me over the edge. They'd be free of the luck, good or bad, that now plagued their peaceful and well-ordered tower. As sometimes happened with invalids.

The net creaked. I laced my fingers around two of the larger knots and held tight.

Below, the tower disappeared with its neighbors into the

depths, growing indistinct long before the cloudtop obscured everything. Farther down, the songs said, the tiers grew together, even some of the towers, as the bone cores expanded out, filling the hollows of old quarters. Even farther down, well below the clouds, lay legend. The oldest songs sang of a bone forest, and the people who climbed it and lived because they kept going higher. And so we still climbed.

Except me. I sank lower, at least for now.

After a lifetime of swinging in my cage, edging lower, then swinging again, I reached Elna's tier. She hooked the net basket with a bone crook, the one she used for bringing in market baskets. Perhaps this very basket. It reeked of onions. Elna and Nat pulled on the crook together and drew the basket onto her small balcony. I climbed out and sat on the ground for a moment, catching my breath.

Elna tugged on the rope twice, and the councilman and his guard yanked up the empty basket.

Far below, the clouds glowed pink with sunset. With All-moons so near, we were flush with the kind of light that faded quickly. The kind that sank to cinder only a few hours after it kindled. Elna's quarters were ruddy with the declining sun.

I looked around my prison. The same walls and tapestries of my earliest memories, but smaller as the inner wall thickened. One day, the tier would be filled with bone, and no one would live here. For now, Elna hummed Remembrance—sung at All-moons and Allsuns—in the kitchen. And Nat. He looked at me now as if I'd made the skymouth with my bare hands on purpose. "You're bad luck," he grumbled. But I saw worry behind the anger. He needed to pass his wingtest too.

I wanted to snap back at him, but fighting with him would make things worse. I pressed my lips together.

Elna emerged from the kitchen to shake her head at both of us.

"Serves you both right." She handed me a piece of lentil flat-bread.

"I don't see why I'm punished," Nat said. "I'll miss training. I'm not the numbhead who went out."

She swatted him. "You didn't stop her. And you closed the shutters. What do you think?"

He looked down. I saw myself through his eyes for a moment. Not Kirit the sometimes-sister, wing-friend of his childhood; now just the spoiled high-tower person who took his mother's attention and got him censured.

"I wish I could change it all," I said. I wanted him to remember what we'd been. Who I was before I moved uptower. To know that I was still the same person, still his friend. His almost-sister.

I tried hard not to care where I was, or about the wingtest and whether we'd miss it. Tried hard not to think of my mother, who'd left me behind. Elna was angry, sure. But with Elna, that didn't matter. She held me close and I breathed in the scent of her skin, the onions she'd cooked. I relaxed, until she murmured, "Our Kirit, skyblessed."

I groaned. So did Nat.

"You two."

"You heard the Singer. I'm not skyblessed."

Elna dipped her head in agreement. But over dinner and until she went to bed, I caught her looking at me with the same blend of reverence and horror that she'd given to the Singer.

Later, I wished she would wrap me up and tell me things would get better, as she had when I'd come in from flight with a bug in my eye or a scrape from the rough sinew nets.

I touched the Laws chip Councilman Vant tied to my wrist. One side was marked "Broke Fortify, endangered tower." The other held my sentence, "Lowtower labor." Nat's bore the more

general "Lawsbreaker." We would wear them until the councilman cut them off.

Shivering, I pulled my quilt tight around me and curled up
on my mat. It smelled of Ezarit's spices and tea.

I was censured. I hoped for forgiveness. For a miracle.

3

LOWTOWER

In the morning, Nat banged thick baskets and buckets together to wake me. Woven vine rasped against age-dark bone. Elna gave us her cleaning rags. We tied everything on a hemp line and used ladders to descend eight tiers below Elna's, into the no-man's-zone of Densira. The smell of rot and refuse clung to my nostrils.

I kept my eyes on the empty tiers we passed, not on the sky with its tempting breezes and diving whipperlings.

"Whoo," Nat said after a sniff at the stench. He jumped from the ladder onto the tier and stunt-rolled into the darkness beyond, howling like a banshee.

The clouds were so close here. They flowed and parted to reveal even more clouds, always waiting. An occasional dark flicker within them might have been a large bird, or something worse.

I disengaged from the ladder, feeling the sky tug at me. Stepped back from the edge, wingless and disgraced. The inner wall had grown much more down here. Barely enough room to sleep out of the weather and the fall of refuse from above. That, at least, was a blessing. Less space left to clean.

I didn't watch where I walked. One foot landed in a pile of muck.

"Birdcrap!" I yelled. I heard Nat cackle. Then he yelped, backing up fast.

A creature swung out of the depths of the tier, dressed in rags. It charged at us, hooting. A thin hand clutched Nat's robe. Greasy hair dangled, and exposed parts of its body sagged like old courier bags, stretching from arms and buttocks. I looked away.

"Begone. Not yours!" it yelled at us.

Elna descended the ladder, pale as always, though the downtower shadows were easier on her eyes. "Tobiat." Her voice rang firm across the empty tier. "My son, Nat, and his friend, Kirit. They're going to clean the low tiers as a punishment."

Tobiat. Invalids like him, as well as the very skyblind and the mad, were sometimes left behind as the tiers rose. They lived far downtower, on the edges of old quarters, scrounging for scraps. Many fell or starved, especially if they had no family to care for them. Or if their family abandoned them for being bad luck.

Elna handed Tobiat a packet of dried fruit and graincakes. He released Nat's cloak to clutch at it, nodding thanks. "Elna's good people."

"He's chosen this tier to make his nest," she said to us. "This will be a foul mess to start with."

Nat looked from his mother to the hermit, then deep into the tier. His nose wrinkled, and I joined him to see what he saw. Piles of stinking rags, shreds of ladders, broken wings. Too many to count. Tobiat had gathered parts of the tower that no one else wanted. We'd never get it clean enough.

"Why does he keep these things?" I whispered. "He'd be much better off letting them fall away with the rest of the garbage."

Nat shrugged. "Dunno. Not like I knew Ma was keeping him."

Elna secured herself to the ladder again, her wings unclasped just in case. She gripped hard, and she began the climb. "Vant said the guard will check on your progress by afternoon." Her words were as much a promise to us as a warning to Tobiat to make himself scarce.

Tobiat, his mouth full of dried apple, cackled and wandered away, trailing a frayed cloth that had once wrapped his body against the cold. I heard him mutter, "Cleaning, clean, cleaners." He receded into the gloom.

Nat passed me a rag and a bucket. "I wish we could use scourweed." The tough fibers were reserved for Singers, for raising towers.

"Not much grows on the lowtowers," I said. "If we find some, I say we use it."

"I'll keep my eyes open," Nat said. For now, we were a team again, trying to work as fast as possible.

Instead of scourweed, we found an old rain catcher, too broken to be worth lifting higher, and used it as a scoop. Then we started as far from Tobiat's piles as we could, swiping at the mold and bird shit that had accumulated everywhere. I felt sick. Nat looked pretty green too.

"Tobiat," he called, "we need to move your things."

Tobiat had piled wing battens and bits of broken carvings around what was probably his bed. Kept them a safe distance from the small fire pit. He had nothing that looked like metal. If he'd found anything that valuable, it would have been sold or stolen before now. I caught myself looking anyway, like a glitter-smitten kavik.

Other piles had been pushed against the inner wall. One leaked dank vegetable liquid from the bottom.

I kicked at it. "All trash."

With two fingers, I lifted a fetid pile of grayish cloth from the heap. The fabric was crusted with age-browned blood and gristle. I walked to the edge with it and had cranked back my arm to give it a good heave when Tobiat came out of nowhere, howling, "Mine, mine!" He grabbed, the fabric crackling at his touch, bits falling off. Stink rose, though whether from the cloth or Tobiat, I couldn't tell.

"Disgusting," I said and pulled, while trying to keep myself back from the edge. Tobiat shrieked and yanked at the fabric, leaning way out. The thought of him falling, at my hand, nearly choked me. The clouds were too close here. As were the shadows that prowled the clouds.

"Nat!" I yelled. Nothing. "Nat! Help!" and Nat came running, finally. He coaxed Tobiat off the edge of the balcony and calmed him with a piece of goose. When I released the rags, the hermit bundled them into a ball and held them close.

"We are never going to finish," I said. We'd miss the wingtest. I'd lose my best opportunity to avoid another confrontation with Singer Wik. And even if we were to finish in time, we'd have no chance to study. One look at Nat's creased brow showed he was worried too.

"What if we toss everything?" Nat raised an eyebrow. "It would be faster. He's mad, right? He won't miss any of it."

I looked more closely at Tobiat. He wasn't mad. His skull was dented on one side, as if he'd hit something at great speed and lived to forget the fall. His skin was frost-marked where he'd left it bare in the wind. Scars rippled across his face and back, and several bones looked to have been broken and rehealed as they lay. He was more crooked than straight. It must have been very painful. Still, he was aware of us. He'd covered himself a bit better with his rags than before. He gripped the cloth tightly. He was in there, somewhere. We couldn't throw his things down like he wasn't.

"Tobiat?" I said in my softest voice. "We have to clean four tiers, fast, or we'll never be allowed to leave."

He looked at me. "Leave?"

"Yes, we'll leave when it's clean."

The hermit reached out a claw and hooked a finger around one of my cleaning rags. He lifted it gingerly and dipped it in the bucket we'd been using to hold rainwater. So he knew how to do it. Soon he was heaving trash over the edge of the balcony with us, yelling, "Good-bye, good-bye!"

The sun had dipped towards the clouds when the ladder clattered against the tier, finally. Tobiat disappeared. I looked around. The space was clean, but it had taken all day. Three more tiers to finish by the wingtest felt impossible.

A stone fruit pit bounced off my shoulder and rolled across the balcony. I chased it down before it could stick to the newly cleaned tier. Sidra and Dojha from uptower circled and swooped just out of my throwing range.

Once Ezarit and I moved uptower, Sidra had become coldly polite in flight class. She'd grown much warmer to Nat. Since Allsuns, he'd found himself at the center of a swirl of brightly colored wings. He looked amused to see them here.

"Does stink down here," Sidra said. "You were right, Dojha. So far downtower, we're bound to get hit with a bucket's worth of foul if we stay too long."

Dojha blushed. "We wanted to see if you two needed anything from flight."

"Since you're going to miss the last classes before the wingtest," Sidra added.

Sidra's wings shone with decorative thread. Between batten sections, panels had been dyed the color of flowers: red, blue, purple. Hard to miss. Sidra caught me sizing up her colors and grinned at me.

"My father says you got off easy." She sounded like our Magister, strict. Scolding. "Lawsbreaking. Bringing shame on the tower just before Allmoons. The guard said you were playing with lenses on your balcony when it came. Did it run away because you sang to it?"

Sidra had the prettiest voice in flight. When she sang Laws, everyone remembered the words. I was not so lucky.

I pulled back into the shadow of the tier and held my mouth shut tight.

Dojha turned her head sideways as an updraft brushed her wingtips. "Let's go, Sidra. Dinner."

"Right," Sidra said. "See you at wingtest, I hope." She waved to Nat, and I bristled. Then they were gone.

Nat gathered our buckets and rags. The back of his neck was bright red.

I reached for the ladder, but Tobiat rushed up, nearly bumping me off the ledge. "Payment," he said, and held out his hand.

"We can't pay you. We don't have anything," Nat said, frustrated.

But Tobiat's hand wasn't empty.

"Look, Nat."

Tobiat held a pile of bone chips, as filthy as his hands. Nat lifted one, and the rest came with it. They were strung together like a necklace.

"More Laws," Nat said. His eyes went flat, and his voice with them. "Thanks for nothing, Tobiat." But he stuffed the stinking thing in his robe so that Tobiat would let his arm go. Once he did, Tobiat bobbed his head and muttered to himself. He receded back into the gloom.

As we prepared to climb the ladder back to Elna's, I heard Tobiat shout, "Leave!"

❦ ❦ ❦

That night, I huddled in the sitting area. Elna had borrowed screens to make a guest space, but it was still breezy. The fire had gone out. Elna's own sleeping screens, hand-me-downs from my mother, muffled her soft snores. Day after tomorrow was the wingtest. If there was the slightest chance we'd be allowed to take it, I would be ready. No time to sleep.

When two fliers are on the same plane and at risk of colli-sion, the flier with more maneuverability must give way. Tradi-tionally, this is the flier with the wind coming over their right wing.

Tradition. There was a rule for that too. *Traditions meant everyone knew what to do, and did it. Laws were tradition, strengthened to avoid angering the city.*

After a while, I'd recited everything I could remember from Magister Florian's instruction, jealous that our flight group had two extra days to practice with him. That they knew they'd be able to wingtest. I'd never felt so angry at my tower in my whole life. Nor at myself.

"Kirit," Nat whispered.

It took me a while to answer. "What?"

He scooted into my space, his hair sleep-tossed. He didn't say anything for a moment, just looked at his hands. He toyed with old message chips, rubbing them together so they squealed.

"That's a horrible sound," I said. Then I pressed my lips to-gether. We used to talk about everything. Then I rose and he pulled away, and now? I wanted to tell him everything, and now I couldn't. The Singer's fiat forbade me. I held my fears in my mouth. I swallowed what I would have once told him about how it felt to scream down a skymouth or argue with a Singer. I waited for him to speak.

"Tell me what it looked like, at least?"

"The skymouth?"

He nodded, eager to hear.

I could give him that. But where would it lead? To have the whole story pulled from me like a silk ribbon off a package, until I was emptied and Nat was tied up in it. *No.*

He cleared his throat and tried again. "All right. What if I go first?"

Hope rose, tickling the corners of my mouth, as I realized he wanted to fix things, a little.

"You have to see these," he said. He wasn't playing with any old message chips from a kavik. He'd been fingering the strand of chips Tobiat gave him. He'd cleaned them up, so that we could see the rope binding them was frayed blue silk. Much finer than the chips we tied to message birds. Or any Laws chips. The pieces of bone were thicker too. This strand was never intended to be sent by wing.

I looked at the scratches on the chips. The carving included tiny holes, careful etchings. Carvings within carvings. "What is this?"

"I'm not sure," Nat said. "Look." He wiped away a spot of mold on the back of a chip. The scratches took on shape and substance. "It's like a tower map. Each chip is a tier. And there are symbols on the other side. I can't make them out."

"What do you mean? You can read chips as well as I can."

"Look," he said again. And he was right. The symbols weren't made up of forms I knew. These were arabesque curls and sharp cuts. Odd angles. Tobiat had given us something very strange indeed.

I whispered without thinking, "Some of it looks like the marks on that Singer's face." Suddenly, I wanted to go back to worrying about the wingtest.

Nat watched me carefully. "Tell me about them?"

"I want to study." I said it as casually as I could. If I'd had feathers like his whipperling, they'd have been raked around my collar.

"Why? This is so much better—secret Singer messages, diagrams. Besides, if we do finish cleaning and you get to wingtest, you'll be great at Laws. You know them all."

If my voice didn't trip me up. If we could wingtest. Too many ifs.

I didn't want to talk about ifs. I couldn't talk about the sky-mouth. "You think the tower on those chips is Densira or Mond-arath?" I asked, trying to think of anything that would swing Nat's attention.

"It might be a tower far away." Nat looked out into the dark. "Why?"

"Because if you get your wingmark," I said, "you can fly the city until you find it. Without a Magister at your side."

He paled. "If I don't, I'll be stuck here until next Allsuns. No wingmark, no flying past this quadrant. No apprenticeship or wingfights or anything."

Nat loved his mysteries and his conspiracies, but he loved flying more. I'd caught him. Worse, if he didn't pass with full marks, he wouldn't get a good apprenticeship because of Naton's Lawsbreaks. Nat and Elna would sink farther on the tower. And they didn't have far to go.

He tried to play it off. "You worry too much," he mumbled.

"We have three tiers to clean tomorrow," I said. "That's worry enough. I'm afraid we're not going to finish in time, even if Tobi-at's was the worst by far." A few days ago, my biggest worry about the wingtest had been to do well enough that my mother would beg to have me as her apprentice. Now I needed my wingmark to stay clear of the Singer's clutches. And I'd started to fear the lengths the Singer was willing to go to in order to set me up to fail.

The last few days of flight training had focused on sweeps, rolls, and defensive gliding, and I needed work in that area. Ma-gister Florian's recitations and songs were filled with important angles and calculations. We'd missed plenty of last-minute secrets while we were downtower with our buckets.

I hoped Nat shared my worries. "We could study together?" But he'd already retreated to his mat.

So I curled back up on my own mat and tried to recite more right-of-way rules. I practiced the singsong Laws. Easy to sing, easy to remember. Less carving required to pass them on. The rhythms were memorable; the repetition made me drowsy.

My eyes snapped open at movement by my side. Elna was bent over me, furious.

"Where did you get this?"

I scrambled off my sleeping mat and stood, blearily, as she shook the blue silk cord with the strange bone chips at me. Nat was nowhere to be seen.

"Tobiat gave it to Nat!"

I'd never seen Elna this angry. "He did, did he? You're an innocent bystander again?"

A chill ran up my back. Yesterday, Elna had thought I was a skytouched blessing. Now she sounded like she agreed with the councilman.

"You can't leave well enough alone, can you, Kirit? Always have to make a mess."

I reeled on my feet. Was I dreaming? Elna loved me. The bone chips dangled and rattled in her hand. That's what had changed.

"I don't even know what they mean," I protested.

Elna ran her fingers along the age-smoothed bone chips. Her chin quivered. She threw the braided skein of chips on the floor and turned from me. "Leave those things be." She pointed at Tobiat's chips. Her voice broke like a wild whipperling's tethered for the first time to a training line. She began singing Laws. Pointedly. The ones about trespass and betrayal.

I struggled to pull myself from my sleep fog and find the words that would loosen her anger. "Elna, no," was all that came out. A child's whisper. "Please." I picked up the chips. "Tell me what they are?"

The chips turned to ice in my hand.

And I jerked awake screaming, sprawled on the warm bone floor beside my mat.

The real Elna was at my side moments later. Elna who loved me, who had always been there, her hand gentle on my back. She hushed me softly and began to hum a baby's song about Allmoons and Nightwings, like I was a child again.

"Sing The Rise," I murmured, my eyes drooping.

She shifted to the song of salvation. The story of how the city nearly died in the clouds and how the people saved it. In my mother's quarters, Elna's voice had been tight and formal. Here, she sang from the belly.

The Rise began as a children's song, with verses added as we learned to read carvings and to listen to the city sing at Allsuns and Allmoons. She began it low and soft: *"Far down below the clouds, oh, the city did rise. . . ."* She grew surer of herself, even as she kept her voice quiet. She let the notes wash over her. The towers of the city grew in my imagination, in time with the music. Elna glowed when she sang. She repeated the chorus again: *"The clouds fell away, and the people were saved. Oh, the city did rise,"* and I could see her as she might have been, before Nat's father died. Before she gave up teaching. Before Ezarit paid her to watch me and to be my mother too.

My body relaxed as the song wove the air. Elna loved me. The thought was a balm. Then another thought, as I fell into sleep, weighed me down. The next line of The Rise praised the Singers for saving the city.

The wingtest would decide my fate, if I could get there. In two days' time, I would be taken to the Spire by the guardians of the city or I would fly free on my own wings.

ϟ ϟ ϟ

In the morning, a shadow drifted past the open balcony doors. I sipped chicory, and Nat worked over a bowl of dried berries. The bone chips sat on the table between us.

Elna passed us on her way to the midtower market. She'd

tied a satchel of finished mending to her side. I stuffed the skein of chips into my sleeve before she saw it.

"Tobiat didn't get in your way yesterday?" she asked, gripping the ladder tight with both hands.

Nat shook his head. "He helped a bit."

She smiled. "I've found him more helpful when I've treated him with respect."

She began her climb. We watched until her feet disappeared.

Nat took mash to his whipperling. He returned quickly. "Maalik's not here." He grumbled that if someone wanted to send messages using his bird, they needed to ask him first. Then he began rummaging in Elna's storage baskets for more rags.

"Kirit, look." Nat had unstacked several baskets by the inside wall. As with everyone's quarters, the center wall supported the tower. It grew first on each tier and thickened with each year until, on the lowest parts of the tower we could reach, only a few meters of space remained in what were once huge rooms. Barely enough space to land on, if you listened to the scavengers.

The baskets contained things Elna wasn't ready to toss. Nat held a scrap of robe, creased like it had been balled up for a decade or more. I spread it out—two handspans of blue silk striped with dove gray, very faded. A piece of a Magister's cloak. "Elna's?"

"Yes."

"Why did she stop?"

"I think they wouldn't let her teach, after. She never talks about it." He spun on his heel and headed back into the dark. I heard him rummaging. In my hand, the skein of knotted silk cord and bone chips rattled. Some of the chips were shaped like tears and teeth, all were nearly white, flat, and practically soft to the touch. They'd been handled often. The marks and symbols seemed to have been made using traditional tools: bone

scrapers, bone needles, and bone chisels. Only the small holes
drilled all the way through had crisp edges, perhaps made with
one of the few metal drills that remained in the city. Those were
the province of the bridge builders, the artifexes. Like Naton
had been.

The discarded robe in the rag bag and the bone chips in my
hand made me wonder. I fought the urge. Couldn't risk thinking too hard about the Singers.

But Nat lifted the chips and hefted them. "My father could
have made these," he whispered, although everyone had gone
up to the market. The tower was wrapped with ladders and
ropes as people hauled their extra from gardens to the tower
council's farm stores.

"Don't you think the chips are too old for that?" I shifted from
the guest area into the deeper recesses of their quarters. I lifted
a lid on a basket, poked a finger through the handwork that Elna
took in. Searching for a way to switch the subject.

"The holes in the chips. The shadow of an older carving, not
fully ground away. Something's been erased, and replaced." He
jumped as Elna dropped onto the balcony. As she entered, Nat
pushed the skein back into my hand and stuffed the scrap of
cloak into a basket. I slipped the bone markers into a pocket
and prayed they wouldn't clatter too much. Elna had very sharp
ears.

"Forgot my sewing kit. You two had better get going," she
scolded. "Three more tiers to clean."

Ugh. We'd done the worst one yesterday. The next three
likely had occupants too, but anything would be more sanitary
than Tobiat's. We got moving.

My feet were barely off the ladder when we met an occupant of the day's first tier. A woman rushed from the shadows,
her clothes ragged, but less so than Tobiat's. She was so weighed
down by the Laws tied to her wrists, they clattered when she

moved. I couldn't read them before she ran forward and grabbed Nat's bucket. Pulled. Nat leaned back, trying to keep it from her. The two of them spun closer to the edge.

I tried to push them towards the tower's core, towards safety, by placing both hands on Nat's back and shoving. All of us were wingless. None would survive a fall here.

A whoop and a cry made the woman let go of the bucket. Her wind-scarred eyes widened as Tobiat charged in, waving his hands and bellowing. She dodged his hands, then slunk away.

"Looks like we've made an ally," I said, catching my breath. Tobiat looked marginally better than the day before. And I remembered what Elna said about respect. "Thank you for your help."

Tobiat made a face. "Cleaning."

"Yes, and we have to do it fast," Nat said. No time to battle scavengers.

Tobiat glared in every direction, a crooked, unwinged guard. The woman had disappeared into the shadows.

Tobiat stepped to the balcony's edge, then jumped.

I screamed and ran for the edge, expecting to see his weathered form plummeting to the clouds. Instead, I saw he'd managed to land on the lower balcony and roll. "Cloudtouched," I whispered to Nat. "He's gone."

"Could have used him," Nat grumbled. We gathered our rags, wary of every shadow and skitter.

The tier had less junk on it by far than Tobiat's. I dipped my rag in the damp bottom of the bucket and squeezed the cloth nearly dry. Nat did the same. We knelt side by side on the bone floor, scrubbing at crusted spots and stains. When I moved to scrub the central wall, which had pushed far out into the tier, my fingertips and knuckles scraped against the rough bone more than once. I didn't stop scrubbing.

No more scavengers or undertower folk troubled us.

The sun had barely moved by the time we climbed to the next tier. I began to hope we'd make the wingtest after all.

The Singers offered the test to all the quadrants, in four-tower groups, twice each year. Anyone who'd flown at least twelve seasons, as most who'd passed seventeen Allsuns had, could wingtest. Most who attempted the test passed within three tries, and many attempted it. Without the wingmark, no one would take a young flier as an apprentice, no matter who they were related to. If you couldn't fly beyond your home quadrant without a Magister, who would want you?

I tried not to think about who wanted me.

"Kirit, look." Nat had reached the tier before me. He pointed at the small bit of scourweed stuck in a gap between bone plates on a bone spur.

"Yes!" I grabbed the tough nettle and tore it carefully in half. Handed one section to Nat.

After an hour's work on the next tier, a shadow passed once, then twice as a flier circled the tower. We hid the scourweed in a crevice and switched back to rags. I expected Sidra again, and braced for more ridicule. Instead, Magister Florian landed on the balcony. He left his wings set. Not here for a social call, then. He skipped the hellos too.

"You two should consider taking the wingtest *next* Allsuns." A half-year away.

Nat straightened. "Why?"

I swiped at a dark, sticky spot with my rag.

"You're close, but Kirit needs more practice on her turns and on group flight. That last run was not your best, Kirit." He took a breath, giving me plenty of time to remember how I'd fallen out of the turn and nearly lost my bearings. "And now you've spent two days cleaning. You'll be tired, even if you do finish. I don't want to see too many from Densira fail."

I scrubbed harder at the spot. Perhaps it would disappear.

"Magister, with respect—" Nat began.

The Magister held up his hand. "It's up to you. You'll be flying from downtower, already at a disadvantage. Your ability to take the lead in Group is important, and you can't do that well when you're tired. You can do your best, but it might be better to wait until conditions are optimal. Next Allsuns. For Kirit, especially."

I didn't stop scrubbing. I pictured the trades I'd make as an apprentice. My skill at bargaining. Ezarit's appreciation when I finessed a particularly tricky detail. "I will see you tomorrow, Magister."

He didn't smile. But Nat did. "We will both see you tomorrow, Magister."

Florian turned and jumped, wings spread. He caught an updraft and rose almost effortlessly. I hoped I'd be so lucky tomorrow.

"Nice work!" Nat punched my arm lightly.

"What do you mean?"

"He was trying to get you to give up, and you wouldn't let him. I'm sure he doesn't want to lose face before the other Magisters." He paused, thinking. "Now you have to pass the test for sure."

The weight of his words settled on my shoulders, and deep in my stomach.

❧ ❧ ❧

By midday, we still had a long way to go on the tier, but we kept encountering curiously clean corners. The scourweed had helped too. And we needed to eat. As I unpacked the dried dirgeon Elna had sent down in a small basket, I saw Tobiat peeking around a corner. I held out a piece of the dirgeon to him. He darted out, then munched loudly.

"He's going to follow us home if you feed him," Nat said.

"He's helping. Keeping the scavengers away," I said. Maybe the scourweed too. I was surprised Nat hadn't seen it. Besides, I was curious. "What else does he do all day?"

Tobiat reached into my pocket and drew out the blue-corded bone markers. "Mine."

"You gave them to us. For helping, remember?"

He looked at me sharply and handed them back, to Nat. On a whim, I pointed to the faded bridge that Nat had found on the chips. Tobiat squinted, and he sat back on his heels, elbows on knees. His fingers, slicked with bird grease, combed his skeined hair. "Naton's," he said, pointing at the bridge shadow. "Naton's," he said again, pointing at Nat.

Nat dropped his lunch. Tobiat scooted in to retrieve it and gobbled the piece of roasted bird instead of handing it back to Nat.

"It was his."

Tobiat grinned, but didn't say anything more.

Nat held up the skein. "They're not message chips. They're a plan for something?" he asked, raising both in his hands. His fingers curled around the bone chips, as if Tobiat might snatch them away too.

"Cages," Tobiat said before he doubled over with wheezing and hacking. We both backed away. Coughing was dangerous. You didn't want to stop breathing, not for a minute. Tobiat got hold of himself and whispered, "Cages. Delequerriat." The strange word rolled off his tongue like water. Then he sat back on his heels and cleared his throat. After a lot of rattling noise, he raised a gob of phlegm and spat it on the floor.

"Ugh," Nat said.

I swiped at the thing with my rag. It was flecked with blood. When I looked up again, Tobiat had skittered out of sight.

We returned to cleaning, too wrapped up in our own thoughts to talk.

❦ ❦ ❦

By the time the sun came level with our tier, making everything too bright, we still had one more tier to go. The wingtest was tomorrow. The mystery of the chips could wait.

"Hurry, Nat." I scrubbed the scourweed across every surface and tossed garbage.

Somewhere, right then, Ezarit was saving people. Bringing them medicine or making more trades. By now, towers were making a song of it.

To serve the city. Dire need. There was no higher privilege, no rarer service. My mother's bravery was known throughout the city. I pictured myself with my new wings, bringing food to starving towers or fuel to citizens with no heat; I imagined hearing Ezarit's voice, soft and proud, as the city sang *my* name. I scrubbed even harder. I would do this.

We could barely drag ourselves up the ladder to the last tier. "This will take all night," Nat said, going first.

He was right. Even if we managed to finish by dawn, we'd be dead on our wings tomorrow for the test. Still, I followed him up. Heard him gasp as he pulled himself over the ledge.

In the sunset light, the tier sparkled. Clean. Elna stood close to the central wall with Councilman Vant, who looked annoyed. Elna was in a chipper mood.

"Didn't think you two would start with this tier and work down," she said.

"We didn't—" Nat began, but I dug an elbow hard into his ribs.

"We didn't think the order mattered," I finished.

Vant made a *harrumph* noise while he looked around. Finally, his face brightened. "Haven't had the lower levels cleaned

in some time," he said. "Good for the health of the tower."
His voice was jolly, but he wouldn't meet my eyes. He couldn't
figure out how we'd done it.

Neither could I.

"I'll be seeing you and your mother soon," he said with a sour
smile as he reached for my hand. He cut the punishment chip
from my wrist with a small knife, well worn. Then did the same
for Nat.

We were dismissed.

Vant unfurled his wings and leapt from the tier. A strong late-
afternoon gust lifted him in a rising circle around the tower.

Out of the corner of my eye, I saw Elna place a wrapped
parcel by the wall. She climbed the ladder, and Nat followed.
I lingered, hoping to see who she'd thanked with the thick
bundle. No one peeked out from the shadows to claim it. Before I climbed the ladder, I took one of my light quilts from my
satchel and left it atop Elna's parcel. I hoped it would keep him
warm.

4

OLD WINGS

Elna had filled her table with rich things she couldn't possibly have bought herself. Was Ezarit near? She would know what had happened.

I looked behind Nat's and Elna's screens. Nat's whipperling squatted on its perch, several tail feathers dusty and askew.

"Ezarit sent a courier to the tower, with a package for Vant and the goose for us," Elna acknowledged. Maalik pecked at his mash, hungry.

"You sent her a message," I said. It was not a question.

Elna raised her eyebrows. "She needed to know. And you need your strength for tomorrow. Though I couldn't tell her everything." The Singer's warning. *You will not interfere.* If I knew Elna, she'd hinted anyway.

We ate greedily. Nat's fingers dove for the goose fat, and mine scooped up a thick, roasted leg. I saw his frown. He'd wanted that too.

Elna's plate was empty. "Go on, eat." She made a shooing gesture with her hands. "You worked hard. You're testing tomorrow." I pushed the goose leg to her plate and picked up a wing instead. She tried to say she wasn't hungry. When I ignored her, she tore into the leg.

"When I'm apprenticed," Nat said through a mouthful of goose, "we'll eat like this every night."

Elna chuckled. "And you'll need new wings each Allsuns, like Councilman Vant."

"Won't. Ever." Nat reached for the water sack and helped himself. He filled Elna's cup, then splashed water in mine. "I'll be the fastest hunter in the sky. Bring down everything I see."

"Let's hope you don't bring down a friend, then." Elna ruffled his hair. She cracked the leg bone and sucked the marrow out. Nat did the same with a thigh. I set my wing down. Never crack a wing, not even if you might starve.

We were the opposite of starving. We sat at the table near the balcony and watched the lights go down in the highertowers. The stars grew bright in the sky, and the moon bellied above the clouds, full enough to turn the city silver.

"Clear sky," Elna noted. "Good for tomorrow." She stepped away from the table and pulled two bundles from behind the sleeping screen. Our wings.

Nat whooped and spread his out on the floor, then went in the back for a mending kit to shore up a worn seam.

Elna looked sad as she handed me my wings. "Your mother's delayed in the south quadrant," she said. "The tower council brought these down when they delivered the goose."

I shrugged off my disappointment and tore into the bundle, thinking of the green and gold swirls. My new wings. But when the bundle came undone, I found my old wings, newly mended. Elna laid a skein of message chips on top. From my mother. She patted my hand and left me with it.

Kirit, the chips read, *I should be back in time for Allmoons. Southwest is complicated. Meantime, do your best. I won't have you test on new wings after all that happened. You will use your old ones. Liras Viit has mended them well. Be brilliant. You will rise like the sun.*

Nothing more. Old wings, a mother away, and a wingtest for

which I was ill-prepared. I should be flying from the towertop on gold and green to meet the test, with Ezarit cheering me on.

Alone. I would do this alone. Ezarit hadn't returned. The southwest was more important and demanded much, I knew.

A thought took my breath away. Would she return before the Singer came back? Perhaps she didn't want me as apprentice after all. Staying away was an easy way to say so.

My dusky wings with their patches and stains felt far heavier in my hands than they used to. How could I rise if both my tower and my mother were determined to weigh me down?

With that, I snapped back to reality. *Chin up, shoulders back, Kirit.* I would fly the wingtest well enough to keep Wik at bay and take top marks, so that Ezarit would see I was the best apprentice she could choose. And then I could choose to go with her or make my own way.

"Beautiful stitching," said Elna, running her fingers over Liras Viit's patchwork. She patted Nat's shoulder, then mine. "You could work on your mending skills. Never know when you'll need them."

Nat wrinkled his nose, but continued to shore up his wings. I barely hid my expression; I hated mending. I'd trade for my garments, like Ezarit did. After tomorrow.

Tomorrow, we'd be questioned on city Laws and history. There would be a solo flight, then a group flight with students from other towers and citizen volunteers. Group was the most important test: flying among strangers without killing anyone. I had to do well on it all. I could not falter, could not let Vant or Wik or anyone keep me from passing my wingtest.

We'd spent years preparing. Our Magister had drilled us on each element. And tried to dissuade Nat and me from showing up because we'd spent the final days before the test cleaning downtower.

Worse, I had yet to go into open sky since the migration. The thought, even though the Singers had declared the skymouths gone for now and the skies safe, made my dinner feel like a pannier full of guano.

Elna gave me a knowing smile. She remembered what it was like. "Stakes are high. Passage on the first try will make you seem lucky. It will balance the tower's censure." She was trying to make us feel better. "Even on the second try, there are plenty of professions that will still want a strong flier."

But no one wanted you if you were unlucky, or if you happened to attract skymouths to your tower.

"Sidra said some of the group volunteers are hunters," Nat added. He was a fine shot. Good with a knife, too.

"If not the hunters, the guards," he told me while he double-stitched a seam with silk thread. "Sidra said she'd talk to her father if I wanted to be a guard. I would line my wings with glass and patrol the skies."

I barely heard him. As I'd scrubbed the tower, I'd let myself daydream too. My life as a trader. I knew he'd done the same. All that stood between me and that future was one test. Now, holding my old wings, I imagined the roar of air around me as I plummeted and failed. It would be worse than being sent downtower in a basket, because everyone who could spare the time would be watching the wingtest, with lenses. If I fell out of my turn, they would see me.

Everyone but Ezarit.

Allmoons was in two days, which wasn't long. But that would be too late. At least she wouldn't see me fall.

If I could just practice my rolls and climbs once more. If my voice was prettier.

Too dark to fly now. Wingtest started after dawn. Instead, I practiced in the main room. I unfurled my wings, slipped my arms into the straps, stretched my fingers to the harnesses that controlled curvature and, to some extent, lift. The woven harness that held my feet when I flew dragged on the floor with a soft *ruck-ruck-ruck*. I began twisting this way and that, angling my hands to curve the wings' tethers, ducking my head to let the air curl around me.

"You look like you're dancing," Nat said. I jumped. He'd been behind the screen, reading.

"Practicing. You don't?"

He shook his head. "Magister said I'm a natural."

The lanterns grew dim as the oil in them ran out. Elna came in from the balcony and kissed the tops of our heads. She whispered, "Don't stay up too late," and went to bed. Outside, the full moon finally cleared the clouds again, flooding the balcony and the outermost rooms with pearl-gray light. Dark wings chased bugs between distant towers, and the closest towers sparkled under the star-glimmered sky. It was a soft night. Almost as beautiful as an Allmoon.

Someone in the tower had picked up their dolin and was plucking at the strings. The chords drifted down like raindrops.

"Come on, Kirit. We know everything we need to know already. We finished the punishment. Watch the stars come out."

I growled quietly. Nat wasn't nervous anymore. Me, I had everything riding on this test. If I did well, the Spire would have no claim on me. Ezarit would know my worth to her. My luck would be restored. Tomorrow I could begin training to become a trader like my mother. Or I could disappear.

Nat was right; he was a natural. I'd always had to work at it.

I knew I'd pass the first part, Laws. I'd memorized all the songs. The test focused on accuracy, so the fact that my voice sounded like scourweed on bone couldn't hurt me. I hoped. I worried most about Group. Anything could happen then. Sometimes everything did.

I closed my eyes and spun, feeling my old wings fill with the slight breeze. The battens supported two layers of silk that

spread and furled like bats' wings. The wingframe could lock
in position to free the hands, or a skilled flier could use the
grips woven into each wing to rake and angle the wingfoils
during a glide. I felt the grips with my fingers, the leads of the
silkspun ropes that ran to eyebolts drilled at the tips of the wingframe. Singers' wings used tendon instead of silk. For us, silk
had to do.

I imagined myself diving and turning in a clear blue sky.
I imagined leading a group. I had to do well. I had to focus.
But instead of the rules for upwind group flight, or the different
traditions of various towers in the city, I saw the strange patterns on the bone chips Tobiat gave us. My arms dropped to my
sides. My concentration had failed me. No more flying tonight.

When I opened the shutters, I found Nat sitting on the balcony, looking at the moon through a hole in one of the age-worn
bone chips—Naton's plans. I hesitated, one foot on the threshold, then stepped out.

Nat turned and peered at me one-eyed through the carved
chip.

"What are they, do you think?" he said.

The chip made Nat's brown eye seem flat and enormous,
with extra sclera. Like a skymouth's. I pushed that thought out
of my mind. The sky had been clear for days.

I steadied my voice. "No idea." Tried to think of things a
bridge artifex like Naton would want to make. Something woven or knotted. "Probably not a telescope."

He lowered the skein. "Not a good one anyway."

I stood well back from the edge of the balcony, my wings
furled. The night air was cold. A large bat dove from one of the
towers, chasing something. Stinging bugs, hopefully, or a jumping rat. Those were a menace.

Nat followed the bat with his eyes. "Good hunter, that one."

The pause in conversation stretched out. He waited for me

to say something. I scrambled for a topic that didn't include Singers or skymouths.

"Do you want to stay near Densira, Nat? After Allmoons, I mean."

He nodded. "I want to make sure Ma's taken care of. Besides, the best hunters in the north are Densira. What about you?"

I swallowed. Few knew that my mother was thinking of other towers. That would be a betrayal of Densira. And no one could know of the Singer's threat. Or how I might escape it.

"I want to fly with Ezarit. The best trader in the city."

He looked at me sideways. "She's not trying to apprentice you to another tower?"

"We're a team," I said. He wasn't wrong. Everyone understood that it was sometimes necessary for the city to shift apprentices between towers; but not everyone wanted to be the one to go. I wasn't tied to Densira any more than my mother was, so I shrugged.

A week ago, I'd dreamed of seeing the rest of the city. Of living on a tower with bridges connected to a close ring of neighbors. I bet it was a lot more interesting than out here, where everyone knew everything about you before you were even born. I knew it had to be better than living behind the Spire's wall.

I tried to push the Spire and its Singers from my mind, only to return to worrying about the wingtest. "Want to practice Laws?"

He was sighting with his bow, out across the night sky. Aiming for bats, which was bad luck. The skein was back in his pocket.

"Nat!"

"What's it like, do you think, for animals up here?" he mused. "There's a whole lot of eat or be eaten. And they have to do a lot of work. Just like us."

"What's the alternative?"

"We do what the tower council tells us, and the guilds. And especially the Singers. No one asks why anymore."

"No one wants to go back to what life was like in the clouds, before the Singers."

"Who says we would? I have a theory . . ."

Nat always had theories. That way lay danger. "What would you do if no one told you what you had to do?"

"I'd hunt! And wingfight. When I've got my wingmark, I'll fight for Densira. With a new set of wings."

Before I'd moved uptower, Nat had talked about training more whipperlings and expanding to kaviks. The wingfighting was new. Sidra's influence again.

"Do you care about anything but trading, Kirit?"

I couldn't think of one thing I wanted more. If not the power of trading itself, the feeling of connecting towers, knowing I was helping people. Knowing I made it happen. Besides, trading didn't require much singing. Not even socially. Perfect all around.

There were other things I enjoyed at Densira. Watching the wingfights. And carving, though I hadn't done much of that since I was young. Even minding our silk spiders. But trading—finding something of value and exchanging it for something people I knew needed? That was fun. Ezarit loved it. Even when she wasn't flying through a skymouth migration, she'd said it was a good way to rise higher in the city.

Perhaps someday I'd leave Densira and become a trader for a more central tower. Perhaps I'd return and place a bet on Nat's wingfighting team. All I had to do was pass wingtest with full marks.

At the back of my mind, a new thought rose. I cared about one thing more than flying the city: escaping the net the Singer had set for me.

I hummed a Law, trying to get Nat to test me. He finally

responded. "That's Kamik. No going against the decision of the Singers, the council, and your tower." He was right. "Fine. What about this one?" He sang a soft, low tune, almost a whisper.

"Nat, that's awful." He'd sung the dirge for someone lost to a skymouth. He'd sung me my father's death. And almost my own as well. I didn't have to stay out here for that. I grabbed fistfuls of my robe and prepared to sweep dramatically back into Elna's quarters and bed.

"I'm sorry." He ducked his head. His voice grew deeper when he was nervous. "That wasn't funny." He grabbed one of my sleeves and tugged at it, as he'd done when we were children. His hand caught my arm and squeezed. "Really. Sorry."

I didn't pull away; he didn't let go. Like old times again. His hand was cool as the night air. He stood a full shoulder taller than me now, and his arms had become thickly muscled. Mine had gone the other way, wire and sinew. It was the way we flew. I focused on speed, and he tried to work with the bow. To shoot from the wing, he had to hook his straps from the elbow and glide, then aim and shoot. He'd been practicing.

Stars speckled the darkening sky. One raced across the night, fire-backed. "Look up," I whispered. Too late. It winked out of sight. I touched my eyelid, then pointed skyward. Even a falling star deserved respect. We saw where its spirit went, not its body.

Nat released my arm and we sat apart together in the shadow of Elna's blackberry vines. The leaves smelled sharp in the cool. He eyed me.

"You're still worried."

That was an understatement. I was terrified. "It's those old wings. Liras Viit did a good job mending them, but they're not as wide as the new ones. And I've grown some." I steered away from additional what-ifs, other, more secret, worries.

Most of our class had broken in their new wings in the past

few weeks. Wings that were built to carry adults, strung tight enough to execute complex turns. The past few days of Florian's class had likely been filled with wild turns, as new wings reacted slightly differently to students' old habits.

I didn't want to admit that Ezarit was right, at least about the new wings. I'd fly more confidently on the old ones, because I hadn't practiced with the new. I hoped so, at least.

I wished I'd never gone out on that balcony during the migration. Wished I could undo that morning the way Elna unraveled a ripped cloth to mend it again.

"You won't be the only one on well-worn wings, Kirit." Nat used adult wings already. He hadn't said anything, but I knew they were a pair that had belonged to his father, long ago.

"How many times have you flown on those?"

"A lot. Not far, not breaking any Laws. But I've been flying with them for moons."

I'd been too wrapped up in my own concerns about Ezarit's trade run, the new quarters. I tried to picture what his wings looked like in the air and couldn't.

"Look on the bright side," Nat added. "You won't have to patch your new wings up after the test. Or worry about them getting ripped during Group flight. That's lucky." He flicked rotten blackberries off the balcony. "I heard Viit's sons are flying tomorrow. That will be exciting."

"Did Dojha or Sidra say who else would Magister the tests?" Our own Magister Florian, of course. But teachers were not allowed to judge the merits of anyone from their own tower.

Nat shrugged. "The usual, plus one new Magister for Mondarath. And Dix from Wirra. Since Magister Granth is still sick."

I tensed. Dix. Ezarit's former rival. Or Father's old friend. I was never sure, and Ezarit wouldn't discuss it.

"I should study some more. I need to get everything right if Magister Dix is testing."

"She can't be as bad as your mother makes it sound." Nat turned the bone chips over in his hands again, distracted.

"I'm not willing to risk it. I have to do well. Dix can't stand my mother, or me." Before the migration, before she'd flown, Ezarit had lit a small banner for Magister Granth's health, hoping that his coughing disease would pass and I wouldn't be in Dix's path. "She holds a grudge."

"You can't think she'd pull anything in front of the Singers?"

I swallowed. I didn't know. Dix. Old wings. My rough singing voice. And Singer Wik.

"It will be all right, Kirit." Nat sat down beside me. "We'll figure it out. And these too." He fingered the chips. "Whatever they're for."

"Why are you so interested in those, when you should be as worried as me?"

"They were my dad's." Nat rattled the blue skein. "What if they're connected to why he was thrown down? Or with something else about the city? Why Lith fell?"

I listened as his excitement grew. Nat had asked questions and spouted theories since we were little. Why there were skymouths. How the Singers stayed fed when they didn't grow anything. Why the city roared. What had happened to Naton.

"I'll take a closer look at them with you, after the wingtest. We can talk to Tobiat again too."

"If these are Singers' things, the Spire will want them back. Maybe Tobiat stole them from Naton, and that's why my dad was thrown down." I tensed at the mention of Singers, but Nat didn't notice. He turned the chips over once more, then put them back into a fold of his robe, musing. "Maybe we can trade the skein to the Singers for answers." He tied the chips securely in his robe, then looked at me. His brow furrowed in concern. "You're still worried. I'll help you study, if you want."

We sang softly through the short night and the early predawn, first Laws, then calculations and strategies for flying in a group of strangers. The hardest part of going beyond your own towers without a Magister in the lead was gliding from tower to tower without getting tangled, or worse, with strangers who were moving from place to place. We dozed on the balcony, wings by our sides, and woke to find that the moon had fallen again.

We had barely rested and were stiff from sitting on the bare floor.

"Nat, we're goners," I said. "We'll fail for sure."

"Don't worry," he said. "I won't at least. Then I'll put in a good word for you next year."

His bravado now and his temper the night before suddenly seemed much clearer to me. He was as afraid as I was. Tired of being the lowest on the tower. He wanted his future as much as I wanted mine. For the first time in a long time, I stepped outside myself and saw him, saw how much he'd changed.

I leaned into his shoulder, and he leaned back. "We'll both rise."

The sun had edged over the clouds and Elna had only just emerged from behind the sleeping screens when we came back in.

"I hope you didn't sleep on the balcony," she grumbled.

"Not at all," Nat lied. "Just checking the wind for today."

5

WINGTEST

Four bone horns sounded short, bright notes across the morning: one each from Densira, Viit, Wirra, and Mondarath.

First warning. If our feet weren't on the testing plinth by the fifth warning, we would not wingtest until Allsuns.

I fumbled with my straps, my fingers thick and clumsy. Elna finished securing Nat's straps and hurried over, tutting. "Your mother wishes she were here to do this for you."

I wished it too.

Elna's hands were strong. She pulled the bindings too tight at first. She was used to Nat's broader shoulders.

We wrapped ourselves warm and tied our quilted silks close. Nat pulled his hair back from his eyes with a strand of silk. I didn't have time to braid mine properly. It was a mess of tangles.

"Here." Elna pressed something soft and thick into my hands. A knitted cap, made of thick spun spidersilk and hemp. The cap's chevron pattern was tight enough to bind my hair against the wind. She grinned.

"You made this?"

She smiled, proud. I hesitated. I'd need something to keep the cap on.

I unfolded the cap from what it concealed. A glint of aged gray-yellow metal, a shimmer of well-polished glass. My mother's lenses. She'd paid a courier to bring them, but could not come herself.

No matter. Part of her would fly with me today. The lenses had survived for who knew how long, handed up, the straps replaced, dents carefully pounded from the frames. She considered them her good-luck charm.

Hope twisted the corners of my frown. I put cap and lenses on. Tightened the straps myself, until the padded rims pressed against my eye sockets. The lenses guarded my tired eyes from everything I saw: they framed and contained the sky.

A second warning sounded from the four towers.

The Magisters and their council assistants would have secured the testing plinth between the towers and raised the second wingtest flag by now: a blue banner edged in gray. We had to hurry.

Nat and I unfurled our wings and moved to the edge of the balcony. Elna whispered, "Go higher," behind us.

A strong gust swept round the tower. Densira's Allmoons banners kicked red arabesques on balconies above us. They streamed up and towards the plinth. A rising gust. A good sign indeed. We leapt together and caught the wind.

As we rose on the gust, two sets of brown wings emerged from Wirra and another three, gray, green, and brown, from Viit. We were halfway to the plinth when the air grew sloppy. An eddy spilling from the lee of Mondarath soiled the gust. I dipped, then Nat wobbled. We had to shift to another updraft, quickly. My mother's lenses slipped down my nose as I turned my head left and right.

Then I spotted a strong breeze marked by a line of coasting whipperlings. Whistling to Nat, I rolled for the new vent. He followed.

By the time we climbed above the towers, on approach to the plinth, we were drenched in sweat.

"We could have called for a ladder," Nat yelled, his wing's left pinion close to mine.

I shook my head. No ladder. Not for me. No matter how tired
I was. I cupped my wings to slow my approach to the testing
plinth. Checked to make sure the path was clear. The tests
might not have started, but the Magisters and councilors already watched, and judged.

The bone horns sounded. Three warnings.

My arms ached, and the back of my neck. I hoped we would
have time to rest between challenges.

My feet touched the woven plinth. The warp and weft of it
gave slightly when I landed as close to Densira's Magister, Florian, as possible. He dipped his head to me, his face carefully
blank.

Nat circled once more and, instead of sinking, executed a flip
that cut his wind and dropped him square between the two
Singers at the center of the plinth. They pretended not to notice. Nat grinned ear-to-ear.

I adjusted my lenses so they wouldn't slip again. Not during
the tests.

The Singers faced away from me. I couldn't tell if the taller
one was Wik, the Singer who had rescued and then threatened
me. Their bodies were gray turrets in the colorful swirl of wings
and nervousness. I would learn soon enough whether he'd come
today.

Around us, students rested and stretched. They recited tower
names to themselves. More than a few looked worried.

The four Magisters stood at the plinth's four corners, sym-
bolizing the four quadrants of the city. Florian for Densira. Viit's
able instructor, Magister Calli. A young Magister from Mondarath, so recently arrived no one knew his name. And Dix as
Magister for Wirra. She grinned at me, showing as many teeth
as she could manage.

A net stretched below the plinth, strung between the four
towers and tied by sinew. A brown-robed member of the trad-

ers' guild landed beside the Singers at the center of the plinth. The Singers dipped their heads, but did not bow. Finally, a crafter landed, her embroidered wings glittering in the morning light. The city and its towers were now represented. The plinth creaked and swung in the wind. The bone horns sounded a fourth time.

Two more students skidded to landings and found their towers, mumbling apologies. The Singers split from the central group. They carried four silk bags to the Magisters at the corners: one Singer walked south and west; the other, north and east. As the Singer carrying Densira's and Mondarath's bags approached, my breath caught again. Wik.

His profile in the sunlight threw me off guard; I was mesmerized by the silver tattoos. They made him look sharper, more imposing. They accented his cheekbones and his chin.

He smiled at Florian and the group. "I wish you all luck in your knowledge and in the sky." He did not look at me, but the corner of his lip twitched.

My throat tightened. What could the Singer do to me, here under open sky?

He could do anything he thought would help the city, I realized. Anything at all. My exhaustion heightened my panic. At a loss, I hummed Elna's song from two nights ago to myself. It worked surprisingly well. I calmed enough to thank the Singer with a clear voice. He paused to look at me, sending a shiver down my spine. Then he continued his slow circuit of the plinth.

"Don't worry about the test, or Dix," Nat whispered. "The guild is watching. The Singers are watching. The Magisters look out for their towers. You'll be fine."

I bristled because Nat didn't understand, before I remembered that he couldn't understand. I hadn't told him anything.

Florian pulled a bone marker from the bag, but did not look at it.

The observing guilds and Magisters ensured the Singer could not fail me overtly. But the Spire had ways of meddling with outcomes. Ezarit had always been especially careful in her dealings with them. I fretted the possibilities, then realized that was exactly what they wanted me to do.

The temporary plinth and the net beneath swayed in the wind. Bone cleats that had been carved into the tower tops of Mondarath and Viit anchored the thick ropes that held the plinth firmly in the sky. Secondary ties looped through moorings cut in Densira's balconies and Wirra's. The lines were temporary, made of fiber and the strongest silks, not spliced with sinew. They would hold for our needs and be used again for the wingfights. The plinth was not permanent, not like a bridge. Only Singers could provide the skymouth sinew necessary for a bridge. With it, they bound the city together.

The towers below us twisted slightly at each tier, each level a little wider than the one above it, lower levels darkening with age and garbage.

I looked around, praying the skies would keep clear. Several other students did the same. I saw my cousin, the talkative Dikarit, who'd failed Laws and Solo last year. He gestured to me to stand with him, but I waved back, choosing to stay by Nat.

Seven students had arrived so far from Densira. Six from Viit. Only two from Mondarath, and both looked nervous. Nine from Wirra.

At a melodic laugh high above us, everyone looked up. Sidra descended, glorious in her wings, visible from any of the towers. Dojha, following her, looked less sure of her own new wings. The fifth warning sounded just as Dojha's feet touched the plinth. She shook her head at Sidra's back, but didn't say anything.

Florian cleared his throat and addressed his Densira class for the last time. "Welcome, flight," he said formally. He smiled

at Dikarit, but not at me. The cold dawn air ruffled the thinning hair on top of his head. "You are well prepared. Make Densira proud."

Three other flight groups gathered on the platform, tight
knots around their Magisters. I imagined those teachers giving
similar encouragement to their students.

The Singers hummed a low, slow song: a variant on The Rise.
Then the older Singer reminded us of the rules: no talking
beyond what the test required, no leaving the plinth, no quar-
reling with the results. When they finished, the Magisters
bowed to us and stepped away, looking for the first time at the
chips they'd drawn.

Each bone chip contained one of four tower symbols. If a
Magister drew his or her own, he would hand it back.

I hoped the Magister from Viit, Calli, would be our Laws
tester. Ezarit knew her. She was a daughter of Liras Viit, the
wingmaker. The Magister from Mondarath was so new even his
students were strangers to him.

"The old Mondarath Magister was taken by the skymouth,"
Sidra whispered. No one shushed her.

Magister Calli joined the two students from Mondarath. Her
task this round would be short.

Our Magister went to Wirra.

And Magister Dix from Wirra went to Viit. I released a little
air from my lungs. One hurdle passed.

Mondarath's Magister walked to our group. He seemed very
young. Below us, no one on the towers would know yet, but
when they learned of it, they would think us unlucky from the
start. So many students, with such a young tester.

When I looked at him more closely, I realized he was barely
older than my cousin.

"I am Magister Macal," he said. "And you are my first flight
test."

Sidra groaned, so softly that only the flight group could hear her, not the Magister.

"Enough, Sid!" Dojha whispered.

Macal began the test of Laws without any further discussion.

He pointed at me, then drew a bone chip from the silk pouch and said, "Trade."

I was very lucky, then. I began to sing the first Law I'd learned, from my mother.

Fair trade requires freedom, honesty, and speed.

No goods will spoil when a tower is in need.

I heard Sidra stifle a laugh when my voice soured, but I kept going.

No trader lives with jealousy or greed.

Or keeps tithes from Spire or Tower.

When I finished, Macal nodded.

Nat got Safe Passage, which he stumbled on.

Sidra took Spire neatly. That was the easiest, and shortest, law.

None enter the Spire, night or day, unless Singer-sworn, or Singer-born, all in gray.

She held the note and ended with a flourish.

Four more Laws passed. Then it was back to me. When the Magister pulled the chip, his brow wrinkled. He stumbled on the word. "Bethalial." An archaic Law. Birdcrap.

My mind searched for the opening phrase. I knew this. They observed it more in the south, and in the city center.

In the Allmoons time of quiet, let no tower be disturbed.

Let no things thrown down in sacrifice be salvaged or perturbed.

A strange one. No one sacrificed things that weren't broken anymore, even symbolically. Magister Florian had said once that some Laws were traditions from the past, but we must learn them still.

Nat got War, which was dead simple.

No tower will sabotage or war
With neighbors near or far.
We rise together or fall apart
With clouds below, our judge.

Only one tower had tested that Law since we came out of the clouds. The Singers hadn't let them rise for generations. Ezarit said the towers to the west sometimes raided, but that was nothing overt.

The Magister circled Densira's flight group. Voices stammered and stalled, and some sang confidently too. At the plinth's other corners, Laws filled the air and were carried away on the wind.

Sidra received another frown from the Magister as his hand fumbled in the Laws bag. We could tell he'd never done this before. Most testers, Florian said once, could feel the Lawsmarks with their fingers and choose those we were required to know. Like Right-of-Way and Tithing. So far, we hadn't had much luck.

"Delequerriat," Macal said after two false starts. Sidra's mouth moved strangely. "Dele—" she began to say, but cut off before she started a song she could not finish. That was how my cousin had failed last year. I could see Sidra thinking. I didn't know this one either, though it sounded familiar. Sidra was left gaping openmouthed, like a baby bird. The time for her answer passed, and Magister Macal turned from her to the group. "Delequerriat: *The act of concealment, in plain sight, may only be used to turn wrong to right.*"

Macal moved on as Sidra's face turned purple, matching her wings. Dojha took Sidra's hand and squeezed. This couldn't get much worse.

It didn't. The Magister pulled Tithing from his pouch, and Dojha passed it. We'd made it through Laws.

Singer Wik handed a blue-dyed marker to each tester who'd

passed. He gave Sidra a half marker, breaking it in front of her. He passed before me and gripped my marker with both hands. My eyes widened. I'd passed well. He wouldn't dare. He handed it to me, and I quickly tied the thin chip to my wing.

Wik and Macal passed on the plinth. The two exchanged a look I could not fathom. A greeting, it seemed, but fiercer. Macal grimaced and turned away.

The craft representative unfurled a dyed silk and set it in the center of the plinth, anchoring it with thick madder-dyed chips against the wind. The City test. We all turned our backs. One by one, we were beckoned forward and given bone chips to place on each of the city's fifty-eight towers, naming them and speaking of their qualities as we did.

I heard Nat take deep breaths beside me, nervous.

The towers rose in my mind, shaped by late-night conversations with my mother. Her tales of what she'd traded and where gave me a window on my city that few had.

When my turn came, I placed the marker for Grigrit in the southwest. They made honey. My mother traded tea and silks to them to help the sick in the southeast quadrant. My cheeks colored as I thought of her. I placed the markers for the six towers she helped. Heard my voice forming the correct words, but my mind went elsewhere, wondering whether Ezarit was on her way home.

One chip remained in my hand. I looked across the map, checking each in turn. Then I placed the final chip at the center of the city and completed the test with "The Spire is home of the Singers, who protect the city and hold it together for us." Two Singers signaled approval, the woman with the silver streak in her hair and an older man, both covered with silver tattoos. On the other side of the map, Wik frowned. The Craft representative gave me a full marker dyed madder-red for City.

When I returned to Densira's corner, I secured that chip to my left wing, next to the Laws marker. Two tests down; two to go. The markers made a soft clatter at my shoulder as they swung on their ties.

ʼ ʼ ʼ

Before the flight rounds began, Macal motioned to me. "You have offended someone?" he asked quickly, looking around to make sure he was not overheard.

I raised my eyebrows but did not speak. My heart hammered in my chest.

Macal continued. "A Singer has indicated he doesn't think you are skilled enough to pass the flight tests. To a Magister who was upset by his words."

I knew it. The Singer was trying to sway the Magisters, to make me fail. He thought I would have no place to turn but the Spire. Densira would turn away from my bad luck. Even my mother.

"Who was upset?"

"Me."

Macal was only a few years older, but his eyes were sure and clear. He didn't like being played for a pawn.

"Anyone else?"

"I don't know. When I refused to listen, the Singer said he had other prospects. Be careful."

If the Singer had any knowledge of my mother's past, I knew exactly who else he'd try to sway. Magister Dix.

The Magisters gathered to draw tower marks for Solo Flight. At that moment, my fear returned. Open sky. Vast and filled with teeth.

If I wished to fly by my mother's side, or to fly independent of her, I would be in this sky every day. I found the fear in my heart and grabbed it tight. Ripped it out and threw it down to the clouds. My mother could fly through a migration without wavering. I would do so as well.

❦ ❦ ❦

The Laws and City tests gave me a chance to catch my breath atop the plinth and to soothe my shoulders from the ascent.

Magister Macal returned to our corner. He'd drawn us again. Sidra groaned louder this time. Dojha didn't shush her. This time, she took a half step away from her friend, while casting a glance at the Singers.

Macal beckoned to Nat. He would test us in tower order, from lowest to highest. Fine with me. Nat looked like this was fine with him too.

"See you all after Group," he said, and jumped from the plinth to meet the Magister in the sky. He rose moments later on a good gust, and I watched his wings and the many-hued wings of the others carve the sky above the city. The sun caught the edges of their silks and made halos of color in my lenses.

We leaned into the wind, watching the first testers return. One by one, they landed, Nat last of all, his face lit with triumph.

My turn came. Despite my resolve, I felt ice-cold, my muscles suddenly tight. My fingers flexed on my wing grips. I tried to remember Florian's words, his admonitions that I tuck tighter, reach farther. I had to be best at this, with the quadrant watching. I would not let them down again.

Stepping off the edge of the plinth, I looked up and out, as we had been taught to do since our first flight. My wings were set to full. I caught a good gust. Macal flew beside me on the steady breeze. I suspected many eyes were turned on me from the towers and the plinth. The uptower students from Viit, Wirra, and Mondarath had already gone. I was one of the last to solo.

The strange young Magister began his twists and turns, and I silently followed his pattern. I caught the rhythm of it and soon found myself lost in the dance that was flying the mottled gusts and drafts of the city. We lit on a balcony, once. We dove and climbed. Then he made a combination roll and dive, as one would do to avoid a crash in the sky. I swallowed and uttered a short prayer to the city, then tucked my head tight and forced myself forward and down.

Wind roared in my ears. My stomach flipped, and I almost let go of my wings. I held on.

Moments later, I was right side up and gasping. I nearly shouted in triumph. Macal smiled, then tucked his wings to half breadth and plummeted.

I followed quickly, because I had to. The dive wind sheared at my lenses, plowed my cheeks back. So far down. The clouds roared towards us, hard and gray. How could he dive so fast? My wings began to shudder. What if they couldn't take the strain? How would we rise back up? I wanted to shout, to protest.

Was the Magister in league with the Singer? Nothing else made sense. No one dove this fast, not ever, not even in a wing-fight. Terror built in my head, pressed against my teeth.

And then Macal curved his wingtips enough to whip himself into a turn with almost as much exiting force. Though we'd studied it once, it was something I'd only heard of Singers doing, and only when they chased a skymouth. They attacked it from below. Now Macal was doing this, in a wingtest. He expected me to mimic him. Without warning.

I tried to quash my anger and fear. If I was being set up to fail, then I would fail spectacularly.

I pictured the wing seams and patches Liras Viit had only recently stitched bursting under the strain. Me tumbling past the towers. *Don't look down.* If I was lucky, they would fish me from the air before I disappeared into the unknown horror of the clouds. I gritted my teeth and spread all ten fingers wide. The wingtips stretched as tiny battens reacted to the pressure. Then I forced my palm into the curve, fingertips pressing up and back in a painful arc. My body mimicked my hands. I didn't have time to say a prayer or even whimper.

The curve turned my wing into a foil, a rudder in the air. I was spun around and up.

My heart pounded in my ears. My lenses fogged at their edges with the speed. As I leveled off, I couldn't help it, I whooped loudly. We were well out of range of the plinth. Macal joined me in a short whoop as well.

Above us, Florian soared past with a student from Wirra. He gave me what seemed like an encouraging nod.

The last part of the test, climbing, was slow going from our depth. My shoulders ached once more, but I fought for each gust, seeking out Allmoons flags and winddrift to set my path.

Then I was once again level with my mother's tier in Densira. With its empty balcony. I had forgotten to look for Elna on my way back up.

As we returned to the plinth, Macal smiled. "They cheer for you."

At first, I couldn't hear anything but the wind. Macal had sharp ears.

Finally, I heard the strange sound. Students nearest the edge of the plinth clapped and pointed at me. We must have looked like flecks against the clouds, we'd been down so far. How could they have known?

I had little time to wonder who this Magister was and how he knew to fly that way when I landed. My flightmates whooped and slapped me on the back.

"You came up so far, so fast!" Dikarit clapped me on the shoulder. Dix, overhearing, shushed him, shushed everyone.

Singer Wik crossed the plinth and loomed over Dikarit. "You will keep to the tradition of silence and decorum," he said. Then he handed Macal the green Solo markers to distribute, and shot him an extra-searing glance. He turned on his heel, the battens of his furled wings rattling, and strode away without a look at me.

I'd passed. Something else had happened as well out there in the sky. Macal's stunt had set me apart from others who'd been trying only to pass. I had exceeded the test. I looked at Macal as he paced the length of the plinth. He winked. He'd known what he was doing all along.

The city's sounds were distant up here, but I imagined I could hear Elna clapping as I tied my Flight marker to my wings. My fingers trembled with exhilaration. What would Ezarit say about *that* level of flying? The best in the class?

Four students sat on the plinth now. They had failed Solo, or partial-marked several sections, and were not allowed to continue.

The students who remained prepared for the final part of the wingtest, Group. A flight with strangers, without a Magister in the lead.

Guards and hunters alighted on the plinth to join our towers. Nat noticed, of course. He puffed out his chest ever so slightly, ready to impress them.

6

FALL

The Singers placed each tower's student markers in a silk bag. They drew groups for us, and I was grateful for the blind selection. It made the process difficult for even them to meddle with. My chip was drawn for the south corner. I walked across the plinth, still breathing hard from my flight, and looked around at my cohort. Four students, one from each tower, and three volunteers.

They looked back at me, taking note of my patched wings and hand-me-down flying gear. I wondered if they'd heard about me. Kirit Lawsbreaker and the skymouth. I kept my chin up.

After a long silence, one boy said his name softly. "Beliak Viit." The silence rose again, and Beliak fought it off. "After Allmoons, I will train as a ropemaker. What of the rest of you?"

Not a big flying trade, ropework, but Beliak would likely shift towers to apprentice. He needed to get full marks. Viit didn't keep many of its own unless they specialized in wings, dyes, and clothing, or mechanicals like Elna's bone hook. It traded for the rest of what it needed.

The girl from Wirra smiled shyly. "Ceetcee. I work in the gardens, but I wish to train as a bridge artifex, like my father."

Wirra's specialty was woven structures, like the wingtest plinth and bridges. Ceetcee could apprentice at home, as I hoped to do.

Ceetcee fingered her wing traces nervously. Perhaps she needed to impress someone as much as I did.

A girl much smaller than the rest of us said, "Aliati Mondarath." She didn't mention a profession. Mondarath traded herbs and beverages. Including what the Singer used to revive me after I shouted down the skymouth.

"I am sorry for your tower's troubles, Aliati," Beliak said.

"And I yours," Aliati returned to him.

We were all very formal. Very cautious.

"Kirit Densira," I said. "I will be a trader."

My group looked at their footwraps. Especially the volunteers. Yes, they'd heard of me. Then Beliak met my eyes and smiled. "Welcome." Aliati and Ceetcee followed suit.

The Magisters gathered to draw groups. The whispers on the plinth fell silent. Dix pulled her hand from the silk bag, looked at what she held, then turned to grin at us, at me.

My luck disappeared like a lost breeze.

Behind our group, another knot of students and volunteers erupted in laughter. Nat's group. A third group was silent until someone screeched. Sidra.

"You can't be serious! I won't."

I turned my head enough to see what she was protesting, without attracting attention from the Singers or Dix. Sidra pointed at Macal. "Not one more time."

I expected to see the Magisters stifle her protests. Magister Florian often did so when Sidra kicked up a fuss in flight. Instead, they regrouped and conferred. Macal said something that made everyone nod except Dix. Sidra swished her wings.

In other years, someone would have been flown home, someone might have fallen by now. Sure, a few testers had washed out. But no one protested a group assignment.

The Magisters separated. Dix stalked towards Sidra, took her by the arm, and led her to another group. Nat's.

Where we stood, I could not hear their words. Nat's hand gestures and how he tilted his head gave him away. He wasn't pleased with the addition to his test group, but didn't want to offend Sidra. He bowed ever so slightly to Dix. The other students began to speak as well. Something shifted. Dix stayed with the group while Magister Viit left it and walked towards us. Somehow, Nat and Macal had turned Sidra's outburst into a way to spare me Dix's attention. If true, either would make a fine trader. And I would owe them both enormous favors.

At a signal from one of the Singers, Magister Calli led our group to the edge of the plinth. We looked south. We would need to beat a zigzag against the wind, retrieve a flag set on a distant tower this morning, and return. Other groups conferred, picked a first leader, and set out, going west, east, and towards the city center.

You can do this, I reminded myself. Now that I had passed my solo flight, I felt a bit better. Still, anything could happen during Group. Crosswinds, a flock of whipperlings. A wingbreak. Skymouths. Especially with student fliers stressed from wing-testing.

Nat's group launched, with Sidra straining to get out in front. Group was all about flying with others in a tight scrum, and in close quarters. Important skills for heavily trafficked towers, and especially for traders, who sometimes need to carry heavier objects as teams.

The group had likely already decided on leader order, but Sidra's arrival had changed that too. She was positioning herself to lead the flight. I held my breath, waiting for Dix to discipline her, but she didn't. They disappeared, headed east.

I looked at my group. Who would take the lead among us? The city was watching.

Groups worked best when leaders alternated; that I knew from both Florian and Ezarit. Sidra's performance notwithstanding. Perhaps that was why everyone was hanging back. Beliak smiled, awkward. Ceetcee rocked on her heels. We'd be here all day.

I stepped forward. "I'll take first lead." Would they follow me?

Their response was a stretch of quiet. I'd botched it already. I scrambled to fix it. "And then Beliak?"

Beliak nodded. "Then Ceetcee and then Aliati?" Both agreed. The volunteers readied themselves. Beliak and I exchanged nervous smiles.

I called the first formation, based on the direction we were headed and the prevailing wind: "Chevron." Magister Calli smiled. I'd made a good decision. We launched, wing to wing, coordinating and signaling wind shifts with whistles and shouts.

We were a noisy crowd, all working together to find the fastest breezes on which to glide.

We were also a fast group. By cooperating, we flew high. We soon overtook Sidra and Nat's group, which was off course and struggling to keep up with her set path.

I signaled Beliak to take lead after we'd made half the distance. He shifted our formation to dove—a raked arrow—since the wind had grown more variable. I fell back to his left point and took a moment to look around.

Ezarit's lenses were a blessing, especially since I'd adjusted them properly. I could see far with them, was less troubled by sun glare than my companions, and my eyes weren't tearing from the wind.

Below, small flights of patchwork wings followed us for a few towers and then turned back. I'd done the same as a younger flier. Without wingmarks, they could not follow us for long.

We passed the farthest towers I'd been to, out of the northwest quadrant. I quieted as I realized the names of the towers I'd studied all my life went with shapes, twists of bone rising from the clouds just as Densira did.

Here and there, bridges spanned the gaps between towers. As we flew closer to the Spire, more towers were connected by the long spans of sinew. Everywhere, ladders grappled tiers. On balconies and tower tops, families stood and waved. Densira families were doing the same for children of distant towers, welcoming them to the rest of the city.

From my position next to Beliak, I spotted our banner on Varu's top tier and signaled. Beliak acknowledged me with a whistle and signaled for us to land atop the tower before the final leg of the test.

❧ ❧ ❧

Varu was lower than Densira by at least three tiers. The tower was so crowded that hammocks and sacks had to hang anchored from balconies. They'd broken War long ago, though Magister Florian said once that they hadn't done more than plot and make a few raids on neighbors' water and food. In return, Singers took Varu's council, along with their families, to the Spire. They refused Varu any opportunity to rise.

Our landing made a racket, silk wings flapping against wind curls that crossed the tower top. The bone roof was smooth and white, showing no new growth. Cleats and pulleys carved around its edge supported the nets below.

Varu had put out a dried-vine basket for the wingtesters. It held figs and a sour-tasting juice. The new tastes reminded us how far we'd come from home.

I removed my lenses to clean them and looked out from Varu to its neighbors. I saw the Spire clearly for the first time, rising from the city center. I'd studied it for the wingtest, but had never been so close.

Taller than the rest of the city's towers, the Spire differed in other ways as well. Where our tiers rose supported by a central core, a solid wall of white bone wrapped the Spire. Ezarit told me once that the Spire's center was a wind-filled abyss. The Spire's market-bridges, designed by artifexes like Nat's father, hung suspended on pulleys in a ring around its wall. Behind the wall, the Spire held the Singers' secrets close.

From Varu's roof, I spotted gray-robed Singers perched atop the Spire, on a flat expanse of bone that could hold hundreds. More Singers emerged from within, like smoke taken to wing.

Beliak watched them too, as he chewed a fig. "One of my brothers was taken to the Spire, five years ago." He frowned. "His name was Lurai." He saw my look and hurried to clarify. "As a novice. Maybe he's up there, watching us."

I swallowed, realizing Ezarit might speak this way about me if the Singer got what he wanted.

Beliak opened his mouth to speak again, but Magister Calli signaled us to ready for the return flight. I offered Varu's group banner to Beliak and Ceetcee, but they shook their heads. So I tied the banner into my robes. We flew before the wind this time; this was easier and more direct, but harder to spot turbulence. Ceetcee looked nervous.

"We'll work together," Beliak said. "Try bee formation." Ceetcee nodded. Magister Calli took note. I offered to serve as the tail of the bee, in charge of watching for shifts before they hit us. And for large birds of prey or skymouths.

I'd discovered while cleaning Ezarit's lenses that they had a special hasp with a bit of reflective glass inside. I flipped it back and forth, realizing it allowed a view of what was behind me, without my turning my head.

As I showed my group how the hasp worked, Ceetcee smiled. "You are lucky, then, and will bring us the same." She used the traditional way of accepting a favor. I would fly at the tail.

I hoped she was right.

We launched again, lighter for having reached the halfway mark of our final trial.

The wind carried us around Varu, past the Spire, and back towards the northern quadrants.

Ceetcee's path had taken us too low for the crowded towers near the Spire. It was a mistake easily made by someone who'd grown up on the outer edges. A strong downdraft from the towers overlapped our gust and fouled our path. Beliak and I whistled a warning at the same time, but Ceetcee didn't alter course soon enough. Our group's progress slowed as she struggled to find a clear path.

Ceetcee passed control to Aliati, flying nearby. Aliati had seemed quiet on the plinth, and at Varu too. But in the lead, her voice was confident and clear. She pushed us to a tighter formation, then sleeked us around several towers, climbing with each gust. Soon we soared at the towers' peaks, chattering and whistling soft appreciation in the sunlight.

Even the volunteers seemed well pleased with the turn of events. They flew at the center of our formation: two hunters and a guard.

I kept one eye on the mirror and focused as best I could on keeping my wingtips pointed. The Magister fell back in formation, so she was just downwind of me.

She was grinning. "Well traveled," she shouted. I saw the testing plinth ahead and grinned too.

We returned triumphant, my three new friends and I. We were flushed from the flight and windburned. Ceetcee had something in her eye, possibly one of her own long eyelashes. Aliati glowed with her success. Magister Calli walked towards the trade and craft guild leaders and relayed our trip with broad gestures. The tradesman turned my way and bowed. My heart lifted. I'd passed, and very well.

Another group landed, with Magister Macal. They were missing a student. Grim news, but not a disaster. "Left him at

the turnaround tower," he announced. "Broke formation without signaling. Nearly took the group out."

We quieted our celebration.

↘ ↘ ↘

Nat's group appeared in the distance, beating their way back
against the wind. They, too, had all their number. An occasional
speck broke the deep blue horizon line. Birds. Sidra still held
lead, and the following wind drove her hoarse voice ahead of
the formation.

They were just a few towers away from the plinth when a
crosswind hit. I squinted and could almost see it. A squall of
air and a rising cloud, a small one. At first I was glad. The gardens needed rain.

But the squall destabilized Sidra's formation. One of the
hunters fought for balance in the gust. He was blown sideways,
towards Nat.

Nat missed a shouted warning from Dix. The hunter knocked
him off course. He tumbled right into the squall, one of his
wings broken.

I cried out as he careened away from the city.

The wind spun him round, the one wing acting as a blade,
his body a rotor. Nat's legs kicked out, but he fell like a leaf from
a garden, twisting down below the plinth.

Magisters and Singers leapt from the plinth, flying fast,
kicking out with their tailskirts, gliding the drafts to get to him.
The latter set their wings, pulled from their finger harnesses,
and reached arms lined with silver tattoos towards him like
prayers.

I knelt at the plinth's edge, Beliak and Aliati on either side.
We peered over. "Please no," I whispered. Not Nat.

The Singers outpaced the Magisters. Even Macal could not

keep up. Singer Wik reached Nat first and caught him by the winghooks. Nat's spin dragged them both down. Beliak made a choking sound, and I grabbed Aliati's arm with numb fingers. Then the Singer's broad wings stopped their fall. When they rose, Nat dangled limply, out cold from the spin. The Singer's left arm bulged with the strain of lifting him, until he removed a rope harness from his waist with his right hand, then double-glided Nat back to us, suspended like a child.

The other Singer rescued another student from the group, and Magister Dix struggled to right the rest of the flight. The group limped back to the plinth and made tangled, exhausted landings.

Singer Wik dumped Nat in a puddle on the plinth's woven surface.

"This one didn't watch the others," Dix said, as if she wasn't certain anyone should have rescued him. "Naton's boy."

There was a hush from the Magisters. Finally, Florian, our Magister, bent to Nat and shook him awake.

Nat retched and grabbed at the air, his face flushed and angry.

"You're all right," Florian said roughly. "You were rescued like a fledge, but you're fine now."

Nat retched again. He'd failed Group. He wouldn't pass the wingtest this year. But he climbed to his feet. The plinth bounced as he took a step. One wing hung crooked from its strap. The other, battens split, silk torn, drooped against his shoulder.

But he had lived. He had not fallen through the clouds. I reached for his hand, and he jumped at my touch, then held tight.

The volunteer who had careened into Nat, the hunter from Mondarath, had plummeted fast and hard. The Singer who had gone after him returned empty-handed. He landed, ashen faced, then pointed up and intoned, "Jador Mondarath fell in service to the city. Look up to watch his soul pass above. We do not look down in mourning."

More loss for that tower.

The blessing ended, and students and Magisters gathered into tower groups one last time. Dikarit stood off to the side, having passed without trouble. Sidra stood, panting, her face ashen. Dojha and I juggled relief and joy with sorrow. Nat, still gripping my hand, turned away from us, eyes on his feet.

A brass-haired Singer intoned a benediction. The last words from The Rise: *We all fly together.* Even in death. "Go in service to the city," she said.

Singer Wik spoke after her. "Wingmarks will be distributed at tomorrow's wingfights, before Allmoons."

Magisters and students raised confused questions. This broke tradition. Wingmarks were exchanged for the four test marks now, not tomorrow.

The Singers did not explain. They repeated the change. The guild members murmured "Singer's right." As if that explained things.

"Must be because of the fall," Aliati said. Her face was marked with tears. Her tower, her hunter.

"I encourage you who receive wingmarks tomorrow to respect the city's Laws, and those of you who have not passed to try again," the older Singer said, then turned and jumped from the plinth without waiting for a response. Her dove-gray wings momentarily blocked the sun as she soared back to the Spire.

Singer Wik and the third Singer followed without a word to anyone.

Our flight groups lingered on the plinth, confused. The test didn't feel over. I began to worry that the Singers would declare no one had passed, but then I thought about my flight and grew calmer. I'd passed. I knew it. Traditions had been broken, all formality lost, but I'd passed. I caught Beliak's eye, then Ceet-cee's. Waved to them as their groups headed back to Wirra and Viit.

When I realized that Nat had dropped my hand and walked to the plinth's southern edge, my heart sank. So caught up in my own worries. Shame on me. I joined him as he peered over the edge, then at the Spire in the distance.

"It wasn't your fault."

"Bad luck," his voice rasped. He unbuckled his left wing, broken beyond repair, and slid the strap from his shoulder. He hung it over the edge of the plinth and dropped it.

My heart ached for him. "Next Allsuns, Nat. You will pass."

Florian waved us back to the plinth's northern side, and I pulled Nat after me. We would fly back to the tower of our youth together.

Using winghooks, Florian carried Nat. Nat cringed with shame. His remaining wing was secured to the Magister's chest.

They glided away from the test plinth. Sidra sulked behind them, muttering to Dojha. My cousin and I followed, trying to read the changes on the horizon.

I would take my old wings to Viit and trade whatever else I could find to have them make Nat a new wing. I smiled sadly. That would help. But Nat wouldn't have wings for this year's Allmoons. He wouldn't be able to fly in the wingfights or join a hunt.

Meantime, Singer Wik would return to talk with me. But I would have my wingmark by then. I hoped that would be enough to carry me far from the Singers' reach.

Ahead of me, Sidra grew more strident and incensed. *Not my fault,* I heard. *Dix will regret this.*

I felt a twinge of empathy for her, and even worse for Nat. They'd have to repeat the wingtest. Sidra's family would be embarrassed, though they wouldn't have as many difficulties as

Nat and Elna would. Sidra would have to live by her father's rules for longer. Knowing Councilman Vant, that could be why she was raging now.

Sidra caught me looking at her and glared back at me. Embarrassed, I distracted myself by thinking of more ways to help Nat get back in the air. Ways to avoid going near the Spire until I was a well-off trader in my own right. My barely formed plans shredded like clouds when I spotted a figure waving from our balcony.

Ezarit. Home. Her lenses pressed my cheeks as I smiled. Then they fogged as the seal broke with my skin when I frowned. She'd almost made it in time. Perhaps she had seen some of the group flight. Perhaps she saw Nat's fall.

If Ezarit had been home in the morning, she would have seen my dive. She would have told me what it looked like. We could have shared impressions, like a team, like the group I'd just worked with. Like the people who'd helped her deliver the medicines to the southeast.

Instead, she'd flown one way, and I'd flown another. So much sky had opened up between us. The skymouth and the Singer, the wingtest and Nat's fall filled the space.

I glided the distance to Densira, and Ezarit's form grew clearer. She'd put her glass beads back in her hair. The top of the tower danced with light to welcome me home. But silence waited there too, taut like a net.

With a wave from Magister Florian, I broke from the group and went to her.

7

HORIZON

She met me on the balcony and caught me like a child come in from a first flight. Swung me round. She held me at arm's length.

"You've grown. How is it that you are still growing?"

I hadn't grown. It had only been a few days since she left. It had been forever.

Why was she greeting me as if nothing had happened? I grew stiff in her arms, fidgeted like a trapped bird.

Her eyes were soft and golden, fringed with long lashes. On her wind-chapped face, her cheekbones bloomed madder and rose.

She touched the chips I'd tied to my wings. Her face fell into worry. "No wingmark? They must be debating results." Her lips moved as she counted four full chips: *Laws, City, Solo, Group.* "But you passed!"

I nodded. I had so much to say, my lips were sealed by the pressure of it all. And against speaking any of it. I smiled at her and let my eyes speak instead.

"I know how you feel," she said. "When I passed the wingtest . . ." She looked into the distance, thinking. "I was so over the sun about it. Higher than anyone. My mother would have been so proud, then." She returned to me, saw me. "Just as I am."

She hadn't seen Nat fall. She didn't know.

I should have told her then, but I couldn't put words to it. I opened my mouth and closed it again. *Everything is all right,* I thought as hard as I could, *Tell me of our plans, describe our future like you did the trade run so many weeks ago, with eyes glowing and fingers shaping air into promise and power.* I wished those words between us.

She waited as well, her head tilting to one side, eyebrows rising. Quiet buoyed us for a moment while we believed we understood each other. Then silence grew from quiet, expanding up and out, hardening. The silence began to push us further apart.

Ezarit tucked a tendril of hair behind her ear. The Laws chip tied to her wrist flashed white. "Household member broke Laws."

My doing. A hero of the city weighted with Laws.

I wondered what Councilman Vant would ask in exchange for making the chip go away. As I opened my mouth to ask, she began to speak at the same time.

"I have some surprises." She pulled me to the table, handed me a package. A cloud of silk wrapping, bound by complex knots, soft and light in my hands. "But tell me everything," she said. I opened my mouth. Stopped. Pressed my lips together.

"Don't keep me waiting, who was your Group tester?" She did not want to talk about the Laws chip either. She was distracting me with banter, another trader trick. This made me more tense, more worried. Still, I could answer her, and distract her too. "My tester was almost Dix."

She leaned forward, her eyes searching mine. "But?"

"But Sidra protested being tested three times by Mondarath's new Magister, and Nat and that Magister pushed for changes. Calli was switched for Dix. I got Magister Viit. We flew true." I didn't speak of Nat's flight. Somewhere far below us, he was finding the words to tell Elna that his father's wing was lost, that he'd fallen. But I could not tell Ezarit.

"I gather Sidra will be serenading her father with her woes."
My mother frowned and picked at my test marks. She sighed.
"And for Solo?"

"Mondarath. The new Magister. He flew strangely, but I
managed to keep up." *I did more than that,* I thought.

"Strange, how?"

"Like a Singer."

Ezarit's eyes narrowed. "How many Singers have you seen
flying?"

"We've watched them, haven't we? At Allsuns? And Allmoons? And the one who came here to get you? And after—" I
stopped. I'd come treacherously close to the things I could not
allow myself to talk about.

She blanched. "After?"

I could not say. I could not tell her.

"Three Singers attended the wingtest."

"Three always attend the wingtest." She would not let go of
my slipped words. "After what? Which Singer?"

"I've only seen three up close. They were all at the wingtest."
I was not lying. Not yet.

She relaxed, but the distance between us expanded. So many
things we were not saying. The silence of our mutual homecoming deepened. I furled my wings properly to have something to do with my hands. Reached to pull the lenses from
around my neck. They felt cold on my fingers. I held them out
to my mother, who touched them fondly, but did not take the
strap from my hand.

"You keep them."

She was trying to mend things. "They're yours. You need them
to fly. Your good luck." They weighed heavier now, burdened.

She smiled slowly, thinking I'd be thrilled. "I can fly without them too. I had very good luck out there." Her smile grew,

thinking of the adventure. "I want you to have them. When you're a trader, they'll come in handy."

The moment she said "trader," something tight in my chest released with a great whoosh of air. I could hear the tower's sounds again, the flapping of Allmoons banners on the balconies.

She smiled again to see me relaxing. "Tell me more," she said. I shrugged from my wings as she pulled me inside.

I looked around our quarters for things that had changed. A tower chip with Vant's mark sat on the table. She owed him now. She followed my eye to the chip and cleared her throat. "We'll discuss that later. Tell me about the wingtest."

I told her as much as I could, about Solo and Group. About Nat, about his fall. Her hand went to her throat.

"I'll make them down a basket."

"It's not something you can fix with goods," I said more sharply than I meant to. I did not want to fight with her. I wanted her to help me figure out how to make things right.

But she waved her hand, nervous, and turned to her panniers. "It is what I can do. Poor Nat. Poor Elna."

She fussed with her trade goods as if she wished to pull a new wing from one of the baskets. She opened and shut containers, sighing. Turned back to me, gesturing to the wrapped package I still held. She arched an eyebrow. "Open that while I think. More surprises later."

I didn't want surprises. I wanted flying panniers and quilts with deep traders' pockets. A wing for my friend. I untied the complicated wrapping to find a new robe, the markings embroidered and dyes done in layers and shades of green. No pockets. I put it down on the table; I'd wear it for Remembrances, tomorrow, after the wingfights.

"I thought it was pretty," she said.

"Thank you."

"And with that a promise to take you to the Spire, once you've made your first trades."

A chill crossed me, like a shadow. It must have shown on my face. Not the reaction she expected.

"Kirit, you've wanted to fly the city for so long. What has happened?" She frowned.

I pressed my lips shut, knowing that everything would tumble out, and she'd be furious at the Singer. She'd argue with them, be ruined.

Her frown deepened.

"The skymouth. Elna said the Singer returned. Saved you."

I nodded.

"But then he stayed. I imagine he said something to you?"

I held my breath. If Elna had told her that much and she guessed the rest, whatever she guessed, it would be as if I'd told her. I wouldn't have broken the fiat, but there'd be no way to prove that to a Singer, either. I let the breath out. "Only for a moment."

"What did he say?"

"That I shouldn't have lived. He spoke to Councilman Vant, told him to make an example of me. Of us."

Her eyes narrowed again. "Are you sure it was the same Singer who escorted us past Mondarath?"

Singers looked so similar in their gray robes and tattoos, but I thought that was a safe area. I described the hawk nose, the green eyes. As I did, she relaxed. Strange.

"You thought it might be someone else?"

She sighed and looked away. She did. She knew Singers, of course. She'd petitioned them. They respected her. But the look in her eye had been more complex than that of someone expecting an old friend.

I cleared my throat, curious now. "Who?"

"I can't discuss it." She stalked to the back of our quarters to fold quilts. Ezarit was not the kind of parent who folded quilts.

Moments later, as if she'd signaled to them, the aunts burst in with congratulations and questions about the wingtest. Several asked about Nat and tutted uselessly. Dikarit looked exhausted, as I must have, but he eyed my mother's panniers, knowing she'd returned with gifts for the family. I smelled what she had carried home, hints of dusky spices and honey. Only a few towers were successful with bees in the city near those who grew that particular group of spices, far to the southwest. She'd been on the wing for a long time.

The sweep and swirl of a trader's homecoming, with shouts of excitement over small trinkets from distant towers, and the general bustle of preparations for Allmoons that began imme-diately after, kept us from any more discussions.

The relatives did not leave our home until nearly dawn. I woke where I'd pulled my mat to get away from them, back by the center wall, wrapped in my flying quilts. The soft rumbles of the city filled my ears.

Ezarit stood on the balcony, looking at the sun barely peek-ing over the horizon. I found a goosebladder of water from the night before. Carried it out to her.

"When you were very young," she said when I joined her, "I flew to the Spire, determined to get a better life for both of us. I was crazed with losses. Loss of your father, of all that I'd planned for our future. I challenged the Spire."

I dipped my head. I knew this.

She pulled the shoulder of her robe down. Showed me an old scar, long and deep, parallel with her collarbone. I had not known this. She had my attention.

"The Singer who flew against me did not want to fight me. He barely marked me. I was ruthless, Kirit. I won that challenge because I wanted our future back. And I got it."

I held my breath, waiting for her to tell me more.

She took a sip of water. "Sometimes, even when you think the fight is over, you have to keep fighting." Then she turned to look at me. Her golden eyes matched the clouds' colors, far below. "You will get your wingmark today."

"Yes." And Nat would not. Nor Sidra.

"You will need to fight for your own future, Kirit. No matter what."

I didn't understand, but she rose and hugged me quickly.

A shout went up in the pink-tinted light of the city's shortest day. Guards called their teams together for the wingfights.

Allmoons meant three days of wingfighting, festival markets, and ceremonies in each quadrant. I'd been looking forward to it.

Tonight, Densira would light its banners, to remember our lost. We would listen to Mondarath's raw grief, and Viit's, and we would say good-bye to those we'd lost to the clouds as well. My banner would have been among them, if the skymouth hadn't turned. Nat's also, if the Singer hadn't caught him.

On the year's shortest day, the towers lit the Allmoons banners when the moon reached its highest point. The city glowed, a fiery night flower. Each year, it surprised me with its beauty. After a short moment, a monument of light, the banners would fall to ash, and the flower that was the city, stripped of its colors, turned back to pale thorns rising from the clouds.

When we were small, Nat and I watched from our mothers' backs, clinging between their furled wings as our neighbors crowded Densira's roof. The night's dark landscape pricked with one light, two, then all the towers together as the council members from each tower lit the banners. The moon rose above the clouds and hung there for the long night, until it seemed bright as day to our eyes. Our bellies rumbled, hungry for Allmoons morning spice rolls. We wondered what we'd find in the markets the next day. Honey sweets, sometimes, small bone toys. And kites, for the holiday.

Ezarit gave me a small silk bag. "For the markets." She grinned, trying to lift our mood. "Make sure you bargain well." I shook it and heard the clicking of many tower chips. There was enough in here to buy my own panniers and beaded ties for my hair. Or something for Nat, my wing-brother, to whom I owed a debt.

She handed me my new wings.

"Go watch the wingfight." She nudged me. "Enjoy it. I have some things to finish up here before I come."

I unwrapped my wings, and she helped me strap them on. Glorious whorls of gold and green. I was transformed. My mouth ached from smiling so suddenly.

She chuckled. "I like seeing you happy, Kirit."

Our smiles faded at the same time.

"I'd like to take my old wings to Viit, to see if Liras can use parts to repair Nat's," I said.

"A good idea. But after Allmoons."

I agreed. No one did any work at Allmoons. But I would have agreed to anything she asked. A good apprentice already. My wings rustled in the wind. Ready to fly.

Outside, tower citizens who wanted to be close to the wing-fight, instead of watching with their scopes, had already started to glide towards Mondarath and Viit, to the balconies there that had been made into grandstands.

I tucked my purse into my robes, tightened my wingstraps, secured my new cap, and, with my mother's shooshing hands to give me extra thrust, at least in my imagination, prepared to launch myself from the balcony and glide towards where my flightmates and family gathered to watch the wingfight.

To my surprise, I spotted Nat's black curls below a patchwork pair of wings. He circled up on a gust and was overtaken several

times by younger children. Still, my heart leapt a little as he
waved at me and shouted, loud enough for everyone to hear,
"You don't live long in the towers if you can't pull yourself back
up when you tumble."

I waited for him to get close before I took off from our balcony, then let my wings spill air as we flew tip to tip towards
Mondarath.

He caught me at this and scowled. "Don't, Kirit. Fly true."

I nodded, banking away. I arrived at the wingfight well before he did and found space on the Mondarath balcony where
the traders often gathered. Nat would catch up soon, I hoped.

Guards lowered the wingtest plinth and stretched it between
the fifth tiers of Mondarath and Viit. The towers had draped the
balconies facing the plinth with nets and woven platforms.

Atop the towers, guards, hunters, Magisters, and several
younger residents readied themselves for the wingfight. They
tied bands of glass shards to their wings and feet. They sharp-
ened their short bone knives.

                    ❧ ❧ ❧

The horns sounded again, a bright cascade of notes, a sum-
moning.

Skyfighters leapt from their towers two at a time. Their wings
glittered in the pale sunlight. One of Mondarath's youngest
fighters roared. Her wings were familiar. Aliati!

I laughed, happy to see a flightmate in her first wingfight. I
worried for her too. Neither joy nor worry was enough to distract me from what came after the wingfight, when the Singers arrived with our wingmarks, but it helped.

The other team marked Aliati quickly as a weak point in
Mondarath's formation and aimed for her. Fleet and lithe, she
tucked her wings and rolled away from them, leading them into
the path of two older Mondarath fighters, including Magister

Macal. Aliati wasn't as easy to knock into the nets as Viit had hoped, and Macal swooped around their assault like a born fighter.

The crowd in the balcony rumbled and jeered at Viit. A few adults clustered in a corner and subtly exchanged bets, raising the wingfight's stakes. I heard Aliati's name, but not whether they were betting for her or against.

A shout went up. Another Mondarath flier, his wing torn, tumbled into the net. A point for Viit already. The flier pounded the knotted fiber that kept him from plummeting through the towers. His Mondarath teammates reformed, one man down.

The Viit cheers grew louder. "A moon's worth of grains!" someone shouted.

Viit attacked in a pincer formation, again going for the flier they considered weakest: Aliati. She dodged them again, and Macal almost trapped another Viit wingman in an attack from below. Mondarath's strategy seemed to be to use Aliati as bait. From the looks of frustration on the Viit fliers' faces, it would not work for long.

The crush of the crowd and the scent of too many bodies too close together wore me out. I hadn't eaten much since yesterday. I stepped back into the tier, searching for a morsel of food or tea. I unbuttoned the pocket in my sleeve and pulled my bone cup out, then smiled as Ceetcee approached me with Beliak in tow.

She found a sack of water and poured me two sips, then offered me an apple the size of my fist.

I devoured it, core and all.

"You were hungry." She laughed.

"That, and unwilling to toss anything down into the nets today," Beliak said.

Ceetcee smiled at him. A wingtest friendship. There were songs about that. I left them to it and turned to see my mother join the betting corner. Nat landed on the balcony at the same time. The trader crowd shifted to avoid him, pressing closer around my mother.

Nat spied me through the crowd and waved. He didn't smile. Was I supposed to have waited for him, after he told me to go? I couldn't tell.

Sidra and Dojha landed and swept between us, laughing. They didn't greet Nat at all.

"Are you all right?" I asked when I reached him. "Not too hurt?"

"Not too much. My pride, mostly."

"What will you do now?"

He paused for long enough that I raised my eyebrows. I wanted to keep talking to him, to show him, and everyone on this balcony, that he was not alone. That we were still wing-siblings. But I couldn't stand here all wingfight. I also wanted to get Ezarit's attention. To meet the traders.

Finally, he said, "I've been thinking of Tobiat's chips. Figuring them out."

"How? You can't fly the city looking for the tower that matches the drawings." I bit back my next words: *not without a wingmark.*

"I bet they'll let me if I'm escorted. You could fly with me."

A quest that could take days, or weeks. It couldn't happen if I were to apprentice with Ezarit.

"I have a plan," he added, when I'd been silent too long.

The crowd shouted as two Mondarath fighters hit the nets. Aliati and an older guard. Viit was now winning.

"Tobiat was at Ma's after the wingtest. He told me the design on the chips is a Spire secret."

"And you believe him? He's addled, Nat."

"Ma said that too, but he knows more about the Spire than anyone I've talked to." Nat lowered his voice. "He was born there, Kirit."

Given what Nat had been through, I nodded. I looked around to see if my mother was still betting. She was.

Nat waved his hand in my eyes to get my attention. "Really. There's something there. Tobiat was on about 'Delequerriat'— remember from Laws? Something hidden in plain sight. I want to know what the secret is. Or trade the chips to the Singers for a chance to ask questions about Naton, at least."

I kept my eyes on Ezarit and the traders while I mulled Nat's mad plan. "You'd have to challenge the Spire to ask your question, Nat. Like Ezarit did. Can't trade secrets."

"Maybe not, unless the secret is big enough. Tobiat sure made it sound so, though he can't remember everything."

I shifted, suddenly uncomfortable. Had Tobiat drawn Nat into his madness? Nat had followed readily, filling the space where his pride had been.

"I want to go during Allmoons," Nat added.

"Allmoons? Against Laws? What could possibly go wrong, then? You can't mean to fly at night?" I asked and threw my arms in the air. Nat's frown deepened at my tone, but I continued. "Why don't you ask a Singer when they come to deliver the wingmarks?"

His face clouded darker.

He was talking about going to the Spire. Not for a market. Not to trade. To find a way to make the Singers give up a secret. Which the Singers were sworn not to do.

I shivered as I thought about Singer Wik's fiat. No, they did not surrender their secrets lightly.

The hurt in Nat's eyes took the fire out of me. He had a half year of waiting, of scrambling to get by, before he could make his path in the world. Because the Magisters had switched for Group and he'd been paired with Sidra and Dix.

"Come on, Kirit. It'll be like old times."

It could have been me with broken wings. But it wasn't.

"I need to think about it, Nat," I said. I didn't meet his eyes. I looked across the balcony, to where Ezarit stood at the center of a crowd of bettors and traders. She turned to look for me too. Beckoned. I went to her.

\ \ \

Only five wingfighters remained aloft; the rest were in the nets. Macal flew for Mondarath against four Viit fliers. Viit observers were already counting the goods they'd take from Mondarath at the loss. Mondarath bettors shouted at the five men and women gliding in tight circles between the towers. The fliers were cut and bloodied, but still better off than their companions in the nets. Aliati among them, a sharp cut down her arm. She shouted encouragement to her sole teammate: Macal wasn't giving up.

One Viit flier's wing tore on the sharp edge of Magister Macal's pinion.

Ezarit shouted at another bet won. She was in her element.

I pulled a marker from my new purse and held it aloft to see if I could catch a bettor's eye. "One, on that Mondarath," I said, imitating Ezarit. A bearded man took the chip from my fingers. Aliati's team. Macal's. The trader's laugh boomed when a Viit flier knocked Macal hard, nearly into the net.

"You'll learn," he said. "You bet early, before they tire." He clapped his hand against my furled wings, rattling the battens. I backed away. Moved closer to Ezarit. Watched Macal continuing to fight out of the corner of my eye.

When the match had only one Viit flier left aloft against Macal, she put a hand on my shoulder and pulled me into the group. "My daughter, Kirit," she said, introducing me to the men and women with whom she'd been betting.

They wore their tower marks around their necks and in their hair. Not the fashion in our quadrant, where we kept them in

purses in pockets. The one who'd taken my marker a moment
ago extended his hand, "Doran Grigrit. My wife," he gestured
to the trader by his side, "Inaro." She inclined her head, and I
made a small bow to them. In my mind, I pictured the tower
map I'd assembled earlier that day. Southwestern quadrant,
where Ezarit went for honey. Far from here indeed.

"I have arranged," my mother said, "a most fortuitous apprenticeship for you, Kirit."

I heard her words, but there was something strange about
them. That wasn't how you announced your own apprentice.
She seemed to be speaking through the long end of a bone
horn, her words distant and warped. She kept going, but my
mind had stopped listening.

Not partners, then. Not a team.

A roaring sound rose in my ears. One of my mother's best
trading skills was the bait and switch. And I realized too late
that I might be the bait.

I forced myself to listen to the terms: ". . .'s daughter will apprentice with me, and you will work with the Grigrit fliers.
You'll learn much more than I could ever teach you."

There was more roaring. She looked at me, held my gaze. She
expected me to compose myself, to seem pleased. While she
sent me away.

She'd made this arrangement while she was on her trading
run. She hadn't told me when we were alone. She hadn't wanted
an argument.

The horns blew for the end of the wingfight. Viit had won,
but Macal had made it a close thing. Each tower bound the
wounds of the opposing teams' players, even as the winning
tower began to plan how to transport the tithes it would take
from the losers.

All around me, tower markers changed hands, bets were
paid, and treasures pulled from robes. The tower was rich with

trades. Something about Mondarath made people less cautious. My mother laughed, and the beads in her hair sparkled.

My new wings felt heavy on my shoulders. I tugged at the lenses around my neck, wishing I could take them off and hand them back. Instead, I smiled as she'd taught me. *Don't show disappointment; that gives the other trader an edge.*

And behind my smile, locked tight, my voice keened silent and broken. Yoked to an apprenticeship I had no say in. Sent away without warning.

Doran continued talking, oblivious. "Just like fledges. Feed 'em, flip the nest when they're prepared. Mine know they're ready."

"Kirit is a hard worker," Ezarit said, proud of her trade. I wondered what she got in return besides Doran's daughter, but I refused to let it show. I locked my smile and pretended to listen, though much of what I heard was the roaring in my ears. "She's done very well in flight."

He turned to me. "Good! We'll teach you the rest."

I already knew plenty. I'd been watching the best trader in the city. But this was not enough. I prepared my objections, but Doran turned his attention to the group again.

"Tower children don't know half what they should until they apprentice. We'll make sure she learns the right way to trade. And the traditions. My father's still alive. His songs about when we came out of the clouds, and before, they'll make your skin crawl." Doran's eyes lit up at the thought of it. And he was right; my skin was crawling already.

Ezarit still played dealmaker. "Doran has the best trade routes in the south." She jutted her chin, and I saw his quilts were richly embroidered. He was very wealthy, then. "We will make them welcome at Densira tonight, and you will leave tomorrow."

Tomorrow. I stared at her, and she rumpled my hair. "We'll meet in the sky," she said. "Traders are never far. And I know you'll be safe with Doran." For a moment, her face grew serious, and her eyes begged me to agree. Then she became lighthearted again. I did not know what to think.

Doran laughed and reached for a wineskin that was being passed around. He took a pull and pointed outside with his free hand. "Ah, Singers!"

I blanched, then remembered these Singers bore wingmarks. Smiled.

Too late, for Doran saw my look. "You'll learn respect for Singers too, Kirit. I'll have no Lawsbreaking in my tower. Singers saved us. They kept us from fighting to death in the clouds. They found the few left alive, taught them Laws. They learned how to raise the towers faster. On their wings, we rose." Doran actually wiped a tear from his eye, and I nodded, even as I edged backwards.

For all my studies, I hadn't realized how different the south was, how traditional. And Ezarit had traded me there, like a weight of tea wrapped in silk.

The Singers landed, with Councilman Vant right behind. I moved away from Doran and the bettors, towards the gathering wingtesters. One last look at Ezarit, her face relaxed now that she'd done her duty and found me an apprenticeship.

Doran laughed heartily and clapped her on the shoulder. She had the dignity to raise an eyebrow, and he pulled his hand away.

The sun was a pale slip on the cloudtop. The Singers' wings were tinted red with the light. The day neared Bethalial by the old Laws.

"We congratulate Viit on its win," the Singer with the silver streak in her hair said. "We will hurry to get you to your home towers before nightfall."

Behind us, the bantering and the post-wingfight win recapping faded as everyone turned to listen to the Singers. The members of my flight clustered forward. Nat kept to the back, in the section of the tower already fallen into shadow.

The two Singers who bore the wingmarks were the woman with the silver streak in her hair and the older man. Wik was not with them. For that, I heaved a sigh of relief.

The female Singer held the bag of wingtest markers, a thick-spun silk dyed goldenrod. I could hear the markers click together from here.

Sidra joined the press towards the Singers. I kept myself back a little, soaking up the feeling of *almost*ness. The moment before I could hold my future in my hands stretched out—the length of a breath, held.

The wingmark would open the city to me and would free me from the Singer's plans.

A tattooed hand dipped into the bag, then handed gold markers out. First to Beliak, then Aliati. Six more fliers tied wingmarks to shoulder straps. Ceetcee, Dikarit.

Sidra shifted her feet, impatient. She couldn't be serious. Not after recieving partial chips in Laws and Group.

Dojha took her mark. Someone cheered in the background. The bag was nearly empty.

The Singer paused. Her mouth formed a frown, as if she was about to say something distasteful. "The reason for the late awarding of wingmarks was our need to confer with the council. Two fliers performed well in many aspects of the test, but failed in other ways."

My heart skipped a beat. Nat. Perhaps they would let him pass after all.

The Singer continued. "A strong argument has been made in the case of one of these fliers."

Then Sidra held a wingmark in her hands. She turned to tie it to her shoulder strap, caught my eye, and smiled.

I was baffled. How could she earn her wingmark after

the disastrous Group flight, not to mention failing Laws? And arguing.

Ezarit came to stand by my side. Her hand touched my shoulder. "We do not buy our wings," she whispered. And I understood. I waited to hear what Nat's fate would be, knowing that Elna would never bribe the council, even if she had the means.

Ezarit's hand rested on my arm, and I remembered what she'd just done. Doran Grigrit. I shrugged her away. First I would get my wingmark, then I would try to negotiate my own apprenticeship, without her help. And then I would help Nat.

But the bag was empty. The Singers unfurled their wings and prepared to leave. Impossible. Where was mine?

I pulled the test chips from my wing as I hurried towards them, shouting, "Wait!" There in my hands were Laws and City, Solo and Group. I'd passed them all, whole and well. I held them out.

But the Singers shook their heads. The older Singer smiled. "You are Densira? You broke the Silence. In Solo. After breaking Fortify. Your lack of tradition and discipline failed you, set a bad example for others. Try again next year."

All around me the bettors fell silent. No one had thought to put money on that outcome. I heard Doran call for his party. They were leaving. Ezarit scrambled to slow them, to renegotiate.

Many of us had broken the Silence. Sidra especially. But her father had tipped things in her favor. And the Singers, I realized, had tipped things in theirs.

I stood, stunned, at the balcony's edge, as the Singers leapt into the wind. Doran and his wife followed, without a backwards glance.

Behind me, I saw my mother, wan and staring. She could not fathom what had happened, her plans gone to shards around her. My luck had tainted hers. She took a step back, then another.

I looked every direction, hoping for a place to hide and sort this out. Soon, Wik would come to speak to Ezarit, and perhaps she would give me up to them instead. I had to get away, if not to hide, then to rage. Where no one in the towers could see me.

Those from Densira who'd come for the wingfights pulled their faces into careful masks when they saw me. So unlucky. They whispered warnings against my dangerous behavior to each other.

Beyond them, in the shadows, Nat watched me. Then he turned and slipped from the shade-side of the balcony into the sky. In the commotion, no one else noticed.

I slid through a break in the crowd, between figures turned to watch the departing Singers, and edged towards the empty part of the balcony. My neighbors let me go. I was unlucky again, and beneath their notice.

In one quick motion, I opened my wings and flew after Nat. A cold gust pushed me out fast. The tower shrank behind me before I realized he was headed far from the city, into the open air.

8

CROSSWIND

"I'm coming with you," I shouted across the sky, loud against Mondarath's fading noise.

Nat let me catch up with him. "We'll take the crosswind in," he replied.

We were two Lawsbreakers, flying without wingmarks, at Bethalial. *Allmoons' time of quiet.* If we were caught, we would be weighed down with even heavier markers than before. But what did that matter, when we were already so burdensome to our families, to our tower?

"Where are we going?"

Nat's feet dangled at awkward, overgrown angles from his wings' footsling. The wings supported him, but barely. "You'll need to let me draft on your wings for the turn," he said. That was not an answer.

We passed the broken tower, Lith, at the northern edge of the city. The winds here were plainer, less easy to read. They were also less prone to shifts and wind shadows. Few flew the edges of the city. I knew my mother did because the winds were also faster here. But I wondered at Nat. The crosswinds picked up farther south. To catch them on this angle, we'd need to fly a long way into the open sky.

"Turning where?" I asked. I didn't care what his answer was. We were in the open, no tower to turn to, no place to land safely.

My eyes burned from staring hard at the blue, looking for ripples, air currents, skymouths, danger.

We could turn back. The city meant safety. Still, I wanted to keep flying until we disappeared into the distance, until they lit our banners and set us free.

"Into the center," he said. "Soon."

For now, all we had was sky ahead and cloud below. No towers, no colorful wings. No skymouths, I hoped.

Beyond the city, the air felt much colder. We closed on the point where a crosswind usually cut in. Ezarit had said once it was the fastest route to the center, but the most dangerous. In that moment, on that day, we didn't care.

I spotted the cloud drift that marked the windstream first, and whistled to Nat. He turned his head to sight an angle off the receding towers, then whistled back. Time to turn. I took the lead, dipping my right wing low and spreading my fingers in their harnesses to stretch the upward curve of my left wing.

I turned, a blade of fury carving the sky. Behind me, I heard the crack and flap of Nat's wings fighting to cut the same arc. He teetered, then pulled straight and steady. We aimed for the city.

I didn't realize I was crying until my cheeks began to crackle with the cold of the crosswind. The lenses dangled around my neck, unwanted, but necessary. I tucked my arm from my wing and yanked them up over my nose. My cap slipped as the strap dragged on it, but didn't fall.

The lenses. I bet Ezarit regretted wasting them now. She didn't want me by her side. Doran Grigrit didn't want me. Nor Densira. None would have the Lawsbreaker, the skymouth attractor. None would have Nat Brokenwings either. We were nearly castoffs. Unlucky. If we failed again, we could wind up skulking in the low tiers, scraping filth from trash to get by. Unless we flew our own way.

Singer Wik was behind this. The Singers had taken every-thing, even after I'd paid my debt to my tower. The Spire on the horizon caught my eye. In the fading light, the tower was pure and white, surrounded by the city's waving banners.

I would run straight into its walls, like a bird. The tower would shake as I fell.

They would not come for me. I would go to the Spire to find the truth, I'd take them by surprise. They would give me my wings and my marker, or I would challenge like Ezarit had. At first light, I would demand my rights and have my questions answered. Nat too.

Nat flew behind me and back a bit. In my reflecting lens, I saw his clenched jaw, his narrowed eyes. He wanted answers too.

While the city marked its shortest day, grieved its losses, and moved on, we would mark the city. Carve a hole in it. Break tradition.

We would take what it refused to give.

I shifted my gaze, refocusing at the approaching view. As the towers began to light Allmoons banners, the central rooftops blossomed with fire along their edges. Dusk advanced; the city came alight, with the Spire pale and steady at its center.

We aimed our wings, flying direct and angry towards the city's heart.

9

APPROACH

The current we rode carried us high. We looked down over the central towers as the flickering banners faded to ash.

We'd broken so many Laws tonight. I wondered at that. And then I did not even care. I wasn't Ezarit's obedient girl anymore. Where had that gotten me?

A scrim of high clouds and the gaining dark gave us some cover. We were shadows tonight, hidden by ritual. The city's eyes were on its lost. We would be obscured until the moon had fully risen and the banners burned away.

We dove into Varu's shadow, then around. No one peered from its balconies. All were on the tower's highest levels, remembering.

To fly unseen was frightening. I was used to life lived in the open, where everyone watched. In the crush of neighbors at the Allmoons lightings, I'd never thought of what the rest of the city was like, dark below the canopy of banners lit and burning.

The Singers, too, were gone from the top of the Spire. Attending their duties around the city, chronicling the lost. I understood the need for the Bethalial now. *No one but Singer-born or Singer-sworn may approach the Spire at Allmoons.* Well. I was under a Singer fiat, wasn't I? That was good enough for me.

The Spire looked as impenetrable as ever, but no gray wings were about to see us on our mad approach.

We both knew the Spire wasn't empty. Not all Singers attended Allmoons on the towers. Some Singers, according to tower gossip, never left the Spire's walls. They sequestered themselves in order to more closely listen to the city and discern its needs. They turned inwards for the good of the city. That was their sacrifice.

That was also our opening, Nat's and mine. We glided close enough to the Spire that, if it had balconies, they would have seen us. The market nets were pulled up to the top of the Spire, their baskets bound as if for a storm.

"We are the Nightwings!" Nat crowed. Figures from a children's song. "None see us!"

For the first time, I wondered if Singers stayed at the towers after Allmoons. No one flew at night, so they must. No one except Nat and me. We raced the dark now, two shadows in the gloaming light.

Nat took the lead again. "I know where we need to go. Tobiat said the chips were made for something about sixteen tiers down."

We chased the dreams of an addled hermit and a dead man. As my anger ebbed, I grew afraid that we would soon join their ranks. Who was better off, Tobiat or Naton? *Enough.* I shook off those dark thoughts.

Ten tiers. My eardrums grew tight, then released. The clouds swirled too close, too dangerous. We were far enough down that, in any other tower, we'd be staring at filth-clotted walls. The Spire was different. The pristine exterior was decorated with carvings here and there, not filth. They didn't throw their waste down the outside of the tower as the rest of us did. Either that, or they didn't make any waste. Another Singer mystery.

I followed Nat, then flew by his side as we circled the sixteenth tier. No nets here, only grips and cleats where nets once were. He pointed to something rough-looking on our first circuit of the Spire. Not the sixteenth tier down. The fifteenth.

A portion of the wall carved with several markings, made familiar by Naton's bone chips.

"I told you!" he yelled.

And then we were past it. I'd barely had time to process what I saw. But we circled again. As we came back in range, Nat pulled his bow and nocked an arrow.

He'd tied a thin line of spidersilk and tendon tight above the arrow's fletching. It dipped a thin shadow through the air, to his wingstraps. Nat had bound himself to the shaft.

I had no time to question the wisdom of this plan before he aimed and shot. Beautifully. Like a true hunter. The arrow threaded the eye of a bone cleat carved into the wall. Nat pulled on the rope, and the arrow flipped up. Locked tight to the eye. Then the rope pulled taut between Nat and the tower, and he was ripped from our forward flight. I looked under my wing and behind me to see him dangling from the fifteenth tier down on the Spire. That must have hurt.

When I'd left the wingfight and Mondarath, my ears had been full of roaring anger. I realized now how little thought I'd put to this, besides following Nat. That perhaps he'd planned for one, not two, to approach the Spire. Nat knew exactly how he would connect himself to the tower and had planned carefully. No such preparations were in place for me.

I needed to make the next circuit of the Spire on my own. I flew silent, eyes casting left, right, and down for a Singer, for a hint of skymouths or anything else. The cold winds whistled around me. Below, clouds and the towers began to glitter in the rising light of Allmoons. In a few moments, the glass beads I'd woven in my braids and along the edges of my wings would pick up the light and throw it like a beacon to anyone who happened to glance into the dark night sky.

This should have been a day of celebration and joy. Instead, rage cooled into sadness. I was alone in all the city, but for a single friend. *Oldest friend. Wing-brother.*

I completed the circuit and saw Nat clinging to the wall. He'd driven two pitons into the bone during my turn. He worked fast, for sure.

As I passed, he tossed me a line, and I missed it. Cursing, I found myself with a choice. I could circle a third time or turn and beat across the wind to the thrown rope.

The moon would be fully up before I flew around the Spire a third time. Too dangerous. I would turn. I would do this the hard way.

I dipped my left wing and banked a turn out of the breeze. The silk of my wings flapped noisily between the battens, then stilled. As I turned, I lost altitude. Now Nat was above me, and I neared the seventeenth tier downtower. There had been little enough rope before, and when he threw it again, I had to be higher. I strained to find a strong gust.

In the Spire's wind shadow, there wasn't enough unsullied air to lift me higher.

I pulled closer to the Spire, hoping for an updraft. That's when I saw them. Another set of carvings similar to the ones Nat had found, but deeper. And a mark for a handgrip.

We'd been taught to fly to handgrips in emergencies or storms and had practiced clinging to Densira's spurs, but I'd never done it without a net. Nor in the dark. I locked my wing harness with a thumb and withdrew my fingers from both sets of fine controls. My breathing came quicker, and my mouth felt dry as old bone. I crooked my arms in the winghooks and prepared to grab.

I was flying too fast when the grip came within reach. I crashed into the Spire and scrambled my hands along its sides, splintering shards from the wall into my palms as I clawed.

The wind lifted my wings and gave me a moment's buoyancy.

Then the gust strengthened and tried to tear me from the wall, just as my fingers sank through a hole with a deep grip in it. I grasped hard and hoped. Detached my other hand and grabbed double-handed, pulling my body parallel with the wall of the Spire. Clouds, it hurt. I splayed against the wall, powerless to do more.

Nat stifled a shout.

With my face pressed so close to the carvings, I could see holes within the symbols. Much like the chips had, but finger-sized. Slowly I peeled a few fingers from the grip and reached them to the holes.

Nat and Tobiat were right. The chips were a map. To what? To secret Spire gates? That would be worth plenty to the Singers. And to us, stranded on the side of the tower in the middle of the night.

"Can you climb up?" Nat called.

I shook my head. "Wait a minute, and I'll either climb or peel off and try again." I tried to slow my breathing as I peered into the darkness for clues about the quality of the wind this close to the Spire.

My foot began to slip, and I scrambled again for purchase. Mashed myself as close to the wall as I could, fingers still caught in the smaller holes. Something gave behind the pressure of my fingertips. I pressed again.

A grinding sound came from inside the wall. When I looked down, I could see a shadow growing on the pale tower; a distant panel of bone below me began to slide sideways.

As the gate opened, I heard other sounds, like water running down a wall.

Of course they had gates. Secret exits, for when flying from the top of the Spire wouldn't do or they came under attack from a rogue tower.

"Nat!" He'd love this. Perhaps this was enough of a secret

for him, for both of us. Then we could fly home. But to what kind of welcome?

There must be more such gates. If Naton's chips marked them all, the Singers would be eager to have the skein back. Perhaps they would trade for it after all.

The grinding sound continued. I couldn't see much, but I could feel movement in my fingers, and in the bone pressed against my chest. A rush of foul air brushed my cheek. My fingers tightened on the grip in the walls and in the holes.

Nat shouted again. He gestured wildly. His feet scrambled, his legs pumped and a wing jammed against the tower. He tried to climb back up the rope, panicking.

I hung on tight and looked around in time to catch the ripple and the tear in the sky that became a slick maw, blood-black, with teeth that glittered like stars, aimed right at me.

The monster pushed a pulse of raw wind before it. My wings filled with it and pinned me hard to the wall.

I could not breathe. I could not turn and scream—Nat was screaming enough for both of us.

From the corner of my eye, I saw motion in the darkness. Shadows swooped past. A net flew through the air and landed with a slick sound in front of me. The breath of the skymouth stopped pushing at me. I could breathe again.

Gray-winged Singers flew above and below me. One made a high-pitched noise and pulled the skymouth away by the net.

Another threw a second net at me. The ropes, made of sticky spidersilk, smelled of herbs and muzz. The silk tightened around me, cracking wing battens, pressing its cloying scent at my nose and mouth. I could not see Nat.

"Where are you?" I yelled to him as I was pulled from the wall.

The net's embrace wrapped me tight. I was lifted higher, bound in sick-sweet ropes. The stars spun. The moon shrank to a pinhole. Alone, I rose up to it and disappeared.

PART TWO

THE SPIRE

10

FORGOTTEN

Rough bone pressed against my palms, my face, my knees.

I was not falling. Not eaten. But I could not hear the wind.

My eyes were crusted shut. I rubbed the grit from them until they opened enough to reveal blurred shadows. I drew a breath full of filth and dried bone. When I coughed, a pale dust cloud rose cumulus beside my head, then settled, glittering, across my hand.

Tied around my wrist, a gray silk cord held three thick markers. They rattled together when I moved. Laws. New ones. Heavy ones.

I pushed hard against the floor with both hands, then raised my head and torso until the room spun and my heart beat a tattoo in my ears. When I could breathe again, when the pounding ebbed to a dull pulse, I eased onto my knees.

"Nat?"

My words echoed. No reply in the darkness.

My arms wouldn't extend or lift from my sides. I touched left hand to right shoulder to find thick strands of spidersilk. The Singer's net. I grasped it and lifted, intending to peel the sticky silk from my shoulders and back.

My hiss of pain echoed through the room as my skin stuck to the silk. Still, I did not pause. Skin, shards of battens, and wing fell away with the net, broken.

As the pile of discarded net and wing shifted with my movements, the floor rumbled and sighed. I had not caused that sound, but I knew what it was. Below me, the city spoke softly and then grew silent.

Once free of the net, I reached out and touched bone walls in every direction. My markers rattled. I tucked them under the cord to still them.

Now I could hear someone singing, faint notes rising and falling beyond the wall. But as my hands made a circuit of my prison, I discovered no doors, no openings. No way to reach the voice. No breeze here either. Only a rough wall that rose higher than I could stretch my fingers.

Then the darkness shifted. Broke. Far above my head, a small light guttered and held. Someone had set an oil lamp into the wall. The light struck the space in patches and, as my eyes steadied enough to trace it, the shadows of my prison acquired edge and gouge: carvings, everywhere.

On the walls, Singers fought gryphons in the carved clouds; they tore carved wings from a woman, they threw a flailing man from a carved tower.

I had no doubts now. I was trapped within the walls of the Spire.

The bone murals of the prison continued along the floor. I lifted my aching knee and studied a red imprint in my skin: a face carved mid-scream.

Above me in the growing glare of the lantern, a white arc appeared like a moon unfurling: crescent, then half, then full. A carved bone pail scraped against the wall as it was lowered on a rope. The pail dropped into my upstretched hands, and I felt the edges of words. More Laws. *Bethalial, Trespass, Treason.*

Nothing in this room was uncarved, unmarked, except me.

The pail slipped from my hands and clattered against the floor. It wobbled to a stop, and I crawled to it. Inside were a bladder sack and a dried bird's gizzard. I unstoppered the sack and sipped. Water. It tasted like scourweed. I put the bird's gizzard in my pocket.

I muttered my thanks. My voice was a rasp.

"You are welcome, Kirit Notower," a voice said in response, startling me. Before I could respond, the bucket rose on its rope. The moonlight above my head shrank to a hairline crescent and then vanished.

I put my head on my knees, wrapped my arms around my shins, and wept until I ran dry.

Later, I took the gizzard from my pocket and looked at it. They were feeding me. If the Singers had wanted me dead, I would be.

When they lowered the bucket again, I tried to see beyond the light, to see the shapes of those above. I saw nothing, not even their hands. This time, the goosebladder held a weak broth; the bucket, a stone fruit.

"How long will you hold me here?" I shouted at the moon.

The voice responded slowly, "Until you hear. Until you understand." Then the moon in the ceiling slid closed again. Once my eyes had adjusted to the darkness, I could see that it was not closed all the way.

They couldn't leave me here forever. A corner of my pile of silk and netting already reeked of urine and foul. I'd pushed it as far from my bedding as I could.

I heard singing again. I heard The Rise echo down from above.

There was a way out. It was small and distant. And all I had to do to reach it was fly.

My broken wings mocked me silently from the floor.

I put my ear to a wall and heard the pulse of the Spire, the wind sweeping the walls, the bone thickening, the deeper sounds. Of the city beyond the Spire I could hear nothing.

What of Nat? Was he a prisoner within the Spire too? Or had he been thrown down? Worse? Was I truly alone?

I began shouting, hoping they would come to the moon-window again. "You can't hold me here! My tower and my family—"

Would what? They had turned from me. Found me unlucky.

I tried once more. "My mother—"

Traded me away.

"You can't hold me here! You cheated me of my wings, and you cannot hold me!"

I ached to see the horizon beyond the walls. To feel a breeze. See a sunrise. There was no way to tell how much time had passed except by the arrival of buckets.

The total enclosure made my heart pound against my ribs. To calm myself, I listed what I used to see from my quarters in Densira: clouds, birds on the wing, Mondarath, sometimes Viit if the weather was right. Banners. Green plants. Neighbors climbing ladders, crossing far-off bridges, carrying children nestled tight to their breasts as they flew short distances. Sky.

I had always been able to see the sky. There had always been a breeze laced with ice, or wet with rain, or hot with summer. There was no weather here. No sky.

The walls of my prison absorbed blows from my fists, cut my skin when I struck a sharp carving. I sank again to the floor. The walls surrounded me like an unforgiving second skin. When I woke, it was to the grinding sound of the panel above drawing back and another pail. This one contained another sackful of broth, with the gritty must of dirgeon. Those birds ate anything, and it showed in the taste of the meat. I was willing to eat like them at that moment.

The pail still rattled. A bone tool had been tucked beneath the sack, its sharp end wrapped in silk. A carving tool.

"What do you want?" I shouted to the hole above me, not expecting an answer. But then a shadowed head appeared in its halo.

"We keep the city safe," said a voice. "We look for those who could do the same."

My shoulders and legs ached. I turned my head from the light and stretched to see if I could touch both walls at once. Not quite.

"You don't want me. I break Laws. Endanger my tower. My city." I held up my wrist, shaking the markers to make them clatter and echo.

Now that my eyes had adjusted to the gloom, I could better read the markers: *Bethalial, Trespass, Treason.*

"You have indeed." And the window closed entirely.

I was Kirit Notower. *Lawsbreaker. Unlucky.*

I had attacked the Spire. At Allmoons. I'd attracted a sky-mouth. My hand tightened around the carving tool, its silk wrapper. I had lost my friend.

In the dim light, I unwound the silk from the carver's tip. In the towers, we wrote message on bone. Dye was too valuable. Ink unavailable. The Singers, it seemed, had both. My eyes strained to read the marks on the fabric: *Some believe you are more than your crimes. Some believe you can Rise. Are you worth saving?*

I thought about the wingtest. About the way I'd flown. I'd not heard of Singers lifting Lawsmarks, ever. I thought about Wik, his insistence at Densira that I could help the city. Singers could do anything for the good of the city.

They wanted something from me. Perhaps I could make a trade. Convince them to lift my punishments. If I could reach them.

The carvings. At points, deep enough to allow a fingertip to jam into a crevice. Perhaps a bare toe. I pulled my silk foot wrappings off. My toes were soft and pallid in the dim light. My fingers found a place on the wall where someone—another prisoner?—had carved a series of birds in flight, circling upwards. Had they been able to carve the birds all the way to the top? If so, climbing them was better than waiting for release.

The deepest carvings had sharp edges, but my fingers still found purchase and I pulled myself up against the wall. The effort of climbing made the pads on my fingers throb. My knuckles cracked. My toes ached. I stopped, rested, then tried again, pressing my body close to the wall, pushing with my feet and calves until my leg muscles burned painfully. After the first few minutes, my fingers and toes had grown so numb, I could not shake them awake. I fell back to the carved bone floor. It was hopeless. A trick. I was never meant to leave this place.

I did not intend to do so, but I fell asleep again. I did not dream. I woke to find I'd spilled from my silk nest, kicked it aside, slept on the floor. My cheek pressed hard against a carving of the city. I rolled over and muffled a shriek of pain. My fingers had swelled and blistered. I stuck two of them in my mouth and sucked, whimpering. The taste of blood and dust from the room made me ill.

The city was silent now, the Spire too. I tried to guess what day it was—we were past Allmoons, but how far past?

With only the buckets to tell me, I had no sense of when I was. Perhaps it was evening. Perhaps Elna was already cooking dinner. Perhaps Ezarit had returned from another trade. I imagined the conversations, held to them tightly. What would Nat have been doing? And I? I would have been doing nothing, not until I could pass a wingtest without breaking the quiet.

This was no comfort.

Before long, another pail descended. It contained a dirgeon

wing, already broken, its marrow drying out, and, I thought, a smaller sack of water than before. The Singer at the top of this pit had set me a timer. The more time I spent here, the less I'd be fed. Soon, my food would run out and I would vanish. No more bad luck, no more Lawsbreaker.

I drank every drop of water and savored the lone wing.

Another bucket was sent down the next day, with less water and a piece of goose liver. I lay curled in the small pile of clean silk and netting. My fingers had recovered, but my feet, with their soft pads that never had to do much, were lacerated and painful. I could barely walk, even if there'd been room enough to do so. I leaned my forehead against a wall and listened to the city whisper and pulse. I imagined Nat was here too, listening with me to the secrets of the Spire. I whispered our Laws to him.

Bethalial: *In the Allmoons time of quiet, let no tower be disturbed.*

Delequerriat: *The act of concealment, in plain sight, may only be used to turn wrong to right.*

Trade: *No trader lives with jealousy or greed.*

War: *We rise together or fall apart. With clouds below, our judge.*

On the bone wall near where my foot rested, someone had carved a skymouth attacking. It gaped at me.

I took up the tool against it, scratched over it until it disappeared.

Then I found a tiny, uncarved space in the floor. I drew the lines of Nat's profile as I remembered it.

The sharp edge of the carver peeled tiny curls of bone away in its passage. Nat's face looked much younger on the floor. His face from our youth, from before Ezarit and I rose. It was a poor likeness, but when I finished, I had someone to talk to.

I told him everything, in a rush. That I wanted to live, any

way I could. I told him why the Singers wanted me. What Wik
forbade me to tell anyone. I told him what I could do. How I
could help the city.

Nat did not respond. But the Spire did: it whispered secrets
back to me, until I was ready to fly.

❦ ❦ ❦

Covered in filth, my greasy braids matted against my head
like a cap, I stripped all but the last layer of silk robes from my
body and piled them below where I planned to climb.

I left my friend on the floor below me, with my broken wing.
The Spire's whispers pushed me higher.

I heard them as I balanced on the tips of my toes and slipped
and fell. My back arched, and my head struck hard against the
wall. I heard them when I woke again. Hopeful, fearful. Calling for me.

Nat would have wondered at me, I realized. Talking to the
Spire. Starving to death, more like it. *Get up,* Nat would have
whispered. *Pull yourself up.*

And so I did.

I found the carving tool and poked at a blister on my forefinger, let the sack of skin weep. It hurt. I howled with the pain as
I did it again and again, until I was ready. Then I wrapped my
fingers and toes in what was left of the cleaner spidersilk.

The wall was already warm and slick with grease from my
hands. I ignored the pain in my fingers and concentrated on the
lift I got from my legs. I pretended that my toes were part of
the wall and that the Singer above had a rope around my waist
and was hauling me up. I found I could inch my way up the
wall, crack by crack. I pressed fingers and toes into the carved
crevices: faces and wings and clouds and towers, the forgotten
dreams of others who had been here before me. The spidersilk

provided an extra stickiness that held my hands to the wall and let me stop and rest.

My legs and arms started to shake when I realized that the carvings were thinning. At the bottom, there was only a small uncarved space. Now that I was high—at least three tiers, I realized—there were many fewer handholds. The oubliette narrowed at the top, and if I could make it a few body lengths higher, I would be able to place a foot on the opposite wall. I could edge my way up. A big if. Not many more carvings here— a flock of birds, a faint trace of a flower, broken off.

Below me, the floor was dark. I knew now why the carvings below were so clear against the walls. They had been shaded with dried blood, where others had fallen, trying to rise.

Up high, the carvings were brighter: eggshell on bone.

I could see the edge of the crescent now. The buckets had stopped coming, but the window had been left open. A promise, if I could make it.

They waited for me there, the Singers who wanted me, though for what purpose and how long, I did not know. I did not care.

Anything to get out of this prison. I braced myself on a narrow foothold and dug into the wall with the carver. Dried bone curled away. Thin lines became deeper. I was not going for beauty or style. I would not leave a mark beyond a handhold. This was not my last message to my city, to the Spire. This was a way out, nothing more.

My fingers oozed blood when the carver finally splintered and shattered so badly I could not find a sturdy edge. I screamed with pain and frustration. My whole body was rigid.

Would what I'd done be enough? The Spire remained silent. I could not wait for it to speak again. I had to try on my own, a few more steps. I lifted a shaking arm and gripped the carving with my fingers, pulled. Lifted my foot and put it in the last bird on the wall. Placed my other foot on top of it. Grabbed for the new handhold I'd carved and pressed up. I nearly slipped. I scrambled for balance. The carver fell, and it took a long time before I heard it hit the floor.

With shaking legs, I moved my foot and stretched it to reach the other wall. My hipbone popped at the exertion. I had no idea how long I'd been climbing, but my body noted the time in aches.

I missed the voice of my city. The daily sounds from distant towers. The bustle and press of neighbors, the call of friends on the wing. I missed the voice of the Spire, the whispers.

I braced close to the ceiling and lifted my fingers from one handhold. Reached towards the crescent. I was short by finger-lengths.

I roared, pushed off my feet in frustration, and found myself lifting farther than I'd thought I could. My toes pointed hard, my pelvis rocked, my spine and shoulders and everything leaned towards that hole. My fingers seemed to grow, clawing for the crescent. Sinking my hands around the thick edge of bone that was the way out. I touched it with a fingertip on a wild swipe. That touch drove me forward again and up. I grabbed the edge with one hand, then the other. My feet slipped, and I hung for a moment, above the oil lamp, above the oubliette. My fingers slid. I had no strength left to hold on.

11

FOUND

A rush of air. A moment where I touched nothing, not the wall, not the ledge of the window. I flailed, hands cupping emptiness. Then one hand caught a muscled arm, reaching from the gap in the wall. Held tight.

"Easy. I've got you," a familiar voice said. The brightness of the room threw his face into shadow, but I knew his profile. The way he clipped his words.

Wik leaned out of the opening above me. His fingers gripped my wrists tighter as he pulled me up. He turned his head away from me and spoke over his shoulder, almost grunting with the effort. "Tell Rumul she finally made it."

I could not hear a response, but he turned his full attention back to me. My hands locked on to his arms, while his hands circled my biceps. I scrambled my feet against the bone wall and pushed as he pulled. From beyond him, a breeze brushed my cheek. Fresh air. I longed to bask in it.

He dragged me, still kicking, through the hole. The thick edge scraped the last spidersilk from my chest and bruised my ribs. I hit the floor hands first, then my knees connected with the hard surface.

Sunlight struck the bone floor, turning it and the walls bright white, shocking my shadow-trained eyes. All I could see in the dazzling room were gray foot wrappings and the edge of a dark robe.

"Rest," Wik said. He held out a water sack, and I snatched it from his hands. This Singer. I swallowed my first sip, then took another. I spat that mouthful at his feet.

He laughed and stepped back. I was too weak to rise or to try again.

As my eyes grew used to the light, the lower half of the room took shape: a broad expanse with stools and a workbench, all carved from bone, near the wall where I sat. A threshold carved with chevrons and, beyond that, a passageway. Then more light and air. The passage bordered something like sky, though the light was strangely taut, like sunbeams strung on a bow.

I took another sip of the water. Built my strength to move, to rush for the passageway, to shout at Wik. To leave here.

With the sound of swishing robes, two more pairs of gray feet came into view. I struggled to sit straighter, my back and leg muscles protesting each shift in position.

"Kirit, you have broken such Laws." The new voice belonged to another man. It was a smooth voice, the kind Ezarit had always told me to be careful about when trading. The kind of voice that lulled listeners before it struck them down.

This Singer listed my crimes. I could almost hear the songs that accompanied each broken Law: Bethalial. Trespass. Treason. War. I startled at the last. That had not been tied to my wrist.

"Did you think breaching the walls of the Spire was not War? You could be called a traitor to the city." His voice was even, soft. *Mellifluous.* My skin crawled. Beneath the smooth tones, I heard darker notes.

I looked up, trying to meet his eyes. His face was shadowed. The light behind him hurt. "All I wanted . . . ," I began. My voice rattled.

"You wanted to fly the city. To be a trader, like your mother."

Yes. He was so very right, but I wouldn't let him win the point. "Better than her."

The Singer sat on a stool, his knees level with my eyes. Wik and the other gray-robed figure remained standing on either side of him.

"Ah, but you had bad luck, and then the wingtest went so poorly."

"That was *his* doing," I said, lifting a shaking arm to point at Wik.

Wik didn't move. The Singer continued as if I hadn't spoken. His hands, resting on his knees, were silvered with tattoos.

"All traders want to be important. They all look for an edge to make them faster, better than their competition. Your mother is no exception. She fought to gain her edge. How would you be better than her?"

I could not answer that.

He continued, his voice rising and falling. "The best traders help the city. There are songs in their honor. Your mother's run, bringing together the medicines for the southeast? That is already sung in many towers."

Already. I'd been trapped in the Spire's walls for many days, then.

The Singer leaned forward so I could meet his eyes without tilting my head up. I could see the silver marks on his cheeks and forehead. His head was bald, and tattoos curved above his brow. Some symbols I recognized: knife, arrow, spear. Some I didn't understand at all.

"The towers know her wings on sight. You want that. She flies everywhere without fear. You want that too." He pressed his lips together: a dark line below his sharp nose. "But you are a Lawsbreaker. Your tower's only use for you now is as an offering to the city. They will sing no songs for you."

I shuddered. An offering. When I left Mondarath with Nat, I hadn't thought beyond making the Singers give me my wingmark. Now everything was lost. I swallowed. "Is Nat here?"

The Singer looked me in the eyes, with more sorrow than I'd thought possible on a Singer's stern face. "No."

My heart dropped. His word turned my fear into truth. My oldest friend, fallen. His death as much my fault as his own. More so. He had not broken Fortify. I had. My mind went as empty as the sky beyond the city. It filled with a moaning that built as I remembered his screams and the skymouth attacking.

The feet to the Singer's right stepped forward, and a hand shook my shoulder roughly. A young woman's voice said, "Stop that. The sound hurts my ears."

The Singer raised his hand. "Sellis, let her mourn her friend." I was grateful to him, until his next words stifled my sobs to a hiccup.

"Wik is of the belief," he said, "that you have suffered enough losses, Kirit."

I looked up. Rumul smiled, slowly. Beside him, Wik shifted on his feet. "You love the city?"

The city's towers. Its blue skies, the lights of Allmoons. The touch of the wind when I woke in the morning. The towers and the people in them. The songs of our past. I did love it.

"Yes." The barest whisper.

"It needs you, Kirit. If you can grow beyond your anger and your losses, the city needs you."

The girl, Sellis, pressed my shoulder again. "Listen to Rumul."

The honey-voiced man's name. Rumul. He stood up. Walked behind the workbench and took a seat there. Wik and Sellis remained near me.

"Why do you fight us in this?"

I shook my head. I could barely sit, much less fight.

Rumul lifted a thick skein of bone markers from the work-table and rubbed a chip between his fingers. For a moment I thought he held Naton's chips, but these were new, uncarved. Their cord was red, not blue. "You were offered an opportunity to come to the Spire, which you resisted."

I eyed Wik's spit-marked foot. He had not said much since he'd pulled me from the oubliette.

"And yet you flew straight here on your own. Why?" He fingered another chip. The markers were thick. They were Lawsmarks like the ones on my wrist. "Because you knew we had something you wanted. And you thought you had something we wanted too."

I swallowed and prepared to bargain. I *did* have something they wanted: me. My voice. I could help them with the sky-mouths. For my wings. For my life. I lifted my chin, took a determined breath.

Rumul raised his eyebrows. "You still think so?" I nodded, opening my mouth. Sellis jerked my arm and hushed me before I could argue.

"There is dissent in the Spire over letting you live. Wik has argued on your behalf. Has said you stopped a skymouth. Though you didn't stop the one near the Spire."

Wik stepped forward. "She had no time to do so."

Sellis jumped in, saying, "She is headstrong, and she is a Lawsbreaker." She raised my hand and shook my wrist so the marks clacked heavy.

A look from Rumul quieted her.

The room settled into silence, punctuated only by the clicking of the bone markers Rumul held.

"You are no longer a citizen, by Laws," he finally said. "But I would like to make you a bargain."

Sellis stifled a protest. I struggled to rise to my feet, succeeding only when Wik steadied me. A bargain.

"When a citizen challenges the Spire and fails," Rumul said, his voice taking on a new depth, "they are thrown down. However, when a Singer, or a Singer-born, does so, they are allowed to live, if their injuries are not too great. Did you know this?"

I shook my head.

"What has Ezarit told you of your father, Kirit?"

A puzzling question. When I was slow to respond, Sellis elbowed me. I glared at her. "She's told me nothing. He disappeared during a migration."

Sellis snorted. "Your mother is a liar."

I bristled. Though I could not argue the words, Sellis had no right to say them.

Rumul watched me glare at Sellis for a moment. "She is correct. Your father is in the Spire."

"A prisoner?" I pictured the walls of the oubliette I'd just climbed from and felt panic tighten my stomach.

"Not at all," Wik said. His voice was low and clear. He kept his eyes on Rumul's desk, so his bird-of-prey profile was all I saw. "He is injured, but he lives among the Singers."

Rumul produced a roll of silk from his pocket, wrapped around something heavy and something that clattered. He passed it to Wik, who handed it to me. I unwrapped the silk and gasped. My mother's lenses—I'd thought them lost.

A skein of message chips was tangled in the straps.

"The lenses were his once. Your father's," Rumul said. "We are pleased to have them back."

The lenses heavy in my hand, I stumbled with Wik's assistance to the workbench and spread the chips out across the flat top. My hands shook, though the message was not addressed to me. Nor to anyone.

But I knew the hand that had marked the chips as well as I knew my own.

❦ ❦ ❦

You will live, they tell me, Ezarit had written.

For a moment, I thought she'd sent this message to me. Then I saw how faded the skein was. How dust-filled the marks. This was a message as old as Naton's had been.

I brushed a shaking finger across the chips. Felt the marks she'd made. Kept reading.

I traded you and your lies for my life. Your secret will remain with me, and the Spire will make me a fine bargain for my silence. Good-bye, love.

The bone grew slick, and the dust trapped in the marks dimpled from the tears I realized ran down my own cheeks. I did not brush them away.

This was not meant for me. She did not mean me.

I tried to hold on to that thought.

Sellis cleared her throat. She shifted under Rumul's fierce gaze, but made no further sound.

So many secrets. So many things Ezarit had kept from me. I knew she'd challenged the Spire, but to learn our tier was a bribe for her silence? That my father—

Rumul's words suddenly hit home. "My father is here? He is a Singer?"

Rumul nodded. "He was Singer-born. He ventured out of the Spire before he took his wings and was marked a Singer."

"And when he disappeared? When he left my mother alone?"

The room went still.

Wik bowed his head, his hand warm on my arm. "He was Spire-born. It is tradition to return. In the end, he paid a heavy price."

I sputtered. He left us. No price was great enough. "Does he know of me?"

Quiet built in the room. Outside, in the passageway, a voice called out a muted greeting, and another voice responded. A bird flapped its wings and passed into the taut light.

"He knows now," Rumul said. "Ezarit hid you from us. You were seen so much with another woman, Elna, and her son."

Nat. Oh, Nat.

Rumul continued, "Singers cannot possibly know everything. When Ezarit moved you uptower with her, we realized our error." His voice was soft, sorrowful. As if he himself had sustained a loss. "Some Singers feel that if you had been taught properly, you would not be in the situation you are now."

I turned to Wik. "You weren't at Densira to escort my mother through the migration."

He shook his head and began to answer. Rumul held up a hand, leaving the bone chips on the table. "You were a surprise to the Spire. We were curious about you."

"But what would you have done? I am grown."

"True." He frowned. "If Ezarit's plan was to keep you from us, she did a nearly perfect job. But she had something of greater value than she knew."

Me. Breaker of Laws. Skymouth shouter. "My voice." That was my bargaining tool.

"Untrained, your voice is merely awful," Wik said. "But trained, you could truly help the city."

I blinked. My mind, once empty as the sky, was a mess of wind-tossed thoughts and feelings. My father, alive, a sharp, sudden sunbeam. My mother's betrayals, dark clouds. A small thought, that she'd been trying to keep me from the Singers, fluttered back and forth between the two, like a whipperling on a message run.

"I want to see my father," I said, my fingers tight around the lenses.

Rumul shook his head. "He is unable to come uptower, and only Singers may descend below the novices' levels."

"You cannot be serious," Sellis cut in. "You are truly considering this?"

Rumul stood behind his workbench. His stool fell over and clattered to the floor as he turned to face her. "You are a member of council now?" Sellis ducked her head. "You are not yet a Singer, Sellis. You are here as my ears. Have a care."

I tried to understand the layers of this room. What Rumul decided was paramount. Wik seemed to be on my side, in a strange Singer way. And this Sellis? My ribs throbbed from her sharp elbow. What did I need to say to tip the balance? I thought hard, tried to remember all my mother's lessons about bargaining. The arguments I had practiced within the walls of the Spire had been based on one desire: I wanted to live.

Rumul was trying to show me how I could live and still be a part of the city. Thanks to a father I'd never known. A Singer.

How did I feel about that? *No time to hesitate, Kirit. No time to be afraid.*

I tried to consider what Rumul stood to gain from taking me in. How far he'd go.

"What are you offering?" I rasped.

He smiled. "A chance to change your life." The words hung in the air, sweet and tempting. He continued. "You can train as a Singer. You can learn to control your voice, and, with it, help the city. If you prove to us that your behavior is due to your lack of education, then we will reconsider your sentence. Do well enough, and you will join us."

Rumul's tattooed face gave me chills. His voice—I knew better than to trust it. My mind reached for clouds and sky, found only carved walls. Any chance was better than the prison I'd emerged from. Even this chance. I could never go back to the towers, to the way things were. But now I had another chance to stay alive.

"How could she possibly—" Sellis started. She slammed her mouth closed without finishing the sentence, before Rumul reacted.

"It will not be easy, the transition. You know less than a child. But"—he turned to his right and smiled again—"Wik has offered to try to train you."

This man, who had denied me my wings. To be my trainer. I tensed in his grasp. Bit back a *no*.

Rumul continued, inscrutable. "And Sellis will be your novice guide."

Two shocked faces now, mine and Sellis's. Her mouth twitched. Rumul stared her down, then returned his gaze to me.

As I considered my new future, the part of me who'd grown up in the towers shouted against it. "If I cannot do this?"

"If you do not succeed," Rumul said, "your fate is out of our hands. Your Laws, and those of your mother, will—"

"You cannot hurt her. I will not do this if you hurt her." The words were out of my mouth, fierce and angry, before I could think. Yes, I was angry at Ezarit. But that was my fight with her, not theirs. She was my mother.

Rumul put both hands on his workbench and leaned towards me. His scalp gleamed in the light, and his breath was tart with the scent of a recently eaten apple. My stomach growled, unbidden. His wind-chafed face and his tattoos marked his long experience at the top of the Spire. "I will not battle with you, Kirit. You must decide on this life."

I held his gaze. Tried to stay standing by myself, even as my knees wobbled. His dark brown eyes hardened to black.

Behind me, Sellis whispered, "If she isn't leaping at it, she does not deserve the choice."

I turned, slowly, and looked at her for the first time. She was taller than me, with wind-chapped cheeks and lips. Her gray robe framed a face that was all edges: sharp chin, cheekbones, a point in her hairline made sharper by the tight pull of her dark braids. Her eyes a sky blue that was rare in the towers. She lifted her chin higher and held my gaze, silently.

Wik cleared his throat. "You cannot become the best of the Singers now. You are too old." I dropped Sellis's gaze and turned to face him. "But you can fly with us. Live the life you should have had, with proper training. You will see the city in a whole new way with us. You will help your people rise. And you will learn to manage your voice."

"You did not tell me these things when you tried to take me from Densira."

He blinked and tilted his head. "We cannot speak freely of this outside the Spire."

I looked back to Rumul, who raised his eyebrows. Waiting.

Wik continued, "You may not have the training, Kirit, but you have something the Singers need. With us, you can become something more important than a trader."

I pictured myself among the Singers, chasing skymouths from the sky. Helping bridge the towers and keep the city together. I imagined myself returning to Densira on gray wings. Behind me, Sellis sputtered, but Rumul's gaze held her silent.

I closed my eyes. If I said no, I would be Kirit Lawsbreaker. Kirit Notower. What did I have left?

Nat, I thought, *I will not forget you. Nor Elna. I will find your answers inside the Spire, somehow. I will see you again, Ezarit. I will make you proud despite yourself. I will make you miss me.*

When I was ready, I opened my eyes. Rumul watched me

closely. He'd straightened and now held both hands palms up over the workbench. Waiting in one hand was the red skein of blank Lawsmarkers. In the other, a larger bone tablet marked with the Spire's symbol.

I extended my hand through the air between us and placed it over the tablet. Wik smiled a thin, wary smile. Sellis gathered her robes and swept from the room. I could hear her shout an order that echoed through the Spire.

When Rumul tucked the chips back into his robe and pulled out a sharp bone knife, I knew there was no changing my mind. I took the knife and carved my name mark on the tablet, a thin scratch that barely showed.

Sellis returned with a pile of fabric, holding up gray robes banded with bright blue to replace the remains of my ragged clothing. They looked too small for me, but also whole and warm. A younger Singer brought a washing bowl. Sellis handed me a small cake made of grains, honey, and bird fat. It tasted like sunshine might.

The three of them waited as I swallowed my meal. Then I lifted the bone knife again. I pierced my thumb and squeezed the wound hard. A drop of my blood fell on the tablet. It darkened my mark and the Spire's symbol, making both visible.

I was theirs, and they were mine. I was reborn into the Spire.

12

ACOLYTE

Sellis exited Rumul's alcove again without a word, dragging me behind her. She sped through the tier so quickly I gained only a blurred impression of the more ornate wall carvings, their edges shadowed by the sunlight pouring through the tower's apex. We came to a ladder cut into the thick outer wall and spines of the Spire.

"You'd best keep up on your own," she said as she turned to descend. "I won't be slowed down. I challenge for Singers' wings this year."

My aching feet strained to support me as I stumbled after her. The treads had barely enough space for a foot. My blisters and cuts made each step painful; my strained muscles too. I drew breath and tried to look strong. Capable.

"I already passed my wingtest," I reassured her, while attempting to smile over my shoulder.

She paused on the ladder and looked up at me, flipping her dark braids off her shoulders, digging her close-set gaze right into mine. "That means nothing here. Nothing."

I began to respond, but she'd descended again, and my fingers had started to slip. I clutched the slim carved rungs and scrambled after her.

We passed tier after tier, until I whimpered through my teeth each time my feet touched a new rung. On each tier, I heard the swish of robes as people passed, the murmur of conversations, and the sound of wind swirling nearby. On one floor, several voices were raised in song: tenors and altos. Their melody echoed off the wall where we climbed.

On another, lower tier, a group of children scrubbed the floor near the ladder. Two whispered in the shadows, their brushes dripping beside them. As Sellis passed, she hissed at them to get back to work. They stared for a moment longer, steel-blue eyes peering from identical faces, their robes gray with one blue stripe like mine. Then they scrambled back to the group just as an older Singer rounded a curve.

Sellis's gray silk robes had three stripes of blue at the hem. The lowest stripe's edge, undone and fraying, dragged on the risers. I tripped on it twice, then caught myself. Judging by its color and fit, my new clothing must have been intended for a much younger novice. How would I earn my stripes? How would I begin to keep up with Sellis?

She stopped so suddenly on the next tier that I nearly put my foot on her head. Sellis hissed and grabbed my ankle, threatening to topple me. "You will pay attention!"

"I assure you I am trying."

"You are worse than a fledge!"

I could not argue that. Everything within the Spire struck me as strange, as if a tower like Densira had been turned inside out. My eyes ached for sky with each tier we passed; my ears missed the comforting sounds of families arguing, neighbors haggling, babies crying. For a group named Singers, their home was almost as quiet as the sky. They walked it as if they were listening for messages on the wind.

Sellis let go of me, but the suddenness of my change in situation kept me pinned to the wall. No longer trapped in Rumul's prison, but still inside the Spire. I'd given up the sky and the towers in exchange for a life enclosed on all sides by the Spire's bone walls.

Nat might have known what to do; I did not.

"Breathe," Sellis said, no tinge of mercy to her voice. "I won't carry you if you faint."

I inhaled. I would find a way to live in this new place.

We left the ladders and paced half the circumference of the tier. Other girls who seemed to be the same age as Sellis, or older, greeted her as she passed. They stared at me. I felt the pit's grime on my skin, the dried blood on my hands. The way my arms and legs showed beneath the too-small novice robe. I watched my feet, trying not to trip and further set myself apart.

To our left, the passageway beyond the alcoves and classrooms ran to a sudden drop. The Spire's center was a void. Wind whistled as it rose past each tier, up and down the hollow of the Spire.

"To fall into the Gyre," Sellis said, watching me with a level of calm that made my skin crawl, "is to fall forever. You should be careful."

I craned my neck to look past her and saw galleries spaced around the Gyre, carved into the tower's spines. Places to sit while watching a challenge, perhaps. Sellis dragged me on.

She turned suddenly, into a small alcove barely big enough for one person to sleep in. "Here are my quarters." I hoped mine were close by. I could barely stand.

She glared at me again. "You will sleep here." She pointed to the floor in front of her alcove. "They've made you my charge. I name you my acolyte. I do this for Rumul, and so you will do this for me. What I need, you get. What I drop, you pick up. Understand?" Her voice was brisk, businesslike. She didn't care how I answered.

"Rising above your tier again, Sellis?" A boy peered around the corner. "You can't take an acolyte until you are a Singer."

"Special case," Sellis said. "She is just now committed to the Spire."

The boy whistled low and came closer, looking at me. "You came from outside?"

I saw no use in pretending otherwise. "I did."

"Lurai," Sellis said, "you aren't even supposed to be on this tier. Go away."

Lurai. Lurai. The name was so familiar. Beliak's lost brother, yes.

As I remembered, he turned to leave.

"Did you come from Viit? I think I flew wingtest with your brother," I said, hoping I could keep him here another few moments. The last thing I wanted was to be left alone with Sellis.

Lurai's brow furrowed, and he smiled, bemused. "I don't know any brothers. I am Spire, since I was young." And he started to turn away again, but stopped. "What are the towers like? What is your name?"

"Her name is Kirit Spire, and she is not going to fill your head with boring tower talk, Lurai. She has work to do here." Sellis gave him a gentle shove and then, from somewhere within her alcove, handed me a bucket filled with stink. "Get rid of that, acolyte. Bring the bucket back, cleaned. In the morning, I will have mending for you to do."

I waited for her to tell me where to take the bucket. To point me towards the pouring points that every tower in the city had. But she turned her back to me, lay down on her sleeping pad with a sigh, and appeared to fall asleep with no further trouble.

Lurai had disappeared. I stood alone in the darkening tier with a bucket and orders, but no way to fulfill them. I heard rustling around me and knew that other occupants of the tier were peering out of their alcoves to see what I would do.

I considered taking the bucket and dumping it on Sellis, but this would have been a bad way to start my new life.

"Pssst."

The whisper came from near the edge of the Gyre. I shambled over, feet aching, cautious of traps.

"We'll show you." The whisper again, but no body to go with it. "Over here. By the edge."

Now I saw them. The blue-eyed imps from several tiers up. Crouched in the gallery, watching.

"Won't you get in trouble?"

They shook their heads. Twins. Rare enough in the city. I couldn't imagine a parent giving both children to the Spire. They must have been orphans. The Singers took in orphans.

"I'm Moc," one of the twins said. "She's Ciel."

"Kirit," I said. "Kirit . . . Spire." My voice trembled on the last word.

"We're all Spire. Shouldn't matter when you got here," Ciel piped up with her high child's voice. A lock of brass-colored hair hung over her eye. The rest was neatly braided.

"But *we* were born here," Moc added. So much for my theory. "So was Sellis. She thinks it does matter. That's why she thinks she's so much better than you."

I blinked. That was good to know.

Moc took my hand and led me to a double rope. "Pull on that."

I did, for what seemed like ages. My hands throbbed as the rope rubbed them rawer still. Finally a large bin appeared, and I poured Sellis's bucket into it. The smell made me gag. When I was done, Ciel helped me pull on the other side of the rope until there was resistance, then a tug.

"Where does it go?" I asked through a yawn.

"Down." Ciel shrugged. "Don't the towers?"

"Sort of. The towers are open. Trash and stink are thrown down."

Ciel wrinkled her nose. "Must get bad down low."

I frowned. It did.

Moc listened, rapt.

"We keep most things, though," I added. "Guano, for the farms. And for seed finding. Rinds and gristle, to feed the worms that make the dirt."

Moc's eyes grew bigger than I'd thought possible. "We get most of our food from the towers."

That was good to know too. If food came in, perhaps messages could go out.

The children tugged at my robe and showed me where the scourweed grew. I almost laughed. Outside the Spire, scourweed was reserved for making the towers grow. Marked as special. Inside the Spire, it wasn't as hard to use it for cleaning filth.

Moc and Ciel kept up a happy chatter while I cleaned Sellis's bucket. They showed no signs of leaving. Despite how tired I was, I loathed the thought of returning to the silence of Sellis's alcove. Ciel and Moc's curiosity about me woke my curiosity in turn.

We walked the tier right around, talking, and they pointed up and down the Spire to the classrooms, the communal kitchens, and the alcoves.

"The novice alcoves are here and on the lower floors, but the Singers"—Moc sighed—"they're up at the top. With the council on the highest floors."

"Moc, shhh," Ciel said cautiously. "We should go now."

We'd circled back to Sellis's alcove. This one tier was much bigger than any on Densira, and the number of people it held stunned me. I pulled off my outer robe, piled it on the floor, and collapsed onto it.

As tired as I was, with the circle of the Spire's apex brightening with moon, I still could not stop thinking. Did Ezarit already know? Had they given her my tablet? Would she tell Elna? Did they know what had happened to Nat?

Our night flight seemed like a dream, something that had happened to someone else.

Would I be allowed to leave the Spire ever again?

The questions rolled on. My mind gnawed at them, giving me no answers.

In what seemed like mere moments, Sellis nudged me awake with her foot. A new day had begun. I rose from my improvised bed, straightened my robes around me, and went to tend to her needs.

\ \ \

The smell of apples steamed in spices told me where the novices took their meals. My stomach growled, but my heart sank. Ezarit cooked those too.

"They are my favorite," a voice said near the entrance. Wik. Several children seated nearby whispered and pointed. A Singer in the room must have been rare.

Sellis looked at him. "She cannot possibly keep up. She knows nothing about the city. Nothing about flying."

He nodded. "And you and I will help her discover that."

I opened my mouth to protest. I knew as much as anyone.

Wik handed me three smooth bone bowls from a woven basket. "Get us some food. Sellis and I must speak."

When I returned, my stomach growling at the contents of the bowls, they'd claimed low stools. Their heads were bent together. I balked at joining them.

But Wik noticed my glance and waved a hand in welcome. "You have no reason to fear me, Kirit. In fact, we have much to talk about."

I had yet to say anything, or to taste the apples, though sky knew I wanted them. He gestured to the bowl. Finally, he speared some on a fork and passed it to me. "Eat. You need your strength. Today will test you."

For what?

Wik filled me in about "for what" very quickly while Sellis

looked on with a sour expression. "You will begin your education. I am certain you will progress quickly and rise to the level of your peers before you know it."

Sellis snorted.

What did *that* mean? I took the smallest bite of apple. Taste filled my mouth, the cinnamon rippling over my gums and making me want to eat the whole bowlful. I watched the Singer. Wondered what the battles were that had given him his marks.

He saw me looking. Pointed to his cheek. To a spiral inside a circle. "My first turn in the Gyre," he said. "A young man challenged for tier. I was sent to fight him."

I swallowed. This was how Wik took his Singer wings. My mother must have made a similar challenge and won. Not so, the young man Wik had fought.

"Is tier such a hard thing for the city to give?"

"You see?" Sellis threw up her hands in protest at my ignorance.

"Sometimes," Wik said. He smiled, a contrast to Sellis's glare. He didn't elaborate.

Instead, he pointed again, to the pattern that wound around his left eye and over the breadth of his forehead. The mark, another Gyre fight won. "This one made me a member of the council. I fought an old Singer, Mariti, into retirement." He saw my look. "It is our way. You must be willing to sacrifice everything for what you believe, Kirit."

"Willing to kill for it?"

"Mariti did not die. He conceded. He still serves the city as a windbeater."

Concession? I hadn't known that was possible in the Spire.

"It is not a dishonor, among the Singers. Windbeater is a powerful role in the Spire."

Powerful as compared to what? Trading? Perhaps.

Sellis smacked the edge of her bowl with her hand. "When

Singers get old or hurt, they have a place to go. They don't starve. They're not left out to die. We're not monsters." Her expression finished the sentence: all these things happened in the towers.

Was it the truth? I saw in her face that she believed it was. She turned away quickly so I couldn't read anything more into her expression. I stored that knowledge for later consideration as I squinted at a small pattern by Wik's earlobe. A knife. I explored his face with my eyes. A patch near his chin had been left unmarked. A small stretch of skin with no scrawls.

"I wished to mark an excursion there," he said. "But I took my wings instead."

My lips parted. "An excursion?"

"Some leave the Spire," Sellis growled, turning back towards us, "for the towers. I can't believe you don't know this. Tower folk are so—"

Wik cut her off with a look. He flexed his hand on his knee. Took a breath. Sellis's dissent seemed to be getting to him too.

Between bites, I tried to figure out what made excursion so special. Singers left the Spire all the time. The words escaped before I even realized I'd spoken.

Wik laughed. "Before they take their wings, before they are marked with tattoos, some Singers are allowed a special type of excursion. Especially the Spire-born. So we can understand the towers. Just as only a few are given to enclosure—the deep communication with the city that lets us know its needs." He said this as if the words should make sense to me.

At my confusion, Sellis gave an exaggerated sigh. "We should enroll her in the nests. With the infants." She faced me. "You need years of training to become a proper Singer. Years. You can't glide in here and—"

Around us, other novices watched. The room had fallen very quiet.

At a look from Wik, Sellis cleared her throat and held the

dirty bowls towards me. She tilted her head and gestured with her chin. *Move, acolyte.* I found scourweed piled in a corner and scrubbed the bowls until they were no longer sticky and my hands were cut and bleeding again.

When I finished, I rejoined them.

Wik stood. "Let's walk." He folded his hands behind his back and paced away. Sellis and I hurried to catch him.

"Tell me about excursion and enclosure." If I was to learn, I'd need to get started somewhere.

Sellis said, "Enclosure is for those who can listen to the sounds of the city."

"When it roars?" I shuddered, thinking about those days. And what happened after.

She stared like I'd said the most dense thing possible. "The city speaks all the time. And we speak to it. The Singers who are enclosed tell us what the city wants. What it dreams for itself."

I realized that the pocket of bone where I'd been trapped until yesterday was not only my prison. The carvings were too beautiful. Too reverential. That was an enclosure.

"Are there many who do this?"

Sellis shivered. "Yes. But not forever. They take shifts."

"And excursion?"

Wik blushed, confusing me. "Before we take a seat on the council, most Singers are permitted some time abroad. To ensure we do not become too disconnected with our cousins in the rest of the city."

I raised my eyebrows. "To live among the citizens. In the towers."

He nodded.

"In secret?"

Wik stilled, like a hunting bird. He watched me as his lips parted in the briefest possible, most silent response, a breath of a word. "Sometimes."

The thought of Singers prowling invisibly among us made me shiver. I did not know why. It felt safer to think of Singers as gray-robed guardians.

I stayed silent while Wik fidgeted with fuzz on his robe. He wanted to tell me more—this controlled, powerful young man who'd ruined my life wanted to say things to me, I could feel it. But what? And why?

I remembered Ezarit talking about conversations as ways to trade—"They want to share with you. You need to find the right question that gets them to share more than they intend."

Fine. I mulled the questions I had. I thought about what Wik had already told me. I looked at him and waited until the right question rose to the surface of my mind.

Before it had a chance to do so, Sellis spoke. Her voice was scornful. "Your father nearly didn't return from his excursion. Imagine. Falling for the towers."

"It happens, Sellis." Wik cut her off.

That was interesting. "When can I meet him?"

Sellis snorted. "You would need your wings."

The look in Wik's eyes said I must ask no more. I considered shifting the discussion to Naton instead. At least I could finish Nat's journey for him. But Wik had a question for me instead.

"Do you know why we need you, Kirit?"

I shook my head. "But if I must enclose myself to listen to the city, I am certain I will lose my mind. That isn't it, is it?"

For once, Sellis was silent. Her face betrayed her: this was something she did not know. She looked to Wik, hoping to learn too.

Wik continued to pace the tier, the two of us hustling to keep up with him. "Several shouters are already too old to fly. We need your voice," he began.

Sellis snorted again.

"You need training, a great deal of it. This is a skill that you can learn quickly, I hope. Few enough have this ability, and many cannot learn it."

That shut Sellis up.

She tilted her head suddenly, as if she'd heard something I could not. "Rumul requires me."

Robes swishing behind her, she was gone without another word.

Wik remained. He slowed his pace.

"She does not like me," I said.

Wik nodded in agreement.

"You and Sellis are not friends either," I ventured again. He didn't react. "Were you born in the Spire too?"

He chuckled. "I was. My mother serves on the council."

"And Rumul?"

"He respects my opinion, and my mother's. She saw you fly at wingtest. She argued your case."

"The woman with the silver patch of hair?"

Wik gave me a look, but didn't continue. I tried a different line of questioning. "What happened to my father?"

Wik cleared his throat, but kept quiet. His discipline, especially with what he said and did not say, was clearly well practiced. But without his saying another word, I knew. I knew everything and still nothing at all.

"He didn't want to give up Ezarit."

"It nearly cost him everything to return to the Spire. He was enclosed until he could hear the city again. Then he had to fight a challenger in the Gyre, and he was gravely wounded." Wik increased his pace, until he walked ahead of me.

Could a Singer fall in love? That was not the right question to ask, not now. I caught up to him.

"Why didn't they throw him down?" Suddenly I wanted to know everything.

"Why? Because his challenger spared him. And he is useful. Much like you."

"He was spared and is a windbeater? He's like the Singer you challenged? Mariti?"

Wik answered slowly. "I cannot discuss it further." Some sound I could not hear caught his ears. "Time for your class." He was obviously relieved.

Wik was a puzzle. We walked the novice tier, drawing the attention and whispers of younger students. What to make of him?

"Singers and their secrets and machinations, Wik. How do you bear it?"

He stopped and looked at me. "We."

I was suddenly aware of my arms and legs sticking far beyond the sleeves and hem of my robe. My skin went goose pimpled. "We. How do we bear it?"

He pointed to a large alcove. We'd walked halfway around the tier. "It is our sacrifice for the city. We will talk later," he added before he turned and headed towards the ladders.

A Magister standing inside the alcove watched me, her eyebrows raised. I looked past her to the youngest of the novices, all wearing robes like mine. They stared back at me. One near the back squelched a giggle: Ciel.

 ᚹ ᚹ ᚹ

I ducked into the alcove, where the tallest student's head was level with my waist. The room was dim compared to those above, but still ornately carved. Silk cushions lined the floor, and bone benches banked the outer wall.

The Magister spoke slowly, as if I might not comprehend. "Our new novice. You will sit and learn the songs as best you can at your . . ." She paused and looked down her nose at me. "Age."

She seemed only a few years older than me. Her skin did not show the wind wear that Rumul's did.

"I know the songs, Magister." I spoke quietly, hoping to gain a stay, or a quick escape.

"Silence," she said, and her words sounded like a thunder-clap in the hush of the Spire.

I thought of my success with Laws and City at the wingtest and sputtered. I knew everything the city had required of me. Wik must have lied to the Spire as well, in order to ruin my test. I would show them. I jutted my chin higher and waited, standing, while the rest of the class found seats on bone benches and on the floor.

The Magister frowned. "Very well. Sing for us. Show us what you know."

Fine. I would. I thought of what to sing. A song to show I knew Laws? A history?

The only thing that came to mind was The Rise. A children's song. I could not sing that here. I beat the idea back and clutched at Laws. At anything. No words came.

Eventually, as children stared and whispered, I gave up and began The Rise.

"*The clouds paled as we wound up and up,*" I sang, ignoring the gasps. Good, let them know me and my terrible voice.

> "*The city rises on wings of Singer*
> *and Trader and Crafter,*
> *Rises to sun and wind, all together,*
> *Never looking down.*"

As I began the second verse, the Magister waved at me. "Stop. You are worse than I thought. And with our most trea-sured song."

The class of children had collapsed around me in fits of silent laughter. My face flushed red. What had I done wrong? My voice. They were laughing at my voice. I was fierce when I began; now I was only ashamed.

"Moc." The Magister crooked her finger. From behind a taller boy, Moc peered out with an apologetic look at me. "Lead your flightmates, please."

Moc's voice was a tremulous quaver, but his friends joined in, and the sound of young voices filled the room. Theirs was a boisterous retelling of The Rise—but not a version I'd ever heard before. This Rise told of danger, of dying, and of tower fighting tower. This Rise was not beautiful. It put music and memory to fear bred of long privations. It was a warning, wrapped in familiar notes.

In the Spire, even the songs were different.

Nat would have loved to know about this. As for me, I realized Sellis was right: I was worse than a fledge. If I was to get my wings back, I would need to learn fast.

By the time we broke for the evening meal, I had committed several verses to memory. My stomach growled as we walked to the common dining hall. Moc and Ciel took long strides on each side of me.

"We'll help you remember," Ciel said. "We'll practice with you."

"Don't you sleep?"

Moc shook his head and grinned. "We learn a lot when everyone's sleeping."

And they did help me—on that day, and on many days after.

In the dining alcove, the twins seemed to know everyone. They filled their bowls with the day's meal—peas, or potatoes, or spiced bird—and began chattering with other novices before they'd set their meals down on the long bone tables. I was swept up in their conversations and barely needed to speak myself.

Often, I found that we sat near Sellis, who was surly but not outwardly rude.

The children of the Spire swirled around us, eating, talking with both hands and mouths full. They were much like children of any tower. And yet they knew things the rest of the city did not. I wished for the first time that I could have grown up here, that I'd been taught what had really happened, instead of a merely a pretty song filled with lies about the city I loved. There was power in the knowing.

❬ ❬ ❬

The moon waned and filled, then waned again. I mended Sellis's robes, badly at first, then better. Cleaned buckets and her cell.

My throat went raw from singing with the children.

Many evenings, Wik came to test my shouts and to instruct me further.

"There aren't many of us," he said.

I caught his meaning. "You are a skymouth shouter, too."

"Yes, but not naturally. I had to train, and I'm still never certain—" He swallowed before continuing. "Whether it is enough to stop the next one. It has been, so far. I am lucky."

He taught me to aim my voice, by standing across the Gyre until I could shout at him in any wind. He made me do breathing exercises to strengthen my diaphragm and lengthen my shouts. "So you don't black out again," he said.

He frustrated me with his criticisms. "You are not trying hard enough. Your voice doesn't have the right timbre, as it did at Densira. You must try harder."

The harder I tried, the more I was unable to recall what shouting at the skymouth had sounded like, or felt like, and the more I was convinced that I was unable to manage it on demand. What good was I to the Singers if I could not control my voice?

"It's no good, Wik." My voice rasped from the exercises.

"We will find another way," he said. "I must ask the council for permission." He refused to elaborate.

Meantime, we walked the Spire and practiced. Wik and Sellis and I. For Sellis lurked these lessons, and sometimes tried to accomplish the same types of shouts that Wik and I were practicing. Her frustration built when Wik shook his head at her attempts, but she kept trying.

"Most Singers can't, Sellis," he said. "It's all right to not be perfect at something."

"There are many things I haven't perfected—yet," she said, frowning.

The lower tiers we walked through were as richly carved with city and Singer history as the oubliette had been carved with fears and monsters. As we walked, I noticed that at least one place—sometimes less than two hands wide—on each Spire tier had been left bare. We passed Singers paused by those walls, hands laid gently against those uncarved stretches of bone. Their eyes closed as if listening. I wished to understand what they heard, but when I reached out to a wall, Sellis swatted at my hand. "You may not. Not yet."

On the other side of the passage, beyond the steep drop, Singers and older novices flew the Gyre's swirling winds.

I wanted to regain my wings so that I might fly with them.

Sellis saw me watching. "Not yet." She found me more carvings to study. "Soon," Sellis encouraged me as she rousted me from the floor to clean her bucket and her bowl. "Soon," the Magister said as I scrubbed the carvings on the upper tiers clean of grime. "Soon," Wik promised, before asking me to shout for three minutes; my voice turned to gravel.

But I flew the Gyre in my dreams, before the galleries, up to the council balcony, and out through the apex into the blue sky.

And I learned to listen to the Spire in other ways, and through the Spire, the city.

I heard the city's voice in the bone floors, through my feet as I walked, my knees as I scrubbed. I heard its rumbles and creaks, its sighs. I learned to speak to it in secret.

As I slowly learned, I was punished for nearly everything. For getting words wrong. For annoying Sellis. For being in the wrong place when a Singer wanted me somewhere else. I could not say how many infractions, but the punishment was always the same: not bone chips to weigh me down, but more cleaning and carving. My nose was filled with bone dust, and I grew tired beyond measure of being handed the carving tools. My hands thickened with calluses and scars from tracing patterns charcoaled on the walls for me by Sellis, the Magisters, Wik, and seemingly anyone else passing by.

And yet, I learned. Despite everything. Moc and Ciel knelt by me and sang with me while I gouged at the walls or scrubbed the floor. I watched Singers come and go on powerful wings and listened to the songs they sang to each other, citing challenges won long ago in order to support arguments today.

I pricked my ears for any mention of the windbeaters.

When the full moon showed through the top of the tower, the entire Spire stopped to sing The Rise. Sound swept me up in the history. The bravery. The real Rise. I mouthed the words I knew now, still hesitant to sing with them.

I memorized facts about the towers: how high they were, how many had troubled their neighbors. I listened as Magisters discussed balance in the city and how to keep towers from cracking, like Lith. An artifex came to show our class how bridges helped strengthen the towers. With the young ones, I counted the toll of the skymouth attacks.

We had our own songs in the Spire: legends, epics, and heroes the towers could never know about. *"Corwitt Takes the Nest of Thieves," "The Plunge of the Singer," "The First Appeasement."* Through them, I began to understand more of the bone towers on which we lived.

I had not seen Rumul since my release from the oubliette.

The Spire remained quiet, save for the songs and the city's everyday sounds.

And then the day came when I stood before the classes and sang The Rise again, and they sang it back. The Magisters questioned me about the populations of Grigrit, Varu, and others, and I knew the answers without thinking. I knew them all. The sun passed beyond the tower, and the oil lamps came out. My examination continued. Did I know the load-bearing weight of new bone? What was the angle at which a Singer must glide when carrying a child? An adult?

I had memorized the songs, understood the reasons for the answers. I knew so much more now.

The Magister presented me with a gray robe bearing two blue stripes. A robe that fit me.

Sellis brought me a pair of wings. Worn ones, certainly, and not the glorious Singer wings I'd admired, but something to practice in.

My voice, too, had strengthened. Wik seemed pleased.

When I returned to Sellis's tier one night, a small, perfect apple rested atop the folded bedding outside the alcove. I munched the whole thing, sour core and all.

The next morning, Sellis woke me early, saying, "Now I will show you how to fly."

"I know how to fly," I protested.

"You still don't know everything," she said. But she smiled behind her stern words.

She cleared her own bucket that morning. We tightened each

other's wingstraps; ate bowls of boiled buckwheat sweetened with honey together in the dining alcove. Then she showed me how little I knew.

As we exited the alcove and walked the passage outside, still chewing our last mouthfuls, she grabbed fistfuls of my new robe and pushed me over the balcony, headfirst.

In my panic, my kicking legs flipped me right side up. My hands reached out, grasped air, then silk.

In the confines of the Gyre, I took command of my wings and let them unfurl, praying that I would have time to jam my fingers in the grips. A gust caught and spun me. I tried to hold down my breakfast. My fingers locked around the grips, and I struggled to turn before I hit the opposite wall and dashed myself to pieces.

But I did not turn. And I did not hit the wall.

A drumbeat from deep down in the Spire began as my wings filled with a strong gust from below. My plunge ceased abruptly. An updraft carried me, though a moment before, the Gyre had held only the most meager of breezes.

"What is this?" I whispered.

Sellis appeared beside me, smiling. "It is the Gyre, Kirit. Learn to fly here, and you will own the city."

Sellis pointed. I ducked my head to look and saw the windbeaters at work far below. At first I thought they were using sheets of silk, similar to those sometimes used in wingfights, that caught and bent the wind. But their tools were complicated by frames, sleeves, and battens. I gasped. The windbeaters wore giant wings over their arms. They worked in rhythm to the drums, channeling the wind through the tunnel so that it lifted and planed.

"Singers who can no longer fly," Sellis explained as we flew tip to tip, "are still a part of the Spire."

The wind coming up through the center of the Spire smelled

of must and bone and something thick and caustic. Wik had said my father was a windbeater. Perhaps he worked the Gyre below me now. Did he know I flew above? I had my wings now. Perhaps now I would be allowed to go below and speak to him.

More windbeaters gathered, using their misshapen wings to channel the air. A grinding sound floated up to us.

"They are opening the gates," Sellis said. "To build a stronger vortex—to welcome you."

The gates. Like the one I had opened in the walls so many days ago.

I cringed, even as the breeze quickened. The gates' opening made me worry about skymouths. I tucked my legs in my footsling and wished for my lenses.

"Relax," Sellis said, not understanding my fear. "Singers have been doing this forever."

"It's true," Ciel said, leaning out from a gallery. She grinned, her tiny face framed by a circle of sky and sun, far above. Faces peered over the balconies, amused. She laughed at my surprise. "This is nothing. Wait until your first fight. If it's not exciting enough, the windbeaters have rot gas and fire to speed things up."

"Ciel!" Sellis said. "Let her learn for herself."

I glided the Gyre in a circle and watched the windbeaters. Their oversized wings swept and dipped. The winds rose, and I could feel the pressure change in my ears.

Sellis modeled a turn, then a slow dive. I followed her, wobbling. The new wings and my time away from the wind had cost me skill and confidence.

Gyre winds mimicked the best gusts of the open sky, made more complex by the shape of the tower and its galleries. I discovered I could tack quicker, and that the breezes became muddled near the walkways.

Sellis called sharp instructions to tighten the curve of my

wings, to stretch the footsling with my ankles, to look up, not down.

"You'll need to learn to fly with locked wings," she said. "For the challenges. Can't hold a knife and grips both."

"Have there never been skymouths in the Gyre?" I finally asked, as I felt more comfortable in my glides.

My companion did not answer. The drumbeats slowed and we sank to our tier and furled our wings. Ciel ran to a ladder, late for class downtower. I sighed and looked out into the Gyre. "That was amazing."

Sellis tucked her wings away. "Flying the Gyre is for training. We shouldn't enjoy it."

I composed myself, but Sellis's face broke into a glowing smile. The first I'd seen from her. "But I love it anyway." She reached to help me furl the complex angles of my training wings. "Singer wings have more detail. You need to care for them, or they'll wear wrong. Become dangerous."

"I will."

"When I first became an acolyte, learning to fight in the Gyre was my reward for being quick. I had excellent sparring partners—" she began, then stopped. Smiled shyly, her head tilted, listening. I heard nothing. "I am summoned away."

I had so many questions, but exhaustion took me before she returned.

In the morning I woke to find Sellis still not back, and Singers rushing past our alcove. A bone horn sounded. First Moc, then Ciel ran past. "Quickly!" they said, pulling me upright.

I was barely on my feet when the city roared loud enough to knock me back down.

13

SACRIFICE

The Spire shook with sound. What had begun as a low moan far off built quickly, like a fast-moving squall, into a blistering roar, and did not lessen. Soon, the storm of sound battered my skin with its force, emanating from the Spire's very walls.

The birds roosting on the ledges beyond our alcove all rose and scattered into the Gyre and out through the apex with a clapping of wings that shook dust loose everywhere. The Spire's enclosure amplified the city's roar. Everyone within, at least who I could see, was affected by the sound. Students rushed by with their hands over their ears. A Singer fell to his knees.

As suddenly as it began, the sound moved up and out past the top of the Spire and faded away.

When they could stand again, the Singers whispered to one another in worried tones.

A bone horn sounded atop the Spire, and I heard distant klaxons sound in the city.

"Moc," I whispered, "what just happened?"

Already on his way to the ladders, Moc spun on his soft foot wraps. "We've got to get up top to watch!"

I must have looked confused, because he grabbed my arm and began to pull. "This is a big one. The Singers will tell the Magisters and the city leaders what the city wants at Conclave. It's going to be crowded up there."

All the air went from my lungs. Conclave. Elna had said that

when the Singers took Naton, it was for a Conclave. It had been
a long time since the last roar of this magnitude. Usually there
were only rumbles and rumors of rumbles.

I could still feel lingering vibrations in my bones. Neither
rumble nor rumor: the city had made a sound as if the world
was ending.

From down the passage, someone yelled Moc's name, and
my slight companion skittered off again.

I was left alone in a swirl of activity. Everyone knew where
they needed to be. Except for Kirit Spire. Conclave hadn't been
covered in the novitiates' class. Sellis and Wik hadn't instructed
me on where to go, what to do. Once again, I did not belong. I
was the sole still body in a whirl of motion.

Tower children were schooled in a version of what happened
when the city roared. That information was all I had to guide
me now. Singers had recorded the codex of sounds the city had
made over generations, ever since we rose through the clouds.
When the city roared, the Singers weighed a new chip, from a
piece of tower knocked loose by the sound. The bigger the roar,
the bigger the piece. If none had been disturbed, they cut one
from the lowest tier themselves, sized carefully to chronicle the
sound for the future. They bound these in the codex.

Then they balanced the roar through Conclave.

Once, Florian, our Magister at Densira, had told us how the
city had roared twice in his own childhood. He'd turned sallow as he described the second Conclave, the desperation of
the adults around him.

"Weren't you grateful for the Lawsbreakers, Florian?" Sidra
had asked. Sidra's father had lectured us about Lawsbreakers a
few days before. We'd learned that even those who defied the
tower had their purpose in the city.

Florian had coughed. "We were grateful. Their duty meant

that the city was appeased and didn't roar again for many years."
But his face was still sallow, still drawn. He'd lost someone; he
was still afraid.

I remembered now that he'd toyed with a thin bone marker
at his wrist: a Lawsbreak of his own, though a small one.

When he'd gathered himself, Florian explained what came
after a roar, doing his job as our Magister. He spoke of how
those who lived at the margins, those who broke Laws, would
be called into service to the city. That the Singers would come,
weigh their crimes by the bone chips they carried, and take the
ones they needed away.

As I remembered, I felt as shaken as Florian had been. I'd
broken Laws. I broke Bethalial and Trespass. Worse. I still wore
those markers on my wrist. I was sure no one had forgotten.

If the need was great, would they come for me too?

No, I thought, they needed me in other ways. They'd said
so. Still, I couldn't help the fear rising in my gut. Elna said
Naton hadn't been given Lawsmarkers at first. She'd said that
until the Singer handed them to her once Naton was gone, she'd
had no knowledge of his crimes.

If the need was great enough. That had been an enormous
roar. I looked around, desperate for ways to make myself useful. No one said a word to me. They moved around me as if I
was in the way.

That was the last thing I wanted to be. I did not want one of
the Singers who disagreed with my training to find a reason to
add to the appeasement.

The novitiates' tier emptied. The birds scattered by the noise
had not returned.

A tug at my sleeve. Ciel stood close.

"I'll show you where to watch."

I could have said no. I could have hunkered down in the

shadows and waited for Conclave to end. But I choose to follow Ciel to the Spire's apex and watch, like a Singer.

❧ ❧ ❧

Atop the Spire, the city's councilors gathered. The craft and trade representatives arrived as Ciel dragged me up the last rope ladder, for there were no risers carved into the top of the Spire. You had to fly up, or scramble.

Ciel tucked herself behind a spur of bone near the ledge, her wings unfurled for safety. I tried not to cling to her hand: I had not been wearing my wings when the roar began. The wind whipped the robes of the assembled, and those on the ledges below, looking up through the Spire, watching.

Two Singers rode a gust of wind up and out of the Spire, carrying something between them. Metal gleamed in the sunlight. Those watching whispered; a brief sound, louder than the wind.

"The scales." Ciel pointed at the gleam. I leaned to get a better look. The Singers flew a small circuit of the Spire's ledge and landed carefully. They anchored the base of what they carried to the ledge: a brass plate, very old, wrapped with spidersilk, tied to nearby bone cleats. Magister Florian hadn't said the scales were so big. Or made of metal.

A spike of bone stuck up from the plate, bound there by a metal hasp. From where I crouched, it was hard to see the mechanism. A metal basket wobbled on each side of the spike. The baskets teetered and swung until the councilors, crafters, traders, and Singers gathered around to shield the scales from the wind.

A Singer drew a bone chip from a carry sack the size of a baby. Bigger. He raised it high, so that everyone might see, then placed it in the basket closest to the edge of the tower. The scale dipped. City representatives muttered among themselves. They turned to the horizons of the city.

I looked too. At first, all I saw was sky. The wide-open blue made my heart leap. The sky was a drink of cold water. The warm sun, a balm. I had missed both so.

Then I saw them.

All around the Spire, gray-winged Singers approached, bearing nets.

The two Singers who'd carried the scale stood. One was Rumul. The other was the woman with hair as brass-colored as Ciel's.

The arriving Singers dropped their nets on the ledge but did not untie them. Inside, I saw hands and feet, a curled back. No wings. I could hear someone weeping. The bodies were robed in white. Many lay still.

The net closest to us wriggled as its occupant turned, dark curls falling away from a face. I sucked in my breath. Those looked like Nat's curls. Nat, alive?

Not Nat. *Please no,* I whispered to the city.

Brown eyes peered from the net, sun-spotted olive skin below the dark curls. Not Nat. Someone older. My relief was short-lived. *That was someone's Nat,* I knew.

Beyond the Spire, a man circled wildly, shouting as he flew near two Singers carrying a net with an older woman in it. I couldn't hear what he said from where I stood, but amazingly, Ciel heard. "He wants to challenge for his wife," the girl whispered, wide-eyed.

I looked across the gap, past the couple, and saw the edges of the nearby towers rippling with what looked like motes of dust from here: belongings being thrown from nearby towers. Citizens were jettisoning anything that might skirt the limits of Singer patience if another appeasement was required.

My fear for Nat transformed. Rumul's threat against my mother seized my throat. Surely she wouldn't be one of the citizens caught up so? Not after I had signed myself over?

Ezarit's voice whispered in my mind. *You gave them what they wanted. What do you hold in trade now?* I shook my head to clear the sound. Rumul wouldn't. They needed me. Wik had said so. I held myself in trade still.

And if I was not good enough to be a Singer? What then?

If I was still at risk, so was Ezarit.

The Singers approached, carrying fistfuls of bone chips towards the scales. They surrounded the brass baskets, one Singer for each of the towers. The ledge filled precariously with people.

"What are they doing?" I turned to Ciel, but she'd disappeared. I watched alone as more Singers appeared from every direction, their flying nets filled with men and women. All were dressed in white, most clinging to the nets disinterestedly.

Drugged, of course.

"Where have you been?" Sellis whispered to me as she hurried past, Wik close on her heels. "We searched for you. Come with us!" She grabbed my robe and pulled me from my hiding place. "Rumul's orders."

She didn't let go of my robes when I began to scramble after her. I picked up my pace, lest she drag me right over the edge.

The Spire's silence grew heavier as more Singers landed, none making a sound. We reached the gathering around the scales in time to watch them place the first of the chips in the empty bin.

"Wirra," said the Singer as he placed a chip. Bone hit metal. A high sound, a sour sound. The only sound.

The scale barely moved. Another Singer came forward, and another, adding chips from each tower to the basket until it began to drop against the weight of the bone chunk on the other side. More Singers stood by, their hands cradling the chips of the Lawsbreakers. Waiting to see whether those crimes against the city would be added to the weight.

The Singers worked silently, and the citizens who stood with them kept silent too. The man shouting for his wife had been bound and struggled beside her now.

Standing close to the Singers, I heard soft clicks and whispers. Now and then one crouched, putting an ear to the ledge. Something they heard caused them to hurry, gesture more Singers to action. Almost all the nets had been stripped of their Lawsmarkers now.

Sellis pulled me forward.

By now, more than a hundred Singers had gathered atop the Spire. More soared around it. The councilors and the craft and trade representatives, plus the citizens in the nets made over two hundred souls standing on the Spire. The wind whipped robes. The captives shivered in the cold air.

"Densira."

I saw a ragged robe and recognized the face of the woman who had charged at Nat and me in the lowtower.

But no Ezarit. I despised my own relief.

Rumul sang the verses allowed during Silence. This part of Conclave I understood.

> You have each broken Laws.
> Your crimes weigh on the city.
> You have heard it roar.
> You and your towers
> have brought the city to anger.

As he sang, he turned to me. His eyes bored a hole through me, and I froze. How close I'd come to sharing the fate of the cloudbound. For that was what they were. What I could have been.

Rumul's companion sang then. The Singer with the silver streak in her hair. Her voice was a contralto, a contrast to

Rumul's deep tones. *"With your sacrifice, the city will be once more at peace."*

My breath caught as I counted the number of Lawsmarks balancing the scales. The men and women bound atop the Spire. With the size of the roar, the scales didn't sit even until almost all of their chips had been added: thirty out of thirty-five. I'd known the process of Conclave from Magister Florian, if not the reality. Not since the city rose through the clouds had so many been thrown down at once.

A Singer with a hand on the Spire's roof whistled. His face contorted with worry. The woman sped up her song, rushing the words. Everyone atop the tower leaned forward, urging her to greater speed. Finally, she finished. *"We do what is best for the city, though it causes us pain,"* she sang. And she walked to where the first cloudbound was held, unfurling her wings as she reached the edge. She freed a thin man from the net, clasped him by the shoulders, and fell with him into the sky. A moment passed, and we saw them gliding out towards the edge of the city.

The man's feet kicked in the air, but he made no sound. Nothing from him, no shriek, or cry. He was carried away in silence.

Rumul nodded. "He goes well." The head Singer looked to the other cloudbound. More Lawsbreakers had been prodded to their feet and stripped of their nets. Many shivered, their eyes on the horizon. Others stared at us. I forced myself to look back, though I wanted to scream.

Nat, oh, Nat. Your father. This happened to him.

Sellis searched my face, saw my miserable expression, but did not scold me or yank at my arm.

Thirty. So many. Even one was too many. Too much of a weight to bear. I took a step forward. Sellis gripped my wrist and held me in place. Did not let go.

Rumul looked to the gathered Singers and held out his hands. One at a time, Singers in dark gray robes stepped behind one of the cloudbound, set their wings, and flew to the city's edges, where they would let go of their burdens. One at a time, the cloudbound were taken away, all silent save the second to last, a young man who pleaded for his life. "My father," he said, "has money and goods. All you could need. It has saved us before, why not now?"

"Not enough muzz," someone whispered behind me.

"Or he's bargained for his life before," I whispered back, before I locked my mouth against the Silence.

Sellis glared at me and twisted my littlest finger until I wanted to shriek against the pain. "Silence."

This cloudbound man looked familiar too. He'd been at the wingfight, among the traders. He kept begging, even as the Singers frowned and drew closer. They bound his mouth with silk, so he wouldn't disturb the city further in his fall. They lifted him away, to the south.

Some towers gave more than others. Mondarath for debauchery. Wirra for fighting. Many more from the southlands for debts and trespasses. But no one I knew among them. Not Ezarit, not Elna. I wiped my leaking eyes with a corner of my sleeve. Small mercies.

Singers returned and took their posts around the rim of the Spire, ready to go out again to the towers if the city was not appeased. They stood still as carvings, resolute. Wrapped in their duty, though their eyes glistened with tears and wind.

With a shock, I realized that they hated what they did. And yet they did it. Wik stood among them, eyes red.

They waited.

We waited with them.

We stood until night fell, until the gray shapes outlined against the lingering dusk blocked out the stars in the sky.

The crafters and councilors waited. I saw Councilman Vant standing near a ladder, but he did not see me. He scratched his nose and blinked in the cold wind.

Sellis's stomach growled.

This was another part of Conclave I had not known. We marked the emptiness left by the cloudbound with the pain in our stomachs.

Around the Spire, the towers kept silent too.

By dawn, the Singers who had pressed hands and ears to the Spire throughout the night stood. The city's rumbles had ceased.

By noon, we were weak from standing in the wind and our stomach pangs had turned to birds' claws, scraping against our ribs. Moc and Ciel were ashen shadows of themselves. They leaned against the woman who'd sung the Conclave.

Someone passed around a water sack. We each took a single sip. The water tasted sour.

By evening, the city had not roared again. A Singer ascended from below. "The Enclosed are satisfied. The city is appeased."

Rumul and his companion sang the final notes of Conclave wordlessly, marking the passing of the cloudbound, the release of their trespasses from their towers.

As he sang, we looked up to mark their passage, rather than down, to mark their fall.

Then Sellis nudged me with her elbow and jerked her chin towards the ladder. Other Singers had already begun the climb. We were allowed to descend.

‹ ‹ ‹

Sellis moved quickly down the rope ladder, then to the carved steps of the lower tiers. She was eager for food and bed. I ducked into an alcove, still shivering from the fast and the cold of Conclave, and with more than that.

Rumul entered the alcove at last and saw me waiting for him. "You are out of place, Kirit."

Always, Rumul. And yet? "I have questions." I spoke softly, with respect. Tried to still my shaking from the cold, from the ritual.

"You should ask Sellis. Or Wik, when his duties allow."

"I would ask you." *Slowly, Kirit.* I had watched Wik avoid challenging Rumul's authority. Now I tried to do the same. Sellis and Wik had not prepared me for Conclave. There was more I needed to know now, rather than *soon*.

A novitiate brought a shallow basin of rainwater and handed it to Rumul. The young man waited while Rumul dipped his fingers and rubbed at his face. Then the Singer dismissed him with a wave.

I was allowed to stay.

Rumul raised his eyebrows and made a reeling gesture with his hand. I saw his challenge tattoo, faded now, but still visible. A symbol I'd recently learned to carve. A knife.

"Who gives the Singers the right to murder people?" The words had come faster than I'd intended.

He sighed. "How do you not number yourself among the murderers today, Kirit?" His voice was not smooth, not sweet. It was tired and rough.

"What?"

"You attended the Conclave. I saw you."

I waited, not understanding. I'd thrown no one down.

"Did you try to stop it? Did you offer yourself in place of the old man from Viit?"

I had not. My first thought had been to stay as far from the edge as possible.

Rumul continued. "We're all guilty of wanting to stay alive. To do so, we must at times appease the city. The city would destroy us all without it."

"You say so, but I didn't see the city throw those people down."

He reddened. "Your decision, then, is to join them?"

It was not. "I want to know why."

He wiped his dripping face with his robe. "Kirit, there is no more sacred duty than that of a Singer. We keep the city whole. We make sure its traditions are not forgotten. That its people do not throw everything to the clouds. To do so, we listen to the city, appease it, and enforce its rules. Do you understand?"

I felt hunger stretch its wings in my stomach. Thought of how Singers taught the Magisters, who then taught us histories, Laws. "If you maintain traditions, why are songs different inside the Spire?"

"You have seen how people revile us, fear us? Even as they respect us?"

"Yes." Remembered long pauses after the word *Singer* came up in tower conversation.

"Can you guess why we might change the words of our history?"

His eyes glittered in the lamplight. I was being tested. How much of my Singer training had sunk in?

Continue arguing, his eyes seemed to say. *Or prove you deserve the opportunity you've been given.* I cleared my throat. "The songs Singers learn are more frightening. The towers don't suffer as much of our past because they have forgotten. So they don't fear each other."

He inclined his head. "Such as?"

"The clouds. What the time before the Rise was really like."

"War. Horror. The things citizens did to their towermates, to their neighbors, Kirit. The city needed to heal, to come together again, once we rose out of it."

In my mind's eye, I saw the scenes I had learned to sing. Tower by tower, the horrors. "We learn different verses so that we may keep it from happening, without making the rest of the city eager for revenge."

I realized this for truth as I spoke it. The Singers had done this. They had saved the city in more ways than one.

And Conclave—when I lived in the towers, it was used to frighten stubborn children to action. As we grew, we learned that it was a way for the city to release the burden of broken Laws. A way to redeem the offenders.

Now that I had seen what actually happened, I could not hold my tongue. "What kind of people do this to one another?"

He bristled. I'd pushed too far. I saw anger in his eyes. Then he blinked and took a breath. His voice grew softer.

"The city demands much of us in return for shelter. Long ago, we learned to tend it in ways that you already consider barbaric. Very well." Rumul looked at me, both hands held out, palms up. "It is the trial of the Singers to do this. If we ignore the city, we fall. If citizens begin to fight, if we lose our traditions, we fall. The towers crack. Would you go back through the clouds? So many died, coming up. The city may rise with or without us, Kirit. The tiers will fill in with bone and push us out. To live, we must rise too. To rise, we must appease our home when it grows angry with us."

"Haven't you tried to appease it any other way?" I thought of Nat, growing up without Naton.

"Yes." The way he said it, I knew he believed it. But he continued. "We've lost four towers, all on the outer edge. Broken. Lith was only the most recent to fall. So many people have died, Kirit. Thousands, all at once."

My mouth formed an O, but no sound came out.

Rumul looked up at the ceiling of his alcove, which was carved with stars. "That is the sacred trust of the Singers."

I shook my head slowly. "And what do we get in return?"

"Life." He spread his hands like wings.

I thought of what I now knew. I thought of Wik's eyes at Conclave.

"And what of people like Nat's father? Naton?"

I could see he recognized the name, was trying to remember why. I saw the memory rise behind his eyes. His mouth hardened to a line. "He broke Laws, Kirit."

"No one who knew him thinks he would do that. What Laws?"

"Laws within the Spire. He had a great trust from us, and he betrayed it."

"What trust? What did he do?" I could not stop myself, though Rumul's look grew more inscrutable. "I want to know the truth!"

Rumul came to my side and gripped my arm. "Then I will tell you," he said, his voice softer than it was before. The honeyed voice. "Naton was a friend. A brilliant bridge artifex. He knew more about the Spire than most citizens ever will. Naton . . ." He paused. His voice was very sad now. Sad and soft. "Colluded with a disgraced Singer to bring information out of the Spire. It began innocently enough. He saw something during the course of his work; he was curious. But in the end, this curiosity became dangerous. He had learned things that others in the city would pay well for. Knowledge that would have allowed others huge advantages over the rest of the city."

Knowing Nat's own curiosity, I could believe his father had been curious too. But selling out the Singers? I didn't believe it. What was Rumul telling me?

"To whom did he betray you? What was it?"

Rumul turned to look at me.

"Nothing more glorious than being on wing at Allsuns, is there? And Allmoons."

I began to nod. Then I realized the latter for a trap. He had turned his attention back to me. I closed my mouth tight.

He chuckled. "You're learning."

"No one is allowed to fly on Allmoons."

He raised a finger. "No citizens fly at Allmoons." He said it as if he held a greater secret behind his lips. I wanted to draw it out, and I didn't want to know.

"The Singers fly at night?" I pictured myself and Nat at Allmoons. We'd felt we alone owned the sky. We hadn't known. Nat would have loved knowing. And then I realized.

"This is what Naton found out."

Rumul paused and smiled. Then he took a breath and continued. "Some Singers fly at night. An important skill, especially for those who can control the skymouths."

"How is that possible? Nat and I—" I cut myself off, to avoid thinking about Nat. "How do you see the wind? The towers? How do you not collide and fall?" I stopped and thought. "The skymouths?"

He held up a finger. *Patience.* "It is a skill you have yet to learn."

I was distracted. Now that I knew Naton's treason against the city, that he'd found out the Singers fly at night, I wanted to know more about how they flew. But for Nat's memory, I chased the last shreds of the secret down. The bone chips Tobiat had given to us had notes etched on the backs, in what I now knew to be Singer notations. Maybe they held the secret to night flying. And we'd had them in our hands the whole time.

"Who was Naton going to tell?"

Rumul shrugged. "We learned he had betrayed us shortly before the last Conclave. He hadn't yet shared what he knew with his contact, but it was a trader."

"But he never told?"

"He was caught before he could pass the information on. We caught his colluder afterwards, but the notes he'd made were lost in the confusion of Conclave."

"How did you learn about the betrayal?"

Rumul grew still again. Then sighed. "My first acolyte, on his excursion. He discovered the treason." He paced the length of his room, to the hammock, and returned to his workbench. Sat down with a reluctant frown.

Treason.

"The acolyte had taken up with a young, ambitious trader. Naton had told her already that he had information he wanted to sell. She was gathering the markers to pay him. Our Singer kept her from making the mistake of meeting him and turned Naton in." He looked at me significantly.

I drew the truth together in my head, saw it as a whole. The trader, young and ambitious—and who wouldn't be faster at trading if they could fly at night when no one else could?

Ezarit. Naton had intended to give what he knew to Ezarit.

Oh, Ezarit. . . . Kept from breaking Laws by her . . . lover. Rumul's acolyte. My father. My father had betrayed Naton, and kept Ezarit safe, and helped the Singers keep their secrets. *No.*

Rumul read my conclusions in my expression. "You see it now."

I did—and if my stomach hadn't been emptier than the sky before a migration, I might have been sick with it. But the memory of the secret Naton died for tugged at me.

They flew at night. Singers flew at night. And Ezarit had wanted to know how.

Two questions fought in my mind. They raced from my mouth.

"What happened to my father? And how do you do it? Flying in the dark, when you cannot see?"

Rumul smiled. His voice smoothed even more. "You will learn, if you choose. Sellis is training."

He was silent, waiting on my answer. I knew danger still lingered. Rumul's hold on the Spire was stronger than any councilman's. And I suspected Sellis would not be overjoyed to have me along on her training. But this—what a thing to know. And what power to have.

"I wish to learn this," I finally said. "I am ready to learn it."

"You think so? You can understand why it is necessary to keep the Singers' secrets? You understand why our duties, and the ones you saw at Conclave, are necessary?"

My thoughts returned to the Conclave's horrors. I recoiled against the expected answer. *There must be other ways.* Things untried. Then I remembered Lith's dark, cracked form. I considered how to make myself more secure, so that I did not become an offering myself.

I would silence my questions about Conclave. This was what Rumul asked of me. To keep Singer secrets, to help the city.

"Yes." I was determined.

"No going back, Kirit. Accepting this skill means accepting all of what the Singers do. Going deeper into our secrets. Including what you saw during Conclave. When the time comes, you will fight all comers to protect the secrets of the Spire."

"I will never throw down Elna or Ezarit."

He agreed. "As long as you hew to Singer law, we will not need to hurt Ezarit." He paused. "Or Elna."

There it was. My trade. Not what I had planned at all when Nat and I flew through the night. I'd come then to take what was already mine. Now I agreed not just to serve the Spire, but to become it.

He brought out a bone pot of caustic ink and marked my left hand himself, right there. A small spiral, a coil. Like wind in the Gyre. His fingers gripped my hand. The touch of his brush burned, and I bit my lip hard.

No further ceremony signaled my passage. With one mark, I became even more Singer-bound.

"When you are ready, you will challenge in the Gyre," said

Rumul. Just then, Sellis entered the alcove. She stopped and stared at us both, as if she'd caught us in an unwelcome secret.

Rumul smiled at her. "Kirit will learn how to fight in the Gyre. To fly at night. To better guide skymouths. Then you will both be ready to challenge."

Sellis's entire expression changed. "We will be ready."

I swallowed. They spoke in circles.

Rumul turned back to me. "Wik says you are doing well, but you must do this last thing quickly. Before Allsuns. The need is great. It will not be easy. And you must learn to fly as we do."

His eyes met mine, and I sensed he was daring me to succeed in my father's place. Or to fail on my own. For him, I was an experiment. No risk to him, only to myself. The higher I went, the further I could fall.

14

SENSE

Sellis watched me closely, silent questions hovering behind her eyes. She complimented my quick rise to third-stripe and compared her hand mark with mine. They were identical.

"Each council member has their own style," she said, touching hers.

"What is that ink they use? It burns."

She did not take her eyes off her mark. "A Singer secret. They mix it with something from the skymouths. That's what stings and what makes the marks turn silver."

I winced at the thought of gaining tattoos around my eyes like Wik had.

I didn't see him that day. I did not know when he learned of my rise. Instead, I climbed down to the novices' tier and watched the class. They practiced towers, much as I'd learned them at Densira for the wingtest.

When the Magister dismissed them, the novices broke left and right around me. Only Moc and Ciel greeted me.

"Why do they do that?" Around Sellis, the novices gathered and chittered happily, telling her about everything that happened in the Spire. She had the benefit of many eyes. I had two extra pairs only, both trained on me.

"You're unpredictable," Moc said. "You do unusual things. You couldn't keep the Silence."

"You're tall."

"Your voice is still strange."

I raised a hand. "Enough, thanks." I saw things more clearly. Even after showing them how quickly I could learn to be like them, the young Singers-to-be were still uncomfortable. I was different. The Spire didn't like different. "You and Ciel aren't bothered?"

Ciel tilted her head and laughed. "You're new. Everything in the Spire is old and always happens up down up down. You came in sideways."

They liked me for precisely the reasons the others didn't. The twins were tiny and strange, but they were the eyes and ears I had in the Spire. I needed them.

But they'd begun disappearing for days, even before the Conclave. When they returned, their temples bruised, their eyes bloodshot, I asked what had happened, and they tried to explain.

"Training," they had said. "We train to hear better."

The day after my meeting with Rumul, I found out what they meant.

* * *

Wik sent a whipperling to the twins and me. The message chips it carried listed a tier and an alcove. Two levels down.

When we arrived, breathing hard from rushing, I caught a glimmer of metal. Wik held an ancient tool in his hand. Its base was the same shape as the bruises that sometimes appeared at Ciel's temples: a deep purple blotch overlaying her soft, honey-colored skin.

My fingertips brushed the cold lenses that hung from my neck. Wik frowned at me. "You have a disadvantage, Kirit. You do not know how to listen."

This was unfair. I tried very hard to listen. I had already heard the city whisper and roar.

Noting my frown, he shook his head. "When they are very

young, Singers begin training in a different kind of listening. Some use what they learn to better hear the city. Others, to keep track of signals when we fly and fight. Still others use what they hear to see better."

The last pulled me out of my study of Ciel's hair, her complex braids.

Seeing better with hearing?

"Close your eyes," he said, coming to stand very close behind me. I twisted to look at him, and he raised his eyebrows and waited.

I closed my eyes.

Wik pressed one end of the metal tool against my temple.

In the darkness, I felt the pulse of his breath against my cheek. He didn't speak.

A cool strip of silk was placed over my closed eyes and tightened. I tried to pull away, but Wik held me firm. "Don't move."

Then a sound of metal hitting metal. So much metal, I thought as the tool began to vibrate against my head.

"Listen," whispered Wik.

I strained to do what he asked. I heard nothing beyond a muffled giggle on the other side of the room.

"Listen with your skin, your bones," Wik said as he struck the metal rod again. This time, a hum echoed deep within my skull.

"Now we will change something," he said. "See what the echoes do."

I heard robes swish and Ciel tell Moc, "No, that way!" Then silence again. Then that sound vibration as Wik hit the rod pressing into my head. Echoes and vibration surrounded me. They had a slightly different shape, flatter, faster than before, but I couldn't figure out why.

I described it to Wik. "Good!" He removed the tool from my head, the blindfold from my eyes.

In front of me, Ciel stood holding a broad piece of bone. She lowered it and rubbed her arms.

"You see?" she asked.

I didn't, not really. "I see the panel you're holding."

"But what did you hear, before? Think."

I heard vibrations. Waves of sound colliding behind my blindfolded eyes. They hurt. "The vibrations were different when you stood in front of me?"

Ciel grinned. Her eyes glowed as if I'd performed a wonderful trick.

Wik smiled too. "Good." They blindfolded me again, but without the metal rod. "Now try to mimic the vibration the rod made: tilt your head back slightly, open your mouth—yes, just like that—and click your tongue against the roof of your mouth very quickly."

That sounded ridiculous. I lifted the edge of my blindfold with a finger and looked at them. They were surely making fun of me.

"Just do it!" Wik was growing exasperated. He wanted discipline, not questions.

Blindfold dropped, the dark complete, I tried to do what he asked. My mouth gaped open, and I pressed the tip of my tongue against my mouth to make a clicking sound, as I'd heard Sellis do sometimes in flight.

"Faster!" Ciel whispered.

I heard the clicks in my head, but still they meant nothing.

Until their shape changed. Instead of sound leaving me, some of it returned, faintly, as if the noises I made had bounced off something. Echoing. I tried to lift the blindfold again. Wik stopped my hand. "No. Tell me what you heard."

"The sound changed. Like Ciel was holding the chip up in front of me again."

Wik took my hand from the silk blindfold and guided it away

from me, until my fingers connected with the hard slab of the bone chip, an arm's span from my face.

"You heard it there."

"So?" I couldn't see how this was important.

Wik sighed at my tone. Even blindfolded, I could guess the face he made. Frustrated. Full of frowns.

"So. Try it again."

I heard robes swish, then silence. Something had changed, and they wanted me to guess it by making that ridiculous face while clicking my tongue. Fine. Though I could not imagine the dignified Singers doing something like this, I tilted my head back and clicked again, faster this time.

I strained to hear the echoes. "The chip is farther away?"

"How do you know?"

"The echoes are fainter?"

"Echoes? Plural? Listen to what your body is telling you."

And I got it. "Plural echoes. Two objects, farther away."

"Reach out."

I swept my arm in a half circle. Stretched my fingers as far as they would go. Touched nothing. I attempted again to lift the blindfold, but Wik stopped me once more.

"Walk forward two steps, then reach out again."

When I did, my sweeping hand brushed one bone chip to my left, then Moc or Ciel's small fingers, then air, then a silk panel held taut by more small fingers.

"That's very useful, Wik. I can find small children holding objects in an empty room with my eyes closed." I felt ridiculous. Like they were setting me up for a prank.

I heard the smile in his voice. "You learned that very fast, Kirit. Good. You will need to learn much more, even faster."

I waited.

"This is your room now, Kirit. No more sleeping outside Sellis's alcove."

I sighed with relief. That was a very good change.

"But," Wik added, "you will live here blindfolded. If you re-move the blindfold, you will fail the training." His voice didn't waver. He was serious.

Fail. How much? I wondered. Could I fail just this portion of being a Singer, like with the wingtest? Or would I fail the whole thing? I resolved to not fail any of it.

He continued, "When you are ready, you may meet us in the dining alcove for something to eat. But you may not remove the blindfold."

That didn't sound like such a bad task. When I said so, I heard Ciel laugh. Something grated, bone on bone. A lid, being rolled away from the floor. Ciel took my hand and walked me forward five steps. I heard the sucking sound of a windbeat-ers' tunnel, low, near the floor.

My new alcove was seemingly part of the vent system. If I made a mistake and got too close to it, I could be sucked out of the Spire. Worse, whenever I left the alcove, I would know the Gyre's edge was nearby.

"You wouldn't risk me falling. You need me." My voice was almost pleading.

"We need someone who can fly as we do, not someone who stands on ledges and shouts at the sky." Wik's voice was firm. He meant every word.

They bound the blindfold and covered it with another layer of silk. If I broke the second layer, it would be obvious for all to see.

"I don't know how to do this." All I'd been shown was some sort of mouth trick, a stunt with echoes.

"Use your ears, Kirit. Use the feeling in your bones," Wik said from farther away. He pressed the metal rod into my hands. "Few animals fly at night. You must become a bat."

And they said no more. I reached out with my hands, but they were gone. All was silent. And dark.

At first, all I could hear was my own heartbeat. Then the sounds of the city, the passage of robed Singers above and below me, the bones all around me, began to whisper.

With the blindfold tight around my eyes, I was caught within a wall of darkness. My own enclosure. I felt panic stir.

To quiet the noise, I tried standing still where Ciel had left me. I tilted my head back and clicked, my tongue soft against my palate. I experimented with different speeds. The alcove's dimensions were small, though not as small as the pocket where I was first held in the Spire. And this room's exit was an obvious arch. No echoes at all. But I refused to walk out yet, into the jumble of the Spire, and towards the edge of the Gyre. I needed to practice, a lot. And fast.

I explored the alcove with my hands and with the echoes I could make. I tried using the rod and humming. I sensed that the ceiling was low.

A different set of echoes, lower and less sharp, told me something about what was arranged along the far wall. I slid my foot forward and skirted the vent to reach the sleeping pad and the necessaries. Then I curled into a ball and slept.

When I woke, it was dark. My hands went to my face, and I realized it would always be dark until the blindfold was taken away. I lay still and listened, trying to breathe slowly, so that I could hear other things besides my heart pounding.

The rhythm of the Spire had slowed. I heard robes sliding down the bone ladders and across the floors. I heard whispers from passing Singers, but not many. Then I heard a snap of silk and battens, the sound of someone leaping into the Gyre nearby. This was glorious: the sharp sounds wings made against wind, the song a body made when it cut through the air.

I sat up. Others had learned to hear. I could too. I touched my tongue to the roof of my mouth again. It felt fuzzy, like I'd been doing this too much. I clicked my tongue fast, and I found the shape of the space I occupied. When I knew that, I could walk it.

I thunked my shins hard against a bone bench. My own yelp was the loudest sound I'd heard in hours.

Giving up seemed so easy. I had to find my wings by touch.

Still, I pulled them over my shoulders without removing the blindfold. I heard the drag of the straps across my robe. The city whispered blandishments from the walls. A class let out two tiers above me, and I heard the almost-whispers of the youngest novices as if they were much closer.

Focus. I needed to focus.

I shuffled back to the center of the room and made a slow turn. My echoes bounced off the bench differently than the wall. My sleeping mat muffled sound, while the alcove's archway pulled it out into the passage beyond.

I practiced until I could sense the room. My stomach growled, then gave up. My mouth felt thick with thirst. I echoed my way across the room to a hook, where something sounded solid and soft at the same time. I reached out and touched a lukewarm bladder of water. Carefully, I lifted it from its hook. I drank and laughed at what I'd done, coughing as my first success went down my windpipe, rather than my throat.

When I thought I was ready, I stepped out of the alcove.

Sounds washed over me from everywhere. People moved past, close and far, and their sounds battered at my senses. Behind the blindfold, I could perceive shapes rushing at me and away, but the noise was confusing. I stepped back into the alcove and lay down. I could not do this. Moc and Ciel couldn't do this yet, and they'd been practicing for longer than I.

"You can do it," a voice said, from close by.

I sat up. Sellis's voice.

"I did it. You can do it. Let me give you some hints."

She told me how to hold my head straight, how to avoid being distracted by a sound, turning, and losing my way. She told me about the path around this tier, how far away the dining alcove was, and the shapes I might encounter.

"Why are you helping me?"

"Because Rumul won't let me night fly without you." She said it simply, with regret, so I knew she told the truth. "Even if you don't make it, they won't start a night flight without partnered pairs, and no one else is training now. So you need to learn fast."

"Singers fly blindfolded?"

A pause. "Absolutely not. But when you do fly in the dark, you can use your ears to help navigate. Once you learn to hear, you can see where most people in the city can't. It's an augmentation, not a replacement, Kirit."

I opened my mouth to argue, but when I reached out to touch her shoulder, I grasped air. I sounded the room and discovered she'd already gone. Echoes surrounded me instead.

When the Singers began The Rise that night, the sound bloomed in my mind. I started to cover my ears, but then I opened my mouth and sang instead. Singing with them lessened the discordant sounds that I felt through my bones.

My rough voice matched the deep group voice word for word.

Tomorrow, I thought. Tomorrow I'd make my way blind around the Spire. I would not fall.

And then the Singers would let me fly the city again.

\ \ \

The Spire's morning noises woke me. In darkness, I heard whispered orders, the shuffling of feet. Pulleys rattled, and buckets clattered. A whipperling launched from a nearby tier and flutterscreeched away.

I touched my blindfold, then dropped my hand to the mat where I'd put my father's lenses. Ran my fingers over the age-pitted metal, the cool glass.

When I stepped from the alcove this time, I could echo and build an image of the simple room I'd left behind: an empty water bladder hung from a wall, a neatly folded sleeping mat, and, atop the mat, a pair of lenses.

The passage beyond my room felt vast and featureless to my ears. I echoed until I could hear the difference between the ledge and the drop beside the ledge. I unfurled my wings, just in case. My fingers tempted the edge of the blindfold. Stopped. If Wik had lookouts nearby watching me, even Moc or Ciel, they would know. They would tell.

I slid one foot forward across the bone floor, then the next. My tongue touched the roof of my mouth, light and fast. Turning my head from side to side let me sweep the space before me. I made my way across the passage in spurts, avoiding alcoves and bone spurs, to stand with both hands pressed against the outer wall of the Spire.

Thud. My heart pounded. My ears boomed. My hands felt the echoes of the city. I'd made it.

I spun quickly, reversing direction—I hoped—and echoed again. A large shape blocked the open space. It moved before I could sense more than breadth and height. Not Moc or Ciel, that was certain.

"Who is there?"

No answer. I hadn't thought there would be.

With a deep breath, I turned to the wall and felt my way along the carved surface until I reached the ladder. I echoed up and sensed the way was clear for several tiers. When I stepped onto the rungs, I thought of Elna, climbing near-blind up Densira. How knowledge like this could have made her way easier. Safer.

What Nat wouldn't have given to know this. The thought didn't make me sad this time. Instead, I felt a rush of strength. In this, I was stronger than anyone in the towers. I knew now why Singers stood so quiet, so confident.

Distracted, I missed a rung with my foot and grabbed hard with both hands to keep from tumbling. Below me, I heard nothing. No intake of breath, no faint grunt as arms and legs braced to catch my fall. I echoed over my shoulder, and the ladder was clear of climbers. I was on my own.

For the rest of my blind climb, I moved carefully, staying focused. I would think of the towers later, when I had time. When I was safe.

The novice dining alcove was four tiers up from my alcove. I counted the tiers as I passed them, hearing the sounds of footfalls and robes change tone and clarity as I climbed. Where Sellis slept, few seemed to be about. The entire tier sounded empty as I paused to rest on the ladder. An echo-sweep across the passageway caught someone in the act of climbing over the ledge of the Gyre, using the pulley ropes.

As the person straightened, I heard wings being furled. Battens clacked together, and silk rustled and folded. My echoes bounced off broad shoulders again.

"I can see you, Wik." I would not fail in his presence again. "Even with the blindfold on."

He chuckled. "You are quite good at this. Not everyone is. Sellis couldn't sound her way out of her alcove without help for a year."

"And Ciel and Moc?" I stepped onto the tier.

"Their ears are as sharp as yours, but they're distractible." His voice was closer now. I could hear him breathing. "Your focus is good."

I didn't need to echo to know where he was now. My fingers stretched out and tapped his lower arm. I traced the muscle down to the veins on his hand with my fingertips. He froze. I kept my hand on his arm. Tightened my grip, trapping him there.

"Why did you have me failed at wingtest, Wik?"

He stayed silent for a moment. His lips parted, audibly, as if he'd pressed them together before deciding to speak. "The council felt you would be more motivated to consider our offer. And Macal showed you too much with that dive."

The young Magister. I couldn't remember his face very well. It seemed so long ago. But the dive. I remembered that dive. I smiled. "A Singer's dive."

Wik's robes rustled. He pulled his hand away. "Macal is talented, but unpredictable, and young. My brother doesn't hold with all the traditions."

"Your brother?"

"Yes," Wik said. "And a good Magister. He cares about the towers very much. He is trying to convince our mother and the council that he could serve the city better as a teacher."

As I absorbed this, Wik touched my shoulder. I startled.

"You need to keep going, Kirit. You're almost there." He stepped around me and clambered up the ladder. "See if you can smell your way to breakfast," he whispered.

I stood still for another moment, the floor cool beneath my feet. Then I climbed after him, sightless, but not blind.

The noise of the dining alcove on the next tier sounded like a storm: conversations built and lulled. Pairs and clusters of novices passed me, hushing each other when they spotted my blindfold.

Embarrassed, I lowered my outstretched hands and tried to echo as unobtrusively as possible. The moment I did that, my sense of surrounding space began to fade. I stumbled and stopped. Then, taking a deep breath, I tilted my head back and echoed the way that worked best for me. I heard shapes that must have been tables and benches. A jumble of motions around me could have been novices, seated, standing, and walking. I found a table shape near the entrance of the dining alcove where two figures were seated: one broad and larger than most novice shapes, the other slim and sitting ramrod straight.

I sat down at this table, next to the second figure, hoping I'd got it right. I smelled pungent spices.

Fingers tugged at the knots of my blindfold. When it dropped, the daylight in the room made me blink until my eyes watered.

"You did it," Sellis said. "First try." She smiled guardedly. I thought I saw a jealous twinge, but then she brightened. "You understand now," she said.

"With your help," I said. I meant it too.

Wik pushed a bowl of potatoes and peppers towards me. "With enough practice, we'll make you a Singer yet, Kirit Spire."

"What's next?" Breakfast's spices prickled my tongue, and I blew out to cool my mouth. All around me, the sounds of the meal and the room added to what I could see. I wanted to learn more, to know everything now.

"Rest," Wik said. "With no moon tonight, we must rest today." I couldn't imagine why. Not when there was so much to hear.

By the time I returned to my tier, closing my eyes now and then to see if echoing still worked, I was ready to curl up without unfolding my mat. Exhaustion and giddy success netted me and pulled me into sleep.

15

LIFT

Sellis woke me in the dark.

Many Singers were already awake, readying themselves to fly.

In the towers, night was for sleeping. For storing up energy for the next day.

But Singers flew the night. Now that I was learning how they did it, I sensed the power of the skill, the advantages. Night-wings. Like the children's song, but better. They might see the invisible and travel through the city unobserved.

Sellis took me to the top of the Spire, where Wik waited for us. I breathed the fresh air. I wanted to throw myself to it; it felt so different from the trapped stuff that cycled through the Spire.

No moon. The stars were dim. I could not guess how long until sunrise. But I could see the nearest towers. The few lights within. The city slept, though we did not.

"Can you hear?" Wik growled in my ear. He pressed the metal prong to my temple again. "Echo. You will hear."

Suddenly, I could hear too much. I could hear Wik's breath and Sellis's teeth chattering. I tried echoing faster. Sellis and Wik joined me. Faintly, I could hear something beyond them, in the distance, resonating.

I pictured the city before me, the outlines of the towers I knew from my studies. I imagined what could be out there that I could hear but not see.

The forms sounded faint, but very large. They surrounded the Spire.

Oh.

The sounds that my ears strained to hear were the true shapes of the city.

I drew a breath and whispered, "I can hear."

"You will get better at it," Wik said, almost too loud. I realized he wasn't shouting.

My heart leapt. If I could hear the city, I could fly it. Even if I could not see it.

More citizens could learn this, too. If we could hear what we could not see, the towers could help seek out skymouth nests and free the city from their terror.

Sellis must have interpreted the excited look in my eyes. She shook her head.

"The city entrusts us with this knowledge, Kirit. This is not for the towers."

"Why not?"

"Tradition. Since the Rise."

"Singers say 'tradition' when they don't want to explain."

"It's more than that." Wik shook his head, struggling for patience. "It's about our history. About how people work. Traditions hold the city together, like the bridges do the towers. Once, we had no traditions. Only fear and loss."

There had been no traditions in the clouds. Where skymouths and worse roamed free. Where towers had gone to war, attacking each other in fear and desperation. I'd studied. I had sung The real Rise. The Singers' traditions had lifted the city from that darkness.

Now I shivered, chilled.

Sellis, impatient with old history, pulled the conversation back to the night's lesson. "Echoing is a matter of learning to listen even more," she said. "You can hear in directions, see in sounds."

"But it takes practice," said Wik. "Do not assume that you can hear everything straightaway."

But I was surely much better at this than they thought. Perhaps it was like my voice, the shouts I could make that no one else on this blessed Spire could. At least sometimes. When I was lucky. But maybe I could hear differently too.

Then Wik took the prong away, Sellis fell silent, and the city went dark. I could no longer hear the towers spread around me like a flower. No. I was silenced and grounded again. Wik had cut off a newly grown limb. I wanted it back.

I reached for the prong.

Wik tucked it away in his upper robe. "You must learn to make your own echoes out here, as you did inside."

Sellis took my hand and pulled me to the edge of the tower. She nudged me to sit, with my feet hanging over. I balked. I was unwinged, having left my training pair in my alcove.

"We will fly tonight," she said. Her voice sounded more hesitant than I'd ever heard it.

"How many Singers are night fliers?" I asked.

"Most. Everyone has to train to do it, but some don't like it. Many think this one step closer to falling."

"But this lets you see! And hunt skymouths! It's an honor to keep the city safe."

Sellis winced. "This is a charge, not an honor. And you will notice your hearing gets more sensitive for all things. There is a tradeoff. You will be marred."

I looked at my hand and its silver mark. "How?"

"You will hear too much. All the time. Singing will be painful, but you must continue to do it. You will overhear what you shouldn't. You will find crowds abhorrent. It sets you apart."

I already was set apart.

Being separate from the rest of the city was not unusual for Singers. I realized Sellis's cautions held a note of pride. Her concerns were Spire concerns: traditions, skills, Rumul. How much power she had and could gain. How high on the tower you lived didn't matter here. Influence within the Spire and marks did.

Wik had many marks. Rumul had many more. Sellis and I each had just the one, on our hands. Plus the pathways the echoes had begun carving in our brains—those were marks too.

"When do we begin?" I whispered.

"Now," Wik said. He pulled me to my feet and covered my eyes with a silk scarf. Blind. I stood atop the Spire, blind.

"Wait!" I couldn't see where the edge of the tower was, though I felt the solid bone beneath my soft footwraps. The air whistled around me, but I froze in place, afraid to step the wrong way. Nets or no, I did not want to fall.

Wik took my hand and guided me a few steps backwards. Then he let go and spun me around.

Sellis whispered, "Not so fast!" Her voice was loud in my ears. I clicked my tongue against the roof of my mouth, fast, like I'd done in the Spire. My eyes rolled beneath the scarf, searching for sound.

Wik said, "Listen."

And I could, faintly. I heard the wind against the towers and how it wrapped them with soft sweeps of breeze. I could hear gusts too.

We had so many ways to describe different types of wind. *Lifts. Crosses. Constants. Gaps.* I might one day hear them all.

Something low and large echoed ahead of me. The closest tower? Varu. The wind swept over the shape, slowly, then ripped around the higher towers beside it, whistling. Far beyond, Lith lurked, broken and forlorn. I knew it was there, though I couldn't hear it, because nothing else sounded so empty in the entire city.

I knew then that we stood at the apex of the Spire, on the western side, with Varu on my left. That was my compass. The other towers close in sounded whole and twisting. The wind moved among the tiers, and I heard soft laughter and muffled sounds of families gathered together for warmth and comfort. All very faint.

Echoes bounced off the crystals Sellis wore in her hair like shards of sound in a soft cushion. Sound marked where her body was next to mine and, in front of me, defined a broader, taller form. Wik. I reached out my hand. My palm brushed his silk robes.

"Well done, Kirit," he said, removing my blindfold. He lifted two sets of wings from the roof, gesturing to Sellis and me.

The wing frames were covered with deep gray silk. In the dark, they were practically black. Nightwings. Invisible against the sky.

Nat, I thought, *the stories were true.*

I took one set of wings and slipped the straps over my shoulders.

"Already?" Sellis said, hesitating and pale. She looked at me and caught herself. "Kirit's barely ready." But I realized as she spoke that she'd never flown the dark either. I wasn't so far behind her any longer.

My cheeks flushed, but I felt no fear. I knew I could die out there, but it would be among the towers, outside. In the wind. Not forgotten behind walls of bone.

"Frightened?" Sellis said to me.

"No," I said, hoping this would continue to be true.

"You should be," Wik said. "Many things live in the dark. Not just towers and skymouths."

Skymouths. That did scare me. I looked over the edge of the Spire and saw the vast towers widening below us. The dark all around them, swirling to the clouds. Woozy, I had to catch myself before I fell. Sellis and Wik were too busy adjusting their wings. They did not notice.

My hand stung from Rumul's mark as I flexed it to check the buckles on my nightwings. The straps were worn in, but the wings were beautifully made. Nothing like this kind of wing in the whole city. I could almost hear them sing. The wind cut around them with a chuckle, and it tickled my ears.

"Hurry," said Wik. "Sunrise in a few hours."

"Why can't we test sounds at dawn?" Sellis asked.

"Because your eyes tell you what to see then. You need to train your ears."

With that, Wik beckoned me to go first. I leapt from the Spire into the darkness.

As I leaned into my glide away from the Spire, waiting for Wik and Sellis to catch up, one of the worn buckles on my night-dark wings slipped.

The strap screeched. As the bone loop of the buckle continued to give, I could hear the fabric tearing. Before my training, I wouldn't have heard a thing.

My wings pulled taut in the wind. All around me was pitch-black. If the strap broke, I would fall and no one would see me go. I scrambled to set my right wing's elbow hook and reached as far as I could to hold the left strap together with my hand. The movement threw me off balance.

I began to spiral dizzyingly.

"What are you doing?" Wik shouted. When he realized what I held, he ordered, "Turn back now."

I was already trying to turn back. Didn't need to be told twice. I had dipped too low to regain the top of the Spire. I couldn't maneuver, only glide and hope.

I heard the wind curve around something below me before I saw its shadowy outline, barely tinted against the darker forms of depth and clouds. A bridge.

Don't overshoot it. You have one chance.

I could barely see it to time my landing.

I tried hearing the bridge, forcing my tongue against the dry—too dry—roof of my mouth repeatedly, until I made a loud, stuttering sound.

For a moment, my ears shaped the sweep of the sinew bridge. It stretched from Varu to Hirinat tower.

The bridge echo disappeared. I was not yet skilled enough.

I tried to hold the shape I'd heard in my mind. If I could drop low enough to catch the span with something—my hook, a knife, anything, I might stop my glide without falling.

Above, I heard the others glide past me. Wik dove below what must be the bridge. Catching me on this spiral would be risky, even for an accomplished Singer. But he was there to make the last-ditch attempt if I missed.

The strap slipped farther. The bone clasp cracked. And I heard Sellis beside me. She pushed me slightly off course with her backdraft.

"Shift, Sellis!" I shouted. How could she not hear me?

I could sense every change in the wind caused by the bridge and the looming wall of the Spire. If I didn't course-correct soon, one would smash me flat, the other would cut me down.

"Sellis, break windward," Wik yelled.

She finally heard and turned to clear the air. Her turn pulled me back onto a good landing angle for where I thought the bridge was. I kicked my feet out of their strap in time to hook the space where I pictured the railing should be.

I hoped I was right. I needed to be right.

One foot caught, then the other. I landed, sort of, hanging upside down by my ankles. The underbridge breeze swung me back and forth precariously.

The bridge wobbled as Wik landed and hauled me onto the span.

I brushed off his attempts to help inspect my wingstraps.

By feel, I could tell that both straps had been stressed with something sharp. Someone wanted me to fall far enough that I never came back.

Sellis's eyes were wide in the sere predawn light. "I couldn't turn," she gasped, shaking. When Wik held out his hand, she shucked out of her own wings and they checked those wingstraps. They were stressed too, though not as badly. The grips had been weakened as well.

"Where did our new training wings come from?" she asked.

Wik was ashen; his tattoos, almost phosphorescent. The clip he gave to his words chilled me further. "The windbeaters sent new pairs up for the night fliers."

"Windbeaters?" Sellis looked shocked. "But why would they ever—Rumul will—How dare . . ." She fell silent, shivering and looking, in the dim light, much younger and more afraid than I'd ever seen her. She caught me watching, but did not glare or flinch.

Finally, Wik spoke again. "Windbeaters. The Spire is in conflict."

Sellis looked at Wik, then at me. "Please. We must return quickly. Tell the council. Before more Singers fall."

16

GYRE

Wik had produced a sewing kit from a hidden pocket in his sleeve. He dampened a translucent cord with spit, then threaded it through the eye of a thick bone needle. He patched the break with sinew. When he finished, I tested the strap. It felt solid enough for a short flight.

Sellis paced, eager to fly once her wings were patched. Her need to make sure Rumul knew what had happened, and why, was palpable in the darkness.

"We will pursue what happened," Wik promised, when I asked him to elaborate on the windbeaters' actions. "Not now. We must do things carefully."

Not now. Tradition. Carefully. Wik's discipline took patience. I had little to spare.

We flew the short span of night to the Spire. Sellis and I clung to wall hooks outside while Wik worked the gate. We were at a higher tier than the one Nat and I had tried to break into at Allmoons.

A predawn gust cut around the Spire cold and loud. The gate ground open just as sunlight tinged the horizon's dark clouds. We crawled through and emerged on a windbeater tier.

Wik pointed for us to climb back to our tiers, but I planted my feet. I wanted to stay, to confront the windbeaters. To find my father.

He shook his head emphatically. "Too dangerous," he whispered. "In case they're targeting someone."

"Why would they do that?" I was still chilled by the near catastrophe.

Sellis looked like she was too, her usual haughtiness banished. She hesitated beside me, desperate to know more about the windbeaters' intent before reporting to Rumul.

"They can't fly anymore, but they can still meddle," she whispered.

I sat down on the tier floor, stubborn. I refused to move.

Wik's face turned stony. He was unused to being questioned by his charges.

Sellis shifted from one foot to the other, then sat down beside me.

I returned Wik's gaze. "If we may not talk to them because we are not yet Singers, then you must ask them why."

Wik groaned. When we still refused to move, he went to wake and interrogate a windbeater, one he said he could trust.

As he walked away, Sellis stared at me, her eyes wide. "Novices don't question Singers." She didn't look at all comfortable with what we'd done. But she wasn't scolding me.

"We'll get an answer, at least." I hoped I was right.

"It wasn't personal," Wik whispered when he returned. "They couldn't know who would fly those wings."

"Rumul needs to know." Sellis rose, picked up her nightwings, and hurried to the ladders.

Wik watched her go, but I kept my eyes on him. "Why?"

"A few windbeaters have become open to trading favors, though it is not often done," Wik said. "In return for gossip from uptower. Your father, for one."

"And trying to murder Singers?"

"Rarely. They are trying to influence something." He seemed

unfazed, which made me want to shake him. I balled my fists and focused on breathing while he continued, "I can't tell who is behind this. I will find out."

Influence. Meddling. That was what Singers called someone almost dying. I was not comforted, but I let Wik nudge me back uptower while I continued to ponder.

My father traded in gossip.

I could find a way to use that.

The next afternoon, the dining alcove rumbled with gossip, but not the kind that my father would need. A windbeater had fallen, tragically, into the Gyre.

"Who?" I asked Sellis.

"An old crone who thought she'd outsmart the council," she replied. Her chin was up; her confidence had returned. Her hands were folded neatly on the table. She'd downed her meal with relish.

A crone. Not my father. Still, retribution came fast in the Spire. I vowed silently that this would not be my fate.

In the days after, as we continued to train, we saw windbeaters below, practicing wind shifts, as usual. The situation seemed to have settled. But I could not convince Sellis to let me go downtower again. She went so far as to post Lurai by my alcove. It was an honor, she said. An acolyte.

My refusal to obey Wik had alarmed someone, and Sellis was making sure I didn't venture anywhere on my own. I waited for any chance to go back down to the windbeaters' tier, but I was never alone.

We worked on Singer skills, checking our wings well each time. We studied advanced echoing. Sellis and I flew blindfolded. Wik and I practiced skymouth calls atop the tower and on the wing.

We fought more now, testing the younger novices or being tested ourselves against older, just-turned Singers. Bone-knife cuts and bruises from the walls of the Gyre laced my arms, legs, and face like Singer tattoos. Sellis was equally marked.

Some days, the wind patterns were too strong, too complex for us. I bent a batten when I crashed into a gallery. Skidded onto the tier. Sellis fell so far that she had to climb back up on the ladders outside the Gyre.

She was skittish when she finally made it back to our tier.

"I almost fell beyond the windbeaters. That's forbidden. They caught me with a hook."

"What did you see?" I asked.

"They are preparing rot gas below." At my confusion, she added, "The windbeaters throw flaming balls of it into the Gyre during a challenge if it's going too slow."

We began to hear new rumors in the dining alcove, murmurs of arguments in council, of Rumul yelling at someone in his alcove.

Even Moc didn't know what was happening. "Something big," he said, peering over the edge of the Gyre.

Windbeaters gathered by the vents below, practicing new patterns with their huge silk wings.

The Spire's quiet passages clotted with groups of gray-robed Singers who talked almost silently and scattered when approached. I tried to find Wik, or Rumul, but they spent their days on the council tier. By the next morning, Sellis did not appear at breakfast.

"Ciel"—I caught the girl as she sped along the passage— "what has happened now?"

She wordlessly pointed to the Gyre, just as the gusts within rose to a howl. There was so much wind, pushed and funneled through the Spire's abyss so fast, that things not tied down near the balconies began to be pulled into the funnel. A few pieces of silk flew out through the apex. Singers and novices alike ran to grab precious objects and secrete them away.

Rumul appeared on the council gallery, and everyone stopped and turned to look. He spoke, and the wind carried his voice throughout the Spire.

"There has been a challenge. Singer Terrin wishes to address the city. The council has disagreed. He has issued the challenge."

"Singer's burden," the groupings of gray-winged Singers said.

"He will fight for this right, and by fighting, earn his voice, or lose his wings, or forfeit his life."

"Singer's right," the Spire responded. The deep tones of the group's unified voice echoed across the tiers, through the galleries.

Sellis descended a ladder, eyes gleaming. She shouted, "Come on!" to me as she moved fast to find a good view in the galleries.

I followed in her wake, feeling rising excitement overcome the dread that had gripped the Spire for days. This was how Rumul had earned his tattoos. So many fights, like scars crossing his face. This was what my mother had done. And how my father became a windbeater. This was how, someday, I might earn my Singer wings. By fighting in the Gyre.

With everyone else, I turned and let the Gyre wind whip at my face.

ᭅ ᭅ ᭅ

The challenger had traded his gray robes for white. His wings were Singer's wings, a lustrous gray. From where we sat, we could see Terrin had belted his straps double tight. He held a bone knife high in salute to his fellow Singers.

"In defense of the city," Rumul shouted, "I will fight him."

Beside me, Sellis gasped. Far above, Terrin looked paler than before. The rumble from the top tier grew so loud it sounded like the start of a city roar from the wrong direction.

Before anyone could move to stop him, Rumul dropped from the balcony, wings spread. He drew a worn, though still deadly sharp, bone knife from an arm sheath. He tossed it in the air from one hand to the other as he swept around the Gyre.

Terrin checked his straps and leapt, his wings spread full.

The two circled each other, sensing which gusts were powerful enough to lift them up and around. They worked the wind, full of pointed determination.

"I will speak," Terrin shouted. Then he dove, only to shoot up another gust and tear at Rumul's foot, as Rumul passed by.

"Terrin will try to drop Rumul at first opportunity," Sellis said. She paused, swallowed hard, and added, "It'll be his only opportunity."

To me, the challenge seemed much like wingfights at Densira. The fight was smaller: only two men struggled to knock each other out of the Spire, dead or alive. But here, the stakes were higher: the winner spoke for the city, the loser was forever silenced.

"One may win without killing an opponent," Sellis whispered. Her eyes were lamp-bright, and she leaned side to side as Rumul turned. She knew his battle glides, apparently, very well. "He trained me," she explained. "As Wik and I have trained you."

I nodded, still not sure enough of the situation to speak. Asking a muzz-dumb question at this point—when Sellis had just begun to confide in me instead of reminding me how little I truly knew—seemed unwise. I let her continue talking, as it seemed to ease her nerves.

Rumul's glides grew shorter and shorter as he narrowed the horizontal and vertical gaps between him and Terrin. Then he shot forward on a fortunate gust. The smoke of the windbeaters' rot gas preparations had tinted a breeze just enough for him to see it.

Below, the windbeaters drums and the pulse of their wings punctuated the battle at increasing speeds.

"What is it," Lurai asked, coming to stand beside us, "that Terrin wants to say?"

Sellis shushed him. "The Gyre will prove whether it's worth hearing over council's advice." She shook her head. "Terrin was Rumul's friend."

I wondered if there was a song for fighting a friend in a challenge, but I kept my mouth shut.

Sellis kneaded her robes with her hands. She saw me notice and pressed her palms to her lap. "Rumul won't let him live. But he won't let Terrin fall while still alive either; at this point, that would be shameful. For both of them."

Back at Densira, wingfighters fought together in a tangle of jewel-colored wings and glass-spiked feet, of bone and fists and blood and netting. But that was child's play compared to the Gyre. This was the maelstrom.

Terrin tired. His arms shook in his wings; sweat poured down his face.

Rumul was lucky with the gusts, for sure. One caught and lifted him towards Terrin. He took a wide swipe with his knife and almost tore one of Terrin's wings. Terrin turned just in time.

They whipped by our tier, rising, mouths grim, knives sharp. Light spilled over them as the sun broached the Spire's apex. Rumul blinked, dazzled for a moment. Long enough for Terrin to take advantage and get above the head Singer.

Sellis stuffed her hand between her teeth. I leaned forward, watching.

Terrin dove for Rumul, lips parted to shape a high-pitched shriek.

Singers in nearby galleries covered their ears, wincing in pain. I winced too, but could not turn away. Rumul growled and flipped an impossible turn in the tight space, timed to catch a windbeater's gust perfectly. He grabbed Terrin's wing.

With a jerk, he tried to tear the wing from Terrin's back. This angled his own wings against the wind, and he plummeted, dragging Terrin with him.

In a moment, the two men were one body, falling together. Terrin landed a lucky strike with his knife, and blood bloomed on Rumul's robe near his shoulder. Singers were on their feet, mouths open, soundlessly watching. Sellis among them.

Then Terrin's second wingstrap gave way and his left arm pulled, dislocated, from the wing. Rumul rose, four wings bellying with wind, two at his back, two in his hands.

Shrilling with pain, Terrin grappled for a balcony. His fingers scraped the tier as he passed us. The gallery leaned forward as if they too were falling.

A grinding sound. A new gust pulled at us. A gate had opened at the base of the Spire's occupied tiers. Terrin was sucked out still shrieking into the bright city sky.

The gate slammed as Terrin's voice faded into nothingness.

The Spire held its breath as Rumul gathered his strength and rode the remaining Gyre winds upwards to the top of the Spire.

On the upper balconies, two council members reached out to pull Rumul onto the tier. They addressed the galleries. "It is decided."

The galleries replied, "It is decided."

Robes rustled as Singers turned back to their alcoves, order restored.

The council members led Rumul away from the top balcony to tend his wounds. The windbeaters dropped their oversized wings to the floor with a clatter.

In the moment after the beaters stopped channeling the winds, an ear-popping reversal swung the Gyre currents. The force pulled at my cheeks and my robes. Older Singers leaned away from the Gyre to brace themselves.

Ciel, standing too close to the edge of the gallery, tripped and fell forward, over the edge and into the chasm. Her tiny training wings fluttered half open and useless.

She screeched, breaking the post-challenge silence of the Spire. Lurai and I rushed back to the galleries and looked down. A half tier below, Ciel clung to the wall, looking up with wide eyes.

Sellis shook her head slowly. She looked exhausted. "Clumsy." The word echoed around the Spire like a death rattle. There were few worse names to be called in the city. One thing the Spire had in common with the towers. Moc ran to my side and looked down.

"Singers can't fall in the Gyre," he whimpered.

I didn't think. "Help me," I said as I stepped to the edge. Sellis and Moc followed. Lurai hesitated, then joined us.

"Hold my feet." I loosed my wingstraps enough to loop one end around a bone post.

If I fell, if Lurai or Sellis let go my feet, I would fall past Ciel, knock her off her perch, and we would keep falling inside the Spire until the end of the world. "Tighter!"

The commotion I made attracted more attention than the fallen child. Behind me, the sound of running feet; above me, whispered words like *tradition* from the higher tiers; across the Spire, louder murmurs. But I was upside down now, my robes gathered around my waist and my under linens showing pale and undyed as I reached.

"Farther out!" I yelled, and Sellis and Lurai edged closer. I felt Sellis adjust her grip on my ankle and tensed, but she wrapped both hands more firmly, and I stopped dropping. My fingertips grazed Ciel's hair.

"Reach up, Ciel," I said as calmly as possible.

The fierce little girl whimpered. Her fingers clamped tighter around the wall of the perch. She looked up at me.

"You can," I said, sounding more sure than I felt. "Just one hand."

She shook her head again, but I could see her thinking about it. She knew she must.

Behind and above us, an older voice said, "Let her go. Singers do not fall in the Gyre," but Moc was whispering, "Please," softly, not wanting to frighten Ciel or me. I was aware by now that no Singer had jumped into the Gyre and glided over to help. If a novice did not learn to fly the Gyre like a Singer, it seemed they let you fall.

At least in the towers we had tethers for the unsure. Magisters who caught our friends and pulled them back from the clouds. Here, Ciel only had me.

"I won't let you fall, Ciel." I whispered it, but she heard.

First one finger, then more peeled away from the wall. They were rubbed with soot, the pads dented from her tight grip. The fingers hovered against the wall as Ciel checked her balance on her other hand, the place where she'd found to plant her feet.

Sturdy for the moment. Her hand shot up and grabbed mine, then slipped, and I clasped it tightly. Her foot slipped farther. She whimpered again. I tightened my grip and gritted my teeth hard.

Ciel swung from my hand, a tiny, winged pendulum. I dangled from the tier. Lurai and Sellis began hauling us both back up.

"If you were Singer-raised," Sellis muttered. She stopped. "You and your tower-fed bones."

If I'd been Singer-raised, I'd have been slighter, for certain. But I also wouldn't have leapt to save a clumsy child.

They pulled, and I held fast to Ciel, and soon I was back on the flat landing of the tier, my ribs and stomach scraped where they'd struck the edge. Ciel grabbed the ledge and pulled herself up and over, then lay next to me, gasping.

"Clumsy," Sellis said, and stalked away.

Ciel took my hand, and we both looked over the edge of the Gyre, into the dark depths.

Lurai leaned back against a wall, catching his breath. Moc knelt next to his twin. Took her other hand.

The galleries began to clear in earnest.

"Don't tell," Ciel said, her voice rough. "I forgot windbeaters sometimes pull the wind, after. I was distracted."

Moc emphasized every word: "They never did it like that before. That was too much."

More sabotage from below? "Who shouldn't hear of this?"

The twins looked at me as if I was cloudtouched. Many Singers had witnessed the fall. Except the council.

"Sellis has already gone to tell Rumul everything."

Moc grumbled as Ciel watched us. "At least Rumul will play it down. Aunt Viridi would not."

Ciel shook her head emphatically. "Please don't tell her. I was clumsy, that's all. Singers aren't clumsy. Not in the Gyre." Her voice did not quaver. She was determined to sound as tough as any Singer. As tough as Wik.

Realization dawned. *Aunt* Viridi, the older Singer with the silver-streaked hair who had attended my wingtest. A councilwoman. Wik's mother. The twins and Wik were family.

And yet their larger family, the Spire family, had returned to daily tasks, as if nothing had happened. As if, with everything decided, order and balance had been restored.

I squeezed Ciel's hand tighter. Saw Moc's eyes narrow. "What is it?"

"I am not sure yet," Moc said. He lifted a torn scrap of Ciel's robe from where it had caught on the ledge. Balled it up in his fist. "But I will find out."

"We," I said. "We will find out."

17

WINDWARD

In the emptied gallery, I got to my knees, then my feet. Ciel clung to my hand.

"Who has charge of the vents? The windbeaters?"

When she didn't answer, I looked for Moc. He was already disappearing down a ladder. I chased him. I heard Wik call out behind me, but I did not stop. Ciel ran with me, but halted at the landing.

"You'll be fine," I said.

She stared down the ladder. Wik appeared behind her, put a hand on her shoulder and dipped his head to me. She let him lift her up and rested her head on his shoulder. Safe.

If I lingered, I would lose track of Moc entirely. I turned and hurried down the ladder.

I caught up to Moc on the next level. Grabbed his robe and held him by it. "Tell me now—what is happening?"

He pawed the air with his fists. "I am trying to find out!" His voice cracked. "Someone is sabotaging the Spire—your wings, the vents! Other things too. It is not over. It is not *decided*."

He swung so hard that I dropped him to the floor. He got to his feet and began descending the next ladder.

"Why is no one else asking questions?"

"They don't see everything Ciel and I do. Some don't trust us because our aunt is on the council. So they don't listen to us either."

I heard truth in his voice. Followed him down into the depths of the Spire. Someone had sabotaged my wings. Someone had tried to hurt Ciel. If I found out why, I might gain better leverage with Rumul. Perhaps I would then have gossip for my father.

We reached the lowest levels, where the windbeaters lived. Bolts of dove-colored silk lined the halls, and silk spiders' nests clung to corners and to the ceiling. I spotted a loom in an alcove. The walls were covered in carvings. Some bone spurs had been carved so deeply and intricately, they resembled lace and lattice more than walls.

Ahead of me, Moc stepped into the shadows, out of the dimming light.

"They keep busy down here."

"They make a bunch of things. Wings, nets. The plinths for wingtests. Trade them for goods from the other towers," he whispered.

Two aged windbeaters leaned out over the Gyre, large wings spread on the floor behind them. They did not turn as we passed.

"What are they doing?" I looked back. One windbeater's eyes were white, like the skyblind. He was tethered to the floor with bone cleats and long sinew ropes.

"Listening to the wind. Learning to shape it." Moc didn't spare them a glance. "Even the injured can do that, if they're good enough. And if they still have use of their arms and shoulders."

Moc kept walking until he reached an alcove carved into the thickening outer wall. Strange carvings surrounded the room like pipes. Long stretches of hollowed-out bone rose to the ceiling. Some had pulley ropes run through them, or hinged lids. They looked like a group of rainspouts.

A bent form was working the pipes—a man, judging by the breadth of his shoulders, though his robes hung strangely. He moved as if each gesture brought pain.

The pipe covers snapped open and clicked shut, sounding like Laws chips. The alcove smelled like old bone mixed with fresh air. The man's fingers stilled. He seemed to be waiting for something.

I heard a soft clicking. Like echoing.

"Civik Spire," Moc said. The figure did not move. Moc cleared his voice and prepared to shout, before shaking his head instead and touching the figure's sleeve. The man spun halfway towards him. Singer marks scarred the skin around his ruined eyes. The left side of his face had been flattened: a broken cheekbone. Something sharp had taken his right eye.

Sound came sudden to my lips. "Oh."

The figure turned to me fully now, as if he could hear me easier than he could hear Moc.

A rasp, like a gate opening. "Skymouth speaker." He said it slowly, as if he rarely spoke. "I'd wondered when they'd find a new one." His laugh was bitter and ended in a cough.

"You almost killed her last night, you broken old man," Moc said, though his voice was softer now. He turned to me, murmured, "Civik's deaf in the left ear. Once you get his attention, it's all right."

I looked at them both, suddenly aware of how much Moc knew about the tower's comings and goings. He hadn't spotted the resemblance between me and the ruined man before me, though. This was one thing he did not know.

But I knew. I saw it in Civik's hands, his long fingers, so similar to my own. I recognized the rasp in Civik's voice as a worn echo of my terrible singing voice.

Civik knew me only by the tones behind my voice. Knew me as a skymouth shouter. But I knew him for much more.

I held my tongue, for now.

Civik pushed on the walls and grabbed handholds to move away from the pipes. I heard bone grind against bone. Civik's robe shifted with the motion. For a moment, I saw that his body was bound with spidersilk to a bone pedestal. Where Civik's legs should have been, his under-robes ended in a knot. Carved bone rollers at the pedestal's base allowed him to move.

I gasped again.

"Young person who has arrived with the impertinent Moc," Civik rasped, "is shocked at my appearance. It hasn't been that long, has it, since my last battle?"

"Twelve years, Civik," Moc said. He gestured uselessly to me. "But this novice arrived a few months ago. And you almost killed her with faulty nightwing straps. And just now, you nearly killed Ciel, too, with your backdraft."

I bit my tongue so that Civik would not realize anything more about me, and let Moc rage on.

"Could you get something right, Civik? You didn't distract the council from deciding against Terrin. You didn't even stall them. You're dangerous. I should find a new windbeater to bribe."

Civik grumbled. "I am trying, young Moc."

"What is going on?" I said.

They both answered at once.

Civik said, "Moc owes me tools and gossip." While Moc said, "Civik's useless—I won't give you any more gossip, Civik, until you help us."

"You were trying to help Terrin by sabotaging the Nightwings?" I asked.

The windbeater shrugged. "Terrin's argument was his. He flew too early. We could have postponed it. We had our own goals."

"But you weren't supposed to target novices," Moc said quickly. "Wik was out there."

Civik waved a hand. "If the night fliers have a setback, that delays Rumul. Long enough for Terrin to seek more support. And many other things."

Swaying from foot to foot as he thought, Moc looked very

young. I held myself still, listening to what was being said and what was not being said. How many layers of allegiance and independence existed in the Spire? In the city, loyalty was to tower and family first, then friends and allies after. A tightly woven fabric—except when there was a flaw. I thought of how Densira and my aunts had almost abandoned my unlucky mother. In the Spire, loyalty was different, focused on power: on gaining it, on keeping it. Much was dedicated to duty. Still more to the city itself. Then, to other Singers, as long as they were skilled enough and did not break tradition. Singers with Spire family had another layer as well. It reminded me of the Gyre's wind gusts, spun together to form a powerful current that lifted a flier's wings. Or made them fall.

I did not understand all of it, by far. And, from what I'd seen, some Singers valued certain layers over others. If I didn't figure out the connections, those forces would work against me, pull me down.

Worse, I stood in a room with my father, and I could not bring myself to greet him. He was weak and ruined. He'd almost killed Nightwings last night and Ciel today, to aid his own plans. I didn't know him. How could I want him as a relative, much less an ally?

I thought back to Civik's attempts to delay Rumul. To Moc's words. "Why did Terrin need support?"

Moc blew air through his lips in exasperation. "You still don't understand, Kirit."

At my name, Civik's head turned farther. His blind eyes looked like kavik eggs. I shivered. "Kirit?" he whispered and leaned towards me. His cart rolled forward, his fingers reaching out, and I stepped back, involuntarily.

"What happened?" I asked.

At my words, Civik leaned back, and his cart retreated towards the wall.

Moc answered. "He fell, during his last fight. Lost his legs. Destroyed his shoulder. Before that, he broke his hip, but he still fought in the Gyre."

"When did you go blind?" I whispered, circling to stand nearer to Moc. Civik's white gaze followed the sound of my voice now.

"His first fight. A challenger. She devastated him, but let him live. He became a windbeater, but he emerged twice to challenge again." Moc sounded sad and proud at the same time.

"You fought blind?"

Moc laughed. "Singers fight until they can't. Of course he fought blind. You could too, if you got better at echoing."

Of course—as a skymouth shouter, Civik would have also trained as a Nightwing.

"And he can't stop fighting. Civik thinks he's the conscience of the Spire, don't you?" Moc stepped close and tapped Civik on the shoulder. The two were nearly the same height.

"Kirit is a name I haven't heard in a long time," Civik finally said. Then his shoulders slumped. "What tower are you from?"

But I had my own questions. "Years ago, you betrayed Naton Densira, didn't you? Why?"

Civik bent farther with more hacking sounds. Finally he caught enough breath to speak. "Is that what you think? Who told you that?"

I was about to answer when Moc looked up, head tilted. "Someone's coming."

Wik emerged from a ladder well.

"Moc. Kirit. Why am I not surprised? You've caused quite an uproar." His voice sounded stern. His eyes, though. They looked grateful.

He saw Civik, bent down to clasp the man's gnarled hand.

Moc pointed. "Old man's been trying to sabotage things all

the wrong ways. First the wings, then the Gyre blowback. If Ciel had fallen . . ." His voice tightened on the last words.

Wik raised his eyebrows. Civik interjected before Wik, too, could grow angry.

"Moc didn't tell me how to stir things up, just that folks wanted them stirred. Hasn't paid me either."

Moc. The Nightwings. No.

"Fine," Moc said, ignoring my shocked face. "This is your gossip: Rumul has accepted the oath of an adult novice to take your place as a shouter. Kirit. He won't need you anymore once she's trained." His voice was angry and mean.

Wik frowned but didn't contradict him. I knelt next to Wik and Civik.

I put a hand out and touched the windbeater's fingertips. "Not replace. Moc is angry." Civik's fingers were dry and callused. He startled at my touch, then wrapped his hand around mine. For a moment, I imagined that we had always been this way. Then I squeezed his hand hard, and he yelped.

"Why did you leave Densira? Why did you betray Naton?" I would not let go until he told me.

Wik put a hand on my shoulder. "You have it backwards, Kirit. Civik has been trying to help."

"I made a mistake," Civik whispered. "A lot of mistakes. But I am fighting now." His eyes rolled, searching for light he'd never find.

"When he returned to the Spire and lost his first challenge," Wik said, "he was allowed to concede. And then he didn't *stop* challenging. His injuries didn't matter. He kept flying. When Rumul finally beat him, he broke Civik's collarbone. Civik was no longer able to fly beyond the Spire without help. He couldn't return to Densira."

I turned on Wik. "And who are you? Rumul's man? Like Sellis?"

Wik shook his head. "I see the good the Singers do, and I defend the city. But Rumul's decisions have consequences for everyone. I supported Terrin and wanted the city to know what he had to say. I was one of a few who wanted this. There are others."

"What was it that Terrin wanted to say?"

"It has to do with the skymouths," Wik said slowly. "But it has been decided."

Civik coughed, ignoring Wik. "Ezarit? Does she live?" So he did remember. He'd drawn into himself, his arms wrapped around his chest.

"She does," I said. "Though she seems to be at the end of her ability to negotiate with the Singers."

I heard Moc gasp.

Civik hung his head. "That is my fault too."

"What does that mean?"

He answered me. "If I'd lost properly, or had told her everything, she would have had more to bargain with."

Then the timing clicked. Civik's initial downfall. My mother's challenge. Her voice telling me the story, after the wingtest. *I was ruthless, Kirit.* She'd fought Civik. To gain her security in the towers.

I looked around Civik's alcove. The pipes, the smell of fresh air and old bone. His sunken, gray cheeks. The darkness. "Are you in pain?"

He shook his head. Then nodded. "Always, a little. Enough."

"You were a Singer and a skymouth shouter. Why are you down here?"

Wik answered instead. "He challenged Rumul. Who could have killed him." I frowned, though I understood. Wik continued. "But shouters' voices? They're valuable. Civik could no longer fly, but Rumul went to great lengths to keep him alive."

Civik's voice. The rasp of it. Stilling with one shout a skymouth, all teeth and maw and grasping tentacles. That was one power Rumul lacked, except when he could control it in others. I looked more closely at my father. His lips were chapped and cracked. His clothing very dirty. He was thinner than Wik, by far.

Rumul might have been keeping him alive, but it was a very near thing. And I couldn't imagine Civik outside the Spire, being flown by another Singer, in the midst of a skymouth migration. There was something else that I was missing.

My hand went to my throat. "How does Rumul use Civik's voice *inside* the Spire?"

There was a long pause. No one answered me.

"It has been decided," Wik said, looking away.

Terrin's challenge. "What did he want to tell the city?"

Civik's laugh was a sour echo. "Secrets."

Wik took my hand and tried to pull me out of the alcove. I refused to budge. Finally, he said, "Come. I will show you."

He took a long loop of knotted rope from the wall near Civik's alcove. The ladder wells had been filled in below this level. Going below the windbeaters, I remembered, was forbidden. We headed for the Gyre's edge. Wik tied the rope to bone hooks carved in the wall and tossed the loop into the depths of the Spire.

18

DOWNTOWER

We climbed down the rope, far into the darkness below the occupied tiers, until we reached a thick set of nets. Multiple layers of them.

Wik touched my arm. Whispered, "Stay very quiet." Then
he walked slowly towards the center of the Gyre, across the
nets.

An acrid smell grew stronger as I followed his path. The nets
rose and fell with our motion, but also with an odd pressure
from below our feet. I wobbled and fought hard to keep my balance. When I looked down, I could not see anything but shadowy ropes and more darkness.

Wik reached the center of the netting and pulled on a series
of knots. An access gate opened to the space below. He lowered himself through the hole, tugging on my sleeve to guide
me, then closed the gate behind us.

I relaxed my hands, which had tightened into fists. Tried to
calm myself. I would not regret demanding to know. This was
where I'd wanted to be.

It wasn't where I wanted to be at all.

We stood in the center of the nets and Wik said, "Kirit, you
must control your voice in here, as we've practiced. You must
not make any mistakes."

Something moved beyond the nets. Something big.

The hair on my arms rose.

"Do not shout. Do not speak. Just echo." Wik's lips touched my ear, his voice sounded almost inside my head.

My eyes adjusted, slowly. I could now see where Wik's face was, his cheek a different shade of darkness than the shadowed walls around us. I saw the quick flashes of his teeth.

But that was all. Wik was right. This was not a time for using my eyes.

His voice was patient, and urgent. "You will understand soon. Just echo."

I was still learning how to echo and hum; the combination was difficult. Now I hummed through my nose while clicking and tried to remember to breathe. The movement on the other side of the net stopped.

"We would have had to do this anyway, to complete your training," Wik whispered.

The completion of my training was skymouth shouting. I stopped echoing. "Is a skymouth caught in the nets?"

I imagined a mouth opening beside me, tentacles reaching for me, with only ropework between us.

I tried to refocus, to corral in my thoughts. Breathe and echo.

I heard the shape of something beyond the nets. Something large, in motion. I turned and echoed again. More of the same shape, slightly smaller. I could not breathe.

"Not one skymouth," Wik said, his voice close in my ear again. "Many."

I stopped humming. Darkness surrounded me. Wik's hand brushed my arm.

I bit back a scream.

"Many?" My voice rose, and there was a rasp on the other side of the net. Motion. Faster. The ropes bulged towards us.

Something tugged at my hair. My robe. Something that slid and grabbed and pulled. My entire body went gooseflesh. I could not breathe at all.

Wik hummed, and the sinister motion slowed. The tentacles receded. My breath returned, but my mouth was dry. It took time to rebuild my echo. For a moment, I was overwhelmed by the darkness, blinded with fear.

"We are safe here," Wik said, stopping his echo once mine had started again. "The nets will hold."

I kept echoing, hearing the coils and tentacles, the long bodies of the penned skymouths that my hum was defining around us. When they moved, the echo blurred into a confusion of roiled air. "Why?" The nets went dark again when I stopped echoing to ask the question. But even in the dark, I could see the pattern of the nets. I had seen it before, on Naton's bone chips. This was what he had carved. The blueprint for these nets. A skymouth pen.

"Some of the skymouths here will be used for their sinew, for bridges. Some give us the ink that lines their glands," Wik said, lifting my hand and putting his thumb on the mark Rumul had given me. Wik hummed again, and I joined him. The movement around us stilled.

After a moment, he tapped my hand and whispered, "They sleep. Your first test, passed."

"Why keep so many, once you've caught them?"

Wik didn't answer at first. Then, "Why, indeed. You should ask Rumul. The problem isn't that we are keeping them. Singers have always kept one or two for training."

I waited for him to continue. He remained silent.

We stood at the center of the Spire's secrets. Nat would have loved this. "Wik. Tell me."

"It has been decided." His voice was firm. "We should go back up. Check on Ciel." He tugged on my sleeve to draw me away, as if he regretted having revealed any of this.

I did not wish to be left alone at the center of a skymouth pen in the depths of the Spire, surrounded by teeth and tentacle, maw and want. But I planted my feet more firmly, refusing to move. "Tell me now."

"Terrin lost his challenge. If he had won . . ." Wik's voice drifted off. "We had hoped . . . But Rumul and the council demand silence, even among ourselves." He tried to pull me towards the rope gate, to the exit at the pens' net ceiling.

I still refused to budge. This was information I needed. "How can I finish my training without understanding this?"

He cleared his throat. Spoke in a hush. "Some skymouths are bred here, by Singers. And they have been, for a long time."

New skymouths, on purpose. My skin crawled as if I were covered in writhing tentacles. My hands pushed at Wik's chest, as if I could have driven what he'd just said back inside of him. "Why would anyone want to make more?"

"See for yourself," Wik said. "Carefully. Few Singers realize they've gotten more than they bargained for."

I turned and clicked softly, not wanting to wake the huge beasts. The sound vibrations translated to large shapes, caught in pens around the Gyre. *So many.* More than the city could ever use for bridges.

In a corner closest to us, I heard something different: a shape like a pile of worn cloth, but softer. Almost deflated. Those were skymouth shapes, no longer moving. *Stacked neatly,* ready to be turned into sinew and ink for the Singers.

There was an order to the cages. A *purpose* that was the darkest side of the Singers. And Naton had helped them make this.

I felt sick to my stomach. "You are farming them." The realization took my breath away, and I stopped clicking. The nets went dark.

"The skins are as caustic as the ink. We can only use the undersides of tentacles and the bladders, and only very carefully at that. The rest gets thrown down. Or fed to the others."

"Who does the work?"

Wik turned his head up towards the windbeaters' tiers. His profile was lit by the dawn just coming into the Spire, elaborate tattoos across his cheeks thrown into relief. Like a fine carving. I looked away, back into shadows.

"Those windbeaters who are able see to most of it, led by a few Singers who can make sounds that the skymouths can hear and who wish to do the work. Terrin was one."

The sick, crawling feeling built.

"But Terrin knew something he wanted to share with the city." My voice was calm, but my mind raced. Skymouths. *Nat wouldn't have believed this if he'd seen it himself.*

As my thoughts jumbled, the skymouths began to stir again. Another rope dropped from the darkness above. The nets bounced as feet marched across the skymouth pens, quickly enough that the beasts inside began to stir angrily.

Wik hummed to calm them as the gate opened. Then Rumul descended into the pens, crowding us amongst the nets.

"Our acolyte is a quick study," Rumul said, his voice soft and shadowed. "Sellis told me you'd gone to the windbeaters. I'm not shocked Civik's daughter would end up on the forbidden tiers. I wanted to see your reaction for myself."

I remained silent. Afraid. Discovered on a forbidden tier. I could not fathom what he would do now.

Rumul turned and grabbed me, putting his face close to mine. "Do you know why we keep them?"

I shook my head, thinking fast. "Wik would not speak of it. I can only guess."

Rumul relaxed. Let me go. "Tell me." His breath smelled of honey.

"That you keep some alive for training. That you trade extra sinew with the towers for what the Spire needs." It was not a bad answer.

Rumul smiled and turned to Wik. "Well, Singer? Do we have another skymouth shouter?" His voice was softer now. He did not seem angry any longer. *Why?*

Wik continued to echo, lulling the beasts around us to sleep. He nudged me, wanting me to answer for myself. My cheeks grew hot. "I am able to calm them, if that's what you mean."

"Good," said Rumul. His relief was palpable in the dark. "It is what we had hoped. For that, and for your silence."

Wik's trust paired with Rumul's approval should have steadied me, but I realized I was shaking. I did not like the head Singer. Nor these pens. Being trapped too close with both was worse than being trapped in the walls.

Rumul rose to his full height, his bald scalp brushing the rope ceiling of the pens. "You have done well these months, Kirit. You proved correct those Singers who believed in you. You were meant to be a Singer."

"She's still got much to learn, much to practice." Wik was right. I was far from accomplished at the things I was learning.

Still, surrounded by the pens, I was driven to speak plainly.

"I do not want to live out my days down here." *In the dark. With skymouths.*

"The council decides what best serves the city," Wik said. "It is tradition." He said it kindly, but I leaned forward in the enclosure, wanting to argue.

Rumul smiled. "The council has discussed Kirit's case already. Your appeal to allow her down here started that. I've approved the request." A dark look at Wik. "After the fact."

Wik put a hand on my arm. *Slowly, Kirit.*

"She may be allowed to help us in the skies, for the good of the city." Rumul's voice began to soothe my worries.

I would have blue skies, not deep shadows. Tower guards who were glad to see me, not broken Singers. I would be a protector of the city, not a collector of bribes, gossip, and skymouth skins. Relief coursed through me. I could still escape the Spire's bowels.

I opened my mouth to speak, but Wik's hand tightened on my arm.

"In time," he said again. "She's not ready."

Rumul ignored him and faced me. "Sellis tells me you are a strong Gyre fighter. That you have held her to a draw more than once."

"Yes." Recently, at least, though not always.

Wik yanked at my arm. I jerked it away, annoyed.

Rumul put a hand on my shoulder. The shadows obscured his face, but he tilted his head. He could have been smiling. "It is time, Kirit. You will challenge for your Singer wings. You will rise or fall to meet your fate."

"What?" Wik said, too loudly.

I was as surprised as he.

But in that moment, I saw myself dressed in Singer gray, flying wherever I was needed, day or night. I looked at Wik, the tension of his jaw.

"I disagree," Wik said. He tried to step between Rumul and me, but Rumul blocked him with a hand.

"A challenge has come from the towers. The council has determined that it is Kirit's to defeat." He looked directly at me. "Accept, and you will take the wings of your birthright. A true Singer."

A last test, then. One I could pass. I was stronger and faster than any tower challenger. I had learned to fly the Gyre well and quickly. Still, Wik's alarm made me hesitate. What was Rumul up to, overruling my assigned mentor? I hadn't learned enough. I did not understand these twists and turns of Spire power.

"Kirit," Wik said, louder than he'd spoken since we descended.

I straightened my spine, looked into the shadows of Rumul's face. "I will challenge," I said.

Wik made one last attempt. "Sellis should be the one to meet the tower challenger. She has been training longer."

Rumul silenced him, holding up a single finger. "She and one more novitiate will challenge on the same day."

In the quiet, I spoke again. This time with force behind each word. "I am ready."

Challengers would receive several days to try to learn the Gyre, though no Singer would help them. I could practice, ask Wik and Sellis to help me.

Rumul smiled. "Then you will defend the city from this challenge. Succeed and you will become a Singer." He did not need to say again what would happen if I failed.

Around us, an invisible weight shifted and rustled, waking.

Rumul took my arm and led me from the pens with Wik following.

As we emerged in the windbeaters' tier, Rumul spoke again. "You will defend the city against your challenger today, Kirit Spire. Prepare yourself."

19

NADIR

High on the council tier, as the sun brightened the Spire, Singers dressed me in a white robe. They tightened my wingstraps and whispered encouragements. They poured me chicory.

I had been allowed several hours' rest. It had not been nearly enough.

"Be fast," said the older, brass-haired woman. Viridi's sister. "Don't forget to look behind you. Above and below too."

I wished I had my father's lenses, with their reflective mirror. I couldn't find them in the morning when I'd rushed back to my alcove, and couldn't remember where I'd seen them last.

When they finished preparing me, Wik bent low and whispered in my ear, "Be careful."

I turned, eyebrows raised. He doubted me still?

"This challenge comes sudden. That is not tradition. You should have much more training. And days to practice. Choose the weapon you know the best. Be careful." He stepped away. Only for a moment did I feel his hand on mine, when he pulled it from me.

"The challenger has chosen the bow as his weapon," said a young woman at my side. Her brown eyes were hemmed with silver tattoos against her olive skin.

She cleared her throat, pulling my focus to the workbench glittering with sharp edges. Glass knives with bone hilts. Bone blades. Spears. Hooks.

I pointed, making my decision.

The young woman had sun chancres across her dark face. She did not smile as she handed me my weapons of choice: knives. The worn bone hilts had comfortable grips wrapped in sticky raw spidersilk. The blades were new: each a glass tooth so sharp it nearly hummed.

Rumul watched from the edge of the council's balcony, Wik beside him. Sellis was nowhere to be seen.

Moc pulled on my sleeve, suddenly beside me. "The wind-beaters will help you. Look for strong gusts in the Gyre."

I looked down at him while the Singer strapped the triple sheath to my arm. "What did you give them?"

He looked worried. "You need help, Kirit. You're still learn-ing. I had to give them your lenses. You haven't been using them much."

"My lenses! Moc—"

But the Singer securing my robes at the ankles hushed me. "The challenged should reflect in silence. It is tradition."

She finished binding my robes, and I walked quickly to Rumul and Wik. I let my wings unfurl, shimmering in the daylight. My footsling dragged behind me, making a skitter-ing sound on the tier floor. Other Singers gave me a wide berth.

Rumul held out a hand towards me, then gestured to the Gyre.

"Your birthright, Kirit. You've proven that."

Rumul's words shredded the doubt Wik's worries had laid down. I could do this.

Below us, a white-robed challenger waited. I couldn't see them on the downtower balconies, but I knew that they must be close, if not already in the Gyre.

"The challenger has demanded answers we cannot give. They have threatened to rouse the towers against the Spire.

Worse"—Rumul paused and stared at me—"they've broken Laws in the past. You will stop them, for the city's sake."

Behind us, Singers stood together, a wall of gray. "You must not fail."

Far below, the windbeaters readied their giant wings, their rot gas. The vents opened, and the Gyre gust swirled up until it reached me. I leapt into the maelstrom.

∖ ∖ ∖

Singers watched from the galleries as I swept around the Gyre, seeking my prey. The challenger who had come so far and dared too much. The one who did not understand what Singers were willing to sacrifice.

I locked my wings in position and took a knife from its sheath on my arm. The wind kept pace with every move I made, lifting me as I circled. The galleries rustled with whispers as I glimpsed a flash of white from the corner of my eye. The challenger, behind me. They must have clung to the wall below the council balcony until I leapt, then followed me out.

Sneaky. Just as some claimed the Lawsbreaker would be. Just like the Lawsbreaker I had been. I could do a service for the Singers, ending this danger to the city. Prove myself. As soon as I got the challenger off my tail.

An arrow arced wide past me, then clattered against the Gyre wall. Their aim was off. The enclosed space and strange winds gave me an advantage. Still, I swallowed hard and tightened my grip. *Hurry, Kirit.*

The windbeaters' drums quickened, and I heard the wind whistle through the galleries. There was a drop coming.

Another arrow seared far too close, the fletching scraping my ear. The bone point missed its mark, but I was windbit already from the Gyre's howl. The brush of the weapon stung my skin.

By arching my back, I angled my wingtips and slowed my

glide. The challenger hurtled over me, into my wind shadow. I angled away as the challenger dropped like garbage, spinning out of control.

As they fought to find a stronger gust, I moved in above. Looked for the best place to slash the challenger's wings. To end this quickly. To succeed and gain my birthright.

I raised the knife. It glittered from the sun and spun as it split the air.

The challenger turned fast. Shadow and wing, strong arms bent hard to the elbow hooks. Fingers wrapped tight around a bow.

We nearly collided.

Dark curls. Angry eyes.

I spun away at the last minute. Knowing the Gyre helped keep me from dropping us both into the pits.

But it was far too late. I'd seen his face. Knew the shape of it from just one glance.

Black hair; those eyes. His earnest look turned gaunt and scarred.

Nat lived.

He had challenged the Singers? He'd threatened the city?

I searched for a gust to take me higher so I could think. *Not him. Not this.* I found none. The windbeaters stirred the gusts to drive us together again.

Wing against shadow. Arrow against knife. Untried Singer against her challenger. Me to my best friend. Kirit to Nat.

My fight dissolved, crippled by relief at seeing Nat alive. But he, righted now, and flying fast, nocked another arrow.

Perhaps he hadn't realized who he fought. He wouldn't shoot, would he?

I banked fast, trying to reach him. Sheathed my knife. The galleries groaned in protest.

Nat's wings dipped and wobbled. He didn't know how to fly

the Gyre. He was tiring fast as well. But he held his bow horizontal. Drew back the arrow. He looked up to aim as we circled.

When his eyes met mine, his hand wavered. I saw his mouth
start to form my name. Then he clamped his lips shut. His fingers tightened on the bow.

Ducking my head and bending my knees slightly, I dropped
fast. The arrow hummed past me, disappearing into the Gyre's
shadows.

I took hold of the wing grips and twisted into a sharp turn.
The windbeaters saw my maneuver and stirred up gusts to add
more force. I rocketed past Nat and circled above him again,
locking my wings in fighting position.

My fingers brushed the next knife hilt. How could I even
consider it? Elna would have two fallen men.

One of those men was currently shooting at me. Trying to
kill me to win a challenge.

The galleries erupted with stamping feet to match the windbeaters' drums.

What did I want? To be a Singer, I had to defeat him. To be
Kirit, I could not.

I took a deep breath and swerved to avoid him. Shouted as
loud as I could over the roar of the Gyre.

"Nat! What are you doing?"

He drew another arrow from his sleeve quiver.

"I thought you were dead!" I could not stop myself.

"You might as well be," he answered. "A Singer!" The way he
said it warped across the wind. To me, the word sounded more
like "murderer."

He found a fast-moving gust and tried to rise above me.

I ducked beneath him and cut off his wind. When he wobbled and started to fall, I dodged out of the way. One last chance.
We flew side by side for a moment, my right wing grazing the
gallery wall.

"You don't have to do this. I have so much to tell you." If I could get him to drop his weapon and concede the challenge, then perhaps everything would be all right. The Singers would punish him, but he might live.

Though they would certainly punish me.

"I know enough. Your Singers lie, Kirit. They killed Naton for their lies!" He started to pull away, then leaned towards me instead, trying to drive me into the galleries and crush me.

"Your father stole secrets! He broke Laws!" I angled my wing-tip until it slipped beneath his. White silk shuddering, battens shrieking. I held him there, then rolled hard, flipping his wing up in the process.

He tottered, dropping the arrow. I flew away straight.

"Maybe some Laws need breaking," he shouted after me, righting himself. "What secrets did my father die for?" He pulled another arrow from his quiver. He only had a few left.

The Singers in the tiers around us rose to their feet, angrily gesturing. On my next turn, I saw Rumul far above, looking down. His face still as bone. The realization hit me. He'd planned this.

He wanted to test me, to see if I was a true Singer. As my father had been tested.

I wove and dipped so that Nat could not aim. My throat ached from the exertion of talking while flying the Gyre.

The windbeaters accelerated their beats. Somewhere below, my father was among them. Civik, who betrayed Naton. The gusts grew more fierce than I'd ever experienced in the Gyre. The wind yanked at my hair, tearing it free. Nat's black curls formed a tangled nimbus around his head.

They'd promised him answers if he won. What could I promise? A quick death, without falling forever. Or I could lose. I could banish myself to the Spire's depths by conceding. They would keep me alive, but I'd never see sky again.

If Nat won, they had to answer his questions, but he did not know the right questions to ask. I did. If he conceded, perhaps then I could ask more questions. Change things.

We flew opposing courses now, sweeping past each other in tighter spirals. He looked for advantage. I sought a way out.

My first friend. My best friend. Why are you doing this? My initial relief at seeing him alive had become anger.

"You don't know the truth, Nat! You have to give this up."

"No." The word was a sob. "You can't win. Singers can't win."

I am not a Singer, yet. But I cannot lose.

He whirled around, furious again. "I thought you were dead! But you're not! You're strong—we nearly starved these months, with the Laws they gave me. Where are yours?" He was crazed, yelling. I saw the chips hanging heavy on his wrists. His arms were pale past the wingstraps. His hands gripped the bow hard. He was tiring, too weak. But desperate. I didn't have much time.

What could I do to shock him, make him concede? I could tell him the truth. I could sing it.

I cast my voice to carry on the drafts. I sang The Rise to Nat. The real Rise.

> *The city rises on Singers' wings, remembering all,*
> *   bearing all,*
> *Rises to sun and wind on graywing, protecting,*
> *   remembering.*
> *Never looking down. Tower war is no more.*

For a moment, the galleries fell silent. Then a shout of outrage broke through the windbeaters' drums, the swirl of wind. Rumul's voice. "Stop this!"

I continued to sing. Hoped Nat could hear me. Would listen.

A voice on a nearby tier joined me. Then another.

Always rising, never failing. The city forever.
Rising together. Rising as one.

Nat's eyes grew wide as the words filled the Gyre and he
heard the difference from what he'd always known as unassail-
able fact. *This is why there are Singers, Nat. To protect tower
from tower.*

I didn't stop singing until he shot at me again, wildly, his last
arrow nicking my wing.

"Stop this! Kill me already," he screamed. He threw the bow.
It spun in the air, hit the wall, and plummeted into the Gyre. I
heard a cheer from the galleries.

Nat's straps bit white against his shoulders where his robes
had slipped. His face flushed deep red. Buoyed by the song, I
circled in long arcs, looking for a way to knock him into the nets
above the pens, to cut his wings open. To win without killing
him. In the galleries, Singers leaned forward to see better. The
fight had gone too slow for the windbeaters.

I smelled the rot gas before I saw the balls of flame. Heard
them rise last of all. With a whoosh, one hand-sized ball flew
up the tower, then another.

"Monsters," Nat shouted, as a gout flew close to his face and
rose out the top of the Spire. I smelled singed hair.

I could push him right into a rot gas ball and his wings would
burn, but Nat would fall, alive.

I tried not to think about how Rumul would judge me for
sparing Nat. I doubted it would be well.

I twisted in the jumbled wind. "I'm not trying to kill you,
Nat!"

"You'll let me go, then send a skymouth to kill me," he yelled.
"Tobiat warned me about Singers!"

"No! Tobiat is damaged! He's . . ." I spun lower, losing altitude, trying to think. Nat followed me down, battling the gust patterns, and something suddenly made sense. "Tobiat was a windbeater."

"What does that mean?"

"He knew Naton. He watched Naton work in the Spire! He's the traitor."

"Shut up, Kirit!" Nat dove for me, hands outstretched, trying to grapple my wings and drag us both down. We plummeted past gallery walls carved with Singers falling, wound round with flames.

We were well down in the Gyre now, too close to the novices and windbeaters throwing flaming rot gas. I heard Moc shout for me.

I fought my way to an updraft, hoping Nat would follow me, that he was strong enough to follow me.

He did. Barely. His pale wings filled with wind.

"I will tell you what I know," I said. "But you must give up then, you must concede. Promise?"

He whistled. Our long-ago flight signal. Agreement.

I was about to break the Spire's rules, but perhaps it would work. Nat would be left alive. I pointed down. Spoke fast. "Your father built pens for the Spire, Nat. That's what the chips mapped. He built pens that would hold—"

I never got to finish my sentence. Two windbeaters began a new pattern. The Gyre's winds spun me round and knocked me into Nat. My knife dragged across his wing.

Over the roar of the wind, the galleries screamed. And then the wind pulled us apart. I heard a gate open and braced myself for more wind. The windbeaters angled their wings anew, and I was borne up on a massive gust.

A separate gust sucked Nat towards the open gate.

I reached for him, tried to hook his wings, but my fingers could not span the widening gap.

He spun limp, his wings folding as he lost control and was flung into the wide-open sky.

But my wings filled. I was lifted by an opposing current. I'd won. Or the windbeaters had.

The challenger was defeated.

The galleries began to sing. Tradition. A second time through The Rise, this time to welcome a new Singer. Their song, which until that moment had been my song too, lifted higher, and the wind swept me up. I was truly theirs now.

I was a killer. I knew no greater pain.

᠙   ᠙   ᠙

"Come up, Kirit Spire!" Rumul shouted from the balcony.

Wik had to reach out with a hook and pull me onto the council tier. He let me lean against him while the council argued in a corner. Had I succeeded? The battle had been won, but by whom? And the secrets I had shared. The traditions I had shattered.

To my wind-deafened ears, their debate was just more noise. Then they parted, walked towards me, the full council following Rumul's lead.

"Welcome, Singer," he said.

The caustic sting barely registered as Rumul marked my right cheek with a new symbol for winning the challenge: a knife. Honoring my murderous deed. I let it burn, unflinching. I heard Nat's scream again, an echo inside my head as he disappeared.

Now I was a Singer, marked with the death of my challenger.

Now I was Spire, locked within its walls no matter where I flew.

PART THREE

WHAT IS LOST

20

FALL

I released my wing grips and let my arms hang at my sides. My feet touched the bone floor of the balcony, and I wavered at the edge until Wik pulled me by the robe, farther into the tier.

A visibly pregnant Singer brought me water in a brass cup. Cold in my hand and against my lips. I could not swallow it without great effort. The Singer took the cup back and put a bowl in my hands.

"Eat," she said, her brown eyes trying to look deep into mine. "The Gyre's exhausting. You'll feel better soon."

I stared at the bowl. Stone fruit in honey. The sweet smell made my stomach growl, but my fingers gripped the bowl's rim and did not reach for the fruit.

A gray-haired Singer patted my shoulder and handed me a clean gray robe. Another brought a sack of herbs and salve for my scratches and cuts.

Wik removed my novice wings, negotiating the straps and harness over my deadweight arms. I stared at his cheeks, his markings. He'd flown the Gyre. Faced a challenger. Many challengers. How did he go on after?

I didn't ask, and he didn't meet my eyes.

Behind the Singers tending and congratulating me, a low bone table held more of the stone fruit and two additional brass cups. Yes, I remembered. Three of us would fly today.

Even now, Sellis looked over the council balcony, waiting to fly. Vess, a novitiate an Allmoons older than Sellis, paced in the passageway between the tier's galleries and large alcoves. We were on the newest council tier. The highest. The outcroppings of bone here were lightly carved, with areas marked for new carving by novitiates.

The noise from the galleries shifted from a discussion's rumble to anticipatory hush. Sellis waited to be called forward, standing on intertwined symbols carved in the floor: *sacrifice* and *duty.*

Rumul stood beside her, right hand light on her shoulder. He looked my way and gestured to a fourth Singer elder, then turned his attention back to his acolyte.

After Allmoons, Rumul had given me a chance to change my life. He'd told me the past Ezarit had kept hidden. He'd put a burden on me: become a Singer or face the consequences of attacking the Spire.

The Singer sent over by Rumul lifted my wrist, examining my Lawsbreaks. Trespass, Bethalial, Treason. Heavy markers, bound with silk cord. Then she took her bone knife and cut through the skein. The markers fell into her palm.

With my challenge won, I'd proven myself. My burden—my Lawsbreaks—gone.

I'd accepted that bargain. I'd flown the Gyre. My friend had fallen at my hand.

Who was I now? Kirit Densira would have demanded to know how Nat's loss served the city. Kirit Spire could not find the words to ask. Sacrifice. Duty. Tradition. I clenched my teeth. If I'd let sound escape my mouth, it would have been a scream. At the Singers. At myself.

Wik took the still-full bowl from my hands and cleared his throat. "It is not always this hard, Kirit. But if it were easy, Singers would be no better than monsters. Or the worst of the city's Lawsbreakers."

I looked him full in the eyes and opened my mouth, but no sound would come out. I choked on Nat's name.

The gallery cheered as Sellis leapt from the council balcony to defend the city and defeat her challenger.

I looked over the balcony's edge and watched her dive like a silent predator towards her quarry. The challenger circled the far wall of the Gyre.

Sellis drew her first knife. I could watch no more. I turned away.

A novice appeared on the ladder to the tier, carrying a long parcel. The gray silk wrapping glowed in the late sunlight. The knots of the package fell away at a touch to reveal a pair of Singer wings. Mine. No more borrowed novice wings. I did not reach for them. The novice looked at me, curious.

"Kirit?" Lurai's voice. I hadn't recognized him. He was once tower too, though he could not remember. I took the wings and vowed to remember Densira. My family.

"You did it," Moc whispered, appearing by my side. He smelled of flame and rot gas.

Moc. Briber of windbeaters. Stirrer of disagreements that endangered all he loved.

Impervious to my despair, he laughed. "I knew you could."

Of course I could. I'd hunted down my life as Kirit Densira, killed it right off, and had become this person. For what? For a pair of new wings and a gray robe.

I shook my head. No. For the good of the city too.

The tiers roared with satisfaction.

Lurai looked over the edge. "She did that perfectly. Fast. Without breaking silence." A quick glance at me. "Sorry. You also did well."

"Come up, Sellis Spire." Rumul's voice boomed in the Gyre's slowing winds.

Sellis's fight had finished quickly. Flawlessly.

She rose now on a draft, her hair wild across her forehead. Her eyes glittered from the fight. Her left hand still gripped a bone knife wet with blood.

She soared above the balcony and then landed by curling her wings just so. With a shrug, she furled the novice wings and stepped out of them. She took the robe from Rumul's hands and smiled at him as she put it on over her fighting shift.

She turned her head to me, then looked down over the drop. "We did it."

I licked my dry lips. Rasped, "Who did you kill?"

She paused. "I don't know." Turned to the table of food and drink before I could ask if she knew what the challenge had been.

I didn't know what Nat's challenge had been. I would never know.

Lurai held out another pair of Singer wings to Sellis, drawing her back towards us. She smiled brighter still and took them, brushing her fingers across the silk. She touched my wings next.

"We are like sisters now," she said.

I could not find the words to respond. She waited a beat, then looked away, towards Rumul.

He waved her to approach the council members. When she reached them, he marked her hand as he had marked mine.

Novices brought more bowls to the table, this time containing apples and stone fruit.

"Pull yourself together," Wik whispered, giving my arm a shake. "Come on."

I hung back long enough that Sellis left the celebratory group.

"You aren't having second thoughts now?" she asked. "You took your time, and you broke silence abominably, but you wiped your challenger out well at the end. Made me proud."

I shook my head. *Pull yourself together.* Hid my bitterness behind a smile. If Rumul learned that I regretted my choice, I would be at risk again. *Sacrifice. Duty.* No second thoughts. My mind worked through the challenge again, slowly. The argument with Nat. It must have looked so different from above. Nat had been a strong fighter, and he got behind me. No one had yet mentioned what I said to him when we were far down the tiers, just before . . . I hoped the winds were such that they hadn't heard my betrayal.

"You will feel better after tonight," Sellis said, drawing me towards the assembled group. "When the city's mysteries are opened to us."

More mysteries. I smiled at her. She smiled back. Genuinely happy.

"You are no longer tower, Kirit," Sellis said, embracing me. "You will find support in Singer traditions now."

I hugged her back, but I was not comforted. I felt a long hollow drop where my heart should have been. I felt the voices of my mother and Elna crying out. Numb, I stepped forward to join the group on the balcony, looking over the edge.

The third challenge came to a draw. The council grumbled. The pregnant Singer said, "Both fighters fallen, both sets of wings broken. That is bad luck."

Wik asked, "The novice, Vess, what to do with him?"

The group spoke in low tones. My Singer-sharpened ears picked up their words.

"Let him beat the winds," said one gray-haired Singer.

"Return his wings to his tower," said a council member.

A murmur of agreement. Wik cleared his throat. "Who will take the challengers' wings to their towers?"

Rumul looked at the assembled Singers, young and old, arrayed around the balcony. His eyes lit on a man, already standing to accept the task. The third Singer from my quadrant's wingtest.

I spoke first. "I will take the wings back to Densira."

The gray-cloaked Singers around Rumul murmured and raised eyebrows. Sellis whispered, "That is not done."

"I will do it," I said firmly. To make amends. To try to explain.

"You can barely sing in tune," Sellis whispered. "A few more months of practice." Her smile had faded.

But Rumul looked long at me until I met his eyes. I did not blink.

"The families can never know whom their challengers faced," he said, his voice hinting at permission.

"I can stay silent," I said. I agreed to not say anything beyond the ritual phrases.

I could not believe they might let me go.

"You must take Sellis with you," Rumul added. "You will return all of the wings and bless the new bridge as well. Two days after initiation."

I nodded, happy to have his blessing before anyone could argue. Turning, I caught Wik looking at me, amused. Sellis's face contorted in frustration.

"Do you know what you ask?" she said. "You are breaking tradition still, Kirit." She paused, thinking of the task I had set for us. "We will have to sing for them. We might do it wrong. You *will* do it wrong. And the bridge? We are new Singers. How could you drag me into tower duties when we should be celebrating?"

I thought on it. When I spoke, my voice was loud enough for the room to hear. "Who better to sing for them?" Several Singers turned to watch me. "We know the words. We know the blessings. We know their last moments. We should sing."

Rumul raised his brass cup. "Exactly. A fine Singer you make, Kirit."

Now that the opportunity had presented itself, I resolved to connect with the towers as much as I could. Kirit Spire would do her duty for the city. The other Kirit would remember the towers and would speak for them when she was able.

Sellis continued to look at me warily. "You upset things, Kirit." Then she swept away, as angry as she'd been when I first arrived. So much for sisterhood.

❧   ❧   ❧

Within moments of Rumul's decision, the slow drumbeat from below ceased. The windbeaters shut the vents, and the Gyre wind reversed. Slower this time.

When the winds had settled, singing from the lowest tiers reached my sensitive ears. I heard students' young voices and the voices of the oldest Singers and teachers, all wafting up the everyday winds of the Spire.

Viridi approached our group, Sellis trailing behind. She spotted Moc jumping my shadow in the evening light of the Spire and shooed him away.

"You will come with me to meet the city, Sellis and Kirit Spire." She took our hands in each of hers and drew us into one of the tier's smaller alcoves, still in sight of the council balcony. "I keep the Spire's records and maintain its history."

Behind us, Rumul and several council Singers drew close in conversation. The rest of the tier cleared out as Singers returned to their duties.

I found I could make out Rumul's low rumble if I concentrated. Viridi set candles and old carvings in a pattern on the floor. Sellis watched her, rapt. My eyes wandered on the carvings, all old city maps and numbers, while my ears traced the pattern of debate behind me. I heard bone chips click as they were passed among the council members.

"Five towers are crowded to capacity in the southwest, and three in the north cannot be managed much longer. The numbers are to hand," one voice murmured. A long silence followed.

Another asked, "Not enough time for new tier growth?"

"It is too soon," agreed Rumul.

"What about recruiting?" the first man asked. "We need novices in the Spire."

Rumul muttered, "Too late for that. The growth is in the older groups."

More muttering. Terrin's name came up. Then the group walked away from where we sat, and their conversation faded.

Sellis elbowed me.

A response was required. Something to do with the tablets laid before me.

"Kirit, I ask you again, do you know what you see before you?"

I was able to answer honestly that I did not know all of what I saw. Viridi pointed again to the bone panels. "This is our history. The few survivors of the clouds. The loss of so much. And new knowledge." Her fingers touched a panel showing a Singer scouring a tower-top to make it grow.

"Knowing how the city grows is a great Singer mystery. Protecting it from harm, our greatest challenge." She put down the bone chips and pulled aside a silk hanging to reveal a small discoloration in the Spire's wall.

I looked closely. The outer layer of bone had been cut away from the wall. It revealed a deep yellow marrow that seemed to throb.

"You cannot do this on a tower, because the outer layer of the tower's core is much thicker than our wall," she explained. "Even on the Spire's lower levels, the walls are too thick to reach the city's heart any longer. Here, though, we can show new Singers what they fight to preserve."

The marrow was darker than the lymph that sometimes oozed from new grown bone. Viridi gestured us close. The air smelled richer here, a little like my father's lenses.

Viridi took Sellis's hand and held it above the marrow. "Swear, Sellis Spire, that you will guard the city before all else, even yourself."

Sellis did not hesitate. "I so swear." She closed her eyes and held her hand cupped in her other hand.

The voices returned behind us. I twisted my head slowly, looking for Rumul's group. I wondered what they were planning. I could not see them, so I turned my attention back to Viridi and Sellis. Viridi gestured for my hand.

Sellis glared at me from beneath her eyelids as Viridi pulled me closer and held my hand before the city. I startled at the sensation: heat pulsed from the bonecut. The metal smell was stronger.

"Swear, Kirit Spire, that you will guard the city before all else, even yourself."

I thought of the oaths I'd already sworn, the promises I'd made so far in order to keep living. *Pull yourself together.* I considered what I'd learned in the Spire. That there was good here. And sacrifice. Important work, not all of it pleasant. I thought of the city's beauty, as only Singers know it. I pictured myself flying in Singer gray, helping maintain city order and peace. Helping the city. I wanted that. Still. Always.

I imagined flying the Gyre again and standing watch at Conclave, or, worse, escorting a cloudbound Lawsbreaker to his or her release. My hand froze in Viridi's grip.

"Kirit!" Sellis said, teeth clenched. "Singers do not hesitate."

We did not, it was true. "I so swear," I said, emphasizing each word.

Finally, Viridi rose and bowed as Rumul and Wik joined us. She made no mention of my hesitation.

Sellis and I climbed to our feet. She stood first before Rumul so he could make the next mark: the oath tattoo on her left cheek. She looked unflinching into his eyes and waited for him to mark her Singer for all the towers to see. Tradition. We saw the evidence all around us. But Rumul held nothing in his hands. No ink. No brush.

"I advise you to sleep well," he said. "You will be Nightwings. You have one final rite of initiation."

Initiation.

At mention of it, Wik turned away, but not before I could see his grim smile.

We bowed to the Singers. Then we lifted our wrapped wings and carried them with us back to our alcoves.

On the way, Sellis tucked her wings under one arm and grabbed the tender spot on my elbow with fingers shaped like pincers. "I thought you were true, Kirit."

I stared at her.

By my hand, my friend fell this day.

She screwed up her face and stepped forward, until her nose was less than a hand span from my own. "This day was supposed to be perfect, my birthright. I was pleased to share it with you." Her words came from deep in her throat, thick and angry. "But you break traditions. You sat with the city bared before you, your greatest charge, and you barely listened. You had no respect."

"I was listening."

"And trying to overhear the council's discussion too. You may have fooled Rumul and the others. You once fooled me. And now you think you are free to do as you like, but I will watch you, Kirit, every move. Until you reveal yourself a traitor again."

She pushed me towards the ladders, gave me time to think while I descended. She followed me all the way to my tier, her eyes boring into the back of my neck. When I could tolerate it no longer, I turned on my heel and faced her.

"You saw what I did. That challenger was my oldest friend," I said. "How could I hope to prove my loyalty beyond that?"

Her smile stretched thinner and wider as she thought over my words. "How indeed, if your loyalty is worth so little in the first place? You could not even keep silent."

Her words were so loud that it felt as if the very Spire stopped and listened.

In the sudden quiet, she bowed her head. "I love the city, Kirit. And the Spire. All true Singers do. We respect it. I will sing with you tomorrow and honor the dead. But I will be watching too."

I pulled my robes tighter around me. She turned to climb the ladder back to her tier, to await the next part of the ceremony.

"And your voice is still hideous," she whispered over her shoulder as she climbed.

❧ ❧ ❧

The sleeping alcove was heavy with the city's heat. In my mind, Nat fell again, and I could not reach him; then I did reach him; I was sucked through the vent with him; a skymouth opened like a red flower in the air and pulled us towards its maw; Wik shook his head at my stubbornness; Sellis glared at me for lying to her, for letting her think I was something I was not. Not her sister. Not a real Singer. Thoughts swirled and fought, keeping my battle-weary body awake. Drenching me with sweat.

Beyond my alcove, the Spire whispered to me until I could no longer fight to keep my eyes open.

In the midst of my troubled sleep, a dark-cloaked Singer came for me. The Singer bundled my quilts, binding my arms and legs, then leapt into the Gyre at a run, with me in her arms.

My scream was stifled by a rough silk stuffed in my mouth. My face was crushed to the chest of the Singer who held me. We fell, the rush of air battering against us both. She fell too fast to have her wings extended.

At the last moment, she opened her wings and we jerked from the fall, into a slow, downward glide.

I smelled the foul scent of skymouth. I could barely keep from retching.

My bearer whispered to me. Her voice was soft. Her heartbeat didn't break its careful rhythm. She hummed to the pen's occupants and opened a small gate. I could hear what was around us, though I could not see it. Soft tentacles brushed my feet. We were above the pens.

"A Nightwing Singer is born twice," my bearer whispered. "Your past will never return. Only the Singer will return. Make no sounds, no movements." The skymouths stirred at her whispers, and she began her hum again.

She tied me to a bone hook with thick, woven straps. Lowered me into the pen. Left me dangling among the skymouths.

I heard another voice saying the same words and knew that Sellis hung here with me.

My mouth was still crammed with silk, so I could not scream. A tentacle brushed my arm. Something soft bumped me from behind.

I tried pushing the fabric with my tongue, but that made me gag. The skymouths in the pen reached out and touched my arms with their invisible limbs.

A thrashing sound nearby drew their attention.

Sellis.

She could send them into a frenzy. She could kill us both.

I could not scream, or shout, but I thought I could hum through my nose. I closed my eyes and tilted my head back and managed a muffled, nasal, hum.

The creatures slowed. I kept it up, though I struggled to breathe. After a moment, I heard Sellis join her hum to mine.

As the sound we made echoed in the small space of the pen, mouths closed with slick sounds. Shapes of soft bodies smaller than my wings became apparent with my echoes. I stifled a laugh. The Singers had hung us in a nursery pen. I swung on my hook as the smaller skymouths nudged at me like baby birds. Their curious arms bumped and touched and turned me about.

They made not one sound.

Time came to a stop. I had nothing beyond now; I had been nothing before now.

Then I heard a skymouth call from above. I knew those tones. Wik's voice. The tentacles retreated. The young skymouths sank to the far reaches of the pens, pressing against one another.

The gate at the top of the pen opened, and Sellis and I, still on our hooks, were hoisted uptower.

Hands touched my back and sides; a Singer lifted me off the hook, took the cloth from my mouth. I could not stop shaking. My blanket bindings surrounded me, kept me from flying apart.

I heard Sellis gag, then start to cry.

The dark-cloaked Singer took my face in one hand and held me still. She kissed my cheeks.

"Welcome, Singer," she said. Viridi's voice. Her cloak slipped, and I saw the silver streak in her hair, all tied back in braids. She did not release my face. "You bring new ways of thinking to our service. I value this."

With her free hand, Viridi raised a brush and drew a circle on my cheekbone. I winced as the ink burned, and tried not to wriggle away; Viridi held my face tightly.

She gave me a drink in a brass cup, and I took it without question. Muzz. It would let me sleep again.

In the dark, I heard Rumul's whispers as he marked Sellis and welcomed her too. I heard what sounded like a kiss in the dark.

My vision faded.

When I woke in the morning, I was back in my alcove, on

my sleeping mat. I rubbed my hair clean with ash and tied my gray robes as I'd seen Wik do. I passed by Sellis's empty room on the way to the Singer's dining alcove. Morning shadows had grown short on the Spire's walls.

The dining alcove was empty, save for Sellis. Her fresh tattoo looked red around its silver edges: a spiral in a circle, like the marks on our hands. I wondered what mine looked like.

I opened my dry mouth to speak, but Sellis beat me to it.

"Do you remember?" Her voice was kinder than it had been the night before. After the first ritual, before the initiation. Perhaps we were sisters again. That was safer for me, certainly. I doubted the peace would last past my next mistake, my next disruption of what Sellis thought her future would be like. But now I knew Viridi valued my presence. Perhaps Sellis would soften in time. Perhaps starting now.

I waited her out, cautious. I remembered too much. She waited too. She was better at it than I.

"The pens?"

Her voice a mix of fear and wonder, she said, "They brought a skymouth into the Spire. For us."

My face must have given me away. She hadn't seen anything last night. She'd been too frightened.

"You've known? How could you know?" She thought for a moment. "You've been sneaking around the Spire. Going where you were forbidden."

"I haven't." This was partially true.

A few days ago, I might have told her about meeting my father, about the windbeaters and the vents below. We would have talked about what had happened the night before. I might have broken the silence and told her more. Now we stared at each other in silence. Not truly sisters after all.

"Why would Rumul not tell you?" I asked, finally.

She flinched. Looking down, she spooned grain mash into

her mouth and chewed deliberately. My stomach growled. She swallowed. "I have decided not to go with you to return the wings. Rumul can send someone else besides us."

This, after everything. After what we'd both been through. After what I'd done to help her survive last night. She would have panicked until they pulled her up.

"You dare, Sellis? When you have been sneaking behind the council's back with Rumul for how long? What would Viridi think? Wik? The others?"

Her cheeks darkened. A lucky guess, now confirmed. "You wouldn't dare."

"Nor you. I am as dedicated to the city"—I put a heavy emphasis on the last word—"as you are. We will return those wings to the tower. Honor and tradition."

Now we each held the other's secrets. It was a wary peace.

Wik found us in the dining alcove, chewing in silence. When we had finished, we climbed to the Spire's roof and knelt before the council.

Viridi took my hands in hers. She smiled, encouraging. Proud.

I sang the words, the ones that had echoed up the Spire each morning from the first day I was freed from the walls. "*I give myself to the city, to its rise, to ensure against its fall.*"

My voice's burr had been accented by my training. My hearing had grown sharper too. The combination was unsettling. I heard the tone I was supposed to sing, the one every Singer knew. I heard it underscored and slightly soured by a second tone, as if I spoke with more than one voice. That undertone was what the singers wanted. My skymouth voice. They would tolerate a voice that broke Silences, a voice that challenged and would not quiet, if it meant they would get what was needed. When I finished singing, Viridi smiled, then moved to stand before Sellis.

She sang clear and proud, her eyes on Rumul.

Then we stood, turning to face the council. We rehearsed once with them the song for those lost in defense of the city. I sang it true this time.

Singers came forward to check our wings for us. Strong fingers tightened straps. My wings tugged at my shoulders as someone adjusted a batten in its sleeve. We had a long flight ahead.

Rumul faced us. "You will fly southeast to Narath tower and present the second challenger's wings to her relatives. Then to Ginth, to present windbeater Vess's wings. By day's end, you will reach Viit and the new bridge that connects that tower to Densira. You will bless the bridge. You will not linger."

A bridge for Densira. They had rewarded my tower for my sacrifice. I was glad to hear it.

"Once the bridge is blessed, you will cross to Densira," he continued. *To Elna. To Ezarit.*

A council member came forward, carrying Vess's wings, along with those of the Narath challenger. Beneath them lay a spare set of wings, the battens broken beyond repair. The silk torn.

Rumul explained, "Because we cannot return the Densira challenger's wings, you will take these."

So Elna would have a pair of wings that no one could ever use.

The council spoke all around us. "Singer's duty."

Sellis and I repeated the words. I felt them echo in my stomach.

It was time to fly. We lifted our burdens and strapped them to our chests.

Atop the Spire, the sun rose over our brethren. We unfurled our wings and engaged the fingertip grips, then soared for the first time as Singers among the towers, to show the city what we had become in its name.

21

RETURN

Narath tower was the height of the southeast. From our approach, we could see Narath had at least two tiers on its closest neighbors, and its gardens bloomed green and lush. Alerted by kavik messenger, residents had gathered on the top of the tower, many families' worth. Sellis's challenger had been popular.

Though I carried the challenger's wings, I realized that I did not know her name.

"Who was she?" I asked Sellis again as we prepared to land.

"A challenger," Sellis responded in clipped tones. "They will name her."

Unsettled, I stepped from my footsling and cut my glide, dropping to the tower with practiced Singer's grace. Sellis landed beside me at the same time. The Narath residents whispered. Bowed to us, but not too deeply.

The tower's councilman stepped forward. His robes were embroidered at the shoulders with green and purple chevrons.

"Our daughter Dita Narath dared challenge the city," the man said, giving me a name to work with. My breathing eased.

"Dita fought well," I answered. "She has honored your tower by elevating a Singer."

"She would fight well," the councilman said. "She was of Narath."

The crowd murmured again, a soft, pleased sound. They

were not shamed here by Dita's challenge. Within the murmur, my ears caught a sob and someone being hushed.

I passed Dita Narath's wings to the man who had greeted us, and Sellis handed them a silk banner to be dyed for Remembrances.

"Would you sing with us?" the tower councilman asked formally.

We would.

Sellis's voice was thinner than usual, but I carried us both. The voices of the tower flowed around the rough edges of my voice, until we all sang together. The sound was beautiful.

"We will return to sing her honors," I promised. Beside me, Sellis nodded. The tower's gathered crowd stepped back from us. Turned inward to pass the wings to the center, where the sob had come from. We were no longer part of their grief.

Sellis took off first, and I followed. It had felt too easy, that.

When we landed on Ginth, our shoulders ached from the distance. This was how my mother flew. This was how traders moved, from east to west and then up around the gusts of the city.

On Ginth, only one person greeted us. Vess's older brother, by his age and looks. The tower's gardens were spare, and the brother's chest was not broad like the men of Narath. Instead, shoulders rounded, his cheeks sunken, he stood bowed around the emptiness of his stomach. To my knowledge, Vess had never spoken of Ginth.

"I barely remember Vess," he said sadly. "Though we are grateful to the Singers for taking him. Two others starved in our tier that year."

Sellis spoke of her friend without hesitation. "He has a beautiful voice. And has added much to the life of novices in the Spire." She drew a breath. "But he was not strong enough to defend the city. He will continue to serve the Spire, but you will not see him again."

Vess's brother sadly accepted the broken wings. We did not sing with him: Vess was not dead.

"On your wings, Singers," he said. He watched us depart. I ducked my head below my wings to look back at him growing smaller on the tower's roof.

❧ ❧ ❧

By the time we landed on Viit, the sun had crossed the top quadrants of the sky, and my shoulders were numb. Sellis didn't complain, but I winced as I furled my wings. I carried only one extra pair of wings now, strapped to my chest, but the flights had been long.

Viit had prepared a meal of goose meat and apples for us, left out in large bone bowl, but no one waited to greet us on this rooftop. A bridge blessing required that they await us below, and on Densira. We ate in exhausted silence.

Flying the city was so different from what I'd thought it would be. It was lonely and quiet in the sky, with too many thoughts tugging at my attention. And attention was required to stay aloft on the city's drafts and gusts. We'd flown above the city's day-to-day traffic, and I'd watched the colorful wings weave in familiar patterns below, wanting to join them once more.

The bridge blessing was a simple ritual. When we had eaten, Sellis flew across to Densira without a word to me, and I descended to the Viit balcony where the sinew and rope spans had been anchored by one of Viit's Spire-trained artifexes.

Bone hooks and eyes had been carved carefully around this tier and incorporated into the cable system to help distribute the load of the main cables. The cables wrapped the tower's bone core, secured with a complex series of braids and tethers.

Pulleys brought from Wirra allowed the bridge's artifexes to tend it during wind shifts and periodic rebalancing. More support cables ran to tiers above and below.

Near the core, a surprised whisper. "Kirit! You live!" I looked up to find familiar eyes: Ceetcee. She wore the tools of a novice artifex on cords around her neck: bone hooks and cutters, a thick awl for splicing ropes.

She clasped my fingers in hers: the first time a non-Singer had touched me in half a year. I did not want to let go of her chapped hands, though she smelled of dried skymouth sinew and rope.

"Well met, Artifex Viit," I greeted her formally, after a moment. Sellis waited on the other tower. I could not linger, no matter how much I wished to do so.

Ceetcee loosened her grip and stepped back too, then bowed. "Well met, Singer."

Two more Viit artifexes stepped forward and bowed. I saw Beliak peeking around a spine in the tier. Of course. As a ropemaker, he would be here.

"You are welcome, Artifexes," I replied, reminding everyone that the bridges were Singer-gifts to the towers. I added, "And gladly met."

The artifexes showed me their work. It was a great honor to tie a bridge. It was also nerve-racking. If the bridge was tethered wrong, or if Singers and artifexes had miscalculated the balance of the towers, a tower's core could be weakened. Its growth could be slowed.

Every tower resident learned bridge songs as fledges, whether they had a bridge or not. During my Spire training, I'd learned even more. I knew tension and binding songs. I'd seen how long-lived bridges were maintained and supported with new material, until a tower's core became too wide to accommodate the bindings, and then the sinew fell or was cut away. I'd examined remnants and drawings of failed bridges, and those of bridges that had survived almost down to the clouds.

I hoped this bridge between Viit and Densira would last that long.

Singers whose focus was on bridge building and working with artifexes had attended and assisted the work on Viit and Densira. Our blessing was a formality. An honor for any young Singer, yes, and not just because of tradition. The first Singers to cross would test the bridge for all and take on the burden of risk. Our sacrifice for the good of the city.

The skies above the bridge were clear. I wondered if Singers waited beyond the towers, watching. I wondered if they would intervene if a bridge ever failed during a crossing. I suspected they would not. Tradition. Sacrifice.

The ties looked secure. The braiding, careful. The secondary cables taut but not straining.

Ceetcee and her superiors watched me carefully. Confident in their work.

Beneath the ties, the bone core felt cool to my touch. So different than the heartbone. I was supposed to look for discoloration or signs of strain. There were none. The release points that would allow the artifexes to widen the wrapping's girth as the core expanded looked much like my wingstraps, but thicker and heavier. Viit's and Densira's artifexes had a lifetime of bridge tending ahead of them.

When I completed my inspection, Ceetcee helped me remove my wings. Her eyes were wide, but her hands held steady as she placed the silk and battens in my arms. We would hold our wings, showing respect for the work of the artifexes.

Across the span, at Densira, I knew Sellis had gone through the same steps. It was ritual.

"Singers risk everything for the city," I sang, knowing Sellis had done this also. I saw her gray shape appear at the top of her end

of the bridge. We mirrored each other, from across the towers, so that our feet would touch the knotwork and sinew of the bridge at the same time. Tradition.

I felt the towers watching as I began my slow walk down the bridge's curve. The careful pattern of ties and woven fiber kneaded my feet in their soft gray wrappings. I did not use the handrails. My hands were full.

"Be well, Singer," someone—I thought perhaps Beliak—whispered behind me.

The gap between Viit and Densira was wide. The two towers were hung with washing, with blackberry vines on Densira and small apple trees growing in buckets of guano and silage on Viit. When the bridge was opened, Elna would be able to cross almost unassisted, to see friends and take work in Viit, and even to cross from there to Wirra on a lower bridge if she wished. The bridge meant greater freedom for all of Densira, and new connections for Viit, as well.

The span creaked beneath my feet. The sound of new cables. As time passed, it would become more pliant, until the artifexes tightened it. Neither Sellis nor I sang as we crossed the new span. We were supposed to ponder the span and its broader purpose.

The bridges served a second purpose: the connections they made strengthened the towers. One of the Singers' bridge building songs carried a dark reminder of what could happen if those towers did begin to grow apart: they could list, develop cracks, and worse. Bridges were occasionally awarded on the basis of those calculations, often conveniently timed for a novitiate's rise to Singer. It wasn't necessary for all towers to have bridges. After all, Densira had been growing fine without a bridge for a long time. A generation, I now realized. Naton and Ezarit. Their punishment.

A punishment I'd erased with my sacrifice.

Sellis had stopped to examine a series of knots on one of the vertical cables that kept the bridge from flipping or twisting in the wind. I waited for her, unable to move until she did. She took her time, knowing I could not continue to Densira until she let me.

My mind wandered. If traders were able to see some of the patterns of power and connection as they flew the city, had my mother seen where bridges were constructed and known that Densira's lack of one was her punishment? Her tower's reprimand? Would she answer me honestly, if I were ever able to ask her my questions?

At last, Sellis began walking again. We both echoed now, as we descended out of the tower's hearing, searching for weak points in the pattern the bridge cast on the wind, the shadow it threw below it. I heard only the sounds of the towers, strong and true.

When Sellis and I passed in the middle of the bridge, we turned back to the artifexes waiting on Viit and Densira. We sang, pitching our voices, *"This bridge will keep the city strong."*

The artifexes cheered. A distant Ceetcee kissed a distant Beliak in celebration.

The corners of my eyes crinkled painfully close to my new tattoos. Their joining made me happy.

Sellis and I walked backwards for the second half of the crossing, eyes on each other, and on the way the bridge moved beneath the other's feet. Sellis moved achingly slow now. *Densira.* I was so close. The artifexes of Densira had woven this half of the bridge plinth. I wonder who had apprenticed as artifex there, and who had trained them. Naton had been Densira's previous artifex.

Half this bridge may have been Viit's work, but everyone watching our gray forms cross knew the bridge was Densira's honor. Densira's luck. A gift from the Spire.

The sinew creaked again and the base swayed beneath my feet. The pliant spans felt so different from the Spire's hard edges. The careful knotting and studied connections, the expanse of cloud below: the opposite of the Gyre.

Above us, the sky sparkled, blue and simple. The sun hung lower than when we began. Our robes looked lustrous in the light.

Walking was much slower than flying. Especially when one walked with Sellis. She had stopped again, studying a knot intently.

Turning briefly, I saw a child's face looking over the edge of the highest tier with a scope, watching from Densira. Growing up on a tower without a bridge meant many things. Isolation and privation. Risk, as Densira creaked alone in the stronger winds. The child above me would know less hardship and more connection to his neighbors. I envied him already.

For once, the sky between Viit and Densira was clear of flight classes and the brightly colored wings of the young. In a few days, there would be a market here, and the new honor would brighten the city. Children would fly crimson kites from the tiers and the bridge as Allsuns drew near. Nearly a half year had passed since my wingtest.

I'd had a kite, long ago. A bright bird on a string. Flown with my nearest wingmate, whose wings I now bore to his mother.

On the other side of the bridge, Sellis cleared her throat loudly. I'd paused in my walk, remembering, and she could not move until I continued my backwards approach to Densira. She waited on the bridge, bored with her game now. Eager to reach Viit and finish our tasks. My reflection, robed in gray.

My arms tired from holding my wings before me, and I suddenly longed to reach the other side as well, if only to be able to wear my wings again. Against my chest, the pair of wings that replaced Nat's wings pressed and rubbed as I walked.

Families gathered quietly around Densira's bridge tier, waiting to cross the bridge, to shake hands with their friends in Viit. Our passage had made it safe. Only a few more steps.

I could hear already some of the discussions from Densira's upper tiers. I heard Sidra's voice, I thought, saying the size of their tier had been reduced by the bridge ties.

Already frustrated by Sellis's slow passage across the bridge, I was angered by this minor infraction. Complaining while Singers risked their lives.

But no, I heard another voice, this one more like Sidra's, begging for silence. The first voice had sounded older. The younger voice spoke of honor, saying, "Mother, for once, be reasonable." Silence fell again.

When I looked ahead, I saw Dojha, from my flight class, standing with one of my cousins at the end of the bridge. Next to two artifexes. By the tower marks tied in their hair, I suspected they were from the south.

Dojha looked nervous. She reached to greet me with a shaking hand. "You are welcome here, Singer," she said. Sidra's mother's muttering continued in the shadows. They thought I could not hear her.

But I was a Singer now, for better or for worse. I was expected to show my old tower a Singer's power.

"You do not keep silence here. You have no reverence for the city," I said. "I will turn back." The old Kirit Densira shouted at Kirit Spire, who'd just spoken. *How could I turn back? This bridge would help Elna.*

Someone in the crowd gasped. If a Singer turned back, the bridge would be taken down and strung elsewhere.

The sound of a slap echoed through the tier. My hand

stretched as if I had struck the mutterer myself. No more sounds came from the back of the tier.

Sidra emerged from the shadows, her face flushed. I expected her to glare at me, but she smiled instead.

Dojha looked at me. "Do you wish this person given Lawsmarks, Singer?" Her eyes held mine. Afraid. For her bridge. For her friend's family. Now that I had the power to tie weights, how would I distribute it?

How, indeed.

Sellis would already have pulled the markers from her robe. I hesitated. I'd exercised Singer power, and now I had to enforce the consequences. All our lessons said so. Tradition dictated.

I shook my head. "I was shown mercy, once. I entrust the artifex to assign a marker if needed. Densira can teach the noisy one another way."

Dojha's look of concern turned to relief. "We will ensure it."

I made the final step from bridge to tower. Sellis and I put on our wings, on opposite tiers.

Dojha stepped aside to give me room, saying, "You honor us, Singer." So formal.

I remembered her trying to help before the wingtest. I'd thought she and Sidra had been teasing. Perhaps I'd misread. They had concerns of their own. Sidra especially. And now we had all changed so much. The distance between me and my former tower suddenly felt overwhelming.

I fell back on tradition and Singer training, saying only, "Your bridge is sturdy and well built. Please make good use of it. You honor the city and the Spire when you do."

Dojha and my cousin stepped out onto the bridge, and Densira began to celebrate.

I looked around me, at my old tower. Familiar faces looked back with unfamiliar reverence and fear. I did not see Elna. Nor Ezarit.

The bridge ceremony complete, I waited for Sellis to join me for our second duty. The awkward silence stretched out until Sellis landed on the tier.

I tried to clear my throat, find my voice. I could not.

Finally, Sellis said, "We have another duty to discharge, and the light is fading. Where is the mother of the young man who challenged the city?"

My burden pressed at my chest. Wings for Nat. Another silk banner.

Councilman Vant stepped forward to greet us. He bowed so low his furled wingtips nearly touched the ground. I accepted his greeting with a bow of my own, then continued searching for Elna in the waiting crowd.

"She is below, Singer," Vant said, hurrying behind me. "She asks that you bring the wings there."

Sorrow bloomed. I stopped walking. A near silent hiss from Sellis, and I was under control again.

"It is tradition, if the family wishes. We will go down to her," Sellis said to the crowd. She and I secured our wings and bowed to the remaining citizens on the tier.

"On your wings, Singer," said the guard who had once stood watch outside my tier, who had called me Lawsbreaker. He bowed to me now.

Sidra stepped to the ledge and pressed an apple into my hand. She didn't look me in the eye. She wore apprentice Magister robes, blue-gray with a stripe of gray. So much like an acolyte's robes, I was caught by the similarities.

Sidra's respect, and that of the guard, was Singers' due. Sellis didn't blink at it. It was her birthright. It was part of what I'd wanted when I'd agreed to fly the challenge. But there, on my former tower, it felt hollow. I was grateful for the silence I was required to keep, for tradition's sake. But I wondered at all the changes in Densira. In myself. At how open and unprotected the tower seemed to me now. At the strangeness of a center core in a tower, rather than a Gyre and walls.

Sidra bowed to Sellis as well. Macal stood behind Sidra and looked at her proudly. Their hands clasped when she finished her bow. Another new thing. So much change.

Sellis nudged me, then turned away from the crowd. *Do not linger.*

She opened her wings and left the tier's edge, then circled, waiting for me to show her where to go. I looked at my former councilman, my former family and flightmates one last time, then unfurled my wings, stepped from the balcony, and rode a breeze down to Sellis.

\ \ \

The tier we sought was far below the bridge and speckled with the garbage of those above it. There, living quarters were pressed a little closer to the edge by the growing central core than they had been six months ago.

Elna stood at her cookpot, stirring. Did not hear us clatter onto her balcony. The scent of what she cooked was new to me. Something with a heady spice.

Finally, she turned. The light of the setting sun behind me etched her face in stark relief, her wrinkles and jowls. As she navigated towards me, her fingertips brushing the room's spines and furnishings, I realized she could not see me in the glare. The skyblindness had grown much worse. A thin silk tether around her waist kept her from the edge of her balcony. Like a child. She kept one hand on it.

"Elna," I whispered, and caught her hand as she passed near.

"Kirit," she whispered back. Then, "You honor me, Singer." Tears filled her near-sightless eyes.

This and her simple formality broke me nearly in two. I did not honor her. I was begging her forgiveness.

Sellis's whispers grew louder as I held Elna's hand. *Cannot linger. Must return to the Spire before dark.* "Kirit. Tradition," she finally snapped. I let Elna's hand go, gently.

From behind a screen, a voice sounded. "Is she here?" The tone was familiar, but had a sad edge.

Then Ezarit stepped around the screen. My mother, here.

She stared at me. Her eyes held worry, a little fear. I stared back, all my words gone from my mouth. She should be out trading. Not here. This was why Singers clung to tradition. To Laws. Surprises conflicted too much with duty.

Sellis seemed confused. She looked back and forth between the two women, trying to understand my alarm. In the time it took her to form the words "who's this?" Ezarit had rushed forward and wrapped her arms around me, wings and all.

Now I understood: Elna had stayed below not because she couldn't rise but because of my mother, because my mother wished to see me. I stiffened, but Ezarit did not let go.

"I am so sorry," she whispered.

"Kirit," Sellis finally managed.

I ignored Sellis. My arms came up from my sides on their own, and my palms brushed Ezarit's shoulder blades. I thought of the scar that ran across her collarbone. From her fight with Civik.

"I met him," I said into her ear. "You let him live." *I couldn't follow your example.* My shoulders jerked with a single sob. I locked my arms against it.

She whispered, so quietly I could barely hear, "I should have told you everything. I thought I was protecting you."

"Tradition!" Sellis pulled hard on my wingstrap. "You will bring shame on us. Rumul will have you enclosed when he hears you cannot keep silent. Cannot act properly."

I didn't care. I let Sellis yank me away from the embrace, but I took my mother's hand. Then Elna's.

I stood between them, taller and robed in gray. I felt their blood pulse behind the soft envelopes of skin that separated us. My mother's words echoed in my ears. *I thought I was protecting you.*

Sellis cleared her throat and glared. I thought of my vows, of the city. I released the two women I loved best in this world. I untied my terrible parcel and prepared for them to turn away from me as well. They would see the truth in my eyes.

With shaking hands, I held out the wings.

Sellis stepped beside me and spoke, because I could not. "Your son has done a service for the Singers," she said. "His sacrifice elevated a new Singer to protect the city." It was the third time we'd spoken the ritual of the honored fallen today. Now it sounded so hollow, so empty.

I watched Elna's face collapse.

My resolve broke, and I began to shake. To reach out to her. Sellis gripped my arm and pushed it forward, but my mother was the one who took the wings from me. She passed them to Elna as Sellis and I waited for them to bow to us, to release us, as the other families had done.

"Did he suffer?" Elna asked.

I shook my head but did not look at her. Sellis squeezed my arm hard, reminding me of how much tradition I broke here.

I could not breathe. *By my hand.* He didn't burn to death. He wasn't eaten by a skymouth. He fell whole and true, a failed challenger, a hero of the city. The song wound its way through my mind. I had asked for this. I'd made it happen.

I looked Elna in the eyes. The light that filtered down to her tier through the tower's shadows made her cloud-covered irises shine strangely. She might not have seen the guilt in my face. But my mother saw.

"He did not suffer," I promised them. Elna's tears fell freely, and I rushed to give her what more I knew, hoping my words would help. "He was thrown out a vent."

The ceremony had gone completely awry. Sellis, in her anger, would tell Rumul about my actions the moment we returned to the Spire. There would almost certainly be punishments. Still, Elna's face seemed lighter now. As if my words had helped. I could hope. I ached to tell them how sorry I was, but Sellis's grip bruised my arm.

My mother nudged Elna, and they bowed.

Ezarit stepped forward and stared long and deep at me. We had no more time to talk. I hoped Ezarit could see what my eyes begged her to see. I wanted her to know that I was trying to do the right things, to make the best trades I could. To help the city. To keep her safe.

We exchanged no more words, but I understood her better now. I hoped she could see that in my eyes before they filled with tears.

ℓ ℓ ℓ

We left before I could give Sellis more things to report to Rumul.

When I leapt, I risked a look backwards, beneath my wings. Elna's and Ezarit's faces glowed from the balcony, on light reflected from the clouds. Looking for a last glimpse of us.

I did not blink or make a sound. I let the evening wind dry my eyes to salt. Hoped it was too dark for Sellis to see my face.

She began to whisper at me as soon as we'd cleared the tower.

"Too dark already, thanks to you. We will, for appearance's sake, ask to sleep at Viit."

She had not suggested sleeping at Densira. That would have been too much mercy.

"I will send a whipperling telling Rumul of your actions."

She had more than enough tradition-breaking to silence me now. To send me downtower or have me enclosed.

I drew a jagged breath, composed myself. Thought about what would draw her attention away from me. What I could trade now.

"I think we should risk going back tonight. The council should hear about Narath."

She was quiet for a moment. "Narath? The first tower?"

"You didn't notice?"

Her silence told me everything I needed to know. I'd heard pride at Narath in the celebration of their challenger. Not grief. Not hopelessness. The Singers would certainly see more dissent from them soon. I explained this to Sellis.

"I heard nothing of the sort," she said.

"Rumul sees the value of my insights. He has forgiven my Lawsbreaks. Why can't you?" I decided not to bargain with her. I would speak my mind, not caring whether I earned another punishment. Duty. "Spire-born are sometimes very deaf to what tower words mean. I might break tradition, but I can help you understand the towers."

A long silence as we flew nearer to Viit. "I see your point," Sellis said. I hoped her flat tone meant she was giving my words serious thought. We angled around Viit. Headed for the Spire.

Another few heartbeats, and Sellis began to echo. I joined her. Soon the shapes of the towers, grown closer at this depth, were clear around us. We found a breeze that would take us faster towards the Spire.

We passed into the purple night, the towers glowing across the heights with warm lights. The city had grown so full while my heart had grown so empty.

22

ATTACK

As we passed Viit, I heard a disturbance, an echo in the wind that should not have been there.

Sellis fell quiet. She'd heard it too.

Then she began to hum again, turning left, then right on the breeze. Trying to find the source of the echo. The disturbance sounded like bubbles in the air. Like occupants of the cages in the Spire.

"Skymouths," she said.

We rode the darkness alone. No one in the towers could see well enough, or hear well enough, to know we were out here. Only the giant hungry mouths of the sky.

"You could try to divert them," Sellis added, her voice hopeful.

"I've never done it for long," I whispered back. "Or on the wing." I wished Wik were there.

"Look." Sellis pointed around the curve of Viit's lowest tiers.

In the dark, I opened my mouth wide and echoed until I heard the curve of a tentacle. Then more. The enormous limbs, curling.

A huge skymouth prowled Viit. My throat squeezed in fear. I heard Sellis swallow, hard.

"There are more, Kirit." She said it in a rush. "We need to get out of here."

I fought the urge to flee. We were Singers. We protected the city. "We must help them, Sellis. We should wake Viit. And Wirra. They can sound the horns."

"We can't fight off an entire migration by ourselves." Her voice edged with strain. She angled her wings to lift herself higher, preparing to race back to the Spire without care if she was seen.

"Wait!"

"What would you do? I can rouse the Spire." Sellis and I carried no weapons beyond our short knives. Our flight was ceremonial. We weren't prepared for a fight.

But I'd heard something behind another, smaller skymouth in the migration group. I'd heard the sound of silk in the wind. A skyshouter call.

Against the purpling sky, two Singers appeared, their nightwings locked so that they could hold their weapons at their chests, arrows nocked to bows. Their faces were obscured by shadow.

"Ah." Sellis sighed, relieved. She circled, looking for a gust that would take her behind the Singers. "We are lucky."

But my own relief muddled with confusion. The Singers weren't driving the skymouths away from the towers. The group rounded Viit and headed the direction we'd come. "What are they doing?"

Sellis slowed her glide, angling up for a closer look, risking a stall. I did the same, then circled, still echoing. The three long bodies and sinuous tentacles revealed themselves clearly.

"I'm sure they have a reason," she said, finally.

"The skymouths came from behind Viit and are flying towards Densira," I said slowly.

"Perhaps Singers are driving this herd out of the city," she responded, too quickly.

She thought the same thing I did.

These skymouths could have come from the pens in the Spire.

The monsters hovered, waiting for something. Waiting for their masters. Flying low.

"Nat said something, during his challenge," I whispered to her as fast as I could. "He said Singers would send a skymouth to kill him if he conceded."

"That's mad!" Sellis said.

"What if it isn't?"

We both fell silent.

"If it isn't," Sellis said finally, "then there's a reason. There's a mystery we do not know yet." Her voice was firm. "This is a Singer matter. If we'd needed to know more, we would have been warned. If we hadn't lingered, we wouldn't have been caught up in this." Time to go back to the Spire like proper Singers.

I would not obey, not here. Only a few Singers could guide skymouths. Wik might be there. But they were too close to Densira. My first tower. My family.

"We must do something to chase them away," I said.

Sellis frowned and shook her head. "We must not interfere."

My frustration caused me to wobble out of the draft. *Focus, Kirit.* I hissed at myself. Managed to find a weaker gust. Sellis coasted above me, circling away from the path of the slow-moving skymouths.

All I could hear was Nat's voice. *Send a skymouth.* Was that possible? Would we do that?

Sellis interrupted my thoughts. "The council talked about crowding after the challenge. During initiation."

So she'd been listening too.

"They were. Go on."

She didn't.

A herding call from one of the Singers drifted back to us on the wind. The verbal nudging of "away" and "here" that Wik had taught me for use in the pens. With a sinking feeling, I knew that Wik was one of the Singers flying with the skymouths. And they were guiding a migration towards Densira.

Finally, Sellis spoke again. "It is for the good of the city, Kirit. Whatever they do." She was quiet for a moment. "We should offer assistance."

Pieces fell into place in my mind. Things Civik had said. And Wik. Then something Tobiat had said, long ago.

Terrin had wanted to work with the towers. He didn't have enough support to change the council's direction on this. Cages. Delequerriat. Singers did their best for the city.

Too many skymouths in the pens for just bridges and training. Too many.

"Sellis! This is what Terrin challenged for. He wanted to change something. This!" I felt sick as I realized what this was. Another way to control the towers instead of working with them.

Sellis shook her head. "We aren't in the Spire, Kirit. We cannot argue a decision here. Challenge, if you want. See whether you share Terrin's fate."

Some Singers and windbeaters had supported Terrin. Others had fought before him. Naton, once he realized why he was building the pens. Tobiat. Nat, even though he hadn't realized what he was doing.

If there was dissent within the Spire, there could be dissent outside of it too.

I signaled to Sellis that I would not follow. Someone needed to warn the tower. To warn those on the lowest tiers especially, for they were most at risk. Elna. Ezarit. The salvagers. Tobiat.

Sellis broke from my side to fly behind the Singers. Perhaps to witness what they did.

I tried to think, keeping to my circuit. Witnessing was not enough. I had to try to help, to change their path.

But how could I interfere besides throwing myself between the skymouths and Densira?

If these were Spire skymouths, they might recognize me and turn faster from their attack. Then again, they were being goaded by more skilled Singers. They might not listen to me. Or hear me at all.

And if the Singers turned them towards me? Could I stop them? I could be devoured, or I could fall from the sky like a stone if a tentacle struck me.

If I did not die here, would the Spire throw me down? Or would I become Kirit Notower again? Worse than Lawsbreaker. I would be outside the city, apart from it.

The skymouths were moving again, circling Mondarath on Densira's near side.

The Singers signaled. Sound struck my ears: *Forward.* They were on the hunt.

A bat chased insects on an opposing air current to my glide. It darted fast on a tangential gust that carried it direct to the top of Densira.

I followed it. Once the Singers saw me, no one would doubt my intent.

But the Nightwing Singers dove, followed by Sellis's bright day wings. They were not headed up the tower's height, to attack from above as dawn broke. Instead, they circled closer to Elna's tier.

I dove lower, echoing.

Elna emerged on her balcony, feeling her way among the few vegetables she'd grown. It didn't matter to her that it was not yet light.

One skymouth, a small adult, saw her and began a slow turn.

"No," I said.

Sellis spotted me and hissed. Tried to block my path with hers. She missed as I dodged down and away, echoing to see better in the dark.

Nat's mother, my Elna, turned at the sound of wings passing close in the dark. At the sound of my clicks.

"Who is there?" she said. "Tobiat?" The hope in her voice broke my heart.

We dove past too quickly, and I had to turn again to reach her. Sellis, flying by my right pinion, tried to entangle me as I banked right, then up, then down. The tower was too close on my left.

Trapped. She had trapped me as she'd done in Gyre practice. I cast about.

Down, then.

I dove.

Sellis followed, hard on my heels. I tightened my grips, raked my wings back.

I twisted until I was in a searing dive, the dive that Macal had dared me to do at my wingtest. This dive ended in a sharp parabola before I plunged into the clouds.

Just as before, the airflow at the cloudtop was enough to power a climb. I pushed hard into it, using my grips to control curvature and angle. The battens tightened and formed new angles and arcs. It was glorious, all this speed. And now I controlled it with a Singer's precision.

I stretched my fingers painfully into the curve and shot upwards, faster than I'd fallen, headed straight for Densira and the skymouth that was opening itself up, a red tear in the sky that Elna could not see. She turned her head this way and that, trying to hear who startled her.

I drew in breath, preparing.

She could not see the danger, even as a mouth opened wide, then wider still, and neared her tier.

I slowed enough to pass between her and the skymouth, and I began to shout the monster down.

The sound of my scream echoed against the inside of my skull. It bounced off the tower. I breathed in through my nose and let more sound out of my mouth. As Wik had taught me, I supported everything from deep in my stomach and pushed out, so the very air shook with the noise.

I tried to make a shield over Elna with my scream. To push the monster away with my voice. The sound expanded and spread. The skymouth slowed. Elna stood openmouthed, stunned. I dove through the sound of my own voice and flew down, hoping the predator would follow.

I heard Wik shout a warning from the back of the group. The Singer in the lead was cursing my name.

Then I was through my wave of sound, and I could not hear behind me.

I knew Sellis would draw her ceremonial knife and come for me, but would the rest of them follow? Would the skymouths?

Looking back, I saw Sellis flying just above the skymouth that trailed me closely. Sellis's knife glinted in the moonlight.

I led both Sellis and the skymouth away from Densira. The night breezes were strong, and we moved fast on them, far from the tower that was my home.

I did not care what happened now. Singers could take me and throw me down. Elna would live to see Allsuns and bid Nat a real good-bye.

I realized that I cared about her more than I did the city. I would protect her against any challenge. Use myself as a weapon if I had to.

With a scream, Sellis attacked my wing, a slicing arc aimed to break battens. She caught a wingtip, and I spiraled away, losing altitude and control as the silk tore. The rip stopped at the first batten. The rest of the wing held, but I could not control my fall. I spun away from the Singers and their monsters, and fell towards the empty tiers of Densira and the waiting clouds.

The wind screamed in my ears. I grew dizzy with spin and fear. Sick welled in my mouth, hard terror against the dryness. I tried to work my legs from the footsling in order to use my feet to keep the rest of me from being dashed against a tower.

The clouds rose quickly to meet me.

I tangled in my wings.

Fell, blinded by the rush of wind.

❧ ❧ ❧

With a powerful jerk, my wings were nearly ripped from my back.

Someone had hooked me. I dangled, then I rose.

I was dizzy, but alive.

Who had me? In the night, with my captor above and my wings in the way, I could not see.

I tried to speak, but my voice was a croak, muffled by my wings. My throat felt like I had swallowed scourweed.

From a slit in the mess of torn silk and broken battens, I saw a double shadow pass across the uninhabited tiers of Densira. One flier, one flown. We flew so far downtower, the bone core had nearly grown out to the balcony's edge.

We cleared Densira's curve, and my bearer found a strong vent. We began to move fast into the open sky, headed beyond the city.

Not a rescue, then. Cloudbound. I imagined what it would be like to fall without the towers around me.

But the air shifted, and a cold breeze flapped the torn wing silk near my face. We turned again, back towards the city. A dark shape rose from the clouds, rough edges blocking the white towers on the horizon.

Lith. *Only the most recent to fall,* I heard Rumul say again. The most recent tower to send citizens tumbling into the clouds.

We approached the broken tower top from the city's outer edge. It was still dark. No one on the other towers could see us this far down. No one looked this way, if they could help it.

I struggled, hoping to slow my captor.

A hard shake stilled me. "You always have the worst timing, Kirit."

Wik's voice. The voice I'd grown to trust. The voice of the man who had led a pack of skymouths to attack Densira.

I kicked and flailed. Tried to loosen my arms from my wing-straps. I would have rather fallen.

"Stop! I wouldn't have let them harm Elna."

I didn't believe him. I did not want to hear him.

He picked up speed, despite my struggling, and turned just before he flew right into the dead tower. As he turned, he tossed me hard at Lith. I tumbled through the air towards the filthy tiers. I heard my wings make another loud rip as he let them go.

I landed hard and rolled to a stop against a bone spur. Dust billowed around me and made me cough. The tower groaned.

Wik did not follow me in. When I looked behind me, I saw nothing but sky. He'd flown away. Stranded me here.

Left to die?

My hand rested on a dusty pile of feathers. Bones snapped beneath my palm. Lith smelled of rot and decay.

The sun broke the cloudline. I caught my breath and checked for broken bones, moving feet and arms carefully.

Around me, Lith glistened darkly in the dawn.

My throat was dry from my screams and my robes were torn from the fall. I would not last long here.

A wail echoed against the dark bone: my voice, burred and painful.

At least no one was around to hear me.

I was little comforted by that thought, until a shadow peeled from a wall and limped towards me, jittering and waving one starvation-thin arm.

"Look who fell!" Tobiat peered down at me, his robe flapping in the shadows of the dead tower.

He sidled closer, bringing a familiar Tobiat-stench with him. I lifted myself up to sitting and looked at him.

"Where did you come from?" I said. But he didn't answer.

The wind coursed through the tower. The pitted bone whispered like a cracked flute.

Had he been left to die here too? Tobiat danced his feet back and forth. His old breaks creaked and stuck out at odd angles; he looked like a broken kite. But when the day brightened enough that he saw the color of my robes, he whistled and backed away.

"Singer." He warded the air with his hands. Began to disappear into the shadows.

"I won't hurt you." I didn't want to be alone, not now, not on Lith. "You remember me, right?"

"Tobiat, it's me, Kirit," I tried again. "Nat's . . ." My voice failed. Nat's what? Friend? Murderer? I couldn't say it. "Remember the cleaning? At Densira?"

I rose and shrugged off the remains of my wings. Tobiat continued to back away.

"How long have you been here?" I asked gently, hoping to keep him near. "Who brought you here?"

Instead of answering, Tobiat ducked into a hole in the blackened wall.

I crawled after him, deep into the broken core of Lith. The tunnel we passed through was neither smoothed by age nor worn away by rot, though Lith smelled like rotting bone. This tunnel had been gouged with sharp tools, recently, to make passages.

The tower's core was hard and cold. Where layers of bone had been peeled back to the marrow, the scent of rot lingered. I brushed a spot with my fingertip. It crackled and compressed at my touch. Nothing like the warmth I'd felt when Viridi let us touch the city.

Wind blew the gray dust of the tower from my finger. We emerged from one tunnel and crossed an open balcony. The floor's odd angle made me wish for my wings. We stood on a dead tier, within a dead tower.

Cracks latticed Lith's core, deep black lines on blackened bone. Nothing grew here except the resilient scourweed and lichen. No families made their homes here. No ladders hung from balconies, no banners. Lith was nothing like the towers of my childhood, and nothing like the Spire.

Tobiat didn't seem to care. He'd threaded a line of silk through the tunnels. As he walked, retracing his steps, he gathered it up into loops. He didn't look back.

"You talked to Nat before he challenged the Spire," I said. This time, at "Nat," Tobiat froze in place. "Why did you let him do it?"

"Wind was right," Tobiat answered gruffly.

"You were a Singer once, weren't you?" I asked, but he was silent.

We entered another tunnel. The gouges looked fresh here, as if someone had dug deep to make new passages between hollows. This passage ended in a narrow cell, walled on all sides and crowded by the central bone core. Two oil lamps glowed weakly in the darkness.

I saw a nest of rags. Smelled the stench of long residency and rotting meat.

Tobiat skittered away from the bedding and placed a small sack of water precariously atop a tripod. He cackled softly as I licked my lips.

A basket of wilted greens waited near the fire, spices and herbs nearby. Bird meat was drying on a rack. Tobiat hadn't lived this well at Densira. Someone was taking care of him. Keeping him alive.

The old man crouched by the fire in his cell. Smoke wound its way out through holes drilled low in the wall. The tower's walls sighed and moaned with the wind; ghost sounds made by a dead tower teetering dangerously on the border of bone and sky.

He peered at me from under heavy eyebrows. "Singers. Sky-mouths."

"How did you know? Why did you tell Nat?"

"Nat," he said again, echoing my words.

My throat constricted. I heard Nat falling again, sucked out the vent. I should have tried harder to save him.

"Kirit," came a whisper from the cell's far corner. Not Tobiat's voice.

The ceiling was very low there. I crawled to the pile of rags, my hands needled by the rough bone floor.

The pile moved at my approach. A tangle of black hair. A glint of white robe spattered with old blood.

Nat.

23

SURVIVAL

My head spun at the sight of him. "You survived the fall?" I reached out and touched Nat's arm, hoping.

He flinched, and I pulled my hand back, still reeling.

"How—" I began, then stopped. When I fought him, he fell. That was part of the how. He lay injured before me, while I knelt there whole.

I stepped back, nearly knocking the water sack into the fire. "I don't understand." *By my hand he fell.*

Tobiat crawled to Nat's side and lifted the rag blanket away. I saw clearly what I'd done. His left leg, broken and splinted, but seeping. His right, torn in long gashes. His ribs, his arms, his head. Wrecked and bleeding, still. His broken form looked so much like Tobiat's.

I knelt at his side. If his wounds healed badly, he would be as crippled as Tobiat. Unable to hunt or fight. Unable to fly? His fate would be tied to a single tower and those willing to care for him. I knew Nat well enough; that would be the worst of all the injuries.

Injuries I caused.

Tobiat's breaks had never been set, never properly healed. And Elna had looked out for him. Someone would do the same for Nat.

I looked closer, thought more clearly. Nat's left leg had been splinted. The gashes on his right were roughly bandaged. His ribs and arm also. I saw the start of a poultice heating beside him, though it was missing some elements.

A whipperling nested in a fold of fabric by Nat's feet. Maalik. Nat's bird.

Someone had found him and brought him here. Someone cared for him. "Tobiat, did you do this?"

"Some!" Tobiat laughed. He pointed at the rough bandages. "Others too."

Someone with enough knowledge to make a poultice. A splint. Someone who could fix Nat and make him straight again. Straight enough to fly.

"Who?" I turned and nearly caught Tobiat. He skittered away. "Who comes here? Who brought you here to tend Nat?"

Tobiat echoed me. "Who comes here? Kirit comes here."

Kirit did indeed. And Wik had brought her.

Nat's eyes opened again. This time they stayed open, blinking at me. Not looking away. They were angry eyes. Fierce hunter's eyes. I, his prey.

"Didn't you hurt me enough in the Spire?" His voice was rough and filled with pain. "You've come to finish the job?"

No. "Never." *Never again.*

"Liar."

I heard again the sound of his arrow passing close to my ear. He had known what he was doing too. I watched his jaw clench and looked for clean rags to rebandage his wounds.

When I found none, I tore the hem of my new gray robe. The rip of silk broke the silence.

"Stop," Nat said.

"Please hear me, Nat."

"Singers hear." Tobiat chittered behind me. He waved his arms above his head. I recognized a windbeater pattern.

"Tobiat," I said, "you were in the Spire. You know how things work."

He mumbled. "Bargains. Bribes."

"Right! I made a bargain. I had to."

Nat didn't answer. He watched me from narrowed eyes.

"How did you survive the fall?" I started to reach out again, then drew my hand back.

He went quiet. Looked older for a moment. Harder. Gaunt. The hollows around his eyes weren't just from pain. Since All-moons, he'd been under Singer punishments. Weighted with Laws. A broken set of wings.

"How did you survive?" I repeated, though I meant so much more than the challenge now. "And Elna? Did Densira help you?" Elna too had looked gaunt, her eyes much worse, when I saw her. I'd been too caught up in my own guilt to realize.

The look he gave me told me all I needed to know. Worse than unlucky. They had become pariahs in the tower.

"I hunted," he said proudly. "Ezarit gave us everything she could, when she could. No one would trade with her for weeks, until the Singers did. I kept us all fed. Went lower on the tower than anyone has in years."

While I ate well in the Spire, Nat had taken care of everyone.

"How did you survive the fall from the Spire?" The third time I'd asked. Despite my shame, I could not ignore the fact that he was dodging my question. I caught his gaze. Held it.

"Tell," Tobiat shouted, chuckling. So close to my side that I jumped.

Nat took a stuttering breath. "Tobiat taught me how."

My face must have shown confusion, because Tobiat laughed again.

Nat coughed. "I didn't go to the Spire to die. I went to survive. To gain the right to tell the truth my father knew."

"The Singers would never let you speak a truth about Naton."

Even my mother had been held to secrecy. Had bargained for it. Another realization swept over me. Ezarit hadn't known who she would have to fight either, in her challenge.

Just as Nat hadn't come to fight me. That match had been Rumul's doing.

"I had to try. We had nothing left but the truth. And Naton wanted people to know that Singer secrets are killing the city." Nat's voice was older, deeper. Even as injured as he was, I heard the strength in it.

"I know their secrets now," I said. Some of them, at least.

"Spire secrets!" Tobiat shouted, and spat at me. A gob of phlegm landed on my foot. "Keep them in the tower!" It sounded like a caution.

"What does it matter anymore?" I raised my arms, palms up. Now Nat watched me intently as I argued with Tobiat.

"Tradition!" Tobiat shouted.

Nat looked between us, then took a deep breath. "Tobiat told me a way to survive, if the windbeaters could be bribed."

My jaw hung open. Tradition indeed, Tobiat. "You bribed the windbeaters?"

Now Nat looked very uncomfortable. "Elna did."

"To win?" I was shocked. She knew how to do this?

"If I could win." This time it was Nat who looked away. Both of us, complicit in this fall.

I reached out and touched my once-best friend's shoulder. "I did not want you dead. I am happy you are not."

His face creased with a small smile that folded into a wince. "I am glad I'm not either. Nor you. But that challenge was never meant to be a fair trial."

If I'd known who my challenger was going to be, I also would have bribed the windbeaters to let him live, as he'd done. I sat back on my heels.

Nat tried to raise his head, licked his lips. I brought him the goosebladder of water and let him sip at it. "We need to get you medicines. Herbs. Honey to keep out infection."

"Soon." Tobiat nodded.

Not soon if there were skymouths lurking near the towers. No one would get through. "Not with Singers on the wing."

"Why would you want to be one of them?" Nat spat.

I searched for words to describe the enclosure. The feeling of learning my fate and my past. Rumul's enticements. *You were born to be a Singer.* It had felt like hope within the walls of the Spire. A way to survive.

I took a deep breath, hoped he'd believe me.

"What I learned about the city, Nat, and about what Singers do, what they've done in the past—I thought I could help."

Tobiat waved his hands emphatically. "Singers help kill."

My mouth hung open. I stared at Tobiat. "That's not what I mean."

"But you were trying to kill me," Nat said.

"You were trying to kill me too. Why did you keep fighting, once you saw me?"

He blanched and lay back. "I wanted to know. We needed a better life. We had a plan. Why did you?"

"I thought I could win and save you. And, yes, I wanted those wings. To try and change things. Some Singers disagree with Rumul." He was weakening, needed rest. But I pressed him again. I was newly ruthless. "What did you give them? And to do what?"

Nat coughed, each jerk causing him to stiffen in pain. I tipped more water to his lips. The sack felt very light. Not much water left to us. He sipped.

"Take more."

He handed it back. "You feel guilty. Don't. You made your choice to be a Singer. Live with that. Change your course if you feel you should, but don't feel guilty."

I bristled. "I wouldn't have flown the Gyre if you hadn't chal-lenged, Nat. I wasn't near ready. So if I am a Singer now . . ." I paused. Was I still a Singer? Someone who killed people? With skymouths? And did I still want to be? "If I am a Singer, you helped make me one."

Turning away from our argument, Tobiat grabbed the blad-der and an empty satchel and crawled back through the tunnel, yelling, "Singer. Sing. Singing." He left me alone with Nat, who began to doze again while I thought about the Gyre fight, the Singers. The skymouths.

❧ ❧ ❧

Nat yelled himself awake from a nightmare that had him grasp-ing the air with his hands.

"Shh." I held his hand, and he didn't pull away. "You have more lives than a nest of silk spiders."

He grinned. A real Nat smile, from before everything. "Can't give up. Worse than falling."

"I didn't give up." I realized it was true. I had found a way to keep going. That was part of who I was. And part of who Nat was, also. We fought hard to live.

As the space around us grew pale with early light, I realized we had a bigger fight ahead of us. If Rumul knew we were alive, he would do everything to change that. We knew too much. *I* knew too much.

The truth was a gift I could give Nat.

"Nat," I whispered, as he tried to find a more comfortable spot, "Singers fly at night. Nightwings are real." I was nearly bursting to tell him how it worked. The old Nat would have loved to know. Would have been desperate to heal fast in order to try it himself.

He only looked tired. "One of too many secrets kept by the

Spire." He shifted position, trying to escape the pain. "Like what happened to Naton."

It had been decided. The challenger was defeated. We keep the silence.

Still, the words rushed from me. "I know what happened."

I'd betrayed Nat in the Gyre. But my father had betrayed his father, so many years ago. How many layers of betrayal did it take to work the cracks in a friendship—especially one like ours—and break it apart?

I took a deep breath. "Your dad discovered that the Singers could fly at night. He was going to trade the information. To Ezarit."

"Ezarit? Why?"

Now I couldn't bring myself to answer him. The words stuck in my throat. *Because she wanted power and standing.* She wanted it even before my father disappeared. She wanted to be the best and the fastest trader. No matter whose life she risked.

It was too close to a confession. Like mother, like daughter.

"Someone found out Naton was trading Singer secrets?"

It would have been so easy to echo his word—*someone*—and leave it at that. But I couldn't keep things from him anymore.

"My father. He was in love with Ezarit, but he was Spire-born. He was trying to protect the city. He didn't know—" I stopped. Civik knew.

Nat hitched himself up so that his back was propped against the wall. He looked for the water sack, but Tobiat had taken it with him.

His lips were so dry. I wished Tobiat would hurry back.

"And that's why the Singers threw Naton down? Because he stole their secret?"

I pushed a strand of hair back behind my ear. "Yes."

Around us, Lith creaked. The floor rumbled.

Nat shook his head. "That might be half of it."

I stared at him, not understanding. "My father told me himself."

Nat rolled over, groaning. I tried to help him, but he pushed me away. "Let me do this."

With his finger, Nat traced from memory a pattern in the dust. After staring at it for a moment, I realized I knew a part of that pattern well. Even upside down. The skymouth pens. But the rest of it baffled me. Nat misunderstood my confusion.

"It's one of the carvings from the back of Naton's bone chips. Though it doesn't look like instructions for night flying. It looks architectural."

So even now, I'd not been told the whole truth. I sat back and studied the drawing. "What do you think these are?" I waved my hand over a tiny mark on the pattern, then another similar one.

"Elna called them Spire holes."

I thought about that. The holes marked tier after tier. There were even more near the thick pattern that I'd recognized. But the holes marked tiers where there were no pulleys or pens. "Why would Naton drill so many holes?"

Nat shook his head.

"Where are the chips now?" If we could study them together, we could connect the secrets. Figure out Naton's message.

He wiped the dust flat. "We traded them to the windbeaters. They didn't want them at first, but Elna knew what to say. That they were from Naton."

I could only imagine what kind of sabotage the windbeaters could get up to with that map. The ways they could foil Rumul, or those like him. The thought gave me pause. We were trapped in Lith, but Naton's chips could still cause havoc.

But another question still bothered me. "How did you know about the vents?"

Tobiat crawled back through the wall and interrupted. "Me!" he hooted.

"Elna said she went looking for Naton after he disappeared, after he was thrown down. She flew as far downtower as she could, around the city. She didn't find him."

"Found me!" Tobiat spread his arms wide. "Shiny present for the artifex's wife."

Nat looked at me, dirty and wounded, and rolled his eyes. Squeezed my hand quickly. I squeezed back before he let go. Almost like old times.

"How long have you been here?"

"Days," he whispered. "Shot through that vent in the Spire, got banged around, and fell again. Landed hard. Then someone found me. Brought me here."

"Who?" I asked. This was important. Tobiat had said, *Wind was right.*

"I never saw. But then your Singer brought Tobiat to take care of me." Nat laughed until he coughed, and his eyes closed again. He passed into a restless sleep, exhausted by our conversation.

Wik. I heard the dark Singer's voice in my memory: *I wouldn't have let them harm Elna.* Felt him catching me while Sellis flew on. So many secrets in the Spire. So many currents working round each other.

I crawled past Tobiat, back through the tunnel, and onto the empty, black balcony. I leaned against a crumbling wall and looked up at the city that had risen beyond Lith's broken tiers.

24

HIDDEN

A shadow passed the balcony. One shadow, but two people: Wik, carrying Elna.

When Wik set her on the ledge, Elna stood for a moment before her legs wobbled. She caught herself against a spur, then sank to the ground and began to crawl towards the tunnel. Towards the sound of Tobiat's voice. She'd been here before. But to fly like that, without wings, blind, after a near attack. She was stronger than I'd ever imagined she could be.

Wik stood on the thin balcony, furling his wings and looking to the horizon. I resisted the urge to push him off.

Elna disappeared into the tunnel, and I followed. She hadn't realized I was there yet. I watched her tend Nat, listened to her clucking at him. She touched Nat's wounds gently and reached into her satchel for a packet of herbs. Pulled back the gray silk, but kept it to reuse. "Who has been here?" she asked.

"Singer," said Tobiat.

Elna dipped her head. "On your wings, Wik."

Wik, who had followed us to the tunnel's mouth, said, "Not me. Kirit."

Elna paused in her work, and her face brightened. "Where?"

The tiny grotto had grown very crowded. I stepped closer to her and put my hand on her shoulder. But I turned to Wik. "Whose side are you on?" I put timbre into my voice. As I'd been taught. How could someone know all that Wik knew and not do something to stop it?

Elna touched my hand. "We trust him, Kirit." It was almost enough.

"Why?"

Tobiat chuckled and gestured to Elna. "Trust," he said. "Can't remember why."

My softhearted, gentle second mother. The woman who never picked a fight, who was always two steps ahead of us as children. Her chin hardened as she ran fingers along her only son's broken limbs, ably adjusting bandages and applying salve as if he had just tripped while running in Densira.

"I went looking for Naton after Conclave. I left Nat with your mother, who was pregnant with you. I spent days at it, all through Allsuns. Broke my eyes, it turned out. Too much sun. Slept in a hang bag down every tower around the Spire for days in the winds. But I never found Naton. I found Tobiat. Hanging by a wing from an abandoned tier on Bissel. Birds had already started pecking at one of his eyes."

She turned her face towards him, smiling fondly. "I don't know how long he'd been there, but he was alive, and he was wearing a Singer robe."

I held my breath. I'd been right.

"I figured if I could make him well, he might tell me of Naton's last days."

"How did he get there?"

Elna quieted and turned to Tobiat. Waited.

Tobiat cleared phlegm from his chest and spat. He coughed for a few seconds more, then drew a long breath.

"Challenge." He cackled.

The sun was going down. Tobiat would babble until it came up again. I tried to hurry him. "Who did you challenge?"

Nat's eyes were open; he was listening too. Tobiat spat again, hitting his first gob with the quivering mass of the second. "Young Rumul. For Naton."

"Why did Rumul want this so badly?"

Wik stepped in. "A Singer historian found a set of bone plates hidden far downtower. They showed Singers using skymouths to hunt in the clouds, and Rumul saw the potential. There was not enough dissent to stop him. Not then. The council brought in an artifex. Called it tradition. Before the Rise, they said, Singers had trained skymouths to defend the Spire. They stopped long ago. Rumul thought it necessary again."

My jaw hung open. Those? To defend the city? No. That wasn't what Wik had said. He'd said the Spire.

"How long have people been trying to change this?"

I'd asked Wik, but Tobiat answered. "Too long. Too slow."

Wik nodded. "Rumul had the votes in council and strength in the Gyre. He had many of the windbeaters too. With some towers rebelling against tithing and Conclave especially, Rumul has fought hard to keep order. Singers were afraid to have another Lith. He gained more supporters. Inside and outside the Spire."

The southern towers, I thought. Where the Spire got its apples. Its muzz.

"We have only recently been able to shift the balances," Wik continued.

All those people. The towers.

I turned to Nat. "What were you willing to die for to have spoken aloud?"

And he looked at me full on, for the first time since I'd found him here. His eyes looked harder, and sadder, than I'd ever seen them. "You mean, what did I risk killing a friend for?" he said.

I winced, but stood firm. Waited for him to answer.

"I wanted the city to hear what Naton knew, and what Tobiat knew, but couldn't say." He paused. His voice was deep and
firm. Determined. "I wanted them to have to sing it from the
towers. That the Singers kept skymouths. Used them against
the city."

No one would have listened to someone like Tobiat.

Except someone had. Nat had. Elna had.

Nat said, "After you disappeared and Singers told everyone
I'd attacked the Spire, they weighed me down with Laws. I had
to hide during Conclave, or they would have taken me." He
paused and drank the tea that Elna held to his lips. "I went so
far down. Into the clouds, Kirit."

Into the clouds. The nerve that had taken. The desperation.

Nat kept talking. "What I found down there, the city needs
to know that too."

I looked at Wik, who shrugged, confused.

"In the clouds, I had to hide often, letting gryphons and skymouths that were the size of whole tiers pass by." Nat swallowed. "It was dark down there. I stumbled around a lot. Nearly
fell off the edge of a tier more than once. Then I tripped over a
nest of them. Hiding. Tiny ones, little bigger than my hand."

"Them?"

"Littlemouths. They live in the towers. But they're not like the
ones that migrate. They're small. No sharp teeth. They climb.
Can't fly. They eat waste and weeds. Not people."

"Then they're not skymouths." I thought of the baby skymouths in the cages. Those had been big. They'd had teeth.

Nat reached into a basket by his side and pulled out his
hands. His palms formed a seemingly empty cup. "Look at it.
Feel it."

I turned to Wik, questioning. He began to echo at Nat's
hands so that we could better see what he held. I joined him.
There was something soft in Nat's hands, for all that they looked

empty. I reached out a fingertip and touched an eye ridge, the crease of a mouth.

The creature was something like a skymouth, a baby skymouth, but much smaller. Large, wide-set eyes, a ridge of glass teeth, but not the sharp edges that gouged and tore. Grinders.

The creature nestled in Nat's hands.

Wik was doubtful. "Another kind of skymouth?" He crossed his arms and frowned.

Nat shook his head.

Tobiat made a sound that was part yelp and part laughter. "Same kind." He stared for a long time at Wik.

I turned too. "What does he mean?" I watched Wik's expression shift from confusion to understanding. To horror.

He spoke in a rush. "The Spire's skymouths are bred there." He reached to touch the tiny creature. Hesitated and pulled his hand back. "It's not night and day. The city needs the sinew. Needs the bridges. Singers have kept a few skymouths for that purpose since the Rise. Rumul argued in council to breed more, bigger mouths. They got more than they bargained for."

Elna bent her head.

"Why was he allowed to do this?" I couldn't believe what I was hearing. Was the council truly that weak? The Singers that easily led? Why had no one challenged?

"Not everyone knows. The skymouths aren't exactly easy to see down there, and so their true number goes unobserved. The shouters and the council know. There's been gossip, but there have been accidents too. And the council has to be careful. Rumul's beaten every challenge so far."

"Terrin."

Wik frowned. "Others too. Civik, long ago. Rumul is too good in the Gyre and has many windbeaters on his side. He bribes them well. When Rumul kept winning, we decided to try to work for change in different ways."

"Sabotage."

"And changing minds. It's slow and dangerous. There are more dissenters among the younger Singers. A few of us try to blunt the effect of Rumul's policies."

"Why can't you tell the towers? Or kill the skymouths?" My outrage brought the pitch of my voice close to a scream.

Wik smiled weakly. "The needs are too great. Rumul has consolidated too much power and removed most of the strong-willed among the council. Only Viridi opposes him openly, and then very cautiously. She—we—have been trying to secure windbeaters we could trust, biding our time. Too much so. Rumul's trade with the wealthiest towers has enhanced the Spire's food; the towers themselves enjoy more bridges, nets too, though they fear the skymouths as everyone does. The wealth keeps Rumul popular. The fear keeps the towers under his thumb."

Tobiat moaned. "Secrets, secrets."

I ignored him and pushed forward. "You are trying to stop it? And Viridi too?"

When Wik nodded, I continued, "Yet she let Terrin be destroyed? She—" I stopped. I turned and looked past Nat. To Elna. "You knew. Naton worked on the pens. He told you."

She blinked and frowned. "I knew something was wrong. I knew he thought he was doing something important for the city, but then he had questions. He gave me the chips before they took him, but before he could tell me what all the marks meant, he was gone."

"Does Ezarit know?"

Elna shook her head. "No one outside the Spire but me. Naton smuggled the carvings on a necklace to me, for safekeeping. If I'd said anything, I would have been cloudbound. And Nat—" She put her hand to her head and turned towards her son's sickbed. "Now you know everything."

Nat threw a bandage in the fire pit, nearly knocking over the tripod, enraged but unable to rise. "I would have told the city! We could have gathered the towers together. We could have done something. Not waited to build support over generations. And now we're stuck here."

"You would have died trying, like Naton," Wik said. In the dim light, his eyes reflected the oil lamps. His face, etched with the marks of his battles in the Gyre, looked grim.

"Just like we'll die here. Once they come for us," I said. "We are two Singers missing, with Sellis gone to report me to the council. They will come looking. They'll search the towers for me. And they will then find you."

"Then we have to rouse the towers, tell them!" Nat said. "They will fight!"

Wik said, "The towers no longer know how to fight. They know how to break things, like Laws, and make minor rebellions. They know how to issue a challenge to the Spire, because that is what they've been trained to do."

"Trained to guard, and to hunt. But only within their own quadrants. Trained to Fortify. To hide. Only a few fly the whole city." Nat's voice was bitter and mocking as he sang, *"Tower by tower, secure yourselves. We watch while others suffer. Call it unlucky. Turn away."*

"And Singers decide which towers gain connections," I said. "Which can rise. Which fall in the path of migrations."

"But"—Wik gestured to the blackened walls around him— "we do not wish another war. Wars break towers. People die. Fighting throws the city into mayhem, and worse. We cannot sink to that. That is what we were before the clouds. We were not a city."

"Are we a city now?" I asked the question. "The towers humbled and begging for Singer attention. For freedom to speak? Who can fight this?"

Tobiat pointed his crooked finger at Wik and me. "Singers fight."

Wik agreed. "One of us must gain audience with the council. Try again to stop Rumul. His last wingfight injury has not healed well, though not many know it. I will go back. If I fail to get them to hear me, I will challenge, and then Kirit will get to the windbeaters. Convince them to support us."

"You want me to go down beneath the Gyre again?" I was suspicious. "You just said Rumul has too many windbeaters on his side."

"Civik sent Moc with a message after you and Sellis departed. The message in Naton's bone chips swayed more windbeaters. He said he'd found places where Naton drilled the extra Spire holes. He thinks Naton meant to use them to undermine Rumul. He also says that some see a way to use the holes, where before they only knew defeat. We could gain more support." Wik pulled a small wrapped package from his robes and held it out to me. "He sent these as his promise."

I took the package and slowly unwrapped it. Glass and metal gleamed. Civik's lenses. Heavy in my hands.

I stared at Elna and Tobiat, then at Wik. Perhaps Tobiat was not so damaged after all, nor Elna so gentle. "Who else is part of this? Why doesn't Ezarit know?"

"She was already too much at risk," Elna said. "The Singers watch her."

Because of me.

"My brother has tried to help, while on excursion," Wik said. "Though he sometimes acts too quickly."

Wik's family: Spire-born, all of them. They had siblings, cousins, parents all around them, as the tower-born did. And they got to keep their families, as long as they remained Singers. His brother—Macal. "Then Magisters can help."

"Some, yes. Some, like Dix and Florian, are Rumul's."

Nat pushed against the floor with his hands. "You Singers have had your chance. I will tell everyone. The towers will take the Spire. End this."

Elna pressed firmly with her hand, stilling him. "A few more days yet." Her eyes said more than a few days.

My hair fell across my face, and I tucked a lock behind my ear. "Wik shouldn't reveal himself if we can help it. If I return, I can try to lodge a challenge before the council can stop me. Rumul, trying to silence a new Singer that he's just elevated? That would raise some eyebrows among the broader Singer ranks, and the windbeaters too."

"Sellis has likely already spoken against you to the council," Wik said. "You'd need to sneak in, or they'll throw you down. Wait until dark. Then come."

Nat looked at us, darkly angry, the old wing-sibling long gone. "If you don't succeed this time, I will find a way to stop the Singers from outside the walls."

Elna put her hand on his. Then I put mine over hers, and Tobiat joined me. Then Wik clasped our hands together. We were five for certain, set against the might of the Spire.

"I was wrong to hope this would all go away," Elna said.

"We will make sure Naton's message gets out," I promised. *One way or another.* I hung Civik's lenses around my neck. "Can you get a message to Macal? Tell him he's needed at the Spire? Would he understand?"

Wik pulled a Spire marker from his robe. Made a symbol on it with his knife. Gave it to Nat. "Send Maalik to Mondarath with this."

Below us, the tower shook anew.

Wik and I crawled back through the tunnel, leaving Elna, Nat, and Tobiat in their hiding place.

When we reached the balcony, we could hear a bone horn in the distance. Calling the city elders to the Spire.

"Something is happening," Wik said.

"Not another Conclave?" Not so soon.

"I will find out. Will try to slow it, if so."

Before I could say anything in response, Wik leapt from the tower. I was left to address the biggest hurdle of returning to the Spire: wings. Sellis's knife had ripped mine, and my fall had made it worse. Four of us, trapped on Lith, with one working wing among us.

And a Singer who had so far kept secrets from both tower and Spire.

I looked about the abandoned balcony, then crawled back through the first passage, rummaging through the discarded refuse of Lith.

I would find a way to turn one wing into two. I would figure out how to get into the Spire without being seen.

Then I would make the Spire tell its secrets to the city.

25

TRUTH

As the day warmed, I descended through Lith's broken tiers with increasing desperation.

Tobiat brought more strong silk rope with him, and he insisted on joining me while I picked through the tower. I couldn't stop him. Nor could I keep him quiet. I struggled to focus. He smacked his gums together and rambled.

He hummed an old tune. Sometimes sang a verse. I listened, despite myself. This was another song long fallen from the city's memory. More than that, I noticed that when he sang, Tobiat's speech made more sense. He could remember longer sentences.

When Tobiat said, "Lith song," I smiled, even as I searched.

"I don't remember much of that one," I said. I expected he wouldn't either.

"Many bridges ran to Lith," he sang, the legend clear and true. My jaw dropped. *"They traded easy and made things beautiful."*

Now Tobiat did not skip or mumble. He sounded whole when he sang. His memory intact. I listened harder. I'd never thought to ask him to sing.

> *But they grew jealous of the Spire,*
> *tried to raise their tower higher, without Singers' help,*
> *nor Spire's blessing.*
> *Men found Lith who wished to fight.*
> *They made it grow,*

they made it strong.
They angered many, Lith cracked and died.
Singers helped them flee, made survivors beg shelter.
  Plenty perished.
No one came to sing their dead.
City punishes those who forget.

Tobiat's song ended. Amazement washed over me, along with new appreciation for Tobiat. Then he shouted, "Roar!" as the city rumbled again.

I shuddered and sped up my search efforts. On one tier, we found a crafter's studio, the floor broken and treacherous. A spine wall had caved in, and the bones scattered across the floor were big enough to be human.

If any of this tier's residents had survived, they'd left everything behind when they went. Tools had blown against the central core and lay covered with dust: needles and saws and nails. Metal. Things I'd seen in Rumul's chambers, in the wing-maker's studio, and nowhere else. No one had risked coming back to Lith to salvage, even though the need was great. I gathered what I wanted: needles—even a metal one—awls, bone battens from a pile.

"Rise." Tobiat held up a carved bone panel. It was gray with dust, but much lighter than the darkened tower. He cleaned it with a corner of his ruined robe.

The panel was beautiful. The carving crisp and confident. Cleaner even than the carving in the Spire. Our bone tools could not compete with the artistry. The sharp wings, the flowing hair of the fliers.

We'd lost so much.

"Oh," I said. "The clouds."

The swirling cuts that ridged the panel's surface could be nothing but clouds. In every direction. Even thinking about clouds all around made me squirm. The panel must have come from the Rise. Part of our history.

At the center of the bone tablet, a woman with a marked face lifted a wingless citizen away from a hunting bird. A Singer saving someone. Not the whole city. One person.

This was almost too humble for the Singers. Most often, their carvings showed Singers lifting the towers themselves, filled with people. My hand, which had carved this very scene in the council tier as a novice, flexed at the memory.

We'd lost so much. We'd lost ourselves.

"The towers sing one version of The Rise, and the Singers know another," I said.

Tobiat nodded. "Secrets."

"But what if that's wrong? What if secrets are destroying the city?" I traced the carving with a finger. Tucked it into my robe.

"Fear Singers. Sing. Fear."

Sure. The towers refrained from fighting because they were afraid of the Singers. I could see that. But Tobiat shook his head, frustrated. That wasn't what he'd meant. "Do you mean to say that the Singers are afraid?"

A bob of the head. A cackle.

"They're part of the city, not something separate," I murmured. "We have forgotten."

"Maybe, maybe," said Tobiat. He singsonged, *"City punishes those who forget."*

What else had we forgotten? How much more could the city lose if Rumul remained unchecked?

We returned to the hideout, Tobiat munching on some gristle he'd pulled from a pocket. I turned over thoughts in my mind, frustrated from the search.

How many generations ago had Lith fallen? Recently enough to haunt the city. How could we keep tragedy from happening again without resorting to Singer methods? Were the stories and

songs true? How would I fly away from here in time to meet
Wik?

I had one good wing, a needle and awl. Battens.

I spotted Elna's satchel on the floor and remembered how
heavy it had felt. I looked inside. Under the herbs she'd carried
when Wik had flown with her, and her sewing box, she'd tucked
the silk and the furled, broken wings from the Spire, the ones
I'd presented to her.

I began to hum The Rise, softly. Soon, Elna, Nat, and Tobiat fell asleep around me, heads nestled on arms, legs tossed
by dreams. Nat snored.

I pulled the silk and wings from Elna's bag, took a piece
of dried goose from our stores, then crawled from the cell
and retraced my path until I found my wing and its broken
mate. Lifting them, I could see that the tear in the right
wing was devastating. There was no repairing the shredded
silk, unless I could summon Liras Viit to this broken tower.
But I had Nat's ceremonial wings. One was less damaged
than the other.

I could patch his better wing with mine, stitch the stress
points and make them whole. I ripped out the seams and dis-
sected his broken wing, pulling the silk from the battens. My
fingers lingered on the torn silk, imagining Nat's wings as they
shredded in the Gyre.

Using the tools Tobiat and I had found and Elna's kit, I
patched myself new wings with the silk of both his wings and
mine.

I hid what remained, but did not throw it over the edge. Nat
was not strong enough to come after me, not yet. He'd want to
fly before he was ready. Too soon.

A rustle in the pile of silk and battens I'd pushed into a corner made me jump. A bulge moved. My skin prickled with fear.
Perhaps I should have thrown it over.

When I peeled back the silk, I saw nothing. Carefully, I put my hand out. I heard a cheeping sound and saw my dried-goose dinner disappear into an invisible mouth.

The little skymouth. I shuddered, despite myself. A stowaway, and a thief.

No. It was a garbage eater. Perhaps these littlemouths helped the city too.

I carefully laid the silk back over the creature and let it eat undisturbed. Began to hum The Rise again.

I pressed the seams on my wings with the heel of my palm. Tugged at them. They seemed solid. Solid enough to get me to the Spire, at least.

A gust of wind caught the wing's edge and lifted it. I pulled the straps over my shoulders, tightened them against my aching muscles. No one else to help me. My fingers brushed the lenses' cold metal. I thought of my father, of Ezarit. Of the bargains they'd made.

I imagined them fighting in the Gyre. Imagined Civik falling, his body breaking. My mother, wounded, a knife cut to her chest. Saw again Terrin's fall. The young woman who'd challenged Sellis. Nat. Heard the wind in the Gyre, felt the heat from the skymouth's maw.

My humming had become a keen. I bit it back.

At a scuffling sound from the tunnel, I turned, prepared to face Tobiat. But Nat pulled himself through, lowering himself to a sitting position against the wall. Elna followed.

"You're going," Nat said, panting.

"Yes. Right now." I looked at him, at the wounds I'd caused. Looked at the worry on Elna's face. I might not have another chance to say it. "I am sorry I fought you."

He frowned. "I fought you too. But you're right, what you said before. I made you a Singer. It wasn't exactly how we'd planned it."

I could feel my face flush with anger. They'd made a plan but hadn't figured out a way to share it with me. "I thought you died! I thought I killed you!"

Nat held his hands up. "I'm not fighting you now." His voice was still tired, and resigned. "Besides, someone from the towers needed to try and fight. Someone needed to fight."

I took a deep breath and blew my anger away. He was misguided, headstrong, and more than a little right.

"Someone will fight. Me. Once I find Ezarit," I said, squeezing his hands. "You heal."

I had to fly. Now. I couldn't undo what had happened. But I could try to keep it from getting worse. I lifted the lenses. Blew in them to keep the glass from fogging.

Elna coughed. "Hurry," she said. "The Singers will be out again at dark."

Her words reminded me that I'd made a bargain too, with Rumul, so long ago. *Your Laws, and those of your mother.*

Trapped here on Lith, I had forgotten the full consequences of my betrayal.

Ezarit. I fought to keep my hands from shaking. I had to find her before I went to the Spire. I had to make her come to Lith, to hide. If I flew fast enough, I might reach her before Rumul's people did.

I tightened the last strap as much as I could.

"What if Ezarit won't listen?" The sadness in my voice surprised me. Ezarit had always done things her own way.

"She fought to keep the Singers from knowing about you; she tried to find a place in a tower that had more power in the city; one that could protect the two of you better than Densira. But Grigrit required an apprentice in order to consider it. She'll listen."

I understood a little better now. The bargain she'd made with Doran Grigrit. Her desperation after the wingfight. "She should have told me."

Elna nodded. "We both should have told you. And each other. I thought my silence would buy your lives."

The sun began to sink below the clouds, turning the sky pink and red.

Silence. Tradition. Secrets. I'd thought I was keeping Elna and Ezarit safe too. Now we were stranded on Lith. Now I had to hurry.

I stood and tightened my other strap, then stepped through the footsling, ready to fly. The sun was setting as I checked the wind at the balcony, low on the city's darkest tower. What Elna and Naton had sacrificed for, and Ezarit, and Nat too, I needed to finish. As soon as Ezarit was safe.

I unfurled my new wings, my lopsided, mismatched pair that was everything I was at the moment: stitched together pieces of my friends and family.

As I leapt from our hiding place on Lith, they watched me go. I stuttered in the breeze until I learned to balance on the unmatched, patched wings. If I were attacked, I would not survive it.

The patchwork wings wobbled. My lenses swung on their strap and banged against my collarbone. I reached carefully to still them and my right wing dipped precariously. I fought to right it, twisting my arm up, just as a small tentacle wrapped around my wrist.

"Bone and blood," I whispered, more startled at the touch than anything. The littlemouth had stowed away with me.

The tiny creature worked its way up my arm and clung to my shoulder. I slipped my hand back into the grip on my right wing. My path straightened immediately, but I still fought for altitude. My neck prickled as the tentacles felt their way forward, dragging the small sack of the skymouth's body behind it. Its hide was rough and dry, not wet like its bigger, fiercer cousins.

The creature pulled itself over to my left shoulder, which was higher ground, I supposed, since the right one kept dipping as I fought to control my new wings. As it settled there, the slight weight change steadied me. The wings soared better. They lifted me, finally, to the clearer air.

"Thanks," I whispered to the tiny monster hugging my left arm, my shoulder, and my back. "Enjoy the ride."

I began to hum again, softly.

The towers rose over me, tinted blue-violet and blackberry hues by the setting sun. At this level, only a few scavengers might have seen me by mistake, but soon I'd rise to a level that didn't have such downdrafts. It would be safer, but if a Singer— or someone loyal to them—saw me there, I would never reach my mother in time to warn her, nor the Spire in time to challenge Rumul before they threw me down.

I would simply disappear. Like Naton and so many others.

Densira and the edge of the city drew close. I found an updraft and circled gently with it, aiming higher. A dark shape passed above me. Two Singers, flying wing to wing.

I dodged around the tower, taking extra time to circle Densira and avoid them.

When I emerged from the other side, the Singers were leaping from a balcony, carrying a burdened net between them. The person in the net struggled.

My mother's voice drifted down the many tiers to my sensitive ears. I was too late.

26

REVOLT

Ezarit shouted at the Singers who carried her away from her tower and towards the Spire. She cursed them, then tried to bribe them. She was still negotiating. But the Singers ignored her.

I tried to climb faster, but my wings would not permit it. I had no weapon to use against the Singers. And my mother wore no wings. My attack would doom her if they chose to let the net fall.

The Singers who bore my mother to the Spire faded quickly into the distance. The city's towers turned to shadow and darkness.

I stumbled along in the twilight air, frustration filling my eyes. Freezing on my cheeks. I kept flying. I could not fail in my goals.

* * *

Even the long days before Allsuns had moments of darkness. The last of the sunset's colors disappeared below the clouds. Oil lanterns flickered in the nearby towers as people drew close with their families.

I hummed quietly, hearing the city as well as seeing it for a short time. The darkness thickened, and I heard the Spire ahead of me.

As my echoes struck the Spire's solid-seeming walls, they revealed hidden hollows and panels. I glided close to the one I needed, the access gate closest to the pens. I pulled my fingers from a wing grip and flexed them.

ۑ   ۑ   ۑ

In the dark, I clung to the Spire's side, a mottled shadow against the bone-white wall. Wik waited for me inside, and Civik, but it was up to me to break in without being caught. Above, Nightwings launched from the Spire and flew into the city. They did not see me.

I had to get inside the Spire, fast.

I traced my fingers along the wall until I found the pressure points that opened the gate from outside. One stuck, then depressed. I heard the sound of a panel rolling back. This was a small gate. I furled my wings before pulling my upper body through.

I entered the Spire sideways, on my belly, near an empty alcove in the windbeaters' tiers. I heard heavy snoring nearby and cinched my footstrap to keep it from clattering against the floor and waking my neighbor.

Hidden on the windbeaters' tier, I waited and tried to think how to find Wik or Civik. On the tier's far side, I saw a small shadow work its way past a moonlit patch. I held my breath and sank back against the alcove wall. Hoped.

When Moc passed by on silk-soft feet, I reached out and grabbed his robe.

He bit back a screech. "I was looking for you! Wik said you would come back."

"I need your help. And Civik's." We kept our voices low.

Moc caught sight of my lenses, still hanging round my neck. "He gave them back to you. Windbeaters don't do that."

"Perhaps he's something more than a scheming windbeater, Moc. He might want things to change too. Ask him."

Moc slunk off in the direction of Civik's alcove, and soon

both returned. Parted ways as Moc climbed from the tier to find Wik. *Hurry, Moc.*

Civik tapped my hand with a finger. "Council's already met to hear from Sellis about your interference. Rumor is you're cloudbound."

"I'm not cloudbound yet. But they were going to hurt Elna."

Civik bobbed his head and shrugged. "Maybe. Maybe Wik would have diverted them."

"People still would have died. We have enough troubles without Rumul making more."

He frowned. "He's still got too many on his side. No one wants to see more towers fall. No one wants war. Our plan is to work slowly." I could see his face as the brief moonrise brushed our side of the tier. He looked afraid, and very old. My heart sank.

"You sent me these," I said, holding his hand to the lenses. "Why?"

"They're yours now. Not mine. I can't do anything with them." His fingers traced the lenses' edge. Then one finger touched my nose. Hovered away. Then his hands covered my face. Softly, he used his fingers to see me.

I held still, hoping Wik would come soon. I'd never talked to Civik alone. When he didn't move his hands from my face, I stepped back and caught his fingers in mine.

"It is time to do more," I said, squeezing his hands. "I need you to get windbeaters who share your views out to the Gyre at dawn."

He nodded. "I can do that. They know what's possible now that we have Naton's chips. We looked at the holes he drilled in the walls. The weak points he created but never had the chance to finish. But Rumul still has influence down here. We have to be cautious." Civik hesitated, caught between hope and doubt.

At the sound of footsteps tripled by a bone cane and the swish of robes on the passage outside the alcove, we both fell silent. We barely breathed until the noises passed. Where was Wik?

I tried to think of something that would make him act beyond his fear. "Do your rumors tell you who they've caught and brought to the Spire?"

Civik shook his head. "Who?"

I paused, thinking of Ezarit's scars, of what she did to Civik in the Gyre. I didn't know how he'd react to the news.

"Who?" He tightened his grip on my hand. Then, as if he could read my mind, he said, "Ah. Yes. Ezarit." The way he said it gave me no comfort. I should have stayed quiet.

"I can't let them hurt her either."

The old windbeater frowned. Then he tapped my lenses again. "You are right. Now is time to fight, and to speak."

I breathed out, relieved. I would have his support if I fought in the Gyre. I hoped he could gather enough of the others. But I needed more than that. "I need better wings, Civik. And a good blade."

My father let go of my hand. Rolled back and forth on his cart. "We do not have those things down here. The Singers took all the nightwings we've made. And there are no blades among the windbeaters. You must get them elsewhere."

There was a scuffling sound, and Moc tumbled into the alcove. "They've blocked off the council tier. I can't get past the guards. Can't get to Wik."

"They kicked me out earlier," Ciel said, appearing behind Moc. "No flying, either."

New plan, then. I couldn't use the ladders to get to the council. I couldn't fly. And Wik was somewhere up there.

"Moc, you need to help me sneak into the pens. Right now."

He started to argue. "They'll see you."

But Ciel said, "I know how," and pulled me from the alcove, towards the galleries where the windbeaters worked the Gyre. She grabbed one of the ropes that ran down the Gyre's sides and handed me a large bucket. It still smelled of stink, but it was empty, and big enough to hold me, if I kept very still.

But the bucket couldn't hold my patchwork wings. I stripped them off. Felt the small skymouth wrap itself tighter around my shoulder.

I tucked myself as best I could into the bucket. Both twins and Civik, working the ropes together, lowered me down on the cable to the knotted ropes of the pens.

They worked fast, and when the bucket came to rest, I rolled out and ducked into the shadows beneath an overhanging gallery. They reeled up the bucket and disappeared.

Alone in the dark, once all had grown quiet again, I crawled to the center of the nets and let myself into the core of the pens. Felt the captive skymouths bump against the ropes and poke the thin points of tentacles out as I passed. I hummed, and the tentacles receded.

When the skymouths settled, the littlemouth still at my shoulder loosened its grip. "Oh, no you don't," I whispered, then tucked it into my robe, by my ribs. I tightened the fastenings to secure it. "You'd be like dinner to your cousins."

Too close beside me, someone coughed, and I jumped. In the darkness, I could make out a tall form with broad shoulders.

"You made it," Wik said.

"I did." My heart pounded from the scare. "How did you get away from the council tier?"

"I told Rumul someone needed to check on the pens. He told me to get them ready to migrate again tomorrow and then return. The council will discuss Ezarit's fate in a few hours."

Worse and worse.

"How did you know I'd come here?"

"I didn't. I'd planned to ask Moc to help find you, but he's made himself scarce."

I wanted to laugh, but it was too awful. "He was looking for you. You passed each other. One going up, the other coming down." I grew serious. "We need to get back up there."

He wrapped a hand around a thick rope. "They will try to stop you from reaching the council and issuing a challenge, Kirit. Rumul says that the city is already angry. That a sacrifice needs to be made."

"Did you try to challenge?"

Wik bowed his head. "I began the process. No one would support me. Not with another Conclave possible if the city keeps rumbling. They are frightened. They don't want to lose my vote on council, if I fail. We were so close to breaking him before the city—" He stopped. Dragged his fingers through his hair. Exhausted. "Instead, I tried to blunt Sellis's attacks on you, tried to keep them from tearing apart the towers looking for you, the traitor Singer. I told her I'd disposed of you already, but that did not satisfy her, or Rumul."

I couldn't imagine it would. "They wanted to dispose of me themselves." Cloudbound. The first sacrifice at Conclave.

"Yes."

"Why should I believe you? You led the attack on Densira."

"I was trying to foil it, Kirit."

"But you didn't."

"No. But I saved you. And brought Elna to you."

That was true. "They have Ezarit now, up there."

He met my gaze. "She's being held in Rumul's enclosure."

I thought of Ezarit, encased in the walls of the Spire as I once was. "I can't get to her there."

"If you win your challenge, you can free her."

"And if I lose?"

Wik was silent. The nets creaked. "Then I will challenge

without support. Like Terrin. And more people will die tomorrow."

I thought of Nat, and my mother. Of the enclosure's carved walls. Of the skymouths. I had to try.

Wik reached into the sleeve of his robe and removed his knife and its sheath. He handed these to me. They were heavy in my hands, and the glass blade was dark as the night. I bound the sheath to my arm.

He said, "I've been down here too long. They are watching everyone. Every tier. How will you get to the council?"

"It's better if you don't know."

He stared at me. "You are a Singer, Kirit. Truly. The kind we need." He leaned close, his eyes fierce. "Don't let them tell you you're not." He climbed quickly from the pens and onto the next tier. Then he was gone, leaving me alone, surrounded by skymouths.

When I echoed, the Singers' skymouths sounded like soft objects, bobbing in the pens. Their tentacles trailed across each other. In the far corner of the pens was a different shape, less buoyant. Not moving.

Any breeding program had successes and losses. I thought of Nat's whipperlings, his search for the fastest ones. Of my own silk spiders. We didn't feed the ones that didn't make enough silk. There were always culls.

I hoped I was right, that it was the same here. Skymouth culls didn't need their skins any longer.

The rigging and cages designed by Nat's father for these pens almost seventeen years ago filled the center of the Spire. I stood on the side, echoing, until I found more still shapes. Beyond them, I could hear the harder objects, the pulleys and cams that raised the pens when the Spire rose.

I imagined how far the cages had risen in the intervening years, and what horrors they'd hosted.

Then I took a deep breath and, humming softly, entered the pens. The littlemouth squirmed against my chest. Gripped tighter. I kept moving, gathering the piles of skymouth skins I'd spotted a moment ago.

I walked the outer edge of the pens, humming. The skymouths quieted, though tentacles still reached for me, curled round my ankles.

A roar on my left drew me towards double netting held fast with spidersilk, thick tendons, and something else. Metal wire. Metal. The desperation of that shocked me. The reinforcements were recent and rough-hewn. The big skymouth Wik spoke of at Lith—they must have enclosed it here. And it did not want to be kept. I backed away quickly and gathered the last few dead and dying skymouths from the pens' edges. My arms filled with them. The deflated bodies and slack limbs slopped over my hands and dragged on the floor, tripping me. Their acrid stench burned my nostrils.

I returned to the center of the pens and put down my burden. I echoed and saw the culls. A dozen of them, piled at my feet. Either they couldn't survive or their keepers didn't want them to.

The pens shifted and creaked as their occupants grew restless with the smell of death so near. I hummed while I worked, hoping it would calm them enough to stay their movements.

All the culls were recent, dying now or dead within the last day or two, by my guess. Several were as large as my wings. Not big enough to be farmed for sinew, so left to feed their brethren in the pens.

I took Wik's knife from my sleeve and dragged its point across the first cull's skin, separating the hide from the muscle below. I wasn't sure what I was doing would work, but I had to try. More rank scent filled the room. I gagged and prayed it wouldn't get worse.

It took an hour to get what I needed.

Above, the night sky showed through the distant opening at the top of the Spire. When I'd begun my task, it was still dark. Now the apex was starting to lighten. The city rumbled again below. I stood on the pens, covered in the gore of dead sky-mouths and looked up into the Gyre. The galleries and tiers rose to the distant circle of sky.

I put on my lenses to protect my eyes from the increasing burn in the air. The skymouths' skins stuck to my fingers as I worked.

Good.

I took the skin peeled from the culls and pieced two slip-pery edges together on my lap. Then I took out the metal nee-dle I'd found on Lith and clumsily tried to thread a thick vein through the needle's eye in the dim light. *Faster, Kirit. Work faster.*

I pushed the needle through the skins, denting my fingers and drawing blood when I had to, pushing too hard.

My arms ached, and my knees grew numb from kneeling as I seamed one hide to the next. Soon, I held an acrid cloak of shame and death that clung to me wetly when I wrapped my-self in it, making me shudder.

"Clouds," a small voice whispered, just above my head. Moc had climbed onto the pens. He helped me adjust the cloak so that it hung low over my face, dripping and filled with an un-bearable musk. I was grateful again for the lenses, which kept the worst of the gore from my eyes. I tried to breathe through my mouth, tried to avoid throwing up at the stench.

Then I left the pens, and, using the slops rope, began my slow climb up the inside of the Spire, wingless, and, I hoped, com-pletely unexpected.

I lifted my hand. It was a shimmer in the air. I was as invis-ible as a skymouth.

27

CHALLENGE

Once I climbed from a prison within the walls of the Spire, half starved, my skin torn. Once, I begged for my life and traded my will for a pair of wings.

I would not beg this time. I was a Singer, and a citizen. They would hear me. They would free my mother. They would find another way to protect the city. They would admit what they'd done in its name.

I clung to the refuse ropes, lifting myself up arm over arm, past the windbeaters' tier. Unseen, I glimpsed my father rousing his peers, preparing them. I saw a closed vat over a new fire. Rot gas, heating. My face grim beneath my hood, I continued to climb.

Above me, the Spire's mouth opened, distant and toothed with the last of the night's stars. I had to reach it, and the council's tier below it. Each tier I passed brought me closer.

After ten tiers, I rested an arm on the railing of an observer's gallery and flexed my aching hands. The skymouth skins had thinned and turned silver where they had rubbed too hard against the fibers of the refuse ropes.

A bone hook clattered to the floor of the tier. My clumsy hand had knocked it loose from its prop against the gallery wall. A Singer must have left it there to push challengers away from the walls. I looked around the tier, a novice level. Saw only one bleary-eyed, gray-robed acolyte trudging with a bucket towards the pulleys. He didn't give the noise a second look.

The wind knocked things over, shook things loose. Now I was the wind, come to knock at the Spire's walls.

Once the novice had finished disposing of his stink, I returned to the refuse rope and continued climbing. I had to move faster now. The ropes would soon be put to hard use.

A breeze wound its way up the Gyre. Were my wings with me, it might have lifted me slowly up the last few tiers. I didn't have time to look down to see if the breeze was natural or created by the first of the windbeaters working the vents. I had to climb.

Hand over hand, feet twisting in the ropes for extra purchase, I climbed alone, save for the kaviks that passed me and tried to coat me with their waste. One hit its target, my shoulder, and the white goo splattered. The guano slid off the skymouth hide and continued its fall into the Gyre. I remained unmarked, hidden. "Incredible," I whispered, thinking of the littlemouth in my pocket. My voice sounded strained and worn.

The dark night and the dimness of the tower helped me climb past many tiers without incident. But I had been lucky for too long. The refuse rope jerked against my hands, and I clung to it, yanked upwards at a fast clip as someone hauled on the rope from above. I saw a face peering over the edge confused. Lurai, looking for tangles in the rope and finding none.

My heart rode high in my throat, threatening to choke me. I was so close. Then the pulling stopped. I swung on the rope as it halted its rise. Above me, Lurai circled his tier, headed for another pulley. One that worked.

Relief slowed my heart a bit, but I knew this was a short-lived reprieve. I had to climb faster.

Lights began to appear in alcoves. Oil lamp sprites moved up and down ladders. I heard whispering, but could not make out the words through my cloak.

I heard a familiar melody. What sounded like Ezarit's voice, muffled, singing The Rise. The city's version. At least it sounded like Ezarit's voice, from very far away. With a clatter, followed by shouts, the song broke off. But not for long. Another voice, from a much closer tier, boomed across the Gyre. Wik. Singing The Rise in response to Ezarit. He sang the Spire's version to her, telling her the truth. It was a subtle rebellion. One that cheered me on. Five tiers to go. Four. I sweated and choked inside the cloak. My skin stung from the still-acrid veins that I, in my hurry, hadn't scraped away.

Below me, windbeaters began practicing their dancelike movements. The edge of my cloak flapped, slapping at my feet. The rope twisted, and I scrambled for balance. The novices just waking and the windbeaters not aligned with Civik would spot me soon. *Hurry, Kirit.*

A pair of carvers dropped over the gallery edge nearest the Spire's opening and hung suspended above me. They spoke quietly as they continued work on the fierce decorations scraped into the newest Gyre wall.

I was nearly to the council's tier, but I could not move without them seeing the rope shake.

As I wavered about what to do next, my foot slipped. In my scramble to recover, the sewn-together hides began to slide from my head and shoulders. I could not hold them in place and still keep climbing.

With one hand, I managed to grab the trailing edge of the cloak I'd made from dead skymouth culls before it fell away completely. I hung, revealed, at the edge of the council tier. Air struck my skin where the hide had touched it, painful and raw.

With arms on fire from the climb, I slung the cloak over the tier edge and grabbed the nearest gallery railing. Pulled myself up and over it. I rested for a moment, a pile of oil-damp, foul-smelling girl, my cheek pressed against the young bone of the tier. My scalp burned. Some hair had torn away when the cloak slipped. The palms of my hands bled. The skin on my arms and face was red from contact with the hides. I pulled my lenses away from my face and down to my neck. I shooed off the pain as one of the carvers approached.

"All right, Singer?" she said, curious at my appearance. My lack of wings.

"Very," I said with all the breath I had. "Special training for night flying," I added.

She shrugged and went back to her work. Rumul may have had Singers searching for me, but he'd failed to inform the novices. My familiarity to the carvers, from many days of punishment as I had learned the Spire's ways, was now another kind of invisibility. I approached the council unchallenged, dragging the cloak behind me.

The council huddled in Rumul's alcove, crowding the space and spilling into the passageway.

Below, more voices began to sing. The morning ritual of The Rise had begun. Sound surrounded me: the story of the city and how the Singers saved it from ruin. In her enclosure beneath Rumul's alcove, my mother might have been able to hear the singing as I had, once.

A shout from the rooftop broke the song's rhythm. I crouched behind a spine as an older Singer climbed down from outside and rushed to Rumul's chambers.

"Fliers approaching! A Magister and four others," he said.

"Who summoned them?" Rumul's voice rang clear over the song coming up from the tiers below.

The council broke its huddle. I hauled the stinking cloak back over my head. Obscured myself. *Delequerriat*, Rumul.

Several Singers began speaking at once. Over the tumult, I heard Wik say, "Let them land. Perhaps they have found Kirit."

The other Singers murmured agreement.

This was my cue. I could rush into the alcove and challenge Rumul while the council waited for news.

But I could not move from my crouch. My muscles had seized after the long climb, my toes were asleep. I watched the visitors land on the roof above and be escorted down to the tier. Only when Rumul emerged from his alcove, the council behind him, was I able to feel my feet once more.

Macal had returned to the Spire. He'd brought Beliak with him. And several traders. He must have told the trade council that Ezarit had been taken to the Spire.

Macal stepped forward, but Wik held up his hand and stopped his brother from speaking. One tan-robed trader, his hair beaded with glass like my mother's once was, cleared his throat.

Rumul spoke before the trader could. "We did not summon you to the Spire."

"We thought we heard horns," the trader said. "Macal said we were summoned." He was layering the truth. I could tell from the set of his jaw. Macal nodded in support. Met Rumul's glare with raised eyebrows.

The trader looked over Rumul's shoulder, eyes searching, perhaps for Ezarit.

Several thick-shouldered Singers climbed up the ladders from downtower. Rumul had called for reinforcements. Once they closed ranks around him, I would not be able to get close enough to challenge him. I would be captured. I racked my tired brain for ways to get around them. Then Ciel burst past me and ran to the assembled Singers.

"I saw her, Kirit, she's in the novice's tier! The traitor!"

The guards reacted by unfurling their wings and diving into the Gyre. The fastest way down.

Sellis's voice came from the alcove. "I told you she wasn't dead yet."

My path cleared, I pushed past the traders, past Macal and Beliak.

"Hey! Hands off!"

"You pushed me."

"I didn't."

I barely registered their confusion. Then I remembered. My cloak shielded me still.

Invisible, I made it all the way to the council members who had gathered in a gray crowd around Rumul.

Wik stood close to Rumul, arguing with him. Rumul watched him as a gryphon regarded its prey. The council was slowly backing away from Wik.

I pushed my way into the circle. "I challenge the Spire," I said as loudly as I could.

Rumul and the council members turned left and right, searching for the speaker.

I pitched my voice so that the traders and Sellis and the carvers in the Gyre could hear me. "I demand to be allowed to fight as a Singer for the good of the city. I challenge you, Rumul."

I reached up and grabbed the skymouth cloak with my bare hand. My fingertips burned as I pulled it away, more hair going with it. I let it drop to the ground and stood at the center of the council, just inches from Rumul.

Council Singers gasped and whispered. The traders looked shocked. Macal and Beliak folded their arms, blocking the alcove's exit.

Rumul stared at me, then pointed to Wik. "Drop her into the enclosure as well."

"No," Wik said. "Once a challenge has been put forward by another Singer, it must play out."

"Singer's right," several council members said. So there was dissent, even here.

Viridi, who days ago had held my hand to the city's mystery, its very heart, stepped forward. "It is tradition," she said. Several more council members shifted uncomfortably. They knew she spoke truth.

Another tradition was for Rumul to win in the Gyre. His face held the map of his wins. But the knife wound from his fight with Terrin had not healed easily. I had a chance.

"I challenge you, Rumul, and bid my life for my mother's," I shouted again. Loud enough to be heard in the tiers below. "I offer it for the good of the city."

The morning song stopped. Singers and novitiates turned their eyes to the council tier. I heard the low grinding sound of a vent opening and felt the Gyre wind deepen and quicken.

Rumul's jaw clenched. His tattoos curled and folded as his frown deepened. "You had such promise."

I met his eyes. "I still do."

He did not respond.

Sellis shoved a council member aside and pushed into the circle. She looked long at Rumul before she turned on me. "I take the challenge up in Rumul's name. There will be no concession."

"Singer's right," the same group of council members spoke again, joined by more who had stayed silent when I issued the challenge.

Wik groaned. Sellis was young and whole. She was an excellent fighter. I was tired from my climb, hungry from my days away from the Spire. Wik began to step forward, to take up my challenge for me. I would not allow it. I held up my hand and met Sellis's eyes.

"I accept."

Far below, enormous white wings edged the windbeaters' tier. They began to move, creating eddies and whorls in the Gyre. The wind picked up.

Singers stepped back from us, gathering weapons for us to select. A rustle of silk and clatter of wing battens nearby nagged at the edges of my attention, but I refused to turn from Sellis's glare. The challenge began now. Here. I would win, or she would. One of us would die.

Only when Rumul pulled her aside did I drop my gaze and look around me.

Wings surrounded me. Viridi, Beliak, and Macal held theirs out, straps ready for me to slip over my shoulders. Wik held a different pair. They were tea-stained, with a kestrel stamped on the silk. As familiar as home. My mother's wings.

I reached out to touch them. Drew the straps over my shoulders and tightened the buckles.

"I would see her."

Rumul started to argue my request, but Sellis whispered to him and his face changed. "Open the enclosure."

They took me to the moon-window above the pit and I looked down on her, curled far below.

She peered up, unable to see who watched her.

"I cannot make the same choice you did," I said. She sat up, listening. "But I understand why you made yours."

"I wanted to know you would be safe," she whispered. Her voice carried up the walls of the pit, and my ears helped it the rest of the way.

"There is no safety here," I said. I turned so the council could hear my words as well as Ezarit. "The city must know what I know. Why should I die silent?"

She reached her hand up, towards me. I reached through the window, towards her. We were separated by the deep pit, but I could feel her there with me. A breeze cooled the stinging rash that had risen on my hands. I closed my eyes and imagined she wrapped her arms around me and held me until I stepped away.

I walked from the alcove across the passageway to the council tier.

Without waiting on tradition, I leapt into the Gyre.

❧   ❧   ❧

As I hurtled from the ledge, the windbeaters whipped the challenge winds higher. The churning gusts confused me. Some vents buoyed me up; others seemed to disappear from beneath me.

Heavier gusts began to rattle from far down the tower. The carvers grabbed their tools and pulled themselves from the walls. Singers and novices ran to the galleries to watch.

I locked my wings in fighting position. Reached into my sleeve and undid the sheath. Wrapped my fingers around the hilt of Wik's glasstooth knife. I felt a small tentacle wrap my arm, then release it.

My throat closed. I had forgotten my small passenger. I had doomed the little skymouth too.

The windbeaters were my hope. If Civik had convinced enough of them that I was worth the risk, they would support me. If not, or if he was still convincing them, then I could fly right into a void and drop like a stone.

I could not know how well Sellis would fly these gusts, nor what she was armed with. That was the right of the challenged. My own knife—Wik's knife—smelled acrid. Like skymouth skin.

Taking a tactic from Nat's fight, I circled the Gyre and grabbed a carved post below the council balcony—the traditional launch point. If she chose that, I could get behind her.

The spectators roared and looked above me. My guess had been right. Sellis soared over my head, carrying a long bone spear in one hand and a glass knife in the other.

She locked her wings in fighting position and dropped quickly, searching for me.

I pushed out from the wall, twisting into my glide, and circled on her heels.

She made a sharp turn and came at me from the side, intending to crush me against the Gyre wall. Her eyes searched for the best angle to take me out quickly.

I'd seen Sellis fight in the Gyre, and I'd trained with her. I knew the tricks she used. I slammed into her before she could build up speed. Knocked her into a spin that sent her against the far gallery wall. Her pinions clattered against the carvings.

As she fought to recover, I began to shout.

"You know the truth, Sellis. So should the others."

We were high enough that we could be heard by many of the tiers. At my words, the galleries rumbled. Not everyone here knew what was done in the Singers' name. Not even Terrin had gone so far as to speak the truth before he won the right to do so.

Tradition.

Sellis would never break the Silence. She would never allow me to do so.

Whose permission did I need to speak? No one's.

Tradition had created a place where Rumul could breed secrets. I was finished with tradition.

My voice rang rough and barbed across the Gyre.

I shouted the truth for Ezarit, who could not hear me. For Naton and Elna, who were not here. I shouted to the traders from Naza and Bissel, and to the shadows I saw gathered at the Spire's roof.

"Below you, in the pens, we have bred monsters. This has been done in the city's name. You were lied to on purpose. The city was deceived."

"Silence!" Rumul roared from the balcony.

The Singers were so caught up in the fight, and in my words, they did not notice the growing audience on the rooftop. As Sellis and I circled higher on the maelstrom, I thought I could see Ceetcee, Sidra, Dojha, Dikarit, Aliati, and citizens from nearby towers, gathered to witness. Macal had summoned them. I squinted at their robes and colorful wings, dazzled by the bright light of Allsuns.

Sellis threw one of her knives. It flew past my ear and clattered down the carved wall.

She shrieked in frustration. "Shut up, Kirit! You cannot speak! Not until you have won!"

But I kept shouting and more. I sang. I sang of the tiny skymouth in my sleeve. I sang of the attack on Elna the night we blessed the bridge. I sang how Sellis had hung back. How she would have let a blind citizen die.

She paled at this.

I sang to the Spire the horror that the Singers had made, so that no one could deny knowing, so that none could stand by, robed in ignorance and tradition any longer.

As Sellis and I wheeled in the Gyre, first high, then low, I could see the galleries and watch some of the other Singers' eyes widening. Novices turned to each other, whispering. The council shattered as several members ran for the ladders, hoping to reach the windbeaters and force them to drop me from the sky. Too late.

My voice cracked as I sang of Naton, Tobiat, and Civik, one gone, one broken beyond repair. One lost, then found again.

A rumbling dissent sounded from the very walls of the Spire, even as I continued singing and shouting the Singers' crimes.

A gust lifted me higher again. The windbeaters supported me.

But I did not stop. I shouted the Spire's triumphs too. I sang how the Singers saved the city, how they kept its people from warring against one another. How they collected our stories and kindled our culture. I sang Tobiat's story of Lith.

Finally, I sang the skymouths. My voice grew hoarse, but I sang their past and their present. I sang the pens and the truth about the migrations.

I was still singing when a horrified Sellis threw herself at me. "You lie!" she said. "You will be silenced!" She stabbed at my side with a long bone blade.

And then I screamed, with all the sound that I had left. I had run out of words. I screamed and screamed and screamed.

28

RELEASE

Sellis did not land a second blow. She instead circled with her third knife still aimed, listening. Not to my screams. To the city. From deep in the Spire, the rumbling rose. It built to a roar. The watching Singers clutched their ears.

My scream poured from me anew. My voice, echoing down the Gyre, mixed with the city's anger until the Spire shook. Sellis wobbled in her glide, too stunned to make the turn, and crashed into a wall. Where sharp bone tools had carved deep gouges long ago, the Spire's walls now oozed yellow ichor.

Sellis's hands came away from the wall, and she fell backwards. Her hands were stained yellow with the city's blood.

My shout continued, though my voice had begun to falter and fade. Then another voice joined mine: Wik's, strong and deep. Then a third, elderly and tremulous, but shouting from the windbeaters' tier. Civik. My father. I found my breath again, my voice, and continued to scream.

"You must stop!" Rumul dove from the council tier as he shouted to be heard. "You are breaking the Spire. The city."

He hurtled like an arrow towards me.

"The Spire isn't all of the city, it is just one part!" I shouted back. The Gyre echoed with sound.

Rumul's wings were tucked tight. He aimed to knock me into a pen or a vent. He did not intend to fight. He plummeted, willing to sacrifice himself for Singer secrets, for the Spire. The force of him hitting me knocked my breath out. I was silenced.

But Wik and Civik continued shouting.

Rumul and I fell past the occupied tiers. We fell past the windbeaters.

Fell until Sellis, blind from noise and fear, struck us both. She hit me again with her last knife, slicing my arm. As she struggled to right herself, she knocked Rumul loose with a bone hook gripped in her other hand.

Rumul hit the nets above the pens first, and I fell hard beside him. He struggled as something held him there, pulled at him. A tentacle grazed my leg.

The sounds of the Gyre merged with a new noise from the pens. The skymouths. They were screaming back at me. I was so close to them, my head rocked with pain, and I pulled my arms from my wing grips so that I could cover my ears. I found my breath and resumed shouting. The sinew nets pressed hard against my knees and elbows. Beside me, invisible limbs pulled Rumul's arms and legs in different directions. He screamed with the pain.

Some of the smaller skymouths gathered beneath me. I could feel their snouts bumping the netting. One grazed its teeth over my hand, a soft gesture. They pushed on the net and then moved backwards as a group, then they pushed forward again. I could not understand what they were doing, but I rose and fell with their motion. I rolled. They pushed me towards the edge of the pens.

The smell was all around me. The musk. My skin burned with it still.

I smelled like them. And they were screaming like me.

We shook the tower with the horrible pitch of our voices. Then the Spire trembled worse than ever before and a terrifying sound wove between my voice and the skymouths'. A sound like a giant wing breaking. Louder. The bone walls of the Spire began to crack.

The Spire shook again, and the city roared, sharp and piercing. I heard a sound no city dweller lives to describe: the sound of bone splitting.

The cracks began to run through the tower, but while another tower would have cracked across its center core, across a tier, the Spire cracked vertically. From one carefully drilled hole to the next, the breaks ran along carvings, forming arches and circles. In many cases, the breaks started where Naton's carving had gone deepest.

The Spire itself moaned and shrieked as the bone walls of the tower split and cracked. I squinted as entire panels fell from the walls and daylight poured for the first time into the Spire. Novices blocked their eyes. They ran from the winds and the suddenly open tiers. Teachers tried to put wings on their students, to get them aloft.

The tower rumbled, and more walls shattered.

Holes opened around the pens. Naton's tools had cut deep there too. Wind whistled over skymouths escaping the pens and squeezing themselves out of the Spire, suddenly free. The screaming faded as they scattered.

The pressure of invisible bodies gathering beneath me lessened, then disappeared. The netting sagged, and I sank into the depths.

A rough howl shook the tower. Sinew broke and metal snapped as the last giant skymouth's pen twisted apart with a rush of air. The monsters were free.

"What have you done?" Rumul moaned. The line of his collarbone ran jagged beneath his skin and his legs were splayed, broken. Now freed from grasping tentacles. He could not move.

For the first time, the Spire was open to the elements, to the eyes of the city. For the first time, its tiers were unguarded. Singer-bred monsters flew in and out of the gaps in the walls, mouths open and searching for prey.

Sellis circled above us on a gust let in by new air. "What has happened?" Her voice pitched high and panicked. "What has—"

A whistling roar cut off her words. The biggest maw I'd ever seen opened howling and red behind her. Her robes puckered as invisible limbs grabbed her waist, crushed her wings. Drawn backwards, like she was being sucked out of the Spire, Sellis flailed, her arms and legs towards us, her head thrown back, before the mouth swallowed her whole.

The monster turned, the wind from its passage pushing me into the sagging net. A torn wing hung from its invisible mouth, rising to the top of the Spire and out, into the sky, into the city.

I turned to Rumul. His face was sallow and waxy, his eyes closed.

"Sellis! It took her!" I yelled, but he did not respond.

Wik appeared on my left and reached his hand out. "Grab my hand, Kirit. Hurry." He helped me stand.

I followed him up a ladder to the windbeaters' tier, then looked down. Two Singers, one with a large cut on the back of his head, the other with a torn robe covered in dust, braced Rumul's legs on his folded wings, preparing to move him, unconscious, to safety.

The Spire stopped rumbling.

Civik lay crumpled beside the gallery, his wings beside him. With his mouth open, he looked as if he was still shouting, silently now.

"It took his last breath," Wik said. "Shouting with you."

When I took Civik's cold hand in mine, I found Naton's bone chips wrapped around his fingers. I left them there with my father as Wik pulled me towards the next tier. Naton's holes had not weakened the ladders here.

"Moc? He was down here with the windbeaters. And the novices?"

"Being evacuated to the towers. They're safe." Wik climbed faster.

After three tiers, my arms were shaking. I could not lift them to the next rung. All around us, Singers gathered pieces of the Spire and tended the injured. The Gyre seemed clear, though with the walls blown open, it whistled with a complex wind. "You have to fly, Wik. You have to get to the top of the Spire. I am too slow."

In answer, he unfurled his wings and locked them. Held out his arms to me.

Lifting me up, Wik made a running leap from the tier, and we plummeted into the Gyre. He found a gust glittering with sunlit bone grit, and we lifted, circling slowly higher.

I expected a mouth to open above us, or behind us, at any moment. I echoed, but heard and saw nothing. The mirror in my lenses showed me only Wik's robe and his wingstraps. Below us, the nets and the scattered windbeaters receded.

As we rose, Wik called to different tiers, asking after the injured, shouting instructions. Singers waited by the galleries, making ready to fly up after us, but waiting so as not to foul our wind. More flew from the holes in the walls, searching for cracks and signs the Spire was about to collapse. The first of these, a woman Wik's age, with a bruise ripening on her cheekbone, reported back as we reached the top of the Spire.

"It's lacework out there, all open to the city," she said. "But the breaks are evenly spaced. The tower seems to be holding, at least for now."

"Find weapons," Wik instructed her as he set me down. She descended a ladder and ran down the passageway below, following his orders.

"This is what Terrin feared would happen. That the skymouths would escape," Viridi said. Her silver-streaked hair was dusted with bone shards. Her voice cracked. She held Ciel's hand tightly. "We were wrong to pen them, to breed them."

Another Singer interjected, "We'll need weapons if the towers attack."

I flexed my arms and bounced on the balls of my feet, trying to work some feeling back into my legs. "The towers attacking? That's what you're worried about right now?" My voice was rough as scourweed.

The Singer turned to look at me. Who was I to speak?

Wik said, "Listen to her."

"She's won the right to speak," Viridi agreed, silencing any doubts.

"Skymouths are loose in the city." *My doing, in large part.* I knew this. I would make it right.

Macal ran up to us. "The Spire may stand, but everyone knows its secrets now." He gripped my shoulder in thanks. I winced, then spoke again.

"So now the city knows. And now the city suffers. We are still Singers," I said. "We must do our duty. We must catch the skymouths."

We would be stronger working together. No more separation between tower and Spire. I spotted Beliak on the council tier, helping clear large pieces of bone. "Tell the nearest towers to spread the word. Skymouths are loose."

Beliak yanked at the Bissel trader's robe and they climbed onto the roof of the Spire, unfurling their wings as they went.

I turned back to Viridi. "My mother."

"She is safe. Lurai and the traders pulled her from the enclosure when the Spire began to crack. They've taken her to Varu, to let her rest."

A shout from the Gyre. Singers climbed the pulley ropes

laden with weapons. More gathered on lower tiers. They waited for instructions, ready to fly.

What if they would not follow me?

"What you did . . . ," Wik whispered.

"They'll sing of it," Viridi finished for him.

"Not yet," I said. "Not unless—not until—the skymouths are caught."

Beliak returned. "Varu is sending as many people as it can to warn the nearby towers, and the traders are flying to the city's edges. Guards and hunters are ready to fight."

"We have to work together." I turned to Wik and Macal. "All of us." They would follow the three of us, united in purpose. Spire, tower, and me—who was both at once.

With a worried look, Wik ran his hand through the air near my cheek, where ugly welts had replaced the rashes raised by skymouth oils. They no longer burned, but I could feel the passage of air across them, and it made me shiver. I steadied myself as his green eyes met mine and then looked to the horizon, which had emptied of birds.

Sacrifice. Duty. This was what we shared.

From around the city, we began to hear the klaxons. Bone horns sounded warnings, at first from Varu and the towers near the Spire, but soon rippling out. So many.

"We must fix this," I said.

Wik shouted over the edge of the balcony, to the Singers and older novices assembled below. "We will catch the skymouths. Save the citizens first. Worry about the Spire later."

ʯ　ʯ　ʯ

At Wik's words, the Spire's chaos was replaced by years of training. Singers grabbed weapons and found their fighting groups. I returned Wik's knife and found several of my own, along with

a bow and a quiver of arrows. Beliak lifted a set of drugged spidersilk nets.

"Eat," Ciel said, holding out a fistful of dried goose meat, a
sack of water in her other hand. When I took some, she circled
the tier, making sure Singers drank and ate before they flew.

I chewed, exhausted. The food gave me strength, for now.
"We need more fighters, more guards." I grabbed Macal's sleeve.
"Get the whipperlings."

To my surprise, he ran to do what I'd said. The Spire's whipperlings were dispatched with hastily carved message chips.
Anyone who saw them could read the danger, the need to fight
together.

Viridi found me another new pair of wings, Rumul's own
spare set. They were big on me, but tightened fine to my shoulders.

Wik strode past, on his way to assemble his own flight of
fighters. Hunters had begun to land on the roof. I caught up
with him.

"We have to warn Elna and Tobiat and Nat. Lith isn't safe."

He frowned. "I'll make sure they know."

Around me, Singers snapped into action as they'd been
trained to do, protecting the city at a moment's notice.

Soon fliers flew formation from the top of the Spire. We
heard horns blowing farther away. In the distance, on Amrath
and Ginth, I saw Allsuns banners and gardens being hastily
pulled in. Atop many towers, guards' glass-edged wings sparkled in the sunlight as they massed for a fight.

The Singers rose to join them as the sun climbed high into
the sky.

It was Allsuns. The day when towers remembered their
fallen. Looked up in their honor.

But this year, the traditional Remembrance songs would have
to wait.

Flight teams joined, not tower by tower, but as groups. Singers and traders, Varu and Naza, Grigrit and Viit. Mondarath guards flew with Amrath councilwomen.

We flew, and the city flew. Wings of all colors, gray and yellow, bright-dyed and faded. Flew to fight, to protect, all of us, together.

I leapt from the Spire. Five Singers, three able older novices, and two council elders followed me. We were joined by two hunters and a trader from the south.

"Flew with your mother once. Hope you're as good as she is," the trader said grimly. She locked her wings for fighting.

We spread out in a chevron pattern, sweeping around Varu, then southwest, searching for monsters.

From the closest towers came whoops as the hunter-Singer teams netted the first skymouths. Then a scream, hastily cut off.

We found our first skymouth tangling with Ginth's guards. They circled a turbulent space in the air, just out of reach of its arms.

One of my hunters, armed with a bone spear and a set of nets, began to climb, his spear at the ready.

"Go with him," I shouted to the councilors. I took the novices and the second hunter and circled to reinforce the guards.

The hunter could not see where to aim his spear. I looked at the guards. They circled, guessing where to fire their arrows. We'd wind up shooting each other this way.

"Use your nets," I yelled.

Soon, the skymouth was trapped in a confusion of spidersilk and fiber nets. It yanked at its traces until I hummed it calm.

"What do we do with it now?" a novice asked.

What indeed. Taking them back to the Spire and tying them down would only repeat the problem. I circled the group once, thinking. The hunter with the bone hook yelled, "It's getting loose!" and threw his spear. The net stopped jerking.

My heart broke. This was not right. None of it was. "Make sure it is dead, then leave it on Ginth, with a guard."

The sun stayed high, and the net, as they tied it to Ginth's rooftop bone cleats, glistened pink and damp. As the long day stretched on, I realized that the hunters and guards who fought with us were in danger. It was not night, but they still flew blind.

A shadow passed overhead, then Wik circled to position on my left pinion.

I smiled at him, then heard another flier on my right. From beneath a borrowed pair of nightwings, Nat grimaced, pale and determined.

"Elna and Tobiat are safe," he said in response to my startled look.

"Nat, you can't fly now!"

"Everything's braced and bandaged," he said. "Once I got up in the air, I was fine. The challenge will be landing."

I shook my head, angering him.

"I'm a hunter, Kirit. I have to fight." He set his wings and nocked an arrow to his bow with a wince. "Besides," he added sadly, "someone needs to help you clean up this mess."

The two flew on either side of me, Singer and Lawsbreaker, my future and my past. One in Singer gray, one in black silk: Allsuns and Allmoons.

They flew as if they were my escorts. I did not want to be elevated like that. Like Rumul had raised himself above his peers. Above reproach. I set my jaw, stubborn. It was a protection I would not—could not—allow. We all fought as equals.

"Fine. We will each lead a flight. We need fliers who can see skymouths with each group." I scanned the flight following Wik. He saw what I intended. Signaled a skilled Nightwing to team with Nat. I heard the Nightwing begin to echo as Nat and his Singer eyes peeled away from us.

"Wik, find Ceetcee and Beliak. Help them. Tell the Singers you see to team up with tower fighters."

As we flew away from Ginth towards the west, we crossed another group flying in dove formation.

"We've bagged three," their leader shouted. Aliati. She smiled ear to ear, buoyed by their success. The Singer at her side whooped as they turned and headed east.

Across the city, more emerged to fight than hide as the word spread through the towers. The traders, including Ezarit, made sure word spread faster than the skymouths.

I rearranged flights as I saw them so that each group had Singers who could echo.

We continued to hunt the air around the farthest towers for escaped skymouths large and small. Netted as many as we could. This was not the skymouths' fault. This was what they were bred to do. We would capture them now, then figure out, as a city, together, what could be done.

When we left the Spire, the sun was high. Now we flew through the long day into dusk, seeking out the invisible.

In each tower, children and the old had been sequestered behind shutters and huddled close to the tower cores. Rooftops bristled with guards and volunteers. Bone horns sounded alarms.

"This is what the Rise must have been like," said a Singer novice, flying by my wing for the moment.

No, this is nothing like the Rise. "This time, we all work together."

I called for the flight to shift formation.

My flight assembled around me, wings to my left and right, bristling. The glass edges of the guards' wings glittered.

"On your wings, Singer," a hunter called. I looked around. She meant me.

I was the eye of my flight group. I shook myself awake and resumed echoing. Around us was open sky, then a curve of a tower. Below, fresh horror. A medium-sized skymouth, twice as large as my wings, crept towards the tower, its path confused. It zigged and zagged, not attacking, not yet.

"Net!" I said, signaling to those nearest. A big net of drugged spidersilk rustled as the novices unfurled it behind me. I did not take my focus off the skymouth. It moved below us, drunk with freedom, towards the tower.

We circled until the skymouth was directly beneath us and dropped the net. The monster fought, but the novices finally cinched the ties shut and secured it to the tower. I doubled back to make sure there were no more following this one.

From above, Beliak whistled, then dove to fly at my wingtip. Wik was behind him. "Finding fewer of them now, Kirit. Still some out there, but they're hiding. Now what?"

I looked out across the city, hearing its towers as much as I saw them. "We have to stay vigilant, but we should start to rest in shifts. Fixing this will take time. Find places for the Singers to bunk on the towers for now." My voice sounded tired.

"What about the skymouths?" Wik asked.

I closed my eyes for a second. "We're not taking them back to the Spire."

He agreed. "And we can't free them. They're too dangerous."

The thought of more killing, even skymouths, made me lose my way for a moment. I tried to think. What would Ezarit do? What would Naton do? Ezarit might find a way to use the skymouths, to keep them for their sinew. Naton might build something to help hold them, away from the occupied towers. They'd trade bad for good.

But many of these skymouths were bred for killing. Even

drugged in nets, they were still dangerous. One of my fighters had lost a toe, bitten off after he flew too close to a net.

My fliers grew tired. My own arms and legs ached, my mouth was dry with thirst. Fearing we would make mistakes if we grew too tired, I looked for a tower that did not yet have a flight or two of fighters already resting on its roof.

"I'll scout for a tower that can host us," Wik said. He found a breeze that took him southwest and slowly faded into the distance.

As I watched him go, I realized the rash on my hands from the skymouth's hide had faded, along with the skymouth's scent. The caustic oil had finally dried and peeled away. As I flew an updraft, my exposed skin pulsed in scrawls and etchings along the lines where I'd seamed the hides.

In the distance, Nat's dark wings and those of the Singer flying with him led a line of hunters returning, seeking a place to land. I sighed with relief.

Then the sky opened below us. An enormous mouth, readying to swallow us whole.

The monster of the pens. The one that had devoured Sellis. It had tracked us through the night, hiding and waiting. Now it was upon us.

"Scream, Kirit!" yelled Beliak. "Shout it down!"

I tried. A sour sound, almost a bark, came from my throat. My voice was ruined. I had screamed too long in the Spire just this morning.

So I gripped my knife and dove instead. Angled to meet the thing sideways, its teeth as big as my hands; its eye, oiled and deep like the sky.

No chance this monster would stop, once it got through us. Not until the whole city was stripped bare and ruined.

I dove, my glass-tooth blade aimed straight at its giant eye.

I flew close enough that I could smell it: that acrid scent combined with smoke and blood. I tried to hum, to calm it, but the monster rolled its eye, flipped over backwards and fled, jettisoning behind it an acrid cloud that made breathing near impossible.

I choked on the cloud, wobbling on my wings.

"Kirit, where are you?" Beliak called as Nat's flight crossed the skymouth's path. I shouted a warning and tried to right myself.

Nat heard me. He whistled a turn. The Singer in his group signaled wildly and tried to order him back into line.

No! I was upright again, and climbing for them before I knew it. This time, I felt the scream in the back of my mouth, and I hoped that I was strong enough. Loud enough. Horrible enough.

The maw opened. I put myself between it and Nat.

The skymouth grunted and lashed tentacles in all directions. It scrawled motion in a sea of wings, tearing down one flier after another. In the midst of a pass, I jerked to a stop. The skymouth gripped me around the waist with a tentacle and pulled me in towards the rows of teeth. My rough scream had no impact on its intent. My voice faded in my mouth. The monster began to squeeze.

Behind me, Nat held his shot and yelled my name.

The skymouth now loomed as wide as a tower, as angry as the clouds. It shrieked and grabbed even as it drew me in. The fliers dove to stay clear of it, while still trying to make it release me. Arrows studded the invisible giant, but they served only to make it angrier.

The bone battens of my wings began to crack in its grip.

And then I heard a squeal, too high-pitched to be Singer or skymouth. The sleeve of my robe squirmed, then deflated. The littlemouth. I echoed, trying to see it, though I didn't know if I could in all the noise and confusion.

Yes, barely.

The tiny mouth pulled itself along the tentacle of the monster, a soft moving shape against the harder arm. It cheeped and squeaked, sharp-pitched and noisy, like nothing I'd ever heard. When it reached the maw, moments before I did, it was sucked past the glass teeth. The tiny skymouth spread its limbs, reaching for purchase, stretching. It grasped a flap of the mouth and didn't let go. It reached for another, and another. It began to choke the monster from inside.

The giant skymouth thrashed. Tentacles loosened as it clawed at its own mouth.

I fell away from its grip, and when a gust from the skymouth's struggle hit my wings, I rose with the wind until I leveled off on a steadier gust. My wings still bore me up.

As soon as I was steady enough, I turned and flew at the skymouth one more time. On the monster's other side, I saw Nat dive towards it, arrow nocked to bowstring.

I pulled my own bow and nocked an arrow. Aimed at its eye.

Nat was now out of my sight, hidden behind the bulk of the skymouth. The monster rose between us, reaching and reaching. I dove forward.

The air around me took on the sound of gust and the throttled whisper of tentacles thrashing through the air. My glide became turbulent, but I kept going.

The strangling skymouth, fighting its own internal battle for breath, could not control its limbs. I could see its eye, the size of my head, and hear the liquid in its echoes. I held my bow steady.

My elbows ached against the winghooks. My left forefinger and index held the bolt steady against the bow sight. The rest of my hand gripped the bow hard. The gust I rode now was a steady one, and I'd set a straight course. I checked the wind one last time as I drew the bowstring back to my cheek. I held until I was sure that I would crash directly into the creature if I missed, giving me a chance with my last knife. And then I opened my mouth to scream one more time, drawing all my breath. Hoping I had enough strength left in my voice.

Screaming rendered all other actions, fighting and flying and shooting, sharper. I had become an arrow of sound aimed at the most terrible creature in the city. The monster began a slow turn towards me.

No! The turn of its head would lose my mark.

I panicked and fired as fast as I could. My arrow hit the eye at its nearest point, straight through: white arrow into vast deep pool of dark eye. The tentacles stilled and drooped. The monster began to fall from the sky.

As it tumbled, another acrid cloud spewing in its wake, one long limb reached and wound around my foot. Dragged down, I felt another tentacle wrap around my neck. I looked above me and saw fliers circling and diving.

This is a good trade. Me, for my city. If they sing Remembrance at the end of this long day, those I love will sing of me too.

And then we fell, the monster and I, flipping over and over, weight over wing. Wind tore at my robe and hair as we plummeted towards the clouds and the sharp edges of the broken tower of Lith.

More tentacles squeezed my waist and throat. I realized that I might never feel the impact.

29

RISE

When I woke, it was to cold air and dense clouds, to slick acrid smells and the sound of the wind whistling across blackened bone.

I moved fingers and toes carefully, thankful for even this minimal range of motion. Pain was everywhere. I was grateful for that too.

I moved my right leg and shrieked. A blur of bone tangled in gray cloth, soaked with blood.

I turned my head in time to get sick on the floor and not all over myself.

My fingers touched my lenses, tried to wipe them clean of fog and splatter. Carefully, with my left hand, I pulled them away from my face. The dim light of the cloudbound tower was enough to show me finally what the hides had done to my skin.

Silvering paths, swollen and red on the edges, wormed across my hands, palms and backs both, in curls and blots.

I was marked everywhere the hides' seams had touched me. My fingers brushed my cheek and forehead, and I felt ridges there too. They curved and curled like the ligaments of the sky-mouths I'd covered myself with. My hair was burned away in places. I could feel the scars on my scalp. Only my eyes, nose, and mouth had been spared, where the lenses held the hides away.

I swallowed dryly. I needed to see where I was, and find water if I could.

Testing one arm, then the other, I found I could move them without screaming. Careful not to move my leg too much, I sat up slowly. My wing was stuck. It wrenched me back, and I moaned in pain.

"Kirit?" a voice shouted from far away.

"Here!" I tried to call out. My voice sounded very loud and rough in the silence. "In here!" I wanted to laugh. I did not know where I was, but I kept shouting until a shadow crossed over my face. Someone stepped into the tier and jostled whatever was pinning my wing down. I groaned again.

"Oh, Kirit." Ezarit's voice. I felt her light touch on my cheek.

Behind her, Nat said, "I told you we'd find her," and Wik chuckled softly.

"Your song will be very long, Kirit."

They were here. I was here. They'd found me. I smiled weakly. "I'm not finished yet."

Nat came into view, limping on a bone crutch. Wik, the tattoos on his face contorted by a deep frown, appeared beside him.

He handed me a small sack of water.

With Wik's help, I sipped and coughed, then sipped again.

Ezarit tore bandages from her robes, then looked for a way to brace my leg. "We need herbs, honey, and some more battens," she said to Wik. "There are supplies at Densira."

Wik handed the water to Nat. Disappeared from my view. A moment later, he rode a breeze past the tier, headed for Densira.

"Did we get them all?" I asked.

Nat shook his head. "Not yet. Wik and Macal were helping the towers and the Singers work together. The traders have taken the Spire. They've destroyed the pens."

"And the littlemouths?"

"The ones I found are safe. They seemed to have stayed out of sight, in the clouds. They didn't like the skymouths any more than we did."

"We will have to find new ways to make bridges," I said. "No more sinew."

Ezarit nodded. "We will have to find new ways to do a lot of things."

"But," said Nat as he freed me from the tentacles of the skymouth, "there's enough of this monster to last a long, long time."

I hoped the city could make use of that time to heal.

Wik returned with Elna and Ezarit's supplies. Ezarit mixed an herb poultice and bound my wounds, using the remains of my wings to brace my leg. They brushed my new marks with a honey salve, tsking at the strange patterns on my skin.

Ezarit touched the lenses with a finger and smiled at me. "They are lucky, for sure."

Using pulleys and sinew ropes, climbing beside me on sinew ladders, they eased me out of the clouds and to the broken top of Lith, where two more Singers waited.

They'd made a sling to hold me, to carry me back to the city's center.

"No," I said. "I will fly."

Wik began to protest, but the Singer nearest me slipped off her wings without a word. I stood, one-footed, on the edge of Lith, as my friends tightened my wingstraps.

Ezarit approached, waving Nat back. She cinched the second strap tight against my shoulder, then checked the first. "On your wings," she said, then squeezed my hand. I squeezed back, glad she was safe.

The clear blue sky filled with birds. Cooking smells wafted from the nearer towers.

When I unfurled my borrowed wings, the afternoon breeze filled them. I leaned off the edge of the tower and fell into the wind, the footsling bracing my leg. I rose as the strong breeze buoyed me up. Nat was right. Flying was simple. Landing would be hard.

Turning to catch the crosswind, I saw Elna being lifted back to Densira by the second Singer. Ezarit accompanied her. The first Singer rode the sling Wik and Nat carried between them. We passed through the city, and I felt many eyes watching us from the sky and the towers.

Wings of all colors wreathed the Spire. The thick bone wall of the Singers' tower had become a lattice, open to winds and light.

I curved my wings and dropped slowly to the top of the Spire, curling my leg gently and letting a waiting Singer brace my descent. The gusts passing through the lattice played the Spire like a flute: notes rose soft and continuous from the mouth of the Gyre. The tower seemed solid enough, though it would never house Singers again. We had to change. To rejoin the city.

Quietly, beneath the strange new notes of the Spire, I heard singing. On Varu and Narath, and other towers too, my neighbors stood atop their towers, singing new songs and old. Some words were familiar. Some were words I couldn't yet make out. I heard my own name in the mix.

I opened my mouth and sang back, notes without words, my rough harmonies weaving with the voice of the city. Together, we made a new song.

ACKNOWLEDGMENTS

Books don't happen out of thin air. In the case of this book, and all that come after, I've learned so much from many people.

My heartfelt thanks to my amazing editor, Miriam Weinberg, who brings sparkle and light to dark corners, always. Your insights have fractal-ninja powers. To my agents, Russ Galen and Rachel Kory, who believe in this book, this world, and in me, and their doing so set so many things in motion. To Patrick Nielsen Hayden, who gave the book its proper title, and to Teresa Nielsen Hayden, who encouraged me to find my people.

To the artists, production staff, publicity, and sales pros at Tor, especially Stephan Martiniere, Irene Gallo, Lauren Hougen, Heather Saunders, Ana Deboo, Patty Garcia, and Ardi Alspach, and the printers and binders.

To my mentors and teachers. To James D. Macdonald for believing in me when I didn't. To Elizabeth Bear, Stephen Gould, Sherwood Smith, Scott Lynch, and the amazing staff, instructors, and students at Viable Paradise. To Nancy Kress and Walter Jon Williams and everyone at Taos Toolbox. To Gregory Frost, Michael Swanwick, and Jon McGoran for taking in a new transfer to the Philly scene. To poets Heather McHugh, Eleanor Wilner, Charles Wright, Rita Dove, and Larry Levis. To Puckie Thomas, who never let me slack at anything. To Hillary Jacobs and Julie Schwait.

To my colleagues and peers—my Bruisers, especially Kelly

Lagor, Nicole Feldringer, Chris Gerwel, Lauren Teffeau, Sara Mueller, and former Bruisers Wayne Helge, Phoebe North, Douglas Beagley—to Alex Shvartsman, Sandra Wickham, Lou Berger, Oz Drummond, A. C. Wise, Siobhan Carroll, Sarah Pinsker, Jodi Meadows, Jaime Lee Moyer, Amanda Downum, Karen Burnham, Max Gladstone, Liz Bourke, Natalie Luhrs, Raq Winchester, B. Morris Allen, Jay Reynolds, E. Catherine Tobler, Stephanie Feldman, Lawrence M. Schoen, Chris Urie, and E. C. Myers. To the OWW, Codex, B.org, Novelocity, and GeekMom. To Alasdair Semple, who made me a game.

To the scientists and engineers who helped me better understand clouds, wind tunnels, bones, tower updrafts, wings, and foils, especially SkyVenture New Hampshire for the 250-mph experience, Nicole Feldringer, Jason Tuell, Kelly Lagor, and the Lake and Edinger family engineers. Your insights were invaluable. Any mistakes are my own.

To my family and friends-who-are-family, especially my mom, Judy; my sister, Susan; and brother-in-law, Chris; my cousins Beth, Jeff, and Kalliope; Craig and Karen; Geoff, Denise, and Garrett; the Edingers, Harneds, Sinnotts, and Wildes; the Winchesters; Melissa Maddonni Haims, Nanita Cranford, Jennifer Etheridge, Jeff Hugel, Claudia and Jack Etheridge, Wendy and Dan Magus, Nancy Caudill, Sara Costello, Karen and David Beaudouin, and the Henry family. To Charlotte Camp and Rebecca Beach. To the Ginsberg-Joyce family.

To you, reading this book right now.

And to a special place on the Chesapeake Bay near Worton, Maryland, where I first learned how to fly.

Turn the page for a sneak peek at
the next book in the Bone Universe

Available September 2016

Messenger birds launched as one flock from the council platform. Black bodies studded the blue sky in a cloud of purpose. Then each dusky beak pointed towards its home tower, each left leg carrying three new Laws.

The city's councilors watched them go. "Let this be enough."

A junior councilor, still wearing her wingmarks proudly, murmured, "On their wings."

The birds flew northwest from Naza, southeast to Bissel, and to all the towers between and beyond. They used the city's winds to ease their passage. They flew past tiers where families gathered, waiting for news. Where mourning flags flew, new madder-dyed silks fluttering among faded rose rags.

More than half the kaviks crossed the city's center, where the Spire, cracked and groaning in the wind, stood empty. Flaps and cackles broke the morning's eerie silence as the birds diverted around the walled tower, avoiding its gates, its gaping mouth.

The kaviks bore the bone chips tied with spidersilk thread at their black ankles as their ancestors had, curling their claws against the clatter. They made no comment except for a curious tilt when recipients lifted the cords from their legs. A caw for food, which was often slow to come. Puffed feathers as they listened to the new Laws, and the altered Laws, whispered, then sung. Kaviks remembered the words. They remembered everything: the Laws of this generation, the Laws of those that came before.

∼ GROWTH ∼

No tower may use scourweed to elevate
their tiers above any other. No citizen may possess
or store it, stem or seed.

∼ SPIRE (revised) ∼

None enter the Spire, night or day,
unless council-sworn or with council-say.

∼ ESCORT (new) ∼

No Singer-marked or Singer-sworn may fly
between towers unguided.
They will their host towers abide and be cared for
without complaint or reprisal.
Wings they may borrow, but may not own,
lest the city be again divided.

1

CODEX

As children, we learned early that the clouds were dangerous.

Turns out the city wasn't all that much safer.

Between three towers, the council platform hung suspended, its thin profile on the horizon the only thing protecting the city from itself now. Councilors paced, barely visible at this distance, preparing for their morning votes, while I peered at them through sharp cracks in the Spire wall. I wanted to be out there, in the open sky, leading. Making Laws, rediscovering our past, keeping tower from fighting tower. Not here, accompanying Kirit Skyshouter on a cloudtouched expedition into the Spire's remains.

But Kirit and I dangled from tenuous ropes in the Spire's dim afternoon light anyway. We swung within the cracked walls and over the deep gaping center of the Spire because the council and my mentor, Doran Grigrit, had asked it of me.

"No one else can find the codex, Nat, and few want to go in the Spire as it is. She's offering to help," he'd said on the council plinth earlier that morning. "The Singers knew how the city grows, why it roars. How the towers rise. We're on the verge of a new age, with new discoveries, but we need to retrieve as much knowledge from the past as we can, before the Spire cracks further and our opportunity is lost. None of the other Singers have been near as helpful in this effort, not since the new Laws. Take her in."

And here we were.

I hummed a verse of a popular song.

The Spire cracked as a Shout rose up,
freed the city, freed us all.

"Knock it off, Nat. I'm trying to count tiers." Her voice was rough, even when she spoke. The healers said it could stay that way forever.

"That's Councilor Densira to you, Skyshouter."

These days, children sang of Kirit the hero. She was that. She was my wing-sister too, and would always be. But she had faults, and a stubborn streak, and her friends stood a fair chance of getting killed. I knew all about that. Worse, she'd been acting strangely in the past few moons, since the fever. Distant. Obstinate.

"What deal did you cut with Doran?" I said, then sneezed. Bone dust everywhere, even so many months after Spirefall. A cold east-spun wind whistled through the cracks running the Spire's outer wall. The stuff silted the dim light.

She didn't answer. Singers hadn't been keen on helping the council or the towers much lately. A fair number of towers hadn't wanted to help the Singers in a while either. And no one was sure whether Kirit was Singer or Tower any longer. Probably not even Kirit herself.

I took my eyes off of her for a moment to squint at the carvings we swung near. Panels depicting winged battles, sky-mouths attacking with grasping tentacles and rows of glass teeth, tower fighting tower. Singers and their carvings. Their tattoos. The city was well and done with all of that.

Life was better lived in the open towers, not in this walled one. Out in the sky. Not trapped in the Gyre's echoes at the

Spire's center, where I'd nearly died not that long ago. Where Kirit had nearly killed me.

And where I'd tried to kill her in turn.

I sneezed again and the rope swung.

"Quiet, Nat!"

She made it sound like I was sneezing on purpose.

"It's the dust." I kept the irritation out of my voice. The city's hero wouldn't be able to blame the newly elected junior councilor from the northwest quadrant for botching her search. I wouldn't give her any reason to complain.

Besides, I was curious. My mother, Elna Densira, had spoken of the codex with a mix of reverence and fear since Kirit and I were children. She'd said the pages contained our city's survival in numbers: lists of what towers needed shoring up, a record of appeasements. I wanted to see what the city's roars and rumbles over time looked like. I couldn't imagine the heft of it.

We had nothing like that in the towers. Too heavy to carry up, too hard to maintain. Only the Spire and the Singers could keep records like that for generations. But instead of sharing their knowledge, they secreted it away. They practiced crimes against the city in its name.

We knew that now.

After Spirefall, searchers had cut carvings from the Spire walls and sorted through rubble, but the codex eluded them. Then more tiers collapsed, and rumors of rogue skymouths in the Spire began. Most wouldn't go near the Spire now, even if the new Laws didn't forbid it.

If I helped bring the codex back today, that would make me, if not more of a hero, more of a leader, despite having only nineteen Allmoons.

Kirit continued her descent on the gently swaying rope and

I followed, inching down the rough fiber. The silk of my foot-wraps caught on a splinter.

What remained of the Gyre's winds were hollow sounds: bone shards knocked from balcony edges that skittered and bounced down the walls, the flap of a whipperling struggling to stay aloft and in the light, my breath coming fast as I lowered myself down the rope. Once a place to fight for the right to speak, the Gyre resonated now with ghosts and loss.

I gripped the twisted fiber and sinew rope tightly enough that my knucklebones showed hard and pale beneath my skin.

"I wish you'd brought newer ropes," Kirit said.

"Complaining? Not very heroic, Skyshouter." So many songs praised her deeds, her words, her sacrifice. She should know the city had bigger troubles than old ropes.

"If I'd had access to supplies, I would have brought my own ropes," she snapped, looking up.

She always hated when I teased.

In the sunlight, the web of scars across her scalp and face from her burns gleamed silver. I bit back my frustration, and felt a twinge of regret. I swallowed that back.

"Council gave us these." Most of the council had. Three councilors actually, from three separate towers and three different quadrants. These days, that represented a lot of cross-city cooperation. When Doran Grigrit, my mentor; Vant Densira, my tower leader; and Hiroli Naza, Lead Councilor Ezarit Varu's apprentice, first told me what Kirit wanted to do, I'd balked. I'd been tracking runaway Singer fledges since Spirefall and working to address the unrest that was blowing through the city. Important things.

But curiosity won out, and my sense of honor. Lead Councilor Grigrit trusted me to keep an eye on Kirit, and not give her any special treatment. Meantime, Vant had asked me to grab as many Lawsmarkers as I could find on the way, as a service to Densira. We needed those.

"I wouldn't tell Ezarit you're going, or with whom," Vant had cautioned.

Fine by me. Ezarit had enough power to drop me into the clouds if she wanted, even without full control over the council. I was merely a junior councilor. If she had no power over her daughter's doings? That was her problem, not mine.

The bone walls creaked and the dust increased. I imagined myself falling again, wings torn, down the Spire's depths. A feeling I could generate all too easily. And yet? I didn't feel fear here.

Maybe I'd agreed to return in order to prove that to myself. To prove it to her. That I was not afraid of the Gyre, or the Spire, or Kirit herself. Neither afraid nor angry enough to cloud my judgment as a city leader. That was important to know, especially now.

The rope groaned and I paused, looking for the sturdy gallery tier the artifexes claimed still existed. Kirit hadn't stopped. She wouldn't ever stop, not without a solid bone wall right in front of her. "The ropes can take it, but the walls can't, Kirit. Time to pick a tier and get going."

She stayed on the rope. I bristled despite myself. "We shouldn't even be in here. No one else is allowed in. Soon no one will be."

"You can go back to chasing Lawsbreakers if you want." Still descending.

"Not today." She was always like this. I braced for more argument. "You said you'd be quick. Let's just hurry." Besides, Doran Grigrit had hinted there'd be extra tower marks in it for me if we returned with what Kirit sought. "If something happens to the city's hero on my watch, I'll never rise beyond it."

Surprising me, she laughed, but the sound had a brittle edge.

"And I'll never rise beyond it if a city councilor gets hurt in my presence."

She was right. The songs that called her Skyshouter would quiet further, while those calling her Spirebreaker or worse would become even more popular. I didn't want that for her. She'd suffered enough. We all had. She was gaining my sympathy, but she kept talking. "Elna would have my wings for it. And Ceetcee and Beliak too."

Her bringing Ceetcee and Beliak into this, much less my mother? Clouds.

"This is city business, Kirit. If you care so much about what Elna thinks, you should visit." She didn't know anything about us anymore. We'd sent whipperling notes that Elna, who'd helped raise Kirit, was completely skyblind. That Ceetcee would be a mother before next Allsuns. There'd been no reply. Meantime, Ceetcee and Beliak helped me care for Elna as she learned her way in a darkened world. They were caring for me too. And I them.

"Seriously, Nat. You can wait safely up top. I'll be right there. You have enough Lawsmarkers, you don't need to salvage any more. You'll barely be able to fly home with that." She'd missed my point completely and was eyeing my salvaging satchel. The word "safely" burned.

"Always seem to need more these days." I tried to keep my voice light, but this was harder than I thought it would be. We had so much unsaid between us. "I can carry more than you think."

Deep in the Spire, an enormous crack sounded, then tapered off to a rip like battens piercing silk. Echoes of bone striking bone reverberated as a piece of a tier tumbled into the depths. Over this sound rose a rush of wings. Gray- and brown-bodied wild dirgeons and two midsized gryphons shot up from the Gyre in a cloud of beaks and feathers. My favorite messenger bird, a whipperling named Maalik, burrowed into my robes with a squawk.

"Watch out!" The escaping flock surrounded the ropes and rocked it. Scratched us in their passage and were gone in another cloud of bone dust that left us coughing and struggling to cling to the swinging rope.

I held on tight, but Kirit slipped, her feet scrambling to wrap the line again. She grabbed too late for the rope with her knees and dangled for a moment from her fingertips. Her wings, half open for safety, buoyed her in the Gyre's breeze, and I struggled to keep my balance as the rope swung wildly. The gallery wall we'd anchored to creaked.

"Easy!" I whispered through gasps for clear air. Whether I spoke to me or to her, I wasn't sure. Below us, the dark pit rippled with shadows.

If I had to, I could dump the satchel I carried into the Gyre and grab her before she fell too far. I hadn't found anything I couldn't bear to lose yet.

Except Kirit. I couldn't let her fall. Birdcrap. I shifted my grip on the rope, readying to help if she needed me. Her Spirefall injuries hadn't healed well.

"I've got it." Her voice was level, tightly controlled now. Still her arms shook as she gripped the rope. She turned her face away so I couldn't see her discomfort.

She hooked a ledge with her good leg and climbed over a solid-enough-looking gallery wall. "I wanted to search this tier next anyway."

Maalik cackled and climbed to my shoulder, pinpoint claws never breaching my silk robes. He tested my earlobe with his beak, gently. *Yes, bird. Still here.* "Some help you were."

Tossing my spear, bow, and carry bags onto the tier, I followed her. The Lawsmarkers I'd found, plus a few metal scraps, clacked and screeched as the bags hit the floor.

Searchers had turned through the rubble. But scavengers had been here too. The signs were all over. The cages far below, broken during Spirefall, had been pulled to pieces to remove the precious wire mesh inside.

Rubble began to shift and slide as Kirit made her way into the alcove. Bone dust billowed, and she coughed again. "Too much dust," she muttered. "You were right."

At least I was right about dust. Maybe now I could find out why she'd been distant. Ceetcee would want to know why she hadn't answered our messages. "How's it downtower at Grigrit? Dusty there too?" I remembered cleaning a downtower midden once with her, so long ago. I wrinkled my nose at the memory.

She grunted. "Damp. Doran's kept us on the lowtower's dark side. Cold there."

She could have had a hero's quarters once she recovered from her Spirefall injuries, but she'd chosen to live downtower. That must have made her very bones ache.

"Are you maybe a little cloudtouched?" My joke fell flat. I kept going. "Who'd want to live that far down by choice?"

"Singers and fledges don't have a choice," she snapped, but kept sifting rubble. So much for conversation. It didn't look like she knew what she was looking for, that was for sure.

"If the council hadn't taken the Singers' wings," Kirit began again, "I could have used Wik's help here. And Moc and Ciel's."

In previous searches for the codex, Wik had provided nothing, especially under guard. But I didn't say so. "The Singer twins?" I shook my head. "They don't listen. Won't stay in their classes. If we brought them to the Gyre, they'd probably turn scavenger and disappear."

"Nat."

"What? It's been going around." She blinked at my tone, and I bent to hide my dark expression, gathering my weapons from the tier floor instead. Once we'd been closer than friends. Almost siblings. But even then, we'd teased and squabbled. Things were harder now.

"Scavengers aren't hurting anything," she finally said, avoiding a bigger fight.

"They're thieves." She caught my look and frowned. I frowned right back. "I have responsibilities now, Kirit. All Lawsbreakers weaken the towers. Scavengers are Lawsbreakers. They cause disorder that we can't afford. You'd understand if you were on the council." I sounded like Doran and Ezarit when I said things like that. Strong. A leader.

Kirit had been offered a seat straight off, and her choice of mentors. Council had even kept the seat open while Kirit endured her Spirefall wounds and the resulting bone dust infection that nearly took her leg. After Allsuns, when she'd finally recovered enough to hear the offer, they'd asked again.

And she'd said no.

The city needed her, her family needed her, and she'd refused. I hadn't. Nor had Ezarit and Doran. Hiroli hadn't, even though she'd lost her family in Spirefall. She still wanted to help fix the city. In council we learned to debate, worked to keep towers from splitting off or severing bridges, tried to govern without the Singers, even defended towers from raids and riots. It was hard work, and we gladly did it. But not Kirit.

A verse of The Rise came unbidden, the melody learned from years of repetition, the words those she'd tried to teach me in the Gyre.

> The city rises on Singers' wings, remembering all,
>   bearing all;
> Rises to sun and wind on graywing, protecting,
>   remembering.
> Never looking down. Tower war is no more.

The city was coming apart: each tower for itself. As the songs warned.

"Hurry, then," I said. But she dithered, turning this way and that. Searching. "Kirit, really. If you don't know where to look, let's end this. Whatever you want from Doran, there's got to be a better way to get it. I have a vote to prepare for." I hadn't meant to say that last bit.

"Vote? More Laws? Because of the riots?" She must have heard the rumors. There'd been market riots over food, over fair trades. Over Singers walking past. The most recent on Varu, two days ago. There'd been so many skymouth losses during Spirefall, and too much anger from survivors.

"You'd know if you were on the council, instead of making expeditions like this one." It came out sharp and fast. Maybe I'd meant it to. I wanted to fight with her about this—her responsibility—about everything.

Even here, in the Spire's ruins. Especially here.

She met my gaze for a moment. Her shoulders squared. "There haven't been any riots on Grigrit," she said. "Doran runs a tight tower." But then she sighed. "Let's do what we're here for, and argue about that later. The codex should help. And then you will tell me who's getting new Laws this time."

All of them, I wanted to say. *All the Singers. Including the Nightwing Wik. We'd get Rumul too, if we could find his body.*

But we'd been sworn to secrecy until the council was ready. It was our one chance to unify the city, and the timing had to be right.

"Nat," she said again. She reached out a hand, silvered with two Singer marks, and seared with the wilder lines—marks made by skymouth tendons acrid on her tawny skin as she'd fought Rumul to the death. The fight that had eventually cracked the Spire.

I was caught between taking her hand and revulsion. Not at

the appearance of her hand, but at the thought of all she'd done. The Spire had cracked, and the skymouths hidden inside— hidden by the Singers in order to protect the city—had escaped. Many had died. She'd fought then too, and me beside her; Spire and tower fighting together until all the monsters had been captured.

Now she was a hero, but increasingly unwelcome. The city had found its path without her. But Doran had trusted her enough to come here, with an escort, saying, "She's earned another chance, Nat. Her decisions lately notwithstanding, she defended the city once."

Her fingers hung in the air, inches from my arm. Then they trembled and she pulled away. Her brass-flecked eyes, much like Ezarit's, but framed by silvered scars, seemed to plead with me. Then she bowed her head. "I'm sorry, Nat. I'm sorry for your anger."

"You have to pick a side, Kirit. You can't be tower and Spire both. Not anymore."

"If *I* can't be both, who can?"

"Why would you want to? They were monsters. You knew that when you fought Rumul. Before that too." Anger, bubbling up. Singers had killed my father in order to keep their terrible secret. They'd tried to kill me.

Not they. She. Kirit.

"It's not that simple!" Kirit threw up her hands. Dust curled in the disturbed air currents. "Some worked against Rumul, from the inside. Why are you repeating rhetoric when you know the truth, Nat?" The tower creaked again. "Many fought for the towers."

I knew it wasn't that simple. My father had tried the same a generation before.

On my wrist, a faded blue silk cord held a single message chip. One of my father's carvings, found after Spirefall. "They moved too slow. Too many died," I said, each word sent after her like arrows. "You should be angriest of all."

I reached out then, to the Kirit I'd known since childhood, to Kirit Densira, not Kirit Skyshouter, but my hand grasped air. She'd already turned away to search more of the dim tier, and a large alcove nearby.

From the tier above, a floor had collapsed into a pile of rubble in the alcove. A carved stool stuck crookedly from beneath shards of ceiling and wall. Several more cracks ran across the floor where we stood.

"Rumul's office was above," she whispered, turning in place. Getting her bearings.

My wrapped foot slid over the bone floor, testing the seams. The wreckage signified that the floors—tough outgrowths of bone at each new level—could sunder and break without warning.

Working in secret before his death, my father, the artifex Naton, had riddled the Spire with holes. I was glad he'd drilled Rumul's office as thoroughly as he had, but I wished I didn't have to walk through it now.

I looked closely at the fallen ceiling, and the small patch of sky that showed through another hole in the wall. Those weak points had helped us bring down Rumul. *And the whole Spire too, releasing the monsters within.* Now the same weaknesses threatened our safety.

Kirit shivered like she was still feverish. "Did you hear that?"

"Hear what?" Kirit's ears were sharp, even after her illness. Secret Singer training. Echoes. Eerie stuff. Flying at night was good, but the sharp hearing? Disturbing.

I peered into the Gyre. "Just bone chips falling from where we hit the walls, probably," I said. "Don't go thinking everything's a skymouth!" I made tentacle-finger gestures and a face to go with them, wide jaw, tongue wagging. It must have looked awful, but suddenly I was afraid too—of the Spire collapsing, of the clouds far below, of a skymouth lurking, uncaptured and invisible, below—and I didn't want Kirit to see it.

I was a city hero, just like her, at least to some. And a city councilor. A junior councilor.

"No time to be afraid," Kirit whispered. She picked up the pace of her search, pulling shards of bone from the rubble.

The rope we'd descended swung and smacked against the wall. A sudden breeze? The soft scratching sounds could have been my imagination. Then a screech echoed up the Gyre that made my skin crawl. Kirit turned, eyes wide.

"Only bats," I said. *Please be bats.* But a dark shadow circled the lowest visible tiers, far too big for a bat. As it moved, its tail swung and flicked. A beam of sunlight hit it from above. Feathers glistened on broad wings. A long beak stitched up and down as it sniffed the air. I edged back, pulling Kirit with me.

Clouds. Those feathers are the size of my arm.

"There were songs," I whispered. "Old ones. Of things living in the clouds that carried away the dead." *Let's fly, Kirit. What's down there is wrong; it is danger.*

Words from an ancient song echoed in my ear, in an old friend's voice:

> *They eat the stars.*
> *They crack the bones.*
> *They . . .*

Peering over the gallery edge, I struggled to remember the rest of the words. But all was dust and darkness.

ABOUT THE AUTHOR

FRAN WILDE is an author and technology consultant. Her short stories have appeared in *Asimov's Science Fiction, Nature,* and *Beneath Ceaseless Skies*. Wilde also blogs about food and genre at *Cooking the Books* (franwilde.wordpress.com/cooking-the-books) and for the popular social-parenting website *GeekMom*. She lives in Pennsylvania with her family.